DEBT OF HONOR

CARLOS MCCRARY PI, BOOK 9

DALLAS GORHAM

Cover and eBook design by eBook Prep
www.ebookprep.com

March, 2021
ISBN: 978-1-64457-228-3

ePublishing Works!
644 Shrewsbury Commons Ave
Ste 249
Shrewsbury PA 17361
United States of America

www.epublishingworks.com
Phone: 866-846-5123

ACKNOWLEDGMENTS

My thanks to Michael H. Hatfield of Hatfield & Stack, LLC, Attorneys at Law in Tavares, Florida. Michael has litigated numerous Federal and State jury trials to verdict throughout the State of Florida and United States. He earned a Bachelor of Arts from the University of Florida and a Juris Doctor from Cumberland School of Law, Samford University and is a member of Florida Association of Criminal Trial Attorneys. Michael reviewed my manuscript for technical accuracy on criminal law and procedure. Any inaccuracies are solely my responsibility.

My thanks to Richard Kelley, one of the owners of Ford Press in Leesburg, Florida. The company website is https://www.fordpress.com. Mr. Kelley showed me the ins and outs of offset printing. Any inaccuracies in my manuscript are solely my responsibility.

My thanks to my editor Marsha Butler who can be reached via email (swmpwriter@gmail) or by phone (303-931-4698). She makes me a better writer.

ONE

Fallujah, Iraq, 2006

Operational Detachment Alpha 777
Alpha Company, 3rd Battalion
7th Special Forces Group (Airborne), Team 7

The roadblock at the entrance to the Iraqi military recruiting station was manned by Iraqi soldiers. They had blocked both sides of the divided street with concrete barriers leaving a single traffic lane marked by a yellow and black striped aluminum rail which they raised to admit each vehicle. One lane also allowed vehicles to leave. The Iraqis had parked trucks a few feet behind the concrete barricades as a second line of defense.

The Iraqis had been training under the watchful eyes of American Special Forces Team Triple Seven. The Iraqis viewed the Triple Seven with ill-disguised hatred. The Americans didn't care; they were used to being hated. Three of the Green Berets had been sent to observe the roadblock security in action so they could evaluate the operation, and, by God, that's exactly what they would do. If the Iraqis didn't like it, piss on 'em.

Later the Green Berets would debrief the Iraqis and critique their performance at the checkpoint. The Iraqis would pretend to listen, then return to their customary haphazard way of doing (or not doing) things. The Americans were used to that also. The more things change, the more they stay the same.

At least that was the plan.

Sergeant Carlos "Chuck" McCrary and Sergeant Bill Gregg stood near the Iraqi troops, watching and listening.

Chuck was fluent in Pashto, although the Iraqis didn't know that. He carried an MTAR-21 Micro Tavor, a small weapon designed for close-quarters combat. He had two spare magazine that he sure as hell hoped he wouldn't need.

Sergeant Gregg carried an M-16 rifle with a 20-round magazine and two spare magazines.

Sergeant First Class Phillip Franks stood ten yards behind the other two Americans. The grizzled veteran eyeballed the scene through his sunglasses as he cradled his Heckler & Koch MP5 submachinegun with a 100-round Beta C-Mag drum magazine. Ten years older than the other men, he had joined the Special Forces in 1995, well before the Nine-Eleven terrorist attacks. The soldiers in the Triple Seven looked at Franks as an older, wiser brother. By now, Franks had seen and done it all.

When the three soldiers geared up that morning, Chuck had asked Franks why he didn't carry a spare magazine.

"Extra magazines are heavy, and it's gonna be a long, hot day watching these bozos pretend to guard their recruiting station. If a gun battle in downtown Fallujah gets bad enough that I need more than a hundred rounds, we're all screwed anyway."

By two o'clock, the line of vehicles at the roadblock disappeared around a curve in the road between two blocks of mid-rise apartments three hundred yards away.

A black Mercedes limousine with an Iraqi flag flying from an antenna honked repeatedly as it pulled out of the long line of traffic, bumped across the median, and sped toward the checkpoint on the wrong side of the divided street. Its driver lowered his window and waved the approaching traffic out of the limo's way. The limo screeched to a halt at the precast concrete barriers, then tried to wedge its way into the front of the line.

Chuck gripped his weapon a little tighter and stepped forward.

The vehicle that the Mercedes was trying to muscle aside was a battered green minibus coated with layers of road dust and hammered with years of traffic misadventures. The minibus driver cranked his window down and waved his clenched fist as he cursed in Pashto at the driver of the Mercedes.

Out of the corner of his eye, Chuck saw Franks sidestep away from the concrete barricade and sidle closer to the minibus. The dust on the windows was so thick Chuck couldn't see inside. The bus seemed to squat on its rear wheels. *Something heavy in the back*, Chuck thought. *That must be why Franks is checking it out.*

As the three American soldiers looked on, the man in the passenger seat pushed his door open and jumped from the vehicle. Chuck read the driver's lips as he prayed "Allahu Akbar." *God is great.*

The passenger's loose jacket was stretched to cover something lumpy that circled his ribcage.

"Suicide vest!" Chuck shouted.

The passenger dodged around the open door, leapt over the concrete barrier, and sprinted between two trucks toward the Iraqi men lined up fifty meters away at the recruiting station.

Chuck pivoted to Franks and Gregg. "It's a car bomb too!"

Franks slung his weapon over his shoulder and rushed toward his men. Grabbing Chuck and Gregg, he pushed them toward the concrete barricade. "Move, move, move. It's gonna blow."

He tumbled both men over the top of the low concrete wall. As he lifted his leg to vault over the barrier, the minibus erupted like the fires of hell, sending a glowing mushroom cloud into the air and scattering ball bearings and shrapnel in all directions.

Franks lunged toward the ground between the concrete wall and the row of trucks as the secondary explosion of the black limo's gas tank sprayed a shower of burning diesel fuel across the scene of the catastrophe.

The last thing Chuck remembered was Franks laying across him and Gregg as the sky rained debris.

TWO

South Florida, Present Day

"What's that on the beach, honey?" Alicia sat up straight in her kayak to get a better view of the object fifty yards ahead. "Is that a log? Maybe a tree trunk washed up?"

She shoved her paddle into the foot-deep water, sinking it into the sandy bottom to keep from drifting in the breeze.

"It's a dead animal," Harry said. "See the birds eating it? Birds wouldn't tear at a piece of driftwood like that. A dead dolphin maybe?"

"If a dead animal on an Oklahoma highway is called 'road kill,' what do you call a dead animal on a Florida beach?"

"I give up. Maybe 'beach kill'?"

Alicia chuckled. "You got it, babe."

"Okay, what sort of animal is that beach kill?" Harry asked.

"Could be an alligator."

"It's not an alligator, sweetheart. Alligators live in fresh water. Seeti Bay is salt water."

Harry let his kayak drift after his bride of four days. "Could be a crocodile, though. They live in salt and fresh water."

Alicia paddled closer.

"Whatever that thing is, those birds are mauling it. What are they?"

Harry rowed after Alicia. "They're vultures, or buzzards, or something."

Alicia had planned a romantic picnic on a deserted beach. Their hotel had packed a lunch for them, including a cooler filled with Champagne to stow in the deck hatches of their rented kayaks.

"We can't picnic on that beach, Harry. That beach kill stinks to high heaven and the beach is too small to move far enough away."

Harry fumbled his cellphone from the waterproof backpack. "We can shoot a cool video to show back in Oklahoma."

"I mounted a GoPro on my hat. You won't need your cellphone." Alicia switched on the camera and rowed closer. "That's the strangest crocodile I ever saw."

Harry laughed. "You've never seen a crocodile."

Alicia stopped rowing. "It looks like...It could be...Oh my God!"

She dropped her paddle and fell over the side of the kayak, retching like her stomach had turned inside out. Then she splashed to her feet in the knee-deep water.

"For God's sake, call 9-1-1."

THREE

H ank Ramirez called Chuck McCrary at 11:30 on a Thursday morning

Chuck was working at home in his fourteenth-floor office on Port City Beach. The temperature was in the upper seventies in the middle of January, and Chuck had opened the glass sliders so he could smell the salt tang of the Atlantic Ocean. The sea breeze wafted a few clouds across the pale blue sky. His personal slice of Paradise.

Hank never made personal calls during the workday, so Chuck knew it must be important.

He slid the keyboard to one side. "Hey, Hank, what's up?"

"A couple of kayakers found a headless body washed up on a beach in Seeti Bay State Park."

"Do we know the victim?"

"Maybe. CSIs who processed the scene said the guy had '777' tattooed on his left forearm."

"You think he's one of our Triple Sevens?"

"Don't know yet. I've got a set of crime scene photos. Can you meet me for lunch and take a look at them?

"Sure. Where should I meet you?"

"You know that diner across the street from the Precinct?"

"The *South Bay* Precinct? That's over an hour's drive from here. Can you meet me halfway?"

"I'm on duty, Chuck. I barely have time for lunch at all."

"Okay, Hank. But you're buying. Unless I starve to death before I get there."

Chuck's customary morning hunger pangs were already reminding him that lunchtime was imminent. His feeding schedule was breakfast at 6:00 a.m., then a *pan dulce* or bagel around 10:00, lunch at noon, a mid-afternoon snack, and dinner at 7:00 p.m. As regular as animals in a zoo. When he could get by with it, which wasn't often. Life had a way of interfering.

Chuck hated to eat late; he felt like a bear coming out of hibernation. He stopped at the first fast-food restaurant he passed and ate a couple of hamburgers to hold him until he could eat a real lunch. He figured the hamburgers would keep him from starving to death on the long drive south.

Chuck's lunch partner was Hidalgo "Hank" Ramirez. A thousand years ago, Hank had been Chuck's commanding officer in the Triple Seven Special Forces unit. Some people know the Special Forces better as the Green Berets.

By the time the two veterans finished lunch, the diner had mostly emptied. Two Port City cops from the South Bay Precinct dawdled over coffee across the room.

"I brought crime scene photos, Chuck," Hank said. "They're pretty graphic."

"We saw things in Afghanistan and Iraq we can never unsee. These can't be worse. Remember what we found in Ghar Mesar. Besides, I've examined a million crime scene photos."

"Don't say I didn't warn you, buddy." He slid the photo stack across the table, face down.

Chuck flipped the photos over. Good thing Hank had waited until after lunch to show them. Otherwise, he would have lost his appetite. Even so, he swallowed an extra time to keep his *picadillo* and *yucca* down.

The first photo showed a headless body covered in seaweed, washed up on a stretch of beach. The remnants of a shredded gray tee-shirt and khaki

Bermuda shorts clung to the body. Knee socks and one tennis shoe remained on the feet and legs.

It had been years since Chuck had encountered a decapitated body and that was in Afghanistan, not the good old U.S. of A. People could almost expect decapitated bodies in Afghanistan, but not in the U.S. But there it was, sprawled on the beach, plain as day.

That wasn't all: The hands had been cut off too. Chuck's stomach churned.

"How long was the body there?"

"Impossible to tell. That beach is on a small barrier island in Seeti Bay State Park. Only way to get there is on a shallow-draft boat. Two kayakers on their honeymoon stumbled across it or it might never have been found. The turkey vultures and vermin would have eaten the whole thing. Our CSIs hitched a ride on a Marine Patrol airboat to retrieve the body. They took these pictures before they moved it."

"Not a great way to spend their honeymoon. I hope this didn't spoil South Florida for them." Chuck drew the image closer. "The animals didn't leave a lot to identify." He flipped to the next photo, a close-up of the left forearm. Beneath seaweed strings and animal bites three faded figures were visible. "That's three sevens?"

"It's not clear from the photos, but the CSIs looked at the actual tattoo and they're ninety-nine percent sure it says '777.' Buster Cleveland and his partner were assigned the case. Buster remembered I was in the Triple Seven and gave me a heads-up and sent me the photos."

Hank rolled up his sleeve to reveal a "777" tattooed on his forearm. "My design is different from the one on the body, but different guys used different tattoo artists. You never got a tattoo?"

"Nah. My scars are reminder enough." Chuck tapped the photo. "Is the victim a Triple Seven?"

"Maybe. The number 777 also might be a religious reference. I looked it up. It's the Biblical reference for the last day of creation. It also refers to the genealogy of Jesus. The guy may be a devout Christian or a monk from a monastery where members get ritual tattoos." Hank rolled his sleeve down.

The next photo framed the tattoo but included the forearm, where the left hand was amputated at the wrist. "777 is a winning spin on a slot machine," Chuck said. "Perhaps the poor guy loves to play the slots."

"Yeah, a serious gambler. I hadn't considered that. Maybe he thought the tattoo would bring him luck."

"Well, it didn't work too well," Chuck said.

"I hoped you'd recognize his tattoo. The forensics gurus are processing the body. They expect a DNA match, but that takes a few days."

The next photo framed the right forearm. The hand on that arm had also been amputated. It wasn't a clean cut. Maybe an axe or machete? Chuck flipped through the remaining pictures and returned the stack to Hank.

"No hands, no head," Hank said. "Somebody didn't want him identified."

"Too bad Gunner is visiting family in Fargo," Chuck said. "If this corpse is ours, he'd want to know."

Gunner Knutson was an occasional operative for McCrary Investigations, Chuck's private investigation company. Gunner was a former Triple Seven too.

"I called him. Two feet of snow on his parents' front yard and still falling. The wedding isn't until next week, and he's already freezing his buns off." Hank grinned. "He's acclimated to South Florida."

"Yeah, his Viking blood thinned in the Florida sunshine."

The server brought the checks and Hank dropped a credit card on the table.

"You want me there, Hank? To help identify the body?"

"I'm not sure what I want, but this could involve the Triple Seven, so I thought you should know. The body—or what's left of it—is at the Medical Examiner's. Let them finish the autopsy. We'll meet downtown tomorrow morning."

———

The winter sun had reached the tops of the downtown skyscrapers by the time Chuck returned to his home office. Hungry again, he fixed a peanut butter and jalapeño jelly sandwich to hold him until dinner. He took his first bite and Ruby Voight's picture flashed on his phone. *The Yellow Rose of Texas* ring tone announced her call.

Chuck's mouth was full, so he accepted it as a video call, and pointed at his bulging cheeks while mumbling, "Just a minute."

He swigged iced tea and managed to choke down the bite. "Hello, sunshine."

"I wish I were sunshine. It's winter in Austin." She rotated her phone to point out the window. Traces of ice frosted the live oak trees. A sabal palm's fronds were weighted down with frozen rain. The ice made the grass glisten like it was sprinkled with diamonds. Like a Texas Christmas card. "It's twenty-nine degrees in Austin and expected to stay that way for the next five days."

"That's not supposed to happen in Austin."

"No kidding. Where the hell is global warming when you need it?"

"You poor, poor baby. It's eighty degrees here."

"I have more vacation days earned than I can use. I plan to visit Port City next week to work on my tan while the ice melts in Austin. Could you recommend a place to stay? Hint, hint."

"How will the Austin police crime lab manage to process their fingerprints with their best criminalist on vacation?"

"Screw 'em. I get bitchy when I'm cold. I require serious sunshine."

"I know the perfect place. My caseload is medium and I can delegate some. I have a meeting in the ME's office tomorrow morning, but I'll be free by noon. You fly in tomorrow or Saturday?"

"Probably Saturday. I'll discuss it with my boss. I'll try to take off tomorrow afternoon."

"Text me your flight arrangements. I'll pick you up."

"Great idea, lover." Ruby blew him a kiss over the phone and disconnected.

FOUR

H ank and his family lived in Toulouse Bay Village at the south end of Atlantic County. Friday morning Chuck met him halfway—the downtown parking garage of the Port City Police Crime Laboratory.

They rode the elevator to the basement.

Chuck whiffed an odor reminiscent of raw sewage mixed with dead fish and seasoned with ammonia fumes laced with weed killer. "I never get used to that stench."

"It's a combination of decayed flesh and chemicals the medical examiners use in the autopsy suite," Hank said. "The exhaust system does the best it can, but the smell overflows to the corridor."

"That's why they put the autopsy department in the basement. Members of the public who smell that would believe this was Dr. Frankenstein's laboratory. I haven't been here for a while, and my nose has forgotten how noxious it is."

"Your nose should remember better. Once you get used to it, it's not so bad." He drew a small tube of Vaseline from his jacket pocket and extended it to his friend.

Chuck smeared a dab on his upper lip. Hank did too.

The odor intensified in the autopsy suite. The Vaseline made it tolerable

—just barely. Chuck expected to see Dr. Frankenstein, but he was nowhere in sight.

The Medical Examiner, Dr. Anandi "Annie" Mahajan, peeled off her gloves to shake hands. "Hank, I understand you visiting the ME's office. What about you, Chuck? You don't visit the autopsy lab often."

"Hank showed me a picture of the tattoo on the corpse. Several of the Triple Seven unit have tattoos of three sevens. Hank hoped we would recognize the tattoo and it could help us identify the victim."

Annie led them to the stainless-steel refrigerated vaults where bodies were stored. She swung open a waist-high door and tugged out a shelf on rollers. The decay stench threatened to overpower his Vaseline mustache. Hank was a veteran cop who was there frequently, but Chuck struggled to hold down his breakfast. Dr. Frankenstein himself would struggle to confront that miasma.

Chuck visualized half-digested remnants of his Western Omelet spewed across the spotless floor. Not good for his tough guy image.

Until now, this whole concept of a headless body had been merely a crime scene photo—like it didn't have any connection with him. It was an academic exercise in detective work. Now that he was standing in the morgue and about to see the body, the whole grisly scene became as real as a punch in the gut.

Annie tugged back the drape, uncovering the body.

Hank crossed himself.

The corpse's gender was obvious because the nude body lay on its back. Race was another issue. Without the head, the normal cues of hair color and texture and the shape of facial features were absent. The victim had been in the water for God knows how long. Fish and carrion birds had ravaged the body. The skin that remained was light brown, a middle tint that might be African-American, Hispanic, or South Asian. That included half of the members of the Triple Seven, including Captain Ramirez and Chuck, although Hank was a darker brown than Chuck. His blood was Cuban; Chuck's was Mexican-Aztec mixed with Scotch-Irish.

The victim was tortured with a burning tool, perhaps an automobile cigarette lighter or a fireplace poker. Nah, you wouldn't find a fireplace poker in South Florida—no one has a fireplace. The wounds were larger than a cigarette burn. A cigar? Lots of cigars in South Florida.

Chuck's eyes burned and his vision blurred. Whether this man was his comrade in arms was irrelevant. He was—or had been—a human being. No living creature, man or beast, deserved to be treated that way.

The victim's legs and what remained of his arms had a normal amount of body hair. Curly hair. Maybe black? Antarion Billow from Chicago. Billow was a light-skinned African-American. Chuck never noticed the hair on his legs. Was it that curly? In the army the soldier wore long pants, except when training. This body's tan lines indicated that he customarily wore short-sleeved shirts and long pants. Billow had been a civilian for several years. If it was Billow.

Chuck shifted to the other side of the shelf for a closer look at the tattoo.

"It's three sevens, all right. Looks like Boomer Boonliang's tattoo, but I haven't seen Boomer's tattoo in eight years."

Hank glanced at the body. "This body is circumcised; Boomer isn't. Or wasn't the last time we used that communal shower tent in Afghanistan."

"That's right," Chuck said. "I forgot."

"How about Will Gregg?"

"Possible. Dom Navarre has a Triple Seven tattoo, but it has curlicues. What about Hot Dog Franks?"

"Definitely possible."

Hank seemed to take this better than Chuck was. He'd been a homicide detective for a decade or more. Chuck had only been on the force for a couple of years before he left and got his Private Investigator license. Hank had grown a thicker skin than Chuck had.

"We'll know when we receive the DNA results," Annie said.

"Okay," Hank said. "On to other things. Cause of death?"

"The body was in the water for several days and on the beach for an undetermined amount of time, which makes COD difficult to determine. There were no bullet holes or stab wounds. There was one needle mark on his left biceps." The ME pointed. "I discovered remnants of sodium thiopental in his blood, but without knowing how long before death it was administered, I can't tell the dosage. It depends on the dosage whether the sodium thiopental rendered the victim unconscious so they could kidnap him. A lighter dosage would be used to question him. The obvious wounds from torture didn't kill him. They were applied to create maximum pain with minimum risk of death."

Chuck's mind shuddered again at the reminder of the torture. He hoped to encounter the people who did this someday, regardless of whether this poor guy was his brother in arms.

"Any chance the head and hands were cut off after death?" Hank asked.

Annie shook her head. "The decapitation or amputation of the hands was probably the cause of death because the body was exsanguinated. I can't be a hundred percent certain because immersion in water cleanses wounds, but I found ligature marks on his wrists and ankles." She pointed to noticeable grooves on the forearms near the elbows, stumps of the wrists, and the ankles. "Cable ties."

Chuck leaned closer to the wrists. "Everybody on the planet uses cable ties. He was strapped to a chair during interrogation." He formed a mental picture of the victim struggling against the plastic ties…screaming… dying…From the cut marks around the wrists and forearms, he struggled mightily in his final seconds.

Chuck stepped away from the body to compose himself. He wanted to leave, but he couldn't do that to Hank. Maybe Hank had brought him here for moral support. Maybe his skin wasn't as thick as Chuck thought.

"Anything else to add, Annie?"

Before she replied, she glanced at Chuck to make sure he wouldn't faint or puke. "The damage to the ulna and radius of both arms indicate they were severed with a toothed instrument."

He forced himself to look where the ME pointed.

"The sea water washed the blood away, so it's easy to distinguish the bones."

Almost against his will, Chuck leaned closer. "That might be from a cross-cut saw you'd find in any workshop." Unbidden, a mental image sprang at him—a killer sawing off the victim's hands while the poor guy wrestled valiantly but fruitlessly. His gut felt watery. God, he hated this.

"Compare that to the vertebra," Annie said. "The vertebra was severed with a chopping instrument."

Chuck had investigated two beheadings in Iraq and Afghanistan done by religious extremists. "A hatchet or machete?"

Hank shrugged. "Perhaps." He swung back to the ME. "Where are his clothes?"

"They're at the trace evidence lab, second floor."

Chuck's ordeal wasn't over.

———

Hank tapped the button for the second floor. "You heard from Billow lately?"

"About a year ago. He forwarded an email he'd received with a YouTube link to a video of a military dog reunited with its wounded handler."

"I remember that one. Beautiful dog. Anything since then?"

"Nope. I'll call him."

The elevator doors opened and Chuck stepped into the hall. "That's strange. Billow's mailbox is full. I'll text him." Chuck texted Billow to call him or Hank and told him that his mailbox was full.

"I have his parents' contact info," Hank said.

"Me too, but let's not worry his parents. He could be fishing in the North Woods. Give him until tonight to call back."

"It would be ice fishing this time of winter."

Chuck followed Hank to the reception desk. "You have a John Doe brought in yesterday from Rockfish Key. His clothes are in Trace. Who is lead analyst on the case?"

The receptionist glanced at Hank's shield and name tag and entered them on a keyboard. She consulted her monitor. "The headless body?"

"Yeah."

"The analyst is Gracie Oliver. She's in lab six, but it's buttoned up for a clean room. I'll message her that you're here. You two can sit over there."

"We'll wait in Java Jenny's across the street," Hank said. "Please ask Gracie to call or text me when she's free. She has my number."

———

Chuck claimed a table at Java Jenny's and slid a notepad from his jacket. "Let's call the other Triple Seven guys with darkish skin. If we locate them all, the body isn't ours. Why don't you call Barney Wilkinson and Dominic Navarre?" Chuck scratched names on the pad. "I'll find Will Gregg, Toro Torres, and Phil Franks."

"Should we give everybody a heads-up that one of the team may be dead? Kill two birds with one phone call?"

"I wouldn't bother Harris or Boomer. Harris is a redhead, and we determined it's not Boomer. If the body proves to be a Triple Seven, then we'll call everyone."

In fifteen minutes, they finished the first round of calls and ordered coffee refills.

"What did Barney say?" Chuck asked.

"Straight to voicemail. I called his parents and Barney is on a Caribbean cruise with his fiancée. Dom was at his Cadillac dealership. Said to keep him informed. Did you reach your guys?"

Chuck ticked off names on his pad. "Will Gregg was driving in a snowstorm in an eighteen-wheeler somewhere in southern Kentucky or northern Tennessee. The storm was bad enough he couldn't tell which state he was in. And there was a bad signal. He said to email him once we know something."

"He owns the whole freakin' trucking company," Hank said. "What's he doing on the road? And in a blizzard?"

"I asked him. He said keeping his Teamsters membership wasn't enough; he sets a good example for his drivers. Driving in a snowstorm sends the mail-must-go-through message."

"Is there such a thing as too much dedication?" Hank asked. "What about Toro?"

"Toro was asleep. California is three hours behind us. He said he was alive and well despite being rudely interrupted from his beauty sleep after a double shift at the hospital. I promised to keep him in the loop."

"And Phil Franks?" Hank smirked. "Did you wake up Phil too?"

"Couldn't reach him. If he doesn't call tonight, I'll check with HQ at Fort Benning."

"Another fishing trip like Billow?"

"With Phil, it would be hunting."

Hank's phone signaled a text alert. "That's Gracie Oliver. She's out of the clean room."

———

Chuck studied the tattered picture through the plastic evidence bag, even though every face was engraved in his mind. There was an eleven by fourteen print of that same photo framed in the McCrary Investigations conference room, next to Chuck's Bronze Star medal and citation.

A reporter from Associated Press had asked to take a picture of the Triple Seven for an article about Green Berets in Afghanistan. All twelve of them, each holding their weapon of choice, stood on the mountainside. Chuck selected a Squad Automatic Weapon—a SAW. It wasn't his weapon of choice, but other men held other weapons. Chuck figured someone should display the SAW to demonstrate their range of armaments. The background was raw rock with no grass, no bushes, not a hint of green. Captain Ramirez and Warrant Officer Harris Harrison climbed upslope and held an American flag. Sergeant Frederico "Toro" Torres stood on the left and Sergeant Dominic "Dom" Navarre stood to the right. The other eight, all sergeants of various ranks, lined up across the front. The reporter later emailed each member of Triple Seven a jpeg file of the photo.

It was the last picture taken of the unit before Lawrence "Packy" Packard was killed in action by Taliban soldiers in Ghar Mesar.

Chuck touched the image of Packy on the front row. Every Triple Seven had that photo somewhere. Brothers in arms, never to be forgotten. Every man in that picture had had a part in saving his life more than once. Chuck owed everyone in that picture a debt of honor.

Chuck wiped his eyes with the back of his hand. Hank pretended not to notice.

"The victim is one of ours," Hank said, "and he's Antarion Billow or Phillip Franks. We've accounted for everybody else."

Chuck thought back to Fallujah. Phil Franks had saved his life that day…

"Where did you find this photo?"

"It was folded and stuffed into his right sock," Gracie Oliver replied. "At the bottom under the ball of the foot."

"Was there anything in his pants pockets?" Hank asked.

"His pockets were empty except for sand. Nothing in his shoe either. We're analyzing trace evidence in the fabric of his clothes. That was what I was doing in the clean room."

"He was kidnapped, tortured, and searched," Hank said. "Not necessarily in that order. They removed everything that would identify him —except the tattoo."

Chuck glanced at Hank. "How would he have time to hide this picture?"

"Maybe he kept it in his sock all the time. A good luck charm."

"A lot of good it did him."

"Either way," Hank said, "what did Billow or Franks know that was important enough to torture him to death? Whichever guy it was, why the hell was he here and why didn't he call us to say 'hello'?"

Chuck handed the photo back to the analyst. "He was sworn to secrecy?"

"Or maybe someone was monitoring him. His phone was tapped, or his car was tagged with a GPS tracker. Something kept him from contacting us."

"Whatever it was, it must have been pretty damned heavy for him not to call." *What the hell have you gotten me into, Hank?*

———

The two men walked to a Mexican restaurant near the Crime Lab and selected a booth. The server wrote their orders and walked away.

"Buster Cleveland pulled the case? Any chance you can take it, Hank?"

"Nah. Seeti Bay State Park is Downtown's responsibility. Buster was next in the assignment rotation. His partner is Melissa Chan."

"I don't know her."

"No reason you should. You've been off the job five years. Lots of new blood. Lissa moved here from Orlando a year ago. She was an Orange County Sheriff's detective for eleven years. Buster says she's a top-notch cop. Between us, Buster reached his thirty years a few years ago, but he won't retire. If he stays on the job much longer, he'll end up working for her instead of the other way around."

The server brought their meals. Hank smiled his thanks.

"If you worked the case, there's a better chance that the killers would get shot resisting arrest or trying to escape," Chuck said. "You don't want them getting off on a technicality."

Hank peered at Chuck for a long breath. "That's not it. My job is to bring in criminals, alive if I can, so they will face a judge and jury in a fair trial. Buster Cleveland and Melissa Chan will do that too."

"Okay, boss." Chuck spooned salsa on the enchiladas.

"I haven't been the boss for ten years."

"And I haven't been a sergeant. But when you called yesterday, I came. You'll always be boss of the Triple Seven. That means you call Billow's and Franks's parents and give them a heads-up. Once the ME gets DNA back and determines which one is the victim, the death notice shouldn't come from a stranger in the Port City police department. It should come from his commanding officer."

"You're right, but God, I hate to do this. I remember calling Packy's family; then I wrote letters to his wife and parents. Thank God that was the only death notification I had to handle in the Army." He shook his head. "Scoot that salsa over here, will you?"

"Cheer up: All we know is the men are missing. We haven't confirmed a death until we get DNA back. Death notifications come with the territory, Hank. You will forever be commanding officer of the Triple Seven to those of us who served under you."

Chuck's phone signaled a text from Ruby.

At the airport. Boarding now. Arrival should be on time. I crave Cuban food. Among other things. Love, Ruby

Hank noticed his friend reading the text.

"Good news?"

"My girlfriend's plane arrives at 4:10 this afternoon. She's spending a week."

"Good for you. Is she the one?"

"Too soon to tell."

Ruby and Chuck had met the previous October in Texas where Chuck worked with the Austin police to locate his missing cousin. They had three dates in Austin. She'd made two trips to Port City before and after Christmas. It was too soon to talk about love, or marriage, or children, but so far Chuck hadn't uncovered any deal breakers.

Hank reviewed his phone contacts. "I have Billow's parents' contact info from our baseball trip. Another thing, Chuck, if Billow or Franks was here on business, he'd call one of us or Gunner to meet him for breakfast or a drink after work. Nobody's heard from either of them."

"The obvious conclusion is that he didn't want us to learn he was here. Does Billow still work for that printer in Chicago?"

"I think so. Do you remember the name?"

"I'll never forget it. Two veterans founded it after the Viet Nam War. They named it the Bald Eagle Printing Company. Why do you ask?"

"Buster will want us to contact Billow's employer and parents to ask if he's working there and, if he's not, maybe they can tell us why he was in Port City. Fort Benning can tell us Franks's current status."

Chuck had already looked up the printing company's phone number. "I have it. I'll call them. You finish eating." He scooted the plate aside and plunked his notepad on the table.

"Hello, may I speak to the personnel department, please? Yes, I'll hold." Chuck was so hungry it was hard to wait.

"Yes, I'm calling on behalf of Captain Hidalgo Ramirez with the Port City Florida Police Department. We are trying to locate one of your employees. His name is Antarion Billow." Chuck spelled both names. "Is he there? Yes, I'll hold."

He scarfed another bite and picked up a pen. "Yes, I'm here."

A woman came on the line. "We don't have anyone named Antarion Billow, but we had an employee named Andrew Billow. Could that be the guy?"

"Black man, about six foot six? Former Green Beret?"

"That's Andrew, but he doesn't work here anymore."

"Could you give me his emergency contact information, please?" Chuck jotted names and numbers on the pad. "Thank you. How long ago did he quit?" He put that on the notepad. "Did he leave a forwarding address? No? May I talk to Mr. Billow's supervisor? Out to lunch? Please tell Ms. Florence I'll call back in an hour. I presume she'll be back then? Thank you for your help."

Chuck disconnected.

"Antarion Billow changed his name to Andrew Billow. He quit around Christmas. He drew his final paycheck and left no forwarding address. We should call his supervisor. Perhaps she knows why he quit or what he was up to."

Hank picked up his fork. "Andrew? Why Andrew? Let's finish lunch and go back to your car. We'll call Billow's supervisor and put it on Bluetooth so we can both talk."

"Right."

———

Chuck drove to the top of the police garage to ensure a good signal before he placed the call. The ring tone switched from his phone to the radio speaker as the Bluetooth picked up the call.

"Bald Eagle Printing Company. How may I direct your call?"

"Esther Florence please."

"Please hold."

Chuck positioned the phone on the center console. "Take it from here. You're the cop. I'm a lowly civilian."

"You're a taxpayer; that's the highest form of life to us dedicated public servants."

"This is Esther Florence."

"Ms. Florence. I'm Detective Captain Hank Ramirez with the Police Department in Port City, Florida. We are attempting to locate Antarion Billow a/k/a Andrew Billow. We understand you were his supervisor."

"Yeah. The office said you would call. We were real sorry Andy quit. He was a good employee, worked here for five years."

"What was his job?"

"An offset press operator."

"May I ask: When did he quit?"

"Three weeks ago? He come to my office after his shift, and he give notice before Christmas. I offered to go to management to get him a raise, maybe a better shift, but he wouldn't have none of that. I got him an extra Christmas bonus, but he wouldn't change his mind. Said he had a better deal lined up."

"Did he say where he was going?"

"Why you asking about Andy? Is he in trouble? He wasn't the type to be in trouble with the law."

"No, ma'am, he's not in trouble with the law, but he is a material witness in another matter, so we need to talk to him. Where did he go after he quit Bald Eagle Printing?"

"Is he missing? Is that why you called?"

Hank shrugged. "Yes, ma'am. He's missing. Where did he go to work after he left?"

"Wish I could help, captain, but I don't know. He said he'd located a better opportunity in Florida. Him and his girlfriend both. Said it paid so well it was like printing money."

"Doing what?"

"Printers are always looking for good offset operators. It's gotta be the same in Florida as here in Chicago. I asked Andy how much it would take to get him to stay. He said they were paying more than we could match. All I could do was wish him good luck."

"Have you heard from him since?"

"No. We weren't friends or nothing. I was his boss."

"Did he have trouble with anybody there? Did anybody threaten him?"

"You're kidding, right? Nobody would be fool enough to mess with Andy. He was big, and he was a Green Beret. Anyhow, Andy was on good terms with everybody. He's a gentle giant."

"Thanks." Hank gazed his way. "Any questions, Chuck?"

"Ms. Florence, this is Chuck McCrary. Do you recall his girlfriend's name?"

"I remember her first name because I have a friend with the same name, Aisha."

"Could you spell that, please?"

"A-I-S-H-A."

"How about her last name?"

"It was a funny name. Sounded Polish or Hungarian or maybe one of them Russian names."

"Did you ever meet Aisha?"

"She come here once to pick him up after work. His car was in the shop."

"Can you describe her?"

"She wore a head scarf so I couldn't see her hair real good. Brunette I believe it was. Wore fancy sandals with low heels, an ankle-length skirt. Real ornate, it was. She was about my height."

"How tall are you?"

"Oh, yeah, I'm five-foot-five."

"Anything else? Was she white, black, Asian?"

"Asian, maybe. She wasn't quite white and wasn't real dark neither."

"Did she have an accent?"

"Don't everybody nowadays?"

"Sometimes it seems that way, doesn't it. What sort of accent?"

"Hard to tell. All she said was 'pleased to meet you.' I could tell English weren't her first language, but I couldn't tell you where she come from."

"Was she fat, skinny, medium?"

"Real slender, she was. A hundred pounds soaking wet. An exotic face. She and Andy were an odd couple. He was a foot taller than her."

"Thanks for your help, Ms. Florence."

Hank ended the phone call. "What do you make of that, Sherlock?"

"It sounded as if Billow's girlfriend was an immigrant, possibly Muslim—depends on the type of scarf she wore—and he and she were going to work at the same company."

"I don't think Billow is Muslim."

"He wasn't when the Triple Seven was in the Middle East. It would have come up in conversation when we were in those Muslim countries."

"Maybe he converted in Chicago. Lots of black Muslims in the Chicago area."

"If he did, it was after you and I saw him last. Ask his parents about that and about the girlfriend."

"I'll call."

Chuck extended the phone to him.

"I'll use my phone," Hank said. "I don't want this call on the Bluetooth. It sounds so...*public* to someone on the other end. Billow's parents shouldn't feel that someone is listening in, even you."

"Hank, you surprise me with how sensitive you are. You pretend to be a hard-ass, all-business, SOB of a cop. But underneath, you're a marshmallow. I would never think about how a phone call sounds from the other end."

"I cry at sad movies too."

"Should I step out of the car?"

"*Hmm.* Now that you mention it, yeah."

Chuck closed the driver's door and walked to the edge of the deck, surveying the skyscrapers that soared above the garage on all sides. The afternoon sea breeze was cool on his skin. A few minutes later a car window buzzed open. Hank motioned him back to the car.

Chuck buckled his seat belt. "What did Billow's parents say?"

"His mother checked her phone log. Billow called them nine days ago—January 8th. He was in Palm City with his fiancée—Aisha Aubakirovna—he told them."

"That sounds Russian. Was she a foreigner?"

"Let me finish. His parents weren't sure where she was from, but believed it was a former Soviet republic. Billow apologized for not calling them for a long time and told them he was fine. They asked what he was doing and he said it was secret. He couldn't tell them, but he said he was fighting to free oppressed people again—like in Afghanistan—but this time not with a gun. Billow claimed it was better his parents didn't know. If anyone asked, they could truthfully say they didn't know what he was up to.

"Whatever he's into, Chuck, it's illegal. Perhaps there are clues in Chicago. Since that's a soft *perhaps*, the Port City PD won't pay to travel there unless they uncover a hard clue essential to the case. One of us should visit Bald Eagle Printing and talk to Billow's parents. You're the guy with the big bucks. You're also self-employed, so it's easy for you to take time off."

"You're awfully generous with my time and my money." Going to Chicago in the middle of winter was not high on Chuck's Bucket List.

"Well, you said I'm the boss and God knows you can afford the trip."

Chuck grinned. "Okay, *boss*. But the trip has to wait a week." He threw the car into reverse. "My girlfriend arrives this afternoon to spend a week with me. Here, not in Chicago. She's waiting out the icy weather in sunny South Florida."

"But you'll go the week after?"

Chuck headed for the exit. "Yes, but right now, I'm due to pick up Ruby at the airport after I drop you at your car."

FIVE

R uby exited the security area of the terminal with a tote bag slung on her shoulder. She waved and walked faster.

When she reached Chuck, she swung her tote bag around to her back and threw her arms around his neck. Thrusting the length of her body against his, she breathed in his ear. "Oh, god, that feels good."

Chuck returned her squeeze. "Me too."

"Are you glad to see me?" she murmured.

"No, that's a gun in my pocket."

Ruby chuckled, her lips against his neck.

After a minute, they relented and held each other at arm's-length.

"You checked bags? Unless you only brought your bikini to wear and it's in your tote."

She squeezed his arm. "Two bags. One for winter clothes to wear to and from the Austin airport and another with summer clothes for Florida."

They made their way to the baggage carrousels. She handed Chuck her baggage claim stubs. "Let's head straight to your condo. I need a shower, and I'm hungry."

"We can stop at a restaurant."

"It's not food I'm hungry for."

———

After a late dinner, they lingered in the Cuban restaurant. Chuck had missed Ruby. It was great to have her back in his life, even for a week.

"Before we head back to my apartment, we should share one of those fancy rum drinks served in a coconut with a flower stuck in the top. With two straws."

She acted surprised.

"Yes, it's kitschy and touristy, but I'm a local. You should experience the whole nine yards of the South Florida tourist experience. Both times you were here last month, we didn't get out much."

She rubbed the back of his hand. "Good decision, lover. I can go girls-gone-wild on you later."

As they sucked on long, curvy, plastic straws, Ruby and Chuck did what cops do; they talked shop. One coconut drink soon led to another. Since Chuck would drive home, he let her do the drinking. She appeared to enjoy it, and he wasn't much of a drinker. He told her about the body on the beach and that Hank had asked him to go to Chicago.

"You'd have flown to Chicago tomorrow," she asked, "if I hadn't come to Port City?"

Chuck waffled his hand. "Chicago in the winter is not high on my list of priorities. I'll make the trip next week after you fly home. I'll walk you to your gate, then take the next plane to O'Hare."

"Tell me again why this is so important to Hank. The Port City cops already have two detectives working the case, right? Why do they need you?"

"It's not that they need my help necessarily. The Port City detectives don't have the budget to travel to Chicago on such a slim lead. I have the money and the time, so Hank asked me to help out. No biggie."

Ruby took another long pull on her drink. The gold liquid rose in the transparent straw. "Your friend Hank asked you to help out with this case, but you're gonna lollygag with me this week instead of flying to Chicago?"

"What's on your mind, Ruby?"

She finished the last of the rum and coconut. Her hand found Chuck's again. "This is too important to wait. You can't delay another week while the trail grows cold. Neither of us would enjoy this week with that lurking in the corner of our minds. You should fly to Chicago on Monday."

"I can't abandon you in Port City. What kind of host would do that?"

"You won't abandon me. I'll fly with you. Don't worry, handsome. We'll have fun this weekend, then we'll travel to Chicago and work the case."

While Ruby was having her weekend fun, Chuck worried about what they might find in Chicago.

———

Chuck's weather app forecast a blizzard in Chicago. He'd reserved a four-wheel-drive Jeep at O'Hare International Airport before he and Ruby left Port City. He elected not to bring firearms to Chicago. His Florida Concealed Weapon Permit was good in three dozen states, but Illinois wasn't one of them.

Chicago has a reputation as a dangerous city, but Chuck figured the TV news overstated that like they overstate most dangers. Hank and Chuck visited years before, and they spent a delightful sojourn in Chicago. They didn't dodge a single bullet.

As the airplane descended toward the runway, Chuck leaned against Ruby and peered out the window. All they could see was blowing snow. Once again, he asked himself what Hank had gotten him involved in.

Ruby grimaced. "It's ten o'clock in the morning and it's twilight outside. This is worse than what I left in Austin."

He chuckled. "Must be true love for you to flee Austin for sunny Florida only to fly with me to the frozen tundra."

Ruby rolled her eyes.

The snow fell so thick they couldn't make out the terminals as the plane continued to descend. They couldn't even make out the ground. The bump of wheels on the runway caught Chuck by surprise.

"I'm dreading the trip to Billow's parents' house. It's gonna be a nightmare obstacle course," Chuck said.

Ruby stayed with the bags inside the terminal, while Chuck went to pick up the rental car.

As he stepped off the elevator into the parking garage, the sub-freezing wind blasted him in the face. It felt like a frozen sandstorm. Chuck had tried to buy a winter coat before they left Florida, but the local stores didn't stock them. The raincoat he wore was a poor substitute.

The north wind clawed at his hands, face, and ears as he instinctively scanned the parking garage—a habit from his Special Forces days that still served him well over a decade removed from the army. "Situational awareness might save your life," his instructor had stressed. "After you neutralize the first threat, scan for another one to your right, left, and behind you, especially in an urban environment with no clearly-defined battle lines. After you fire your weapon, do a 360 ASAP." Good advice: I'm thirty-five years old and still alive.

Chuck leaned into the wind and trudged to the car rental booth. His exposed skin burned as if frostbitten by the time he lumbered into the tiny booth.

The car rental clerk was bundled in a parka and mittens. His breath puffed out small clouds of vapor in the glassed-in space.

"I expected it to be warmer in your booth," Chuck said with a smile.

"Nah, man. This booth has glass walls. What with wind chill, it don't get above freezing in here. That's why they issue us these parkas to wear, even inside. What's your name?"

"Carlos McCrary."

The clerk completed the paperwork and directed him to his rental car. He instructed Chuck on the best route to travel to Des Plaines in the snow, warned him about the Chicago natives, who were kamikazes on wheels, and provided him with directions to the closest Walmart to buy some winter clothing.

He thrust a keyfob across the counter.

"Thanks for the advice," he said, as he fumbled with a frigid hand to pick up the keyfob.

Chuck skidded on an icy patch on his way to the car and struggled to keep his balance.

Chuck yanked twice before the door opened, jumped inside, and searched the dash franticly for the "Heat" button.

By the time Chuck got to the terminal to pick up Ruby, the car interior had warmed to where he no longer saw his breath.

Ruby was waiting, wrapped in her winter coat. Chuck stopped at the curb and she wheeled out her first bag.

Chuck clicked the remote button to open the rear hatch, but it didn't budge. Frozen like a duck caught on a lake. Throwing open the driver's door, he skidded on another icy patch, slammed the door shut to conserve heat, and teetered to the rear of the car.

The weatherstripping around the rear hatch creaked in protest when Chuck jerked it from its frozen position. He threw Ruby's first bag in and rushed back to the terminal to bring the other bags out, tossing his carry-on in the back seat.

Damn, it was cold in Chicago in January. Chuck had felt this cold in the Afghan mountains in January. That was a long time ago.

Skidding back to the driver's door, he grabbed the door handle. His feet slipped out from under him. He felt like a bear on ice skates.

He tumbled to the icy concrete, and something tore in his left shoulder. He skinned the palm of his hand breaking his fall.

Ruby jumped out of the passenger seat and bolted around the rear of the car.

Chuck waved her to a halt. "Funny, we haven't left the airport and I'm wounded in action." The words puffed clouds of fog.

"No Purple Heart this time, though," Ruby said. She lurched back to the passenger side of the car, leaning on the fenders.

———

Chuck's cellphone rang. He had forgotten to pair his phone with the car's Bluetooth.

"Should I answer?" Ruby asked.

"No. My phone is in a belt holster. Too dangerous to fish it out while we're driving. Let it go to voicemail."

Cars jammed and skidded on the boulevard. Using a cellphone in this weather and this traffic would be suicidal. The ringing continued to annoy them until it switched to voicemail.

Creeping at less than fifteen mph, they lurched down the snowy streets until the Walmart sign flared through the snow, a lighthouse beacon in the twilight. The weather didn't deter the intrepid shoppers and the lot was half full. Chicagoans were used to blizzards.

"You better park far from the other cars," Ruby said, "or you might get banged into."

"Good idea."

Chuck parked in a space a hundred yards from the store. It was tough to do, but he talked Ruby into staying in the car with the heat on, while he tackled the long, treacherous walk to Walmart's entrance.

When he returned, sporting a new winter overcoat, he threw the wet raincoat in the back seat. Ruby leaned over and gave him a kiss on his cold cheek. "Better?"

"Much." Chuck pulled off the thick fur-lined gloves he had bought, but left his muffler around his neck. Damn it was cold. He rubbed his hands together until enough circulation returned to hold his cellphone. Then he checked his missed call. It was Hank Ramirez.

Chuck returned the call.

"Hey, Chuck. I left you a voicemail."

"Yeah. I'm creeping through the damnedest blizzard I've faced since winter in the Afghan mountains, and this is worse. You owe me big time for this, Hank."

"At least this time, no one is trying to kill you."

"Not with a rifle anyway. The way the locals drive, I swear they have a death wish. We passed more wrecked vehicles on the way from the airport than we saw in Kandahar. We parked where it was safe to call you. Whatcha got?"

"Phil's Commanding Officer said his enlistment ran out last month and he didn't re-up. His C.O. doesn't know where he went."

"Franks isn't at Fort Benning anymore?"

"Nope. I traced his cellphone. He hasn't used it in six days, but the last tower it pinged was in Port City."

"He's with Billow."

"That would be a pretty good bet. Why don't you swing by Fort Benning on your way home and poke around? You might find a clue."

"You're spending my money like I was the Federal Government."

"It's for a good cause."

"That's what the congressmen say too. Still costs the taxpayers a shitload of money." Chuck sighed for Hank's benefit. "Oh, well. What's his C.O.'s name?"

"Captain Vincent Hightower. I'll text you his direct phone number."

"At least there won't be a blizzard in Georgia."

"I wouldn't count on it. It's snowing in Chattanooga right now."

Chuck disconnected and called the Billows' phone.

"Heather? This is Chuck McCrary. Ruby and I are running later than we expected. We'll be another couple of hours. We're sticking to city streets and creeping like a turtle. We stopped at Walmart to buy winter clothes; we'll grab something to eat while we're here."

"Is that the one between my house and the airport?"

"Yes, ma'am."

"They don't have a fast-food restaurant inside. Jeff and I were looking forward to you two eating lunch with us."

"Yes, ma'am, we were looking forward to it also, but it's already two-thirty and you and Jeff shouldn't postpone lunch any longer. We're not really hungry anyway. We ate on the plane," Chuck lied. He hoped they couldn't hear his stomach growling over the phone. Hopefully the connection wasn't that good. "Y'all go ahead and eat. We'll get there ASAP."

"You remember how to get here? We're in the same house we were in before. We'll put you in Andrew's room. It's bigger than the guest room. He would like that."

Theoretically, sunset was fifteen minutes away, but the snowy overcast sucked up the light until none reached the ground. Chuck curved into the Billows' driveway and parked beside their minivan.

Chuck drew a long breath and exhaled. His muscles were sore from being clenched. "I feel like I've been driving for days." He rolled his shoulders and drew three slow breaths. Buttoning his new overcoat, he yanked the new watch cap over his ears and contemplated the weather through the frosty windows.

"The snow has abated and the wind's died down. I can make the front door without wearing my new muffler and fur-lined gloves." He grabbed his carry-on bag from the back seat and popped the rear hatch.

"Suit yourself, superman. I'm glad I wore my ski outfit."

Chuck snatched the two heaviest bags from the back. Ruby carried the third bag, closed the hatch, and bounded ahead. She danced, a deer in the forest; he waddled, a walrus crossing a rocky beach.

She clutched the stair rail and stepped into the footprints on the snowy steps. The porch light flicked on. Ruby kept to the footprints all the way to the top. Chuck stepped in the same footprints. The door swung open, and they stomped their feet on the welcome mat.

———

Jeff Billow was a tall, slender black man with salt-and-pepper hair. He stepped onto the porch wearing a turtle-neck sweater. He grabbed Ruby's bag. "We'll do introductions inside where it's warmer." He beckoned the young couple into the entryway and closed the door. "Give me your coats and I'll hang them in the closet. Man, it's good to see you, Chuck. It's been what, five years? And you would be Ruby Voight. Pleased to meet you."

They shook hands, and Jeff hung their overcoats in the entrance closet. He shook Chuck's hand with both of his. Tears glistened in his eyes. "Come in, come in. Heather is in the living room. I told her to stay out of the entryway; it's a deep freeze in the winter."

He opened another door and Heather Billow enveloped Chuck in a warm hug. "Chuck, my boy. It's good of you to come. And this is your... friend? Hello, I'm Heather Billow. Welcome to our home. Can I make us hot cocoa?"

"Yes, ma'am," Chuck said. "I'm frozen through to my backbone."

After the introductions and the *how-have-you-beens*, Jeff led them to his son's bedroom. He closed the door behind them. "Heather keeps up a good front, but she's worried about Andrew."

Chuck was surprised when he spoke of his son as Andrew. "Uh, Jeff, what's this about Antarion changing his name to Andrew? Last time we talked was a couple years ago but he was Antarion then."

Jeff smiled. "He told Heather and me he meant no disrespect, but he was tired of spelling his name. He changed it to Andrew."

"Well, *Andrew* isn't dead; he's *missing*," Chuck said. "We don't know whether the body is him or Phillip Franks."

Jeff rocked his hand. "Fifty-fifty. Not good odds."

Chuck debated telling the Billows about Hank's phone call. He decided to do that once Billow's parents were together.

"I hope our visit hasn't dredged up bad memories."

"No, no, son. You visiting is the best thing that could happen until we know one way or the other. We want to help."

He opened the door. "You two freshen up. We'll serve the cocoa in the living room."

Ten minutes later, Chuck and Ruby joined his missing friend's parents in the living room.

Heather smiled. "It was inconsiderate of Andrew to go missing in January. Why couldn't he quit his job and move to Port City in June? Then you two would have nice weather to hunt for clues."

It had been three or four years since Chuck saw Billow. Hank and Chuck had flown to Chicago in June to watch the Port City Pilots play a three-game series with the White Sox and to visit Billow. The weather had been magnificent.

Chuck remembered examining that headless body and his stomach knotted. Whether it was Billow or Franks didn't matter; the killers would pay. It was killers, plural, because one man couldn't capture either Andrew Billow or Phillip Franks alive. Former Special Forces soldiers were always dangerous.

Chuck shook his head to banish the image.

Halfway through his mug of cocoa, Jeff cleared his throat. "Now that the small talk is out of the way, tell Heather and me how we can help."

Chuck fished a notepad from his jacket. "For starters, tell us about Aisha..." He stumbled over the unfamiliar pronunciation, "Aubakirovna. Did I say that right?"

Jeff smiled without humor. "We had to practice some to learn how to pronounce it without spraining our tonsils."

"You said she was his fiancée?"

"Andrew proposed to Aisha three weeks before they left for Port City."

Heather made a sour face. "He dated that girl for two months. You can't be sure you want to spend the rest of your life with someone in two months."

Jeff chuckled. "I wanted to marry you ten seconds after we met."

"Yeah, but you weren't dumb enough to propose until we'd been on a decent number of dates and met each other's parents," Heather said. "That took two years."

"We waited until we graduated. Andrew's thirty-four years old. It's past time for him to marry. We're lucky they want to marry instead of just shacking up. Times have changed, honey."

Heather frowned. "In too many ways."

"How did Andrew and Aisha meet?" Chuck asked.

"They never really answered that question," Jeff said. "Most folks have a good story to share on how they met their wife or husband. It seemed unusual that Andrew never mentioned how they met."

"How did you two feel about that?"

The muscles in Jeff's jaw tightened. "Heather and I are Baptists and we raised our children that way." He glanced at his wife, then at Ruby. "Are you and Chuck the same religion, Ruby?"

Beneath her light brown skin, Ruby flushed as red as her namesake jewel. The closest she and Chuck had come to discussing religion was singing along with the Christmas carols on the radio during her first visit to Port City in mid-December. They knew the same Christmas carols. That was good enough for now.

Heather shook a finger at Jeff. "Jefferson Clarence Billow, you mind your own business. These are our guests. Don't pry."

Ruby cut her gaze to Chuck as she lifted her mug to her lips. She wasn't drinking cocoa—she was hiding behind the mug.

Heather patted Ruby on the knee. "Sorry, honey. Jeff is too nosy for his own good. Jeff and I met at the Mount Gilead Baptist Church when we were in high school. We were married in that church, and we've been members ever since. We were concerned when Andrew stopped attending church. Later we learned it was after he met that girl."

Chuck welcomed the chance to change the subject. "Did he attend a mosque with Aisha?"

"Not that I know of. I don't believe she's Muslim. The first we learned about her was the day Andrew brought her home to introduce us and announced they were engaged. He opened a bottle of Champagne he brought to celebrate, and she drank with us. I believed Muslims aren't supposed to drink alcohol, and I'm pretty sure she was sleeping with Andrew. From what I am told, Muslims—women anyway—believe in confining sex to marriage."

"She's not Muslim?" Ruby asked.

"But she dressed the part," Heather said.

"Perhaps that's the way everyone dresses in her home country, regardless of religion."

"Maybe. I know she always wore a head scarf."

"They call it a hijab," Jeff said.

"Right, a hijab. She wore that and long sleeves and long dresses. She dressed like a Muslim, but she didn't act like one."

"So, the attraction between them wasn't religious," Ruby said.

"No, the attraction between those two wasn't religion."

"What was it?" Chuck asked.

Heather gave Chuck a look. "Besides the usual?"

"Besides the usual."

"Maybe politics. We met her a handful of times, but we don't know her well. As far as we know, Andrew wasn't interested in foreign affairs until he met her. Then he became interested in political repression in Russia and other countries behind the former Iron Curtain. He said democracy hadn't taken root in the old Soviet Union countries, especially the Asian ones."

"Andrew sprung his fiancée on us with no notice," Jeff said, "and two weeks later, they announced they were moving to Port City. *Bang-bang*, fast. Aisha cast a spell over him. He wouldn't listen to us."

"Did he mention Phillip Franks" Chuck asked, "the one we called Hot Dog?"

"No more than he mentioned any of you boys in the Triple Seven. Why do you ask?"

"Phillip Franks let his enlistment expire last month. Hank Ramirez called me while I was driving here. Franks last used his phone six days ago —in Port City."

"They must have met in Port City," Heather said. "They quit their jobs at the same time. That can't be coincidence."

"I agree," Chuck said. "Where is Aisha from?"

"I'm not sure. One of those 'stan' countries. Turkmenistan or Uzbekistan or Pakistan. Somewhere like that."

Chuck wrote *ends in stan* on the notepad. "Is Aisha a U.S. citizen?"

Jeff shrugged. "That's another thing that concerned us about their whirlwind courtship. Was she luring Andy into marriage so she could become a citizen?"

"And before we learned more about her," Heather said, "*whoosh*, they moved to Florida."

"Do you have a picture of her?"

"On my phone," Jeff said. "They announced their engagement, and I snapped their picture."

"Can you send it to me?"

"Sure."

Chuck's phone signaled. "Got it. Thanks. Do you have her phone number?"

Jeff grunted. "Hell, we were damned lucky to learn how to spell her name."

SIX

Chuck wheeled into the first visitor spot at the front of the snowy parking lot. Snow had been plowed to the back of the pavement, but it was accumulating again. The dirty, white pile was four parking spaces higher than the roof of the car.

"Geez," Ruby said, "I thought it was bad in Austin. We didn't get enough snow to make a decent snowman."

"Pack some in your suitcase; make a snowman once you get back to Texas."

Bald Eagle Printing Company occupied a freestanding building in an industrial district of Elk Grove Village. The sun peeked out and sprinkled the snow on the dormant front lawn with tiny sparkles. The temperature hovered around twenty-five degrees. The weather in Afghanistan hit sixteen degrees during one of Chuck's tours. This seemed colder. Of course, the Army issued the right clothing for an Afghan winter. The memory made Chuck shiver.

He handed the GPS to Ruby. "Stow this in the glove box. This industrial neighborhood probably has no street crime in this weather, but there's no point flaunting the electronic device on the dashboard. It shouts that we're not local."

She stowed the GPS and closed the box. "Ready."

They exited the car.

Chuck rotated a slow 360 to survey the territory. No one on the rooftops. No one in a burqa. Would-be suicide bombers of both sexes hide bombs beneath the religious coverall. No footprints in the snow from a sniper positioned in the hedges.

Ruby noticed. "What are you doing?"

"Surveying the scene for danger. An old habit I learned in Special Forces."

"You afraid of a surprise attack?"

"No, no, nothing like that. But I'm thirty-five years old and still alive. I plan to stay that way. You never noticed me surveying the scene before?"

"Nope, but I've never been in a war zone. I may work for the Austin Police Department, but no one's ever tried to ambush me." She patted his arm. "You keep on keeping us safe, hero." She laughed and pivoted toward the building entrance.

Snow covered the evergreen shrubs on both sides of the entrance to the brick building. A Hunter's Green canvas awning over the double glass entrance doors displayed the company name and street address.

"You need to hold my hand?" Chuck asked.

"I'm pretty good at walking on snow and ice. You should hold *my* hand." Ruby grinned and scampered ahead, nimble as a gymnast.

"That would be bad for my super tough image."

Chuck hiked from the parking lot, placing his feet on the salt-covered sidewalk. Ruby was already inside.

He stomped the snow from his shoes on the rubber mat before opening the door.

Ruby waited in one of the two chairs in the small reception area.

A middle-aged woman talked on the phone at one of the desks. She glanced their way and lifted a finger to signal she would be a minute.

Chuck smiled an "okay" and perused the room. Posters of brochures, catalogs, newsletters, and other products dotted the office. A wooden cabinet held two company softball trophies and a Chamber of Commerce plaque. A throbbing whir hummed from beyond the wall. Noise from the offset presses.

The woman hung up. "Can I help you?"

"I'm Chuck McCrary and this is my associate Ruby Voight. We have an appointment with Esther Florence."

"Oh, yeah. You're the detectives looking for Andy Billow."

Chuck decided not to tell her they weren't detectives. It made no difference.

"Yes, ma'am. Would you tell Ms. Florence we're here?"

"No need to call me 'ma'am'."

"I was raised in Texas, ma'am. I call every woman 'ma'am'."

The woman smiled. "I'll page her."

In a minute, one of two doors on the back wall opened and a chunky woman with salt-and-pepper hair walked through, drying her hands on a paper towel. She tossed the towel into a receptacle and walked over to greet them. "I'm Esther Florence."

They shook hands and Chuck introduced Ruby. "How can I help you, Mr. McCrary?"

"Please call me Chuck. Andrew Billow is missing and possibly dead."

"Oh, God, I hope Andy's not dead. How can I help?"

"We're here to uncover clues. Could we see where Andrew worked, learn what he did, and examine his locker? We'd appreciate it."

"Ain't you supposed to show me your badge or something?"

Chuck drew out his PI license and handed Esther Florence a business card. She studied the license. "You ain't no a cop."

"No, ma'am, but I used to be. I was a robbery-homicide detective with the Port City Police Department before I became a PI. Ms. Voight is a criminalist with the Austin Texas Police Department. She is helping with the case. Captain Ramirez, whom you talked to on the phone, and I were in the Special Forces unit with Andy in Iraq and Afghanistan. Although at that time his name was still Antarion. Ruby and I volunteered to help with the case on our own time. Billow was a brother to me."

"Didn't the Port City cops assign detectives to the case? Why are you two here?"

"Budgetary constraints with the Port City police department make it difficult to authorize travel on a case. The detectives would need to have hard evidence that required an out-of-town trip to investigate, which they don't have. Chances of uncovering something in Chicago that helps discover the killer are slim. Ruby and I volunteered to help the police detectives on our own nickel."

Chuck spread his hands. "Here we are, clutching at straws. In the snow."

"Sounds good to me. Where should we start?"

"How about Andy's locker?"

"It's this way." Florence led the way down a hall, through a break room, and into an adjoining locker room.

"Which is Andy's locker?"

"We gave his locker to a new employee, but I dumped his stuff into that Campbell's Soup box on the top of the lockers. I don't remember what's in there. I figured Andy might come back for it or call me to send it to him. Now that he's missing, I better send it to his next of kin, huh?"

"That would be his parents, Jeff and Heather Billow. Ruby and I are staying with them. I'll give it to them if you like. First, let's see what's in there. Might be nothing but junk."

Chuck reached for the box and his left shoulder pulsed with pain from his losing battle with the O'Hare parking garage. He rubbed his shoulder and Ruby lugged the cardboard box to the table in the break room.

"Thanks, Ruby."

He opened the flaps.

"Wear evidence gloves, Chuck," Ruby said.

"Good idea. I knew there was a reason I brought you along."

Together they inventoried the contents. A Chicago Bulls hat, sweat-stained from long use, was on top. Chuck raised a Bulls sweatshirt with a vivid stain on the right sleeve. The shirt's material was stiff from the ink spill.

"What's that stain?" he asked Florence.

"That's magenta ink," she said. "It's one of the four colors of ink we use on the Heidelberg. Andy, he must have spilled some loading the ink dispenser."

"The Heidelberg? What's that?"

"That's what we call our offset press. It's manufactured in Heidelberg, Germany. It's the best damned press in the business. That sucker costs over a half-million dollars."

"I can't wait to see it." Chuck folded the sweatshirt and put it beside the hat. He lifted out a folded U. S. Army sweatshirt. Holding it to his nose, he smelled fabric softener. Billow must have kept a clean sweatshirt in his locker for emergencies. Chuck refolded it and aligned it with the Bulls apparel. On the bottom of the soup box lay a pair of dirty sneakers. He lifted the shoes and examined them, flipping them over. The right heel was worn to the next layer of rubber. Chuck was repacking the box for his parents when a colorful piece of paper folded into a square fell out of the right sneaker. Mentally, Chuck kicked himself for not thinking to look inside the shoes from the get-go.

Chuck unfolded the paper. It was a foreign currency. The number *200* was printed several times on both sides. He held it where Esther Florence could study it. "Do you recognize this?"

Florence reached for the bill and he yanked it back.

"Let me hold it for you. We don't want more fingerprints on it." He flipped the bill over to let Florence examine it.

"That's not the English alphabet," she said. "Russian? Me, I got a collection of Canadian bills in a drawer at home. They have pretty pictures of Canadian landscapes. Maybe Andy went on vacation to wherever this is and kept it for a souvenir. It's pretty enough."

"Have you seen it before?"

"Nope. Maybe Bailey would know. He's the other Heidelberg operator. We'll ask him when we get to the press room."

Chuck slipped the bill into a paper evidence bag and then into his pocket and replaced the soup box. "Can we stash this here until we finish the tour?"

"Sure. Pick it up on the way out. Let me show you the rest of the shop."

Florence led them through the paper room, the cutting room, the folding machines, the cutters, and into the press room. The huge machine was almost purring. Chuck was surprised at how quiet it was.

"This is the Heidelberg." She gestured at the machine and beamed with obvious pride.

Florence led them to one end and explained what each section did for the print job. She read an entry on the control panel. "It's running a program booklet for a convention in Chicago this April. Five thousand copies."

"This process looks complicated."

"It is. It's a slew of moving parts, starting the feeder system that loads the sheets one at time. Then come four separate printing units, one for each color of ink. Finally, the delivery system grabs each sheet coming off the last press and stacks it on the delivery board."

They stood at the end of the machine until the job finished.

"Hey, Bailey," Florence said, "look at this." She pointed at Chuck. "This here is Chuck McCrary and Ruby...What was your last name?"

"Voight. Ruby Voight."

"Ms. Voight. Right." Florence signaled Chuck to go ahead.

He lifted the foreign currency from the evidence bag and held it for Bailey to examine. "Did you ever see this before?"

"No. Hold it to the light," Bailey said. "Flip it over."

Bailey stepped to the control console. "Hold it under this lamp." He leaned closer to the bill. "Real pretty bill. Good quality printing. Prettier than the U.S. dollar. Where'd you find this?"

"It was in an old pair of sneakers in Andy Billow's locker. I figured, you both being printers, he might have shown it to you."

"Nope."

"Did you and Andy send or receive personal emails?" Chuck asked.

"Such as?"

"Vacation pictures, a funny email from a friend, or a link to an interesting YouTube video?"

"Oh, sure. We all do that."

"Could you tell me all the email addresses you have for Andy?"

"He only used the one. I have the emails on my smartphone." He fished his phone from a pocket. "You want me to forward one to you?"

"Please." Chuck handed him a business card and Bailey tapped in Chuck's email address.

Chuck's phone signaled and he opened the email. "I have it. Thanks. And thanks for your time." They shook hands, and Florence, Ruby, and Chuck walked away.

"May I ask the other employees to check whether Andy used other email addresses?"

"Why not?"

Another half hour and Chuck had Billow's emails forwarded to him from the other employees. He gave each a business card and asked them to contact him if they remembered anything useful or heard from Billow.

"How much training is required to operate that press?" he asked Florence.

"We start a new operator on the Davidson press." She pointed to a smaller machine in the opposite corner of the room. "Most new guys need six to eight months to learn the Davidson. Andy learned it in four months. Like I said, a real smart kid. We kept him on the Davidson for a year on account of we had two printers qualified to run the Heidelberg. Bailey and Simpson."

"How did Andy get promoted?"

"A competitor hired Simpson away. That's why we trained Andy on the Heidelberg."

"How long did it take to train him?"

"Often takes another six months to learn the Heidelberg. Andy learned it in four. Sure hated to lose him." Florence lowered her voice. "His replacement ain't near as smart. He's off today. We may not keep him. The only really good operator we have is Bailey."

———

The blowing snow had returned by the time Ruby toted the Campbell's Soup box to the car. She retrieved the GPS from the glove box, and Chuck entered the address of Billow's last apartment. For twenty white-knuckled minutes, they dodged fender-benders and vehicles skidding at odd angles down the frozen streets.

"This reminds me of a bumper-car ride at the Texas State Fair."

Ruby smiled. "Yeah, but with real cars."

The GPS came to life. "Arriving at destination on left." A 3x5 sign advertising *Chelsea Square Apartment Homes* loomed through the snow. A *No Vacancy* notice swung on hooks from the bottom. Billow's apartment was rented again. No chance of anything being left behind. They risked their lives to drive there, Chuck thought—might as well talk to the manager.

Chuck eased into a parking space. Ruby stashed the GPS. Wrapping the new muffler around his neck, he locked the car and appraised the surroundings before following Ruby to the office. Situational awareness in the absence of a known threat. Nothing moved but snowflakes drifting their way to the ground. His shoes crunched on the newly fallen snow covering the sidewalk. His feet were numb. Street shoes with rubber overshoes aren't insulated like combat boots.

Ruby waited at the door while Chuck paused on the office steps to review the surroundings again. A taxi glided down the street, its tires blazing two narrow trails in the new snow. The snow muffled the noise of its engine.

"Let's go in."

He mounted the steps as Ruby cracked the outer door. Warmer air from the foyer spilled out. They wiped their feet on the mat in the mud room before walking through the inner door.

An elderly man slumped over a newspaper spread on a walnut desk. His head lolled to the side; his mouth open.

Chuck was about to spring into *OMG-he-had-a-heart-attack* mode, but the old man yawned and sat up. He jerked awake from the crossword puzzle he'd been working. He rubbed a hand across his bald spot, peering over his reading glasses. He reminded Chuck of his American grandfather. "We don't have any vacancies, folks. Sorry." He returned his attention to the puzzle.

"We don't need an apartment. We need information."

The manager cackled. "I'm stumped on this damned crossword anyhow. Sure, what would you folks like to know?"

"I'm Chuck McCrary, and this is my associate Ruby Voight." Chuck handed him a business card. "We're trying to locate Antarion Billow a/k/a Andrew Billow. He used to live here."

The old man glanced at the card and dropped it on the desk. He extended his hand. "Walter Waverley. Have a seat."

They sat.

"Private investigators, eh? Why would two private investigators travel from Port City to look for Andy Billow?"

"He's missing. He called his parents a few days ago from Port City but now he's missing. He's a friend. We came to visit his parents and ask around. Maybe we can help locate him. Andrew's parents are worried something bad has happened to him."

"Yeah," Waverley said, "Andy was a Green Beret, weren't he? Real tall, black fellow built like a Chicago Bears linebacker."

"Yes, sir, that's him. Did he give you a forwarding address?"

"Let me check." Waverley swiveled his chair and scooted across the floor to a file cabinet. "This is where I keep the files for former tenants."

Selecting a file, he rolled the chair back to the desk. He flipped the file open and fingered the papers. "I mailed his security deposit to this address." He rotated the file and eased it across the desk.

"That's his parents' address. Do you have any other address?"

"Nope. Sorry." He retrieved the file. "Anything else I can do for you folks?"

"Did you get emails from Andy?"

"Once in a while, he'd send something clever or interesting he uncovered on Wisconsin Dells."

"Wisconsin Dells?"

"Yeah. An article in a newspaper or something online. I'm from Wisconsin Dells. He was thoughtful that way."

"Could you forward me the last email he sent you? My email is on my business card."

"Sure, but why would you want that?"

"To make sure I have all of Andy's email addresses. It might help locate him."

Waverley wheeled his chair to another table where a laptop computer was sitting. He referred to Chuck's business card and tapped the keyboard. "The last email is on its way."

Chuck's phone dinged. "Thanks. Do you have any idea where he is? Did he tell you his plans?"

"Nope. He came by every month to drop off the rent. Always on time and with a nice word to say. You see him, tell him old man Waverley says 'hey.'"

Returning to the rental car, Chuck wondered if he'd ever see Billow to give him Mr. Waverley's message.

———

Chuck parked at the curb in front of the Billows' home. He had bought the collision insurance in case a skidding vehicle side-swiped the Jeep. From the tire tracks in the snow, it seemed one of his better investments. He left the driveway empty for their hosts to park when they finished work. After he scanned the surroundings, Ruby wedged the Campbell Soup box under her arm and crunched through the new snow to the porch. Chuck let them in with the key they had loaned him.

Ruby placed the Campbell Soup box on the kitchen counter. "The box might be dirty and the counter is the easiest surface in the house to clean."

"Your mother would be proud," Chuck said. "So would mine."

He rotated his shoulder to loosen the stiffness. He checked the clock on the oven. Plenty of time to surprise Jeff and Heather with a home-cooked meal. He and Ruby nosed around in the pantry and refrigerator, making a mental shopping list. Locking the door behind them, Chuck consulted the GPS and drove to the nearest grocery store. "How did we live before GPS?"

"The same way we lived before smartphones and the internet," Ruby said. "We didn't know any better."

Two hours later, the aroma of lasagna filled the house. A few minutes later Jeff, then Heather, arrived home.

"What a nice surprise," said Heather. "What smells so good?"

"Lasagna. You cooked it for Andy, Hank, and me last time we were here. Ruby and I wanted to return the favor."

"You didn't need to do that, Ruby."

"Hey," she said, "It was a team effort. We hope you and Jeff enjoy it."

As Heather hugged Ruby, then Chuck, she peered over his shoulder. "What's that Campbell Soup box doing on the counter?"

"That's stuff Andrew left in his locker at the printer. I figured we could poke through it after dinner."

"I'd rather do that now, if dinner can wait."

Chuck gave Ruby a questioning glance.

"The lasagna will keep."

"Help yourself to the box. Now that you're both home, is it okay if I park my Jeep in your driveway? I'm afraid a skidding car will crash into it overnight. Our flight is at 7:05 tomorrow morning, so we'll leave here at 4:00 a.m. We'll try not to wake you."

"Sure thing," Jeff said. "You park the car and Heather and I will look in the box."

When Chuck returned to the living room, the Billows had spread the locker contents across the coffee table. They sat on a couch behind the table. Ruby and Chuck sat in matching side chairs.

The Bulls baseball hat lay beside the Bulls sweatshirt on the far end of the table.

"What's that blue stain on the sleeve?" Jeff asked.

"Andrew's supervisor said it's magenta ink. They use it on the biggest monster printing press I've ever seen."

Heather hugged the sweatshirt to her chest and sniffed once. "I smell fabric softener. Forgive me, but I'm afraid I'll never hug Andrew again. This is something he wore and loved. It makes me feel close to him."

Jeff wrapped his arm around her and squeezed gently.

The sneakers sitting askew on the table reminded Chuck of the foreign money they had stumbled upon. Slipping on a pair of evidence gloves, he removed the bill from his pocket.

Jeff noticed. "Why the rubber gloves?"

"Actually, they're nitrile. This bill may be evidence and we don't need more fingerprints on it." Chuck held the bill where they could see. "This was in one sneaker. It's foreign currency. Does this mean anything to you?"

Jeff squinted at the bill. "Flip it over."

He did.

"Those are Russian letters. I recognize them from stuff on the TV news from Moscow. The first two letters resemble ours: *K* and *A*. The third one is a backwards numeral 3."

"That is the Cyrillic alphabet," Ruby said. "The third letter is a *Z* and the fourth and fifth are *A* and *K* again. It's Kazakhstan. It's 200 of whatever the Kazakh currency is." She studied the bill. "I believe it says *tenge*."

"Why didn't you tell me that when we found the bill?"

"I didn't study the bill at the printer's. I knew we could look closer once we got it back here."

Jeff was fiddling with his cellphone. "Yes, it's *tenge*. T-E-N-G-E. Don't know how to pronounce it."

He faced Heather. "This bill mean anything to you?"

"It might be from Aisha," Heather said. "We figured she came from a former Soviet Republic. Maybe she's from Kazakhstan and gave it to Andrew as a souvenir."

Jeff said, "Andrew was never in Kazakhstan. He must have gotten the bill from Aisha."

"That's good to know," Chuck said. "One other thing, what did Andrew do with his old computer once he bought a new one?"

"He gave it to me," Heather said.

"Did he give you the most recent one?"

"Sure. After Christmas."

"May I examine your computer? He could have left old files on it. I might be able to undelete a document or email to help figure out where he is."

"It's a laptop. I'll get it." She left the room and returned in seconds. "Here it is."

Billow had deleted his personal files, but his email software remained on the computer. He had added his mother's email accounts to his own without deleting his old account. Heather Billow used the same email app. The list of email accounts gave Chuck three email addresses Billow had used, two of them new to him.

Chuck caught a second break in the recycle bin. Billow had deleted his personal files from Heather's computer, but didn't empty the recycle bin. Chuck restored his deleted files and copied them to an external hard drive he traveled with.

The copying would require an hour or more. He joined Ruby and the Billows for dinner.

"We were lucky, Heather. I recovered many of Andrew's deleted files from your computer. I'm copying them to a hard drive. I'll give the files to the Port City detectives working the case. They may learn something useful. At the least, I determined two additional email accounts he used. Maybe we can hack our way into the internet and locate him that way."

Heather's eyes glistened. Chuck prayed they were tears of hope.

After dinner, Heather pushed her chair from the table. "I'll do the dishes, Chuck. I'm real picky how I load the dishwasher. You and Ruby and Jeff relax in the living room. There's a Bulls game on TV."

That night in bed Chuck stared at the ceiling while Ruby breathed softly beside him. *Kazakhstan?*

SEVEN

They landed in Atlanta and walked to baggage claim.

"Give me the baggage claim stubs," Ruby said. "I'll grab a Sky Cap and meet you at the car rental counter. You get the car."

Standing at the car rental counter, Chuck's weather app said it was 52 degrees and partly cloudy. Fort Benning was about a hundred miles south —two hours by the time he rented a car. The temperature at the fort was expected to reach the low sixties by noon.

The low sixties wasn't convertible weather in South Florida, but after a day or two in the Chicago deep freeze, Chuck thought it would seem summery. To Ruby, sixty degrees would be heaven after the ice in Austin, so he rented a Mustang convertible. He planned to drop the top when the outside temperature reached 60.

Twenty minutes later, they were motoring down I-85. The sun was shining and the temperature rising, along with his spirits. Good weather again.

"Ruby, you deciphered the Cyrillic writing on that Kazakh currency quickly. Do you know anything about that area of the world?"

"Nope. My sister Sheila studied two semesters of conversational Russian at the University when I was in high school. I drilled her with flash cards while she learned the alphabet. She paid me with chocolate malts from Whataburger. I spied that Kazakh bill, and the Cyrillic alphabet came back to me."

"What nationality is Aisha Aubakirovna's name?"

"Sorry, when I told you what sounds the Cyrillic letters made, I told you everything I know."

"I'll look it up on the internet. I'll ask Flamer21, my research guru, to research Aisha on the internet."

"Who did you say your research guru is?"

"Flamer21."

"Isn't flamer a gay-bashing slang word?"

"Usually, yeah. I've met him in person a couple times, and Flamer is the only name he gave me. His email address says Flamer21 also."

"Is he gay?"

"Yes."

"*Hmm.*"

"Anyway, if Billow doesn't want to be found, perhaps Flamer can locate Aisha. We locate Aisha, we find Billow. If Aisha gave Billow that 200 tenge bill, she might have left her fingerprints on it."

"Don't hold out hope we'll get anything useful from that bill. I've processed lots of currency. A used bill has dozens of prints overlapped and ninety percent of them are no good because they're covered with other prints. Occasionally I get the most recent prints, but it's a matter of how new the bill is. The newer, the better. That bill from the sneaker was old."

"I'll give the bill to Buster Cleveland to process," Chuck said. "Maybe it will reveal something useful. The other thing that worries me is whether Aisha's fingerprints are in the system. If she arrived from Kazakhstan and holds a Kazakh passport, they aren't in the system."

"It also depends on the date she arrived in the U.S. Before 9-11, they weren't fingerprinting tourists."

Chuck's stomach growled. Glancing at the dashboard clock, he realized they hadn't eaten since breakfast at McDonald's at O'Hare Airport. "My stomach is hollering for Georgia barbecue. You want barbecue?"

"You kidding? I'm a native Texan, same as you. Bring it on."

A LaGrange exit sign loomed ahead. They followed it to State Highway 109. "Ask the GPS to search barbecue restaurants in LaGrange."

"Good idea."

———

Chuck downed a brisket platter with coleslaw and barbecue beans and Ruby ate a pulled pork sandwich.

After lunch they dropped the top.

Chuck closed his eyes and lifted his face to the sun. "This sunny day beats the hell out of blowing snow and frozen streets."

"Yeah, I'm looking forward to the beach."

———

Fort Benning had changed little in the years since Chuck trained there. The flags and fountain at the entrance were new. So were the protesters outside the gate. A half-dozen picketers paraded with signs demanding that Fort Benning change its name.

"I couldn't read their signs while driving. Could you?"

"Yeah. It was something about renaming Fort Benning. Apparently, General Benning owned slaves."

They stopped at the Interstate 185 Visitor Center for a visitor pass and directions to Captain Vincent Hightower's office. His door was open. Chuck rapped twice on the jamb and Hightower motioned them in.

"Captain Hightower, I'm Chuck McCrary and this is my colleague Ruby Voight. She's a Latent Print Examiner from the Austin Police Department."

Hightower shook their hands and waved them into chairs. "Pleased to meet you, Ms. Voight. Are you here to examine fingerprints?"

"Not really, Captain. I'm here to provide a second viewpoint for Chuck."

"You are welcome in any capacity." To Chuck: "I looked you up after you called from the Visitor Center. Your service record is impressive. That Ghar Mesar mission is one for the record books. It seems you invented a new way to use a Kalashnikov." He grinned.

Chuck made an *Aw-shucks* gesture. "Didn't have a choice, Captain."

"I'm an informal guy with civilians; call me Vince."

"Me too. Anyway, my SAW was empty. If I had stopped to reload, the bastard would have shot me from can't-miss range."

Ruby cleared her throat. "What's a saw?"

"Squad Automatic Weapon," Hightower and Chuck said together, then chuckled.

"That's what I was carrying that day, Ruby."

"Reading between the lines of your citation, you clubbed the Taliban to death with his own AK-47. Not many people would think to do that."

"Necessity is the mother of invention. You would have done the same."

"Can I offer y'all coffee while you tell me how I can help you?"

"Coffee is always welcome."

He lifted the phone and ordered three coffees.

"There were pickets outside the gate. I didn't read the signs, but Ruby said they want Fort Benning to change its name."

Hightower shrugged. "You know who Fort Benning was named after?"

"General Henry Benning."

"But Benning was a general in the *Confederate* army."

"The *Confederate* army?"

"Benning fought against the U.S. Army and someone in Washington a hundred years ago named this fort after a local hero. A hundred years ago, he was a hero to the white people in Georgia, and the people who looked like me didn't count."

"I can't imagine how the Army brass justified that decision," Chuck said, "but there you are. Nobody protested the name when I trained here a million years ago. Recent events have made people sensitive about Civil War history."

"And slavery," he said. "My great-great-great grandmother belonged to Henry Benning."

"What do you mean 'belonged'? She was a slave?"

"Benning owned her, same as he owned his cows and his horses. He lived less than twenty miles from here in Columbus."

The coffee arrived. Chuck added a touch of half-and-half and stirred. "In my life, I've met hundreds of people whose ancestors were slaves, including several in the Triple Seven. And people whose ancestors were slave owners, including guys in the Triple Seven. My American grandmother's ancestors moved to Texas from Georgia after the Civil War. It's possible my ancestors owned your ancestors. On the other hand, my Mexican mother is descended from both Aztec slaves and their Spanish Conquistador owners."

"Yeah, that's a conversation stopper, ain't it? Still, you're the one who mentioned the protesters." Hightower grinned. "Don't sweat it. It's ancient history."

"I belong to that club," Ruby said. "One of my Texas ancestors fought for the South and owned slaves. Two of my Louisiana ancestors *were* slaves."

"We're the perfect poster children for modern America."

———

Chuck trailed Hightower's car through a suburban neighborhood that was typically American in every way, except it was in the middle of Fort Benning. Neatly mowed lawns, a scattering of leafless trees, people walking dogs.

"I didn't finish my story," Ruby said. "Another branch of my family from Pennsylvania descended from an ancestor who fought for the Union, was stationed in Louisiana during Reconstruction, and stayed in the South after his enlistment was up. And *his* ancestor fought in the American Revolution."

"You qualify for membership in the Daughters of the American Revolution, the United Daughters of the Confederacy, and the Daughters of Union Veterans of the Civil War."

"I never thought of it, but, yes, I do. *Huh.*"

Vince Hightower parked in the double-wide driveway. Chuck parked beside him and they raised the top. Chuck was prepared to exit the car when he received a text from Hank:

Medical Examiner got DNA results. The victim is Phillip Franks. I will call Billow's parents with the news that he is alive.

Chuck's mind vaulted back to Fallujah, where Philip Franks had saved his life yet one more time. His and Bill Gregg's. Fiery wreckage, the smell of burning diesel fuel, rubble and car parts raining from the sky. Franks laying across Gregg and him as wreckage fell all around them. His head swam.

Chuck crossed his arms on the steering wheel and leaned his forehead on them. This was it. That text shredded the last vestige of doubt about who the headless body was—Phillip Franks.

"Hey, Chuck," Ruby said, "where did you go?"

Chuck shook his head; he didn't trust himself to speak.

Ruby touched his shoulder lightly. "Talk to me, baby. What's the matter?"

He struggled to keep his voice from breaking. "Fallujah."

"Fallujah? As in Iraq?"

He handed her the phone.

She read the message. "What happened in Fallujah?"

Chuck told her about Fallujah. How Phil Franks saved his life and Bill Gregg's. How all three of them wound up in an Army hospital. How Phil Franks was there an extra two weeks because his body had shielded Chuck from the worst of the avalanche of debris. How Franks, despite not being fully recovered from his wounds, rejoined the Triple Seven three weeks later.

Ruby handed Chuck a tissue. He wiped his eyes.

"I owe Phil Franks a debt I can never repay."

"At least it's good news for Jeff and Heather," Ruby said.

"Yes, it's good news for somebody." He got out of the car. "Let's go inside."

Hightower opened the door to Phillip Franks's two-bedroom house and stepped inside the living room. "We haven't reassigned Franks's quarters. Maybe you two will find something useful he abandoned."

"Vince, I just got this text from Hank Ramirez." He read Captain Hightower the message.

"Either way the DNA results would be bad news for the Triple Seven. I'll ask someone from Fort Carson to notify Sergeant Major Franks's next of kin."

Chuck surveyed the room. Government-issue furniture, except for a six-foot mahogany cabinet against the wall. The cabinet had three bookshelves behind glass doors above three rows of drawers.

Hightower regarded the cabinet. "That's not government-issue. Franks must have bought that. Why didn't he move it with the rest of his stuff?"

"Doesn't matter now. Why don't you search the cabinet and I'll do the kitchen? Ruby, you check the bedrooms and bath."

Hightower grinned. "I get to be a detective's assistant. Wait until I tell my kids tonight."

"Sorry I don't have a Junior Detective's badge for you." Chuck tugged on a pair of crime-scene gloves, handed a pair to Ruby, and gave Hightower a pair. "Better wear these."

"Why the gloves?" he asked.

"Force of habit. I trained with the Port City Police Academy. Everyone on a crime scene wears gloves, even those who don't handle evidence."

"This is a crime scene?"

Chuck rocked a hand in a *maybe-so-maybe-no* gesture. "Not my jurisdiction. I'm not a cop anymore."

Hightower tugged on the gloves. "Couldn't hurt. This is your area of expertise; not mine."

———

Twenty minutes later, Chuck returned to the living room.

"The kitchen was empty," he said. "What did you learn, Ruby?"

She spread her hands, palms down. "Zilch."

"How about the cabinet, Vince?"

He gestured to an array of items on the coffee table. "A ballpoint pen, a pencil, three paper clips, one black sock with a hole in the heel, and an old tee-shirt."

"There was nothing under the drawers?"

"The stuff on the coffee table is all."

"I said *under* the drawers, not *in* the drawers. Rule Twenty-three: *Always look under.*"

"Rule Twenty-three?"

Ruby explained. "Chuck made a bunch of rules to use in his investigations. That's the first I've heard of Rule Twenty-three though."

"It means you haven't finished the search until you look under."

"*Under* the drawers?" Hightower said. "How do you look *under* a drawer?"

"When you examine a cabinet or chest of drawers, you remove the drawers and look on all six sides. Also, all six sides of the cabinet or chest."

"Six sides? What six sides?"

"Left, right, front, back, top, and bottom."

"We flip the whole cabinet over?"

"That's the idea."

Chuck opened the glass doors of the cabinet, removed the book shelves one at a time, and handed them to Ruby, who laid them on the couch.

"Let's lift off the shelf unit, Vince."

He grasped the other side and they placed the unit in the middle of the room.

"Nothing on top and nothing on the back," Chuck said. "Let's flip it on its back. We'll examine the bottom. Occasionally people tape something underneath."

"I never realized a person could hide things so many places."

"That's 'cuz you are a normal, trusting person. I, on the other hand, am a skeptical, suspicious, devious, former cop with a cynical outlook."

"I hope you're joking. That would be a sad thing if it were true."

Chuck waffled his hand. "Sometimes it's true and sometimes it isn't. Depends on whether I'm on a case. This week, I'm on a particularly vicious murder case, so I'm a world-class skeptic. You wouldn't believe where I've uncovered drugs stashed—inside toilet tanks, behind air conditioning vents. Even inside a light switch in a garage. Phil isn't a criminal—*wasn't* a criminal—so I didn't do a thorough search of the kitchen. But this cabinet is easy. Let's remove the drawers. Remember: Check all six sides."

Chuck removed the bottom drawer and there it was—the payoff.

On the bottom of the cabinet base was a small World Atlas, about 200 pages. Thin enough to fit beneath the bottom drawer. One page had a corner folded over. Chuck flipped it open. The page was a map of central Asia. A yellow-highlighter circled one country.

"What's that?" asked Hightower.

"A map of central Asia showing the location of Kazakhstan."

A brightly colored paper was stuck in the binding of the book. "The plot thickens."

"Isn't that a bookmark?"

"Yes, but it's more than that. It's a Kazakh 500 tenge bill." Chuck closed the atlas with the bill marking the page and dropped it into an evidence bag. "Billow hid a 200 tenge bill in an old sneaker in Chicago."

"Might be a coincidence," Hightower said.

"Rule Seven: *There is no such thing as a coincidence.* Billow stuffed his bill in the toe of a sneaker. Franks hid his in a book under a drawer. Why didn't they want anyone to learn they were interested in Kazakhstan?"

———

Ruby and Chuck returned to South Florida on Thursday. She sunbathed at the condo pool, and he met Detective Buster Cleveland at police HQ downtown.

Chuck briefed Cleveland on their trip to Illinois and texted him the picture of Billow and his fiancée. "That's all I have on Aisha Aubakirovna so far. It's not much, but Customs and Immigration would know more." Chuck handed him the external hard drive with Billow's files. "Billow used three email accounts: one under the name Antarion and two using Andrew. This drive has his personal files from his old computer that he gave to his mother after he bought a new one. You might learn something useful from it, but the files are from last year and older. Your people can subpoena the email accounts."

Chuck handed him the evidence bags. "Your lab may get Aisha's fingerprints from Customs and Immigration to match what you find on this bill."

"It's pretty-well used."

"Yeah, but that's what I have. We found a second bill that may work

63

better. I don't know whether Aisha handled it." Chuck gave him the atlas he found in Franks's cabinet at Fort Benning and showed him the 500 tenge bill inside. "I checked the exchange rate. Five hundred tenges is about one U.S. dollar. My friend Ruby is a Latent Print Examiner in Austin. She said this bill is almost new. Your people may have better luck with it."

"Thanks, Chuck. I'll keep you and Hank in the loop. Give me until tomorrow and I'll get back to you."

———

Ruby was in the shower when Chuck got home.

He poked his head in the bathroom. "Did you enjoy the pool?"

"What did you say?"

He spoke louder. "Did you enjoy the pool?"

"Lovely."

"You want company? I could scrub your back."

"Knowing us, that would lead to scrubbing my front. That would lead to other wonderful things, but I wouldn't finish washing my hair and scrubbing the sunscreen off my skin. I don't want your sheets to get wet either. Give me fifteen minutes and I'll meet you in the bedroom, clean and dry. In most places."

"Deal."

———

Later, Chuck mixed a pitcher of Margaritas, and he and Ruby sat on the balcony and enjoyed the sunset. He refilled Ruby's glass, then his own.

"What am I going to do about Phil Franks?"

Ruby took a sip. "Are you asking me or asking yourself?"

He reached over and patted her knee. "You are not only beautiful, you are very, very wise to ask that question. The truth is: I don't know who I'm asking. Hank says I should leave the murder case to the Port City cops to handle. Let the law take its course."

"But that's not good enough for you?"

64

He set his Margarita on the end table. "A week ago, that might have been good enough. That's why we have the law. But now? I don't know. I've been thinking about how I owe my life to Phil Franks. How do I repay a debt to a dead man?"

They drank in silence and watched the sunset display its magical kaleidoscope for a few minutes.

"When I was a little girl, my parents took me to a movie called *Pay it Forward*. I don't remember the entire story, but basically this twelve-year-old boy does something nice for someone and asks them not to repay the favor to him, but to pay the favor 'forward' by doing a good deed for someone else. Since you can't repay Phil Franks, can you do something for someone else that would honor your friend?"

"Like when you and I volunteered to help the murder investigation by traveling to Chicago, then to Fort Benning."

"Yeah. Maybe do some more of that."

"That doesn't seem the appropriate order of magnitude for saving my life. Seems like I should do more than that."

"Well, you don't have to decide right now. Sleep on it and maybe something will occur to you."

A few minutes later Gunner texted Chuck that he had arrived home from North Dakota. Chuck glanced at his watch. It was only six o'clock.

"Honey, I just received a text from my friend Gunnar Knutson. I don't remember whether you met him in Austin. He and Snoop worked my cousin's kidnapping with me."

"I didn't meet either of them last year. I'd love to meet them now."

"Gunner was a Triple Seven. He just returned from a family trip to North Dakota. I haven't seen him in two weeks. I'd like to invite him for dinner tonight. That okay with you?"

"Are you cooking?"

"I could, or we could eat out. Your call."

"Does Gunner like Cuban food?"

"This is South Florida; everybody loves Cuban food. It's a state law."

"Let's eat out."

———

Gunner met them in front of *Tres Cocinas*, a waterfront restaurant a mile from Chuck's condo.

Their table was close enough to whiff diesel fumes from the boats cruising toward the Keys or up towards Fort Lauderdale. The easterly breeze blew the fumes and noise out over Seeti Bay.

They ordered drinks and Ruby and Gunner traded life stories—the abridged summaries you tell someone when you first meet. Enough to establish a rapport for future interactions. Ruby skillfully broke the ice with Chuck's traditionally-reserved Viking friend—another thing she was good at.

"So, Gunner, when you're not working for Chuck, what do you do for a living?"

"I work for other PIs too, and I'm a personal trainer at Jerry's Gym."

"Now that you're back from Fargo, maybe Chuck and I will see you at Jerry's tomorrow."

"Chuck works out first thing in the morning. I mainly train the customers who work out after office hours."

The breeze shifted and brought them an aroma of fish cooking over an open grill.

Ruby spread her arms to the breeze. "*This* is why I love Port City. In Austin, we can eat outdoors six or eight months a year. In July and August, it's often a hundred degrees, and in April and November a north wind might freeze your buns off. May and October are best."

After the three of then ordered, Chuck briefed Gunner on their trip to Chicago and Fort Benning. "We'll have a fingerprint report tomorrow."

"How involved are you in this investigation?" Gunner asked.

"Beats the hell out of me. I've got to do something for Phil now that he's dead. I just don't know what."

EIGHT

F riday morning, Buster Cleveland called Chuck McCrary on a video call. "The 200 tenge bill was a bitch to process. Half the population of Kazakhstan handled it before Billow. We managed to identify a thumb and forefinger of Billow and a couple other prints that aren't in the system. The rest were garbage."

"You expected that," Chuck said. "It's disappointing but not surprising."

Cleveland lifted a transparent sleeve in front of his phone's camera. The Kazakh 500 tenge bill was inside.

"This 500 tenge bill from Fort Benning was a different story. We isolated four sets of prints: Billow's, Franks's, and some not in our system. Two of the odd prints from the 500 tenge bill matched the second unidentified set on the 200 tenge bill. We figure those are Aisha's. The other prints are persons unknown. Might be from the guy who gave the bill to Aisha, or someone who mailed it from Kazakhstan."

"That's progress," Chuck said. "Why aren't Aisha's prints in the system?"

Cleveland waved a hand. "Perhaps she's a U.S. citizen. If she was born here, she's a citizen, even if her parents aren't. You know anything about her parents?"

"Not yet. I sicced my internet bloodhound on her trail. Did you learn anything from the Billow's hard drive I copied in Chicago?"

"Nothing useful. Nice try though."

"Have you learned anything about Aisha?" Chuck asked.

"Not much. Now that we have her picture and Billow's, we'll make the rounds of offset printers near where Billow's phone pinged and hope we get a hit."

Cleveland disconnected.

————

Detective Cleveland dropped the cellphone company report on the squad room table where he and his partner could read it. "I'll mark the towers." He wasn't tech-savvy like his thirty-something-year-old partner, but he could read and mark a map—a *paper* map, that is. An image on a computer monitor didn't seem like a real map. Oh, he used a GPS, but you couldn't draw lines on a computer or a GPS screen. Well, you could, but he didn't know how, and he feared he was too old to learn.

Melissa Chan unfolded a giant Atlantic County map on the table.

Cleveland opened a shallow drawer under the table and found a compass and yellow highlighter. "This is the farthest north tower." He marked a yellow X on the first tower's location. Referring to the phone company report, he made another X. "That's the southmost tower. You can fold the map smaller."

"Okay if I cut off the bottom two-thirds?" Chan said. "In Orange County, we didn't make the murder book bulkier than necessary."

Cleveland grimaced. Like Orange County sheriffs, Port City police detectives documented their procedures investigating a homicide in a *murder book*. The book would include the paper map to document how they determined the location of the phone call made from Billow's phone to his parents. Murder books often grew to several volumes. *Screw the way they did it in Orange County*, he thought. *This is Port City and this is my case.*

The paper map of Atlantic County measured three feet by four feet—twelve square feet of paper. The two detectives needed two square feet to document the locations of the cell towers. Chan was such a damned hotshot all the damned time. Still, she was right.

Cleveland swallowed his resentment. "Yeah, good idea." He nudged the map in her direction. "Mark the east and west towers, then trim the map."

Chan plotted the remaining two towers the call pinged. "His phone was moving." She consulted the phone company report and made tick marks on the map. "He pinged off this tower when he placed the call, then the signal switched to this one. Here was the third, and he was on this tower when the call ended." She marked a line approximating the path of the phone. "With the variation in signal strength, this line might be a mile off either way."

Chan entered the street address of the north cell tower into an internet map website. She told the website to list offset printers nearby. Over a dozen business names and addresses flagged on the map, most within the circle of the cell tower's signal. After noting the relevant details, she searched for more printers near the other three cell towers.

In fifteen minutes, she had completed a list.

"This is..." She counted the names and addresses. "...twenty-three potential employers for Antarion or Andrew Billow."

Cleveland was impressed but tried to hide it. "Okay. It's shoe-leather time. Let's show Billow's and the woman's pictures around."

———

Cleveland parked at the seventh printer on the list. "What's the name of this printer supposed to be?"

"Walsh & Knowles Press," Chan said.

The neon sign on the building flashed *On Top Electric*.

"Let's check it out," Cleveland said, opening the car door.

Cleveland opened the glass door and pushed inside. Chan followed. Walking to a waist-high counter, he flashed his shield to the woman who approached the two cops. "We're looking for Walsh & Knowles Press. They're supposed to be at 10300 NW 106th Street."

The woman frowned. "That's this address, but I never heard of Walsh and whatever. You sure you have the right address?"

"It was on the internet," Chan said.

The woman smiled. "If the internet says it, it must be right."

Cleveland threw a *shut-up* look at Chan. "How long has your company been at this location?"

"Two years."

"Okay, thanks." Cleveland and Chan returned to the car.

Chan picked up her phone. "What is the address of Walsh & Knowles Press?"

The phone's generic female voice responded. "The address for Walsh & Knowles Press is 13711 SW Arrowhead Drive, Corcoran Heights, Florida. Would you like the telephone number?"

Chan closed the app.

"Corcoran Heights is way the hell in southwest Atlantic County. No way a phone call would ping off these towers. The company moved." She crossed the name off the list.

Cleveland admired the way she did that; he would not have asked his phone. He would have waited until he was at his laptop in the police bullpen. "Okay," he said, "We have time to visit one more printer today. Who's next?"

———

The next Tuesday, Chan crossed the last name off the list. "Nobody knows either one, and nobody's seen either one. What now, partner?"

What indeed? Cleveland was stumped. "Let's talk to Hank Ramirez and Chuck McCrary. We can meet them for lunch at *El Unicornio*. You call Hank. I'll call Chuck."

———

Ruby and Chuck left his dock after breakfast, planning to spend the morning on his boat, *The Gator Raider Too*, fishing for Red Snapper. They drifted with the Gulf Stream four miles off the coast and trailed two baited hooks in the water. Chuck didn't care whether they caught anything; it was an excuse to spend a few uninterrupted hours with Ruby. She'd extended her vacation another week.

The more they talked, the closer he felt to her. How would she feel about living in Port City? He could enjoy living in Austin, even if it snowed occasionally. Anything for love, if that's what this feeling was. Chuck had been in love twice. Three times, if he counted Teresa Kovacs, but she dumped him twice, so he didn't include her.

In mid-morning, Buster Cleveland called. The cell signal offshore was weak and Cleveland's call kept breaking up. Piecing together the words and phrases Chuck made out, he figured out what Cleveland wanted.

"Buster, I can't make lunch today. I'm on my boat in the Gulf Stream fishing with a friend. How about tomorrow?"

The call broke up again. "Buster, send me a text. A text needs less signal strength than a voice call. Got that? Send me a text." He disconnected.

"That was Buster Cleveland. We had a bad connection. He wants to have lunch with Hank and me to discuss the case. I'll text him."

Buster, I'm on my boat in the Gulf Stream. Lunch tomorrow is good. Text me time and place. Regards, Chuck.

He punched *send*.

"Am I invited?"

"Naturally. You're part of this case even though you'll go home soon. Besides, I want you to meet Hank Ramirez. He's a close friend." *And would be my best man if I marry you,* Chuck thought.

Ruby climbed on the cabin roof and spun a slow 360. "There are three freighters on the horizon and a charter fishing boat a couple of miles that way. I'm surprised there isn't more ship traffic."

"The freighters are northbound. The Gulf Stream flows north at four miles per hour here. Those ships sail in the Stream to save fuel. The southbound ships sail further east, over the horizon, so they don't fight the current."

Chuck's phone signaled a text.

El Unicornio at 12:30 tomorrow. Chan and I have

reached a dead-end. Hank will be there too. Regards,
Buster

Ruby climbed down to the cockpit. "How many more fish should we catch?"

Despite their haphazard fishing, Ruby had landed two snappers and Chuck hooked one.

"We have three good ones in the ice chest. That's enough for a half dozen meals. You done enough drifting with the current? We can cruise home or sightsee on Seeti Bay. Your choice."

"I have something else in mind. There's a fantasy I have that happens on a boat drifting on the ocean."

"Fantasies are my specialty."

Sometimes, Chuck thought, *it's good to be me.*

————

An hour later, Chuck cranked the engines. "How did the reality compare to the fantasy?"

"Wonderfully, although it was bumpier than that first time we did it on Seeti Bay."

"The waves are bigger in the Gulf Stream."

"Okay, I'm ready to sail past a few waterfront mansions on the way home."

"Okay, but put on your bikini before we reach the ship channel. You don't want to cause a shipwreck."

————

On Wednesday, Chuck and Ruby arrived first and claimed a table for five in *El Unicornio*.

"Have you eaten enough Cuban food?" he said. "You fly home tomorrow so we have one more dinner tonight before I chauffeur you to the airport."

"Tonight, let's try a Haitian restaurant. I want to taste jerked pork or jerked chicken before I go home."

"There's a good one a few miles from my condo. One of us can order pork and the other chicken. We each eat half and swap plates." *Like an old married couple*, he thought.

Buster Cleveland and a slender Asian woman walked in. Chuck stood and waved them over.

Cleveland and Chuck shook hands.

"I don't believe you've met my partner, Melissa Chan," Cleveland said.

"It's a pleasure. And this is my girlfriend, Ruby Voight. She's a criminalist with the Austin police. She specializes in latent print analysis."

They shook hands all around.

"Ruby, can you make time this afternoon to help process those Kazakh bills you brought us?" Chan asked. "We couldn't get much from the 200 tenge bill."

"Ruby intended to shop this afternoon," Chuck said. "She flies back to Austin tomorrow."

"That's okay, Chuck," Ruby said. "I'll make time. It'll be fun."

That was another thing they had in common; she loved her job. To Ruby, analyzing fingerprints was fun.

Hank Ramirez appeared at the table. "Hey, guys." He bowed to Ruby. "Chuck says great things about you. I'm Hank Ramirez." They shook hands.

After touching the social bases, Chuck asked Cleveland, "Your text yesterday mentioned a dead-end on the case?"

"Chan and I uncovered…How many printers was it, Lissa?"

"Twenty-three."

Cleveland continued. "Twenty-three offset printing companies within cellphone range of the four towers that Billow's phone pinged three weeks ago. We visited twenty of them. Three had moved or were out of business. Nobody at those twenty printers recognized Billow's or Aubakirovna's picture."

"Any Illinois license plates?" Chuck asked.

"Three, but none on a blue Chevy Blazer and none were U.S. Army Veteran plates."

"Did Billow make other calls on that phone?"

"None. I assume he disposed of it," Cleveland said.

"Did you track the phone's history? Trace its path with its GPS?"

"We tried. He switched it on to use it and off once he finished. His trail since he's been down here is a bunch of disconnected short lines. There's no pattern to it and no place where the phone spends much time. He's too savvy about our ability to track his path."

"Where did you get your list of offset printers?" Hank Ramirez said.

"Melissa did an internet search for offset printers within range of the street addresses of the four cell towers."

"And you uncovered twenty-three?"

"Yes."

"Twenty of those were valid."

"Yes."

"And three were out-of-date," said Hank.

"Yes. What's your point?"

Chuck interrupted. "Those were old printers that had been in business for years. The internet results were out of date. There must be new offset printers in the county that aren't on the map website. Maybe Billow works at a new printer. The right printer might not be near that path you tracked. He switched the phone off most of the time."

Chan seemed frustrated. "Then he could be based anywhere in Atlantic County. He might have used a different phone—one we know nothing about."

"That's right. Maybe you're searching the wrong area of the county or even the wrong county. He could be in Miami or Fort Lauderdale even."

"What should we do?" Cleveland asked.

"The key is the Heidelberg press," Chuck said. "Billow was recruited to run a Heidelberg. Find the right Heidelberg and you'll find Billow."

Cleveland nodded. "Makes sense. How would we determine which printers own a Heidelberg?"

"Telephone them. It's quicker than driving to each printer and showing Billow and Aisha's photos to people. Ask rookies from the police academy to make the calls. They'll be thrilled to get real life experience in police work."

Cleveland gazed at Chan.

She shrugged. "Couldn't hurt."

"Next question," Chuck said, "what did you learn about Aisha Aubakirovna?"

"Quite a lot," Chan replied. "The U.S. Immigration and Naturalization Service said Aisha immigrated to the U.S. with her mother and older brother six years ago. The U.S. State Department granted political asylum to them. She was fifteen. She became a naturalized U.S. citizen last year."

"She's twenty-one?" Chuck asked.

"She just turned twenty-two."

"Where did they come from?"

"Kazakhstan."

"That's no surprise," Chuck said. "Kazakhstan left the Soviet Union, but it is not a democracy. What's the story behind the political asylum?"

Chan consulted her notes. "Aisha's father is Aubakir Yakovlevich, a well-connected former Communist. He's the police commissioner in the capital's security police," Chan said. "He's a corrupt, dictatorial SOB. His wife and son broke with him over his continual disregard of human rights. He's in charge of intimidating or imprisoning the president's political opponents and being a general bad guy. They bolted during a family trip to the Netherlands. They knocked on the door of the U.S. Embassy and requested political asylum."

"Did you locate a car registered in her name in Illinois or Florida?" Chuck asked.

Chan referred to her notes again. "No, but the Illinois Secretary of State's office gave me one funny coincidence. The clerk was typing in *Aubakirovna*, and another car owner's name popped up." She spun the notepad toward me. "It was Duman Aubakirovich, resident of the same address in Chicago."

"The surname Aubakirovich is the masculine form of Aubakirovna," Chuck said. "It means 'son of Aubakir,' Aubakirovna means 'daughter of Aubakir.' Duman is her older brother. Her father back in Kazakhstan is named Aubakir."

Chan made notes. "I'll delve into Aisha and her family."

"I'll supervise the search for Heidelberg presses," Cleveland said.

75

After kissing Ruby goodbye at the airport, Chuck went home. His condo seemed empty. Clint Watson, his brother-from-another-mother, was in class at the University of Florida. Ruby had been gone less than three hours and Chuck was lonesome. Missing Ruby was a good thing, right? That meant their relationship was special, even though they had not yet discussed making it exclusive.

Chuck figured than an exclusive relationship wasn't practical until and unless one of them moved to the other's city. Their relationship had not progressed that far. Neither of them had ever indicated whether they were dating other people. Chuck assumed Ruby dated other men in Austin.

He told himself that it didn't bother him one way or the other. Well, it didn't bother him *much*.

While he daydreamed about Ruby, Melissa Chan called.

"I heard back from the INS on Aisha's family members admitted with her. I confirmed Duman Aubakirovich is her brother. Her mother is Medina Mustafina. The three of them were the only family members admitted to the U.S."

"How many cars did Duman register?"

"I contacted the Illinois Secretary of State again and he has three cars in his name. And, before you ask, there is no registration for Medina Mustafina."

"Patriarchal family. He registered all the cars in his name," Chuck said, "including Aisha's. Any way to tell which car is hers?"

"You said Billow's parents met Aisha. Ask if they remember her car."

"Good idea. Hold on and I'll text them." Chuck put Chan on hold and texted Heather and Jeff Billow:

If you ever saw Aisha's car, can you describe it? Anything helps—color, make, number of doors—anything. Thanks, Chuck

He switched back to his call with Chan. "They're both at work. It'll be a while until they respond. Until they do, I suggest you put all three cars on your BOLO list. We could get lucky and a traffic cop could pull them over."

"Will do. I searched for printers in South Florida with Heidelberg presses. Buster and I plan to visit the ones in Atlantic County first."

"How many did you discover?"

"Seventeen."

"Be alert for Illinois license plates in their parking lots. And don't forget that employee lots may be in the back."

"Right. Talk soon."

While Chuck was grilling hamburgers, Ruby phoned to say she'd arrived home. By the time they finished talking, both patties were burned to a crisp.

Was he falling in love?

———

Life proceeded normally for the next week, but the case of Phillip Franks's murder went nowhere. Chuck's life was treading water. He was making no progress in repaying his debt to Phil.

That afternoon Vicky Ramirez called from her office. In the background, her view of Seeti Bay sparkled on Chuck's phone. Vicky and Chuck were old friends—friends with benefits.

"Let me cook dinner for you tonight, big guy. Like that old song says, 'I've been lonely too long'."

Vicky was third-generation Cuban-American and grew up speaking great English and terrible Spanish. When she and Chuck first met, she asked him to speak Spanish with her to improve her fluency. Once she became fluent, they continued to speak Spanish when they were together. The difference being she had a Cuban accent, and he had a Mexican one.

"Actually, I owe you a dinner, Vicky. Why don't you come here and I'll cook?"

She smiled over the phone. "Make sure it's Chicken Marsala."

The first time Vicky and Chuck slept together she had cooked Chicken Marsala. The dish became their inside joke for a booty call. Chuck would have married Vicky in a heartbeat but she wasn't interested in having children. She was married to her legal career.

At seven p.m., she let herself into his condo with her key. She carried an overnight bag into his bedroom.

Later, Vicky finished her after-dinner Calvados and rubbed the back of Chuck's hand. "What's on your mind, handsome?"

Before he could say "nothing," she continued, "and don't say 'nothing.' You're doing a fair job of carrying on a conversation, but your mind is far away. Is it Terry again?"

The Terry she spoke of was Teresa Kovacs, Chuck's on-again, off-again serious girlfriend for several years. Terry wasn't what Chuck's father would call "a deep-water swimmer." Chuck gave up on Terry the second or third time she bailed on him when his life or their relationship got tough. He always found consolation in Vicky's welcoming arms.

"No, it's not Terry this time. It's a girl named Ruby. We met in Austin last year. I was there working to locate my cousin Emily. Ruby and I've been seeing each other."

"In Austin?"

"Yes, but she's visited me here three times."

"I presume she flew?"

"What difference does it make?"

"I assume that means yes. Who paid her airfare?"

Chuck thought that was an odd question. "What difference does it make?"

"Answer the question, smart guy." Vicky could do a mean imitation of a trial attorney even though her specialty was family law.

"She did."

"All three times?"

"I guess. Maybe she used airline miles."

Vicky smiled her *meaningful* smile—the one where she knew something Chuck didn't know, but should.

"Is she rich?"

"She's a latent print examiner in the Austin Police crime lab, so I doubt it. But I haven't met her family."

"Buying her own tickets means she's either serious about you or…" Vicky grinned. "She loves Port City Beach, and sleeping with you is a way to stay here without renting a hotel room."

"You think she's more serious than I realized?"

Vicky gave him a palms-up. "Or she stays with you because it's cheaper than a waterfront hotel in high season."

"So, she might be using me."

"I haven't met Ruby so I can't say. However, I have known women who look for Sugar Daddies."

"Maybe Ruby invests in the airfare because I'm great in bed."

Vicky gave Chuck one of those looks. "That must be it. She can't find any man in Texas who rings her chimes as well as you do."

Typical of his limited knowledge of women, Chuck hadn't considered either possibility. *She's using me or she's serious about me*, he thought. *Trust Vicky for insight into the female mind.*

"Are you serious about her?"

He waffled a hand. "Not yet, but I could be. Hell, I *want* to be serious, but it's early days, and she lives in Austin. She was here last week."

"Remember Terry. You thought she was the one to build a future with."

Teresa Kovacs had broken his heart—twice. Maybe Chuck was hooked on the Norman Rockwell vision of a family. He wanted his own family so badly that he saw things that aren't real.

"Chuck," Vicky said, "you were more serious than she was. I don't want to see you get hurt again."

"I'll be careful this time. I'll keep my eyes open."

"Ri-i-ight. And you're eating dinner with me, knowing I expect to boff your brains out later. Aren't you worried that ringing my chimes would be cheating on Ruby?"

"Yes. But you're a lawyer. You can think of a loophole, an extenuating circumstance."

"Have you two discussed an exclusive relationship?"

"No. I thought it was too early. Is that a loophole?"

"Does Ruby date other men?"

"We haven't discussed it."

"Would it bother you if she slept with another man?"

"No. We're adults and we live fifteen hundred miles apart."

She gazed at me, wide-eyed.

"Okay. Maybe it *would* bother me, but I wouldn't blame her and I wouldn't be jealous. Or not much."

"Lover boy, you're pathetic," she scoffed and patted him on the shoulder. "You're painting her into a Norman Rockwell painting, but you haven't admitted it to yourself."

"Could be."

"Has Hank met her?"

Hank Ramirez, Vicky's younger brother, once told Chuck that he would welcome Chuck as a brother-in-law, but he realized it would never happen because Vicky was single-minded about her career.

"Yes. Didn't he tell you?"

"I haven't talked to him in a while. We're eating dinner at Dad's house this Sunday."

"I'm sure Hank will tell you about meeting Ruby. She was helping on Phillip Franks's murder case."

"While she was here to visit you?"

"No. She flew to Chicago and Fort Benning with me. Before you ask… I did pay for those trips."

"Anything *you* want to tell me about her? If I'm not getting laid tonight, I might as well be your shrink. Again."

"Hey, I did cook Chicken Marsala. Isn't that an implied contract? Don't give up that easily."

She didn't.

NINE

B uster Cleveland called Chuck at 3:30 the next afternoon. "We revealed a possible lead. You could help run it down."

This was just what Chuck needed to help pay his debt to Phil Franks. He grabbed a notepad. "Sure. What you got?"

"Lissa and I interviewed the personnel manager at Southeast Printing and Binding. It's a year-old printing company at 1422 NW 162nd Street near the Oklahatchee Airport. We showed the manager the photo of Billow, and his pupils widened. He claimed he didn't know Billow, but I believe he does. I showed him Aisha's picture, and the same thing happened."

"Any Illinois license plates in the parking lot?"

"No, but the employee parking is in the back," he said.

"Did you look back there?"

"The gate was locked and the fence is solid wood seven feet high. I didn't want them to click that we're onto them."

"His pupils widened twice. That's pretty slim. You have anything else?"

"Yeah. The nameplate on his desk said *Daniyar Kusainov*." Cleveland spelled both names. "The name might be Kazakh."

"I agree: That's a lead. Nice work. How can I help?"

"You and an operative stake out the company and eyeball the employee cars as they leave. Watch for license plates on our BOLO list. Tail anyone who seems promising."

"That's ten or twelve miles from my office," Chuck said. "In this traffic, I may not make it by five o'clock. Plus, I need to round up an operative. Hard to do on short notice."

"Do your best. If you miss the closing rush, there's always tomorrow."

"Okay. Is there a place to park where we won't be noticed?"

"There's an AutoZone store across the street," Cleveland said. "Big parking lot full of cars, but there's a problem."

"The story of my life. What is it?"

"NW 162nd Street is one of those divided boulevards in that industrial area north of the Oklahatchee Airport."

"Yeah, I'm familiar with the area. I worked a kidnapping case near there. What's the problem?"

"Southeast Printing and Binding is sandwiched between an air conditioning contractor on one side and an engineering and architecture firm on the other, It's in the middle of the block. Drivers exiting the lot turn right, heading west. If the employee lives to the east, they gotta drive west to 15th Avenue so they can U-turn and go east."

"And if their destination is to the west, the auto parts parking lot across the street forces me to turn right, drive to 14th Avenue, and U-turn before I can tail them."

"That's why you need two of you. One of you to park in the air conditioning company lot next door and the other to park at the AutoZone store."

"Thanks for the heads-up."

Chuck disconnected and called Gunner.

"Hey, Chuck. What can I do for you?"

"You at the gym?"

"Yes and no. I'm scheduled to work in an hour, but I'm doing my own workout first."

"Will Kennedy let you off to work for me?" Kennedy Carlson owned Jerry's Gym, where Chuck had been a member since he first moved to Port City. He was Chuck's good friend.

"Ken will do anything you ask. What's the mission?"

Chuck told him.

"Affirmative. I'll meet you there in one hour thirteen minutes."

Gunner and his military terminology—it wasn't a *job* or a *gig*. It was either an *assignment* or a *mission*. He didn't say *sure* or *okay* or *you bet*; he said *affirmative*.

"Park in the lot of the air conditioning contractor next door to the printer. Then call me."

———

Chuck drove his white Dodge Grand Caravan into the first entrance to the AutoZone parking lot at 4:45 and stopped facing the street.

Two minutes later, Gunner passed him on NW 162nd Street and parked his Jeep Cherokee in the air conditioning contractor's lot.

Chuck's phone rang and a bull's-eye appeared on the screen. "Yeah, Gunner. I see you. Did you spot me as you passed?"

"Affirmative."

"Any trouble getting off work?"

"Negative. Kennedy asked whether this mission was about the headless body and I said affirmative. He told me to catch the guy who did it and strangle him with his own guts. What's the mission?"

"Buster Cleveland and his partner suspect that Billow and his fiancée Aisha Aubakirovna work for that printing company. There might be other people of interest to us we haven't identified. I texted you the descriptions of the four cars on the police BOLO. Did you receive it?"

"Affirmative. Let me access it on the screen…Done. I see the list."

"The first three cars on the list are family cars registered to Duman Aubakirovich, Aisha's brother. One of them is hers, but we don't know which one. The other two could be in Chicago or here. The last car on the BOLO belongs to Billow. All four are Illinois license plates. You and I will tail the first two cars on this list that exit the employee lot. See that gate on this side of the printer? That's the access to the employee lot."

"Sounds easy enough. Should I tail the first car or the second?"

"That depends. NW 162nd Street is a divided street. If the first car does *not* U-turn at 15th Avenue, you tail that car. If it *does*, I'll take it. You follow the second car, if there is one, no matter which direction it goes."

"I can't read the license plates from my location. Can you watch for me?"

"No problem."

While they waited for quitting time, Chuck pondered his previous night's conversation with Vicky about Ruby. He thought about how he loved to hear Ruby's voice. Austin was one hour behind Port City. It wouldn't be right to call her at work.

Chuck settled back and selected a country music station on the radio. He was in a giddy-up-cowboy mood. The back of his mind told him something was about to happen, but that part is optimistic. It's also often right.

―――――

At 5:25 a chunky, gray-haired man rounded the back corner of the building. He trudged to the fence that enclosed the parking lot. Chunky worked a combination on the padlock and removed a steel chain from the gate. After swinging the gate open 180°, he chained it to the fence and disappeared back around the corner. Two minutes later a rusty clunker drove through the gate with Chunky at the wheel.

Chuck called Gunner. "Probably the shift ends at 5:30. I forgot to tell you: Illinois vehicles have license plates on both front and back."

"Good, that makes them easier to identify. I'll keep the line open."

Three minutes later a parade of vehicles dribbled out the gate in ones and twos. Florida cars were easy to identify; they didn't have front license plates. Seven cars bumped across the track in the gate.

"Gunner, the eighth car exiting—it's on the list of Duman Aubakirovich's cars. It's an old blue Toyota sedan. The driver's window is tinted and I can't make out the driver's face, or whether it's a man or woman. Whoever it is, they're wearing a black pill box hat with gold trim."

"It must be Aisha."

"Wearing a hat doesn't mean it's a woman."

"Good point."

A red Ford pickup trailed behind the Toyota. Next came a white minivan similar to Chuck's Dodge. Not surprising; at work, Chuck drove a Grand Caravan to be inconspicuous. His minivan was one fish swimming in an ocean of white minivans.

"She's exiting the parking lot," Chuck said, "changing lanes. You ID her?"

"Affirmative."

"Stand by to see whether she U-turns."

Aisha changed another lane, drove a hundred yards, and angled into the left-turn lane.

"She's gonna loop around," Chuck said. "I'll tail her. You watch the other cars as they pass you on the street."

Chuck slipped the minivan in gear and backed out. He eased closer to the driveway. The pickup followed Aisha and the other white minivan did too. The next two cars exiting were Florida cars. Both went west.

The Toyota waited for the green arrow and headed Chuck's way in the second lane, shadowed by the pickup and the white minivan. Neither had front license plates; must be from Florida.

Chuck let another car slot in behind the minivan. A black Chevy Suburban with Virginia plates exited the other driveway of the AutoZone store. Two men were in the front seat. Coincidence? Maybe. Maybe not. The Suburban curved after the minivan.

Chuck punched the accelerator, wedged into the crowd of commuters, and became the fifth vehicle in Aisha's convoy.

The Ford pickup turned first. Then the black Suburban dropped back and another car slipped in between it and Aisha's Toyota. Aisha drove three miles per hour over the speed limit.

There are thousands of cautious drivers in South Florida, mainly elderly, or visitors, or both. But Aisha was neither. Why did she drive so conservatively?

The cars between her and the Chevy Suburban pulled around to pass. But not the Chevy.

Aisha's Toyota climbed the entrance to I-95 Southbound, and the Suburban dropped another hundred yards back. Coincidence? The big Chevy had parked in the AutoZone lot twenty yards from Chuck. It tailed

Aisha for five miles and kept a minimum of two vehicles behind her Toyota.

Rule Seven: *There is no such thing as a coincidence—except when there is.*

The Suburban bore a Virginia plate, but that's not unusual in Florida in January. Thousands of Northerners winter in Florida. Black and dark-colored SUVs are as common as white minivans. Sometime, it seemed to Chuck as if two-thirds of the vehicles on Florida roads are minivans, pickups, or SUVs. Sedans like Aisha's were practically as extinct as the dinosaurs.

Why would a late-model Suburban be parked at an auto parts store? Everything on the vehicle was under warranty. And if they needed a part, why shop ten miles from the tourist district?

If it walks like a duck and quacks like a duck...

Chuck closed the gap and snapped a picture of the Suburban's license plate. Couldn't hurt to run the plate.

He called Gunner. "Did any more cars on the BOLO list come from the printer's lot?"

"Negative. They just relocked the gate to the employee lot. I was about to call you."

"Could you tell whether Billow was in another car?"

"Negative. The shadows are too long, and the setting sun blinded me. Sorry."

"No problem. I need you for something else. Aisha's moving south on I-95. Head this way. Call me once you're on I-95."

Aisha stayed in the slow lane, toddling along at 58 mph.

A yellow Ferrari behind Chuck flashed his headlights. He wanted Chuck to speed up. Fat chance. Maybe his $250,000 sports car sat too low for him to notice the traffic ahead that held Chuck back. Or perhaps he was just an asshole.

Another half mile and the Ferrari discovered a gap in the next lane. He shoehorned his way into the commuters squeezing past. He gave Chuck a one-finger salute. Chuck smiled and waved. His grandma would be proud.

In two miles, Aisha exited at NE 125th Street. The Chevy and Chuck both dropped back to determine which way she was turning before they committed themselves. The other commuters flowed around them. The Chevy and Chuck were rocks in the rapids.

Aisha slipped into the left-turn lane and waited for the light. Two cars lined up behind her, shadowed by the Suburban, another car, then Chuck.

The left arrow shone green. Aisha gathered speed, swinging her gaze right and left at the traffic on 125th. She completed the curve and merged to the curb lane. The two cars behind her sped around her. The yellow light came on. The Chevy beat the red light. The car in front of Chuck didn't.

He was trapped. He pounded the steering wheel with his fist. Funny how often he did that when it never changed anything. Chuck peered under the overpass as Aisha and the Suburban drove out of sight.

While Chuck waited for the next green arrow, he sent the photo of the Suburban's license plate to Buster Cleveland.

We found Aisha. She is driving the blue Toyota on the BOLO list. Heading east from I-95 on NE 125th Street. This SUV was tailing her. We're not the only ones looking for Billow. Please run the plate.

After what seemed like three hours but was likely three minutes, the green arrow lit and Chuck tailgated the car ahead which stayed in the left lane. Chuck angled right and pushed the accelerator, dodging through the traffic. With Aisha driving like a tortoise, he could sprint like a hare and catch her.

The light at NE 6th Avenue switched to yellow. He accelerated through the intersection. The light turned red. He pretended it was pink.

Here 125th Street climbed a bridge over the Florida East Coast railroad tracks. From the high point on the overpass, Chuck spotted three dark SUVs eastbound in the distance. Slamming the pedal to the firewall, Chuck zoomed down the east side of the bridge.

The street curved and became North Bay Causeway near the north end of Seeti Bay. At the eastern end, the causeway terminated in the middle of the town of Seaside at Highway A1A. Seaside had hundreds of blue-collar houses and small apartments built following World War II. That might be Aisha's destination.

Chuck passed like he was running on the moving sidewalk at the airport. A block ahead he made out a white license plate with blue printing. Could be a Virginia plate. North Bay Causeway climbs a bascule bridge over the Intracoastal Waterway. Chuck drove up the slope. The big, black Chevy was three cars behind Aisha's blue Toyota.

The red lights on the bridge barricades flashed to signal drivers that the bridge would rise for tall boats to pass. The bell clanged and the barricades arced across the roadway.

Aisha's Toyota slipped under the lowering barricade, shadowed by one additional car. The Suburban was trapped two cars from the barricade.

The bascule bridge requires seven minutes to cycle, longer if there are several boats. Chuck would never catch Aisha. Time for Plan B.

Rule Two: *When in doubt, follow somebody.*

Chuck couldn't follow Aisha, but he could follow the Suburban. He slowed to a crawl and let three cars wedge between him and the Chevy.

Chuck's cellphone rang and flashed the bull's-eye signal for Gunner. "Hey, Gunner, you reach I-95?"

Chuck's Bluetooth muted the radio and transferred the call to the radio speakers. "Affirmative."

"Exit at 125th Street and head east on North Bay Causeway. I lost Aisha at a drawbridge, but somebody else was tracking her also. A black Suburban with Virginia plates." Chuck read him the number. "Catch up and we'll leapfrog the tail on the Suburban."

While Chuck waited for the barricades to rise, his phone signaled a text from Cleveland.

The Virginia plates were stolen off a sedan in D.C. two days after Christmas. I notified the D.C. and Virginia cops. Can you or Gunner tail them after you tag Aisha?

In eight minutes, North Bay Causeway re-opened. The Suburban jumped a jackrabbit start. Chuck kept up the best he could without attracting the attention of a traffic cop. After three blocks, the Chevy must have realized the futility of catching Aisha and slowed to normal speed. A mile later Chuck slotted in three vehicles behind them.

Gunner called. "I crossed the ICW bridge. What's your position?"

"I passed Fishermen's Pier Park. I'll keep the line open."

"You are three hundred meters ahead. I'll overtake the target enough to make a positive ID of the vehicle. Then I'll drop back and you disengage."

Gunner—he loves military terminology like *overtake* and *disengage* and *meter*. It's a mystery why he didn't reenlist.

Gunner's Jeep Cherokee overtook the third vehicle ahead of him. "I identified the Virginia license plates. That is the target. I'll drop back. Disengage and drop back two hundred meters."

Chuck did and trailed for another mile.

"Boss, the target is heading south on A1A," Gunner said.

"Roger. Shadow them another mile. If they don't turn, I'll catch up and relieve you. It's dark, so I'll close up."

"Hooah." Army slang for *heard and understood*.

Three minutes later, Gunner said, "They're driving onto Venetian Islands. Won't be enough traffic to hide in. You should relieve me before I'm made."

"On my way, Gunner."

Chuck goosed the accelerator and caught Gunner's Jeep. The Suburban was rolling on the main thoroughfare that crossed the first and largest of the Venetian Islands.

The Venetian Islands were chock-full of waterfront mansions almost a hundred years old. The islands were dredged from the bottom of Seeti Bay in the 1920s, a time before real estate developers worried about street crime and home invasions. The streets and picturesque bridges that joined the handful of islands were open to the public. The Port City Beach police and private security companies patrolled regularly, but most of the homeowners took their own security seriously too.

"I'll make the next left, boss. I'll drive parallel on the next street."

"Hooah, Gunner."

The Suburban rolled two blocks with Chuck trailing a hundred yards back. The target hung a right, crossed a miniature Rialto Bridge past the ornamental sign in the pocket park that read *Private/San Marco Island/ Residents Only*, and looped right on San Marco Drive.

Chuck kept them in sight. In the dark, all they would notice would be headlights in their rearview mirrors.

Four mailboxes down, the Chevy curved into a gate in an eight-foot masonry wall that concealed a waterfront estate.

Chuck snatched his phone, swiped the *video* button, and lowered the passenger window. He cruised past the property the Suburban had entered, videoing it and the properties on either side.

Through the closing gate, he glimpsed the brick-paved circular driveway and the huge Mediterranean-style mansion and outbuildings. The Suburban was stopped in a large parking area and four men were mounting the steps to the carved, double front doors.

"Gunner, I trailed them to their destination at 26 San Marco Drive. Thanks for the help. Send me your bill."

"Roger that, boss. Mission accomplished."

Why would four men living in a mansion follow Aisha? No, that was the wrong question.

Chuck suspected the four men were employees of whoever lived in the mansion. The real question was: Why would a mega-millionaire send four men to follow Aisha?

————

Chuck woke up his home computer and ran a property search on 26 San Marco Drive. The good news is that ownership of real estate in Florida is a matter of public record, including the mansion on San Marco Island. The bad news was that the mansion was owned by a Florida Land Trust, a device which hides the owner's identity behind a trustee—normally an attorney. The attorney-client privilege requires the attorney to keep the true owner's name confidential.

Movie stars, police officers, judges, wealthy entrepreneurs, and plain privacy nuts use Florida Land Trusts. Chuck owned his condo through a Florida Land Trust. He had made enough powerful enemies that he didn't want strangers to know where he lived.

Chuck had encountered land trusts in other cases. For the San Marco mansion, the trustee was George Alexander, a local lawyer. Chuck had cracked one case involving sex trafficking of Asian immigrant women after he discovered the same trustee owned several suspicious properties. Chuck used that information to link the attorney to his person of interest.

So far, the San Marco mansion was the only property Chuck had researched. If the George Alexander connection surfaced later, he could use it.

The Atlantic County Property Appraiser's website said the lot measured 150 feet on the street and 170 feet on the canal. The house was built in 1927 and contained over 10,000 square feet of living area in the main house, with six bedrooms, six-and-a-half bathrooms, a fifty-foot swimming pool and a fifty-foot dock. The bungalow above the four-car garage measured 625 square feet plus a deck, with two bedrooms and one-and-a-half baths. The other bungalow with the two-car garage had the same footprint but two stories, so it had 1,250 square feet, four bedrooms, and four baths. The estate was large enough to house a small private army.

Chuck researched the title history of the mansion. The property was purchased in 2003 for $4.5 million by 26 San Marco Drive LLC, an obvious shell company. In 2006, at the height of the nationwide real estate balloon, the shell company made a new loan for $11 million. The bank that made the loan was Kommerzbank Sachsen, a medium-sized bank in Dresden, Germany. The shell company defaulted on the loan and the bank foreclosed during the real estate crash in 2007.

The current owner bought the property from the bank for $1,000 in 2008. That wasn't a misprint: The $1,000 purchase price was as phony as a politician's promise. Following the bogus purchase, the swimming pool and dock were rebuilt and the elevators to the bungalows were added. The property was assessed for tax purposes at $19.8 million.

Most of that information had little value except for Rule Five: *You can never have too much information.* The date purchased might prove useful.

Chuck sent Gunner to make a video-camera pass down San Marco Drive the next morning. That afternoon, Chuck met Gunner at his condo and transferred the video file to his home network where they studied it on a big-screen HD monitor. He forwarded a copy to Buster Cleveland.

"Stop it there," Gunner said. "The first driveway has security cameras on both sides of the gate."

"Yeah. One camera aims onto the entrance driveway by the steel gate. The second aims at the street and the landscaped area between the wall and the street. What's that little box?"

"Let it run one second. Stop. You can't spot them in this view, but there are three boxes on the main section of the wall and one at each front corner of the property. Right there. Those boxes shine laser beams at each other, dividing the wall into four security sections. The boxes on the corners point beams down the property line toward the water."

"Whoever lives there has better security than most banks," Chuck said. "Your drive-by video of the block caught a for sale sign for the house two doors down from our subject. Let's check out the listing."

Chuck did an internet search for 30 San Marco Drive and scanned the real estate listing.

"Enlighten me, O great detective," Gunner said. "What are you looking for?"

"The broker's listing on the website shows an aerial view of the property. For multi-million-dollar mansions, brokers often use a drone to shoot aerial photos of the property and nearby amenities like a park or marina. Aerial shots often include nearby properties. I'm searching for aerial shots of 26 San Marco Drive. Bingo. There's a drone video."

Chuck let it play, then paused it. "There's a shot of 26 San Marco Drive at the edge of the frame." He zoomed the picture and re-centered. "And, bingo. Notice the extra security camera on the roofline at the back? That covers the dock and the yacht."

"What do you think? Organized crime?"

"Or an exiled Eastern European dictator, or an internet tech billionaire, or a member of a foreign country's royal family. South Florida draws serious money from all over the world. Most of it legal. Rich people love to own houses on Port City Beach, especially in the winter."

Chuck entered the address on Google Street View. The Street View camera was tall enough to photograph over the eight-foot wall. Street View gave the two men a view of the front and sides of the mansion as it was two years ago. Nothing out of the ordinary except an excessive number of security cameras on the roof.

Gunner said, "With license plate recognition technology, whoever monitors those security cameras could keep a record of every vehicle that drives in front of the property."

"Which means they have our license plates. If they run the plates, they'll know we don't live on San Marco Island."

"Maybe they're not that paranoid."

"And maybe the federal government will balance the budget this year. Rule Fifteen, Gunner: *Never take anything for granted.*"

———

Chuck called Buster Cleveland. "What have you learned about Southeast Printing and Binding?"

"The guy Daniyar Kusainov who I thought was the personnel manager —he's one of the owners. He has a brother, Aldiyar, and their father, Vladimir. The three of them own the company."

"Might be a clue," Chuck said.

"Melissa and I will do a deep dive into the three Kusainovs. There could be a connection."

"I'll do my own research also," Chuck said. "I have sources you can't use."

"Don't want to know about that," Cleveland said. "I asked the City of Port City Beach to post a patrol car at the entrance to the San Marco mansion and bust the Chevy Suburban with the stolen plates when they come out. We'll learn who else wants Aisha."

Vladimir Kusainov, huh? It was time to burn some more midnight oil.

Chuck didn't learn until the next day that he and the Port City cops weren't the only ones interested in Vladimir Kusainov.

TEN

The next morning the receptionist dinged the intercom while Chuck was reading email.

"Ms. Villa and Mr. Welsh to see you, Mr. McCrary."

"Thanks, Betty."

Chuck's first appointment wasn't until after lunch, and Betty always called him Chuck. The unexpected visitors made her uncomfortable.

"Please offer them refreshments, Betty, and tell them I'll be out in two minutes."

Chuck leaned over and tapped the comforting bulge of his Browning .380 in the holster on his right ankle. He reached back and touched the Glock 17 belt-clipped behind his right kidney. Stroking a rabbit's foot.

He closed all open files on his computer and shut it down. He unplugged the computer and locked it in a fireproof filing cabinet in the storage room. You never know.

As he crossed his office toward the conference room, the locked door between his office and the public hallway rattled. Someone had tried to open it without knocking.

A fist pounded on the door. "Federal agents. Open the door."

Both Chuck's office and his conference room had doors to the hall.

Chuck always entered through the conference room and kept the door between his office and the hall locked.

"Just a minute." He stepped to the conference room.

Closing his office door behind him, he scanned the room. Two dirty coffee cups lurked on the square coffee table that served as his conference table. Chuck had worked there the previous night after the cleanup crew finished. Too late to clean now.

Crossing to the hall door, he opened it. "Hello. Did someone knock?"

Naturally there was no one there.

A man and a woman stood in the hall, blocking the other door. They were so stiff, they looked starched. They could have been wearing signs around their necks that said *Federal Agent.*

The woman, whom Chuck presumed was Ms. Villa, carried a combination purse-briefcase with a shoulder strap and a briefcase handle. Handy thing for a professional woman. Behind her subtle makeup and tightly-wound hair style, Agent Villa's smooth-skinned face and full lips would launch a thousand ships if she smiled. Her pinstriped gray suit with its too-tight jacket was accented with a yellow neck scarf. Pantyhose and sensible black shoes completed the classic Female Federal Agent Fashion Ensemble. Despite her armored appearance, she had a figure that would stop traffic. Too bad she was on duty, and Chuck was going almost-steady with Ruby.

But was Ruby going almost-steady with him?

The man, presumably Mr. Welsh, also wore a gray pinstriped suit. His yellow tie matched the exact shade of Agent Villa's scarf. Did he and Agent Villa coordinate their outfits? He was five-foot-ten and weighed a hundred and thirty pounds if he carried a brick in each pocket. He reminded Chuck of an old movie, *The Thin Man.*

Chuck figured they both wore rubber-soled shoes in case they had to chase him.

Welsh brought a cardboard box. They were planning to haul away evidence. Evidence from Chuck's office.

Why would the FBI be there? Were they investigating the murder of Phillip Franks? Maybe murdering a U.S. Army vet was a federal crime.

Everything from jaywalking to spitting on the sidewalk was a federal crime nowadays.

"Good morning," Chuck said. "My office entrance is here. I don't use that door. I'm Carlos McCrary."

The woman frowned. She approached him with an envelope in her hand. Their rubber-soled dress shoes *squished* on the tile floor.

Villa's white silk blouse was translucent enough to highlight her considerable cleavage behind the suit jacket. She thrust the envelope at Chuck. "This is a warrant to search the premises, Mr. McCrary."

Chuck opened the envelope. The warrant seemed real, but you can't be too careful. "May I examine your credentials, please?"

Welsh presented his. Villa struggled to free her creds from her too-tight jacket pocket. They were Secret Service; not FBI.

"I'm Special Agent Valery Villa. This is my colleague, Special Agent Lionel Welsh."

Chuck reviewed their credentials, then pulled out his phone and photographed them.

"What are you doing?" Villa said.

"I've seen people forge government IDs before. These appear to be genuine, but I don't recall encountering Secret Service creds. May I confirm your identity with your office?"

"Go ahead," Villa said, "the number is on the card."

"I could print a business card like yours on my computer or order them online for ten bucks." Instead, Chuck asked his phone to call the Port City office of the Treasury Department.

Villa seemed pissed that Chuck hadn't used the number on her business card. Too bad. Life is filled with small disappointments.

"I wish to confirm the identities of two people who claim to be Secret Service agents. Whom would I speak to?...Yes, I'll hold."

Villa and Welsh stood in the hallway for the two minutes it required to confirm that two agents had been sent to search his office.

"Thank you." Chuck disconnected and stepped back. "How can I help the Secret Service?" he asked, ever the public-spirited, patriotic citizen.

"You can stand aside so we can execute the warrant."

"I can save you time if you tell me what you're searching for."

"Stand aside, Mr. McCrary."

Okay, they weren't going to play nice. Understandable since Chuck hadn't played nice either. He made an exaggerated step sideways. "Have fun. I intend to wash these two dirty coffee cups in the kitchen. Would you like to search them first?" He held them up for inspection.

Villa sniffed at him. *Some people have no sense of humor*, he thought. Perhaps she was a robot. An attractive robot. Perhaps he should offer to let her strip-search him…

She opened the door to Chuck's office and peeked inside. "That door on the far side of your office. Where does it lead?"

"My storage and file room. My suite has three rooms, each of which has a door to the hall. I don't use the other doors." He lifted the dirty cups again. "I'll be back. You kids have fun."

————

After washing the cups, Chuck returned to the conference room and called Buster Cleveland. "Two Secret Service agents are at my office with a search warrant. I thought you'd be interested."

"What do they expect to find?"

"They won't say. Their warrant covers everything from my underwear to the limits of the solar system."

"Let me talk to the lead agent."

Chuck carried the phone to his office. Villa was sitting in Chuck's chair poking through his desk drawers. He handed her the phone.

She held it as if it wanted to bite her. "What's this?"

"The one criminal case I'm working is the murder of Phillip Franks. I have Detective Buster Cleveland with the Port City Police Department on the phone. He's in charge of investigating that case. I figured he might help you."

"What case did you say you're working?"

"The murder of Phillip Franks. He was a friend. I'm consulting with Detective Cleveland."

"We're not interested in a murder." She handed the phone back to

Chuck. "If the murder were a Federal case, that would be FBI, not Treasury." Her voice capitalized the F in Federal.

She didn't want his help. Maybe if *he* offered to strip search *her*…

Chuck held the phone to his ear. "Did you hear that, Buster?"

"Yeah. Stuck-up bitch, isn't she?"

Villa's cheeks colored.

"She heard that, Buster."

"Screw her if she won't talk to a state cop." Cleveland disconnected.

Chuck shrugged and returned to the conference room. He fired up his tablet and read the day's news. Helpful Chuck, making himself available.

Twenty minutes later, he leaned through the door to his office. "I'm going for coffee. Would you or Very Special Agent Welsh like anything?"

Villa glanced from his desk. "No, thanks. We're good."

"Suit yourself." Chuck got his coffee and resumed his seat in the conference room. *What a waste of taxpayer money*, he thought.

Welsh appeared in the door. "Please unlock your file cabinet."

Chuck handed him the keys. "The little key with the round tab. When you boot my laptop, bring it to me and I'll enter the PIN. My offer to help stands. Tell me what you want to know. Might save us all some time."

Welsh hesitated, glanced over his shoulder before speaking. "What is your interest in Vladimir Kusainov?"

The previous night Chuck spent an hour investigating the Kusainov family and Southeast Printing and Binding. Melissa Chan and Buster Cleveland were on it like hair on a dog, but Chuck wanted his own angle on the situation.

Between eleven o'clock the previous night and ten o'clock the next morning, the U.S. Government learned Chuck had investigated Vladimir Kusainov. Someone decided to search his office and located a judge in the middle of the night to sign a warrant. Someone else assigned two Secret Service agents to execute the warrant.

That was so creepy there were no words to describe how Chuck felt. *Violated…infringed upon…defiled.* What happened to the Fourth Amendment to the Constitution? "The right of the people to be secure in their persons, houses, papers, and effects, against unreasonable searches and seizures, shall not be violated…" The Patriot Act didn't repeal the

Fourth Amendment. Perhaps the Secret Service hadn't received the memo.

Suddenly Chuck wasn't so public-spirited and patriotic.

Chuck sipped his coffee and positioned the cup in the exact center of the coaster on the table. Three points for neatness and style...and stalling.

"What makes you suspect I'm interested in Vladimir...What did you say his name was?"

"Let's not play games, Mr. McCrary. You ran a deep background check on Vladimir Kusainov last night. Our job is to ask the questions, and yours is to answer them."

"Oh, that's clever. Your job is to ask and mine is to answer. I should write that down so I don't forget."

Welsh's face flushed. Chuck hoped he didn't suffer from high blood pressure; he might have a stroke.

Villa materialized in the doorway like a ghost from the crypt. "What's going on?"

Chuck gave her his cop stare. "What is your interest in Vladimir Kusainov, Agent Villa?"

"That's *Special* Agent Villa," Welsh said. His voice was an octave higher—caught by the boss talking out of turn. Welsh was a chastened puppy sucking up to the big dog. Or big bitch.

Chuck ignored him. Didn't even flick the cop stare his way.

Chuck counted to himself. *One-thousand-one. Two-thousand-two.*

Welsh fidgeted. He wanted to say something so bad it made his tongue itch, but he didn't dare usurp Villa's role, since she'd appeared in Chuck's conference room.

At *seven-thousand-seven* Villa's brown eyes narrowed and those sexy lips tightened like a purse string. At *eight-thousand-eight* she surrendered and answered Chuck's question.

———

Villa sat across the table from Chuck. "Vladimir Kusainov is a convicted counterfeiter. That's a matter of public record. He's on parole for the next sixteen years. Since you were investigating him—you being a private investigator—we hoped you had discovered something that would help us."

Chuck had read about Vladimir's counterfeiting conviction the previous night. The image of the Kazakh 200 and 500 tenge bills popped into his mind. Was that what Billow was into? Counterfeiting? Why Kazakh tenges? Was counterfeiting foreign currency even a crime in the United States? Probably. Most things are a federal crime if the Feds stare hard enough. Hell, a simple conspiracy charge sucks you down faster than quicksand.

"That's why you're keeping tabs on him, Very Special Agent Villa? Suspicion of counterfeiting?"

"Not necessarily suspicion. Our monitoring algorithm flagged us that you were researching him. We figured it was time for a fresh look at Kusainov. It's been two years, and we monitor convicted counterfeiters occasionally. Counterfeiters sometimes do it again. Sometimes it's their only skill."

"Did Vladimir do anything to make you suspect he's up to his old tricks?"

"If he did, we couldn't discuss his case with you."

"You just did."

"We can't discuss our cases," she repeated.

"You serve a search warrant to learn what I know, but you won't tell me what you know, and you won't say that you don't know anything. That's not fair, Very Special Agent Villa. What happened to 'One hand washes the other'?"

Villa shrugged and her impressive bosom took a bow. "It's policy."

Chuck struggled to keep his gaze on her face. "Search my files, both paper and computer, all you want. What I know and what I suspect about Vladimir Kusainov isn't documented. It's here." He tapped his forehead. "As a matter of curiosity, how did you discover my interest? Is the NSA surveilling my internet activity without a warrant?"

The National Security Agency sneaks its slimy tentacles into thousands of private lives without regard to the requirements of the Fourth Amendment.

Chuck did that too. People paid him to delve into other people's private lives. The difference was if Chuck got caught violating someone's rights, he could be sued for violating their privacy or thrown in jail. But if you're the government, and they invoke national security, the Fourth Amendment doesn't matter.

Villa said, "We have a FISA warrant. It's legal."

The Foreign Intelligence Surveillance Act covers a lot of sins.

"The warrant is on Vladimir," she said, "not on you. We investigate anyone who clicks on him. It wasn't personal. Your interest in Vladimir was probable cause that allowed us to get the warrant."

"That's interesting, Very Special Agent Villa. Let me confirm I got this right." Chuck ticked his index finger. "First, my investigation indicates Vladimir Kusainov is an American citizen, not a foreigner." He ticked his middle finger. "Second, the crime which you suspect him of committing is in the United States, not overseas." He added his ring finger and tapped it. "Third, you surveilled my internet usage last night in the good ol' U.S. of A. Is any of what I said wrong?"

Villa didn't respond.

"That's what I thought." He lowered his hand. "Tell me how this involves *foreign* intelligence."

"That's above my pay grade."

Somehow that excuse didn't convince Chuck that his rights were being respected.

"You and Welsh are merely following orders."

"Yes."

"That's the excuse the Nazis gave at the Nuremberg trials."

Chuck let the uncomfortable silence linger until Villa squirmed.

"I don't have to tell you anything, but I will, to save the taxpayers' money being wasted on your and Very Special Agent Welsh's salaries. I'm not interested in Vladimir. I'm working with the Port City police on the murder of Phillip Franks. His headless body washed up on an island in Seeti Bay a few days ago. That's the case Detective Cleveland was willing to discuss with you."

Chuck told them everything he knew about the murder.

"What's your interest in the murder?" Villa asked.

"Phillip Franks was my brother-in-arms in the U.S. Army. We were

Special Forces." Villa and Welsh had to know Chuck's military record. They wouldn't drop in on him unannounced without a background check. And if they hadn't done their homework, his Bronze Star and citation and pictures of the Triple Seven hung on the wall of the conference room in plain sight.

"Does the PCPD often ask you to help investigate a murder?"

Despite being the World's Greatest Private Investigator, Chuck decided that making a wisecrack would be unwise. Villa might haul him to the dungeon in chains. Or handcuffs. *Hmm,* he thought. *That might be interesting.*

"My buddy Captain Hank Ramirez is a homicide detective with the PCPD. He brought me in on the case. Hank was commander of our Special Forces unit. He's keeping an eye on the investigation. I was a homicide detective with the PCPD before I became a PI."

"How is Vladimir Kusainov connected to this murder?"

"He may not be." Chuck told her how the Kusainov family owned the printing company and how that connected to Aisha and how Aisha connected to Billow and how Billow connected to Franks.

"That's a long chain with a lot of weak links," Welsh said.

Chuck shrugged. "We're chasing every lead. Southeast Printing and Binding is a lead. We'll learn everything we can about the company and the people. Something might be useful."

"Okay. Sorry to bother you." Villa clutched her purse/briefcase and rose to her feet. To Welsh: "Bring the evidence box."

Welsh handed Chuck back his key ring, disappeared into the office, and returned with the cardboard box. He placed it on the ground beside Villa.

She surveyed the skimpy contents in the box. "We don't need that crap, Lionel." To Chuck: "Where do want us to dump this pile of stuff?"

"On the table is okay."

Villa handed Chuck a business card. So did her puppy dog. "If you learn anything in our area of interest, be sure to contact me or Special Agent Welsh."

Naturally I will, Chuck thought, *right after I pay off the National Debt.* The Feds departed.

Chuck waited ten minutes, then drove to a discount store and bought a half dozen prepaid burner cellphones. Since the U.S. Government had peeked over his shoulder on the internet, they were probably listening to his registered cellphones and reading his emails too. He created a new email account for this case.

It was none of their damn business how he pursued the murderers. This was personal.

Gunner staked out the print shop at quitting time. Before assigning him to tail Aisha or Billow, whichever one showed first, Chuck gave him a burner phone and his secret email address. "I don't trust the Feds. You and Snoop and I communicate on these burner phones and the new email address from now on."

"Roger. Wilco."

In fact, they weren't certain Billow worked at the print shop. His fiancée did, so it was a good bet that he worked there too. Chuck parked on the east side of the drawbridge where they had lost Aisha the day before.

During rush hour, the bridges over the Intracoastal Waterway open on a regular schedule a half hour apart. The drawbridges are timed so boats and barges can cruise from the top of Seeti Bay to the bottom at four knots and never wait for a bridge to open.

Aisha might be leery of potential tails since Phillip Franks was murdered. Even if she didn't know he was dead, she knew he had disappeared. She might cross that bridge every day to lose any tail behind her. If so, Chuck would pick her up when she did it again.

Gunner and Chuck were in position at 4:30. It was Friday, and Aisha or Billow might finish early. Gunner parked next door to the printer. Miles away, Chuck lurked in a McDonald's parking lot east of the ICW bridge.

Buster Cleveland called Chuck's regular phone. He answered on his Bluetooth. "I hope you bring good news, Buster."

"I've had a Port City Beach black-and-white sitting on the mansion since yesterday morning. Two vehicles left yesterday: an old clunker that might have been the cook's and a Cadillac Escalade. The clunker came back two hours later. The beach cops said they saw groceries in the back.

The Escalade returned late this morning. This afternoon the Suburban comes out, but it's sporting Florida plates. Might be a different vehicle."

"Where is the Suburban?"

"Hell if I know. The Beach cops have no grounds to watch them. Beach PD yanked their guys off."

"The estate has a four-car garage and a two-car garage; they might have several Suburbans."

"How do we find out?"

"Did the Port City Beach cops get a good photo of the Suburban with the Florida plates?"

"Sure."

"Send it to me. Let's each compare it with the photo I snapped of the Virginia plates. Perhaps there's a distinguishing mark to confirm it's the same vehicle."

A minute later Chuck's cellphone received the new Suburban photo. He transferred the first picture to his laptop beside him on the passenger seat. He zoomed the photo on his cellphone and held it alongside. There it was: a scrape on the rear bumper to the left of the license plate. The two images were of the same vehicle.

He called Cleveland, who answered on the first ring. "Yeah, I noticed it too. That hickey on the bumper. They noticed you were tailing them. They sent someone out in the Escalade to register the Suburban."

"Or they freaked out at the patrol car sitting on their house. They don't want to be caught with stolen tags. Who is the Suburban registered to?"

"Uptown Trading Company, LLC, in care of George Alexander, a local attorney."

"Aha. That is what we super sleuths call a clue. George Alexander is the trustee of the land trust that holds ownership of the mansion."

"Should we investigate George Alexander?"

"Good idea. I'll sic my cybersleuth on him also. Any idea where Uptown Trading Company is located?"

"No," Cleveland said, "but it's not registered in Florida. We haven't researched other states yet."

"They stole the Virginia plates in the District. Maybe they're from the greater D.C. area. I'll have my guy check Virginia, Maryland, and D.C. We could get lucky."

Chuck disconnected and texted Flamer on his burner phone.

Until further notice, communicate with me on this new number. I have a new secure email address which I will send you. My regular phones and old emails are compromised. Do a deep dive on George Alexander, attorney in Port City. Also, Uptown Trading Company, LLC, probably registered in Virginia, Maryland, or D.C.

Thirty seconds later Flamer sent Chuck a thumbs-up. Nothing to do but wait until Gunner acquired the target, probably another half hour, then a half hour or more until Aisha reached the bridge.

Chuck felt peckish, so he ambled into McDonald's and bought a Big Mac, fries, and a raspberry slushie to hold him until dinner. Or until he passed another McDonald's.

———

At 5:32, Gunner called. "Tally-ho. Aisha is driving the Toyota again."

"Stay on her and tell me whether her route changes from yesterday."

"Whoa, small world. A black Suburban with Florida plates slipped in behind her. Are these the same guys in a different Suburban?"

"What's the plate number?" He told Chuck. "Nope, same Suburban but with Florida plates. There were four guys in that Suburban two days ago. Drop way back. You're outnumbered four to one. No way do I want them to make you. I don't care if you lose them, but don't get made."

After Chuck disconnected, he debated whether to pair his burner phone to his van's Bluetooth. Could the Feds tap that? Rule Fourteen: *When you think someone is out to get you, they probably are.* He did not pair it. The extra security was worth the inconvenience. He texted Gunner:

Do not pair the new phone with Bluetooth. Bluetooth may not be secure.

Gunner texted back:

Hooah.

At 6:05 Gunner called. "She's on the same route. Suburban is four cars behind. She's slowed to less than 25 mph. She's timing it to be the last one across the drawbridge again. Maybe she does that every day."

"Perhaps. We know where the Suburban lives. I'll trail Aisha. You drop off and go home."

"I'm working tonight. I'll be at the gym."

Nine minutes later, the barricades' lights flashed. Aisha's blue Toyota was the last one across the bridge. The black and yellow barriers fell across the highway.

Once she passed the bridge, Aisha drove two or three mph above the speed limit. At Clendening Street, which is southbound Highway A1A in Seaside, she went right.

Tailing a car at night was a mixed blessing. Despite the streetlights, it's hard for the quarry to notice the tail in their rearview mirror because the follower's headlights dazzle them. On the other hand, it's hard for the follower to distinguish them in the traffic unless their taillights are distinctive. Those on Aisha's Toyota were not. There were a million other cars like it.

The commuter traffic thinned. Chuck dropped back another hundred yards. Aisha rolled through a green traffic light on 94th Street next to the Seaside City Hall. Two seconds later, the light turned yellow. By the time Chuck got there, the red light caught him.

Chuck slapped the steering wheel. He had dropped back too far. Nobody to blame but himself.

Three or four blocks ahead, she curved west, probably on 91st Street, but dammit, Chuck couldn't be certain. Between Clendening and Seeti Bay, the town of Seaside stretched westward for ten blocks, each street named after a Pacific island.

The light cycled green. Chuck punched the gas and headed west on 91st Street. Two cars traveled west a couple hundred yards ahead. He couldn't tell whether one car was Aisha's. They slowed at a small roundabout where Tahiti Terrace crossed 91st.

The roundabouts at the intersections of Oahu Lane, Moorea Way, and Tahiti Terrace slowed his progress, like they were supposed to.

West of Tahiti the houses on the south side of 91st became waterfront. In the real estate jargon of South Florida, they were *wet*—meaning waterfront. In this case, they backed up to a finger of Seeti Bay. The houses across the street were not on the water—what the real estate salespeople call *dry*. The modest wet houses were worth a million dollars or more; the dry houses sold for half that or less. South Florida's version of a mixed neighborhood.

By the time Chuck caught up to the first vehicle, he knew it wasn't Aisha's. He pursued the remaining car. A mile later he caught it at another bridge to Seeti Island, a small neighborhood where 91st Street ends at the water. It wasn't Aisha's either.

She had turned on a street nearer to Clendening.

Damn, he though. *I lost her.*

He looped around and traveled back across the Seeti Island bridge, pausing in the deserted street to plan. Nothing to do but sweep that neighborhood between 90th and 92nd, block by block, back and forth like mowing a lawn. Just slightly less boring than watching grass grow.

At Tahiti Terrace, the waterfront portion of 91st ended and Chuck widened the search area to the neighborhood between 90th and 92nd. South of 91st Street, the Town of Seaside gave way to the Village of Seeti Shores. The street name changed from Tahiti Terrace to Madison Boulevard, with modest two- and three-story apartment buildings squeezed onto narrow lots on both sides of the street.

A half-block down Madison, a blue Toyota was parked near a two-story apartment building named "Blue Hawaii." Didn't Elvis Presley make a movie called *Blue Hawaii*? This building was about the same age as the movie. It was built of concrete block and stucco, as common as indoor plumbing in South Florida.

The Toyota had Illinois plates. The parking spaces were unreserved. Chuck couldn't tell which apartment Aisha was in. Hell, she didn't necessarily live in those apartments. She might park there and walk to an apartment across the street. Chuck wouldn't put it past a person careful enough to be the last vehicle across a drawbridge every day. Like they say: Just because you're paranoid doesn't mean they're not out to get you. And Chuck was definitely out to get Aisha.

And he still hadn't seen Billow, although he might have been in the car with Aisha.

The dashboard clock read *7:30*. Madison Boulevard is one-way southbound. Chuck circled the block to 91st again and stopped across the street and 85 yards north of Aisha's Toyota. Backing into a space between another minivan and a pickup truck, he settled in for a stakeout. He was glad he'd eaten that Big Mac; unless somebody stirred, he'd sit there a long time.

By 9:30, Chuck suffered another Big Mac attack, but he wouldn't abandon the stakeout. He considered ordering a pizza delivered to "the white Grand Caravan parked backwards in the 9000 block of Madison Boulevard." Maybe not.

By 10:30, Chuck had finished both bottles of water that he kept in his van, and he needed to make a pit stop. He decided Aisha was in for the night, wherever she was. He started the Caravan and idled down the street, parking near Aisha's car. He lingered until the street was empty of traffic and pedestrians, then stuck a GPS tracking device under her Toyota.

Chuck asked his cellphone where the nearest fast food was that was open this late on a Friday night. It was a Taco Bell. Good enough. He could empty his bladder and fill his stomach at the same place.

At least he wouldn't be hungry when he went to bed, but he was juggling a lot of balls. That wasn't conducive to a good night's sleep.

ELEVEN

B efore heading to the gym the next morning, Chuck read his email. Two reports from Flamer sent at 2:38 a.m. and 3:01 a.m. Did Flamer ever sleep?

The first report covered George Alexander, the trustee for the San Marco Island mansion. Alexander's office was also the mailing address for Uptown Trading Company, LLC, the owner of the Chevy Suburban.

Born in Moscow, Georgy Aleksandrov was the son of Aleksandr Borisov, a Soviet diplomat serving in the embassy of the USSR in what was then the *Deutsche Demokratische Republik*. Aleksandrov was fluent in Russian, German, and English. Once the Berlin Wall fell in 1989, the Communist *apparatchiks* of the DDR and the USSR looted everything they could steal during the so-called "privatization" of government-owned assets.

Aleksandr Borisov sold the newly-privatized Kommerzbank Sachsen, the second-largest bank in Dresden, Germany, to himself and two other high-ranking Soviet diplomats. The next day, the three bureaucrats bought the BAK Bank of Kazakhstan in Almaty, the largest Kazakh city.

Chuck's stomach did a happy dance at the mention of Kommerzbank Sachsen and the BAK Bank of Kazakhstan. Chuck almost said "Aha."

Kommerzbank Sachsen had held the mortgage on 26 San Marco Drive. Did George Alexander live there?

The two Germanies reunited in 1990, and the Soviet Embassy became the Russian Embassy.

With the dissolution of the Soviet Union in 1991, the once-feared USSR ended with a whimper, collapsing from its own inefficiency and corruption.

In 1995, Borisov moved his family to Washington, D.C. His son, Georgy Aleksandrov, changed his name to George Alexander and enrolled in a Virginia law school where he majored in international law. Flamer attached a file from the law school's yearbook with a portrait of Alexander. The picture was twenty-five years old but it was the only one Flamer could find. Alexander had no social media footprint.

Borisov became the Commercial Attaché to the Russian Embassy, a post he still held. Kommerzbank Sachsen continued to pay him a handsome salary to serve on its board of directors.

What does a commercial attaché do? Chuck thought.

Alexander had officed in that building for nineteen years, but Flamer uncovered no evidence that he had any clients. Alexander's name had never appeared in any court filing in any court in Atlantic County, and he had never worked for another law firm or had a partner. How did he earn a living?

Mentally, Chuck tabled that question and read the second email.

The Uptown Trading Company, LLC, was chartered in Virginia in 2001. Despite George Alexander's office in Port City being its legal address, its physical location was in Georgetown, D.C., a tasteful nineteenth-century townhouse, unremarkable on a block lined with tasteful nineteenth-century townhouses. Chuck read the directions from there to the Russian Embassy. An easy six-minute trip on Wisconsin Avenue NW. Uptown's registered agent was Aleksandr Borisov, the Russian commercial attaché. *Hmm.*

The black Suburban belonging to the Uptown Trading Company was newly registered. George Alexander's law office was its address of record. *Hmm* again.

Why was the Russian commercial attaché having four men—

correction: at *least* four men— stalk a Kazakh immigrant living in Port City?

Chuck called Cleveland.

"Funny you called on my day off. I was about to email you. I'm calling a meeting downtown, Conference Room B at 9:30."

"Now?"

"Of course not; today's Saturday."

"Crime never takes a day off."

"But police detectives do. The meeting is this Monday."

"Who's coming?"

"Lissa and I, you, and Hank."

"I'll send you two reports we'll need to discuss. I'll forward copies to Hank and Lissa."

Chuck worked out and thought about Ruby. Multi-tasking. That afternoon he video-called her and they talked almost an hour.

That night he went to bed wondering why Cleveland had called the meeting for Monday. Had he found anything useful? If so, why wait two days to take action on it? Chuck had little confidence in Cleveland's dedication to the pursuit of justice.

———

Detective Cleveland sat at one end of the walnut table in Conference Room B on the fourth floor of PCPD's downtown headquarters. Chuck noticed that Cleveland had positioned Melissa Chan to his right and Hank Ramirez to his left, making his seat the "head" of the table. Probably wanted to demonstrate that, by God, he was in charge. Stationing the other two cops on either side of him made his position clear: Carlos McCrary and Raymond "Snoop" Snopolski may be former detectives, but they were civilians. Helpful civilians, but still civilians.

Chuck didn't care. He just wanted to solve the murder.

Chuck picked the chair opposite Cleveland. He figured Cleveland would have preferred him to sit along the side of the table instead of at the other end—least Chuck's being there suggest that the head of the table was Chuck's seat instead of Cleveland's.

Chuck had sent the two emailed reports from Flamer to Cleveland, Chan, and Hank before the meeting. Cleveland then invited Snoop.

Raymond "Snoop" Snopolski was the last to arrive. He scanned the attendees and lifted his hand in a vague wave. He wore a navy-blue blazer over khaki slacks and white running shoes. The blazer didn't quite conceal the small-caliber handgun in his shoulder holster.

He poured a cup of coffee from the side table and slouched beside Hank. "You called this meeting, Buster. How can I help?"

Cleveland shoved a sheaf of papers over to him. "These are the emails I received yesterday. Sorry I couldn't send them to you before you left home, but I printed them out."

Snoop studied the emails.

Cleveland tapped a finger on the table until Snoop finished.

Snoop set the papers on the table.

Cleveland seemed to be waiting for Snoop to volunteer a constructive suggestion without being asked, but Snoop just sat there. Finally, Cleveland said, "What do you think, Snoop?"

Snoop had carried a Port City police detective's shield for thirty years before he retired and became a private investigator. His fellow cops had nicknamed him "Snoop." He could spend two minutes at a crime scene, remember every clue, and testify a year later at the trial without referring to his notes.

Snoop pushed the emails toward Cleveland.

"I can't add anything you don't already know. A commercial attaché has diplomatic immunity. Commercial attachés are often covers for spy operations. Everyone does that, including the USA and our allies, not just the Russians."

Cleveland scribbled a note. Chuck suspected he didn't know what a *commercial attaché* was.

"You haven't identified the four bully-boys in the Suburban," Snoop continued, "but if you do, they'll probably have immunity. That's the way the Russians work; even the janitors in their embassy building have diplomatic status. That way no one can be subpoenaed or questioned. Or arrested."

Cleveland looked surprised. Apparently, he hadn't known that either, but he had worked only domestic cases since making detective ten years before.

Snoop continued. "As a U.S. citizen, George Alexander doesn't have diplomatic status, unless he's a Russian consul, and we haven't seen any indication of that. Question him and you won't get anything useful. He descends from a long line of close-mouthed Russian criminals dating back to Iron Curtain days. He has no clients, so he's making his money illegally. If you figure out how he does it and uncover proof, you'll have something to hold over his head."

Snoop spread his hands. "I can't wave a magic wand. You gotta do this the old-fashioned way—shoe leather and peeping in keyholes until you catch a break."

"Where is Billow?" Chuck asked. "Is he operating an offset press in the print shop?"

Snoop swiveled his chair in Chuck's direction. "Bud, we aren't sure that he works there. Aisha does, but we don't know that Billow does. Assuming he does, why doesn't he go home at night?"

"Perhaps whatever they hired him to do is complicated...a special job in its final stages. Whatever it is, Billow wouldn't tell his parents what it was, so I figure it's illegal."

Snoop nodded. "And we all know the kind of illegal work that an offset printer does."

"Unless he's printing fake NFL playoff tickets, it's gotta be counterfeiting. It's possible he's staying out of sight until he finishes the job and the funny money is shipped off site. They may have tightened security once Phil Franks was murdered. The essential workers might hunker down until they finish. We've been shadowing Aisha, Buster. Did you or Melissa look for Billow's car in the employee parking lot?"

"No," said Cleveland. "We couldn't see it from the front. A privacy fence surrounds the lot."

"Can't you send a drone?" Snoop asked.

"Not without a warrant. We don't have probable cause."

"The drone's a good idea, Snoop," Chuck said. "I'll use my drone to video the employee lot this afternoon."

"Since when do you have a drone, bud?"

"I bought one for Christmas. I didn't want any of my family to buy me that expensive of a gift, so I did it myself. I use it in the business."

"*Humph*. You ask me, bud, you want a tax deduction for your new toy."

Chuck smiled at his mentor. "That's between me and the IRS. Nevertheless, the drone might help if it confirms Billow is in the printer building."

Cleveland waved the comment away. "Suppose you ID Billow's car in the lot. It might have been there for days. Why hide inside? Could he be a prisoner?"

"Love is often blind, but this engagement with Aisha—his parents called it a whirlwind romance. Billow might be in love with this girl—God knows her picture is pretty enough. But maybe she sprung a honey-trap to get him here and inside that printing company."

"You suspect he's counterfeiting Kazakh tenges?" Cleveland asked. He looked genuinely surprised.

Chuck briefed everybody about his visit from the Secret Service. Cleveland knew about the two tenge bills Chuck and Ruby uncovered. But counterfeiting? Until this meeting, Chuck didn't think that had occurred to him.

"What other explanation could there be?" Snoop said. "You said Billow dropped off the grid a few days ago. Assume he required a few days after he arrived to line up the right paper and inks and make the plates. Once he begins printing, he might not risk being recognized. Hiding makes sense. He holes up in the printing plant, sleeps on a cot, and eats takeout until this is over."

Cleveland cleared his throat. "Why would Billow print fake Kazakh tenges?"

Melissa Chan waved a hand. "I have an idea, Buster."

Cleveland gave her a come-on gesture. "Enlighten us, Lissa."

"I researched Aisha Aubakirovna online. I located some social media accounts. She's a political activist seeking human rights in Kazakhstan. Maybe she feels guilty about the harm her father has done in her former country. I read her blog posts, both in English and in Kazakh. She's quite literate and dedicated."

"You speak Kazakh?" Chuck asked.

"I used an online app to translate. She's a revolutionary. I believe she wants a revolution in Kazakhstan."

"If that revolution is somehow connected to printing counterfeit tenges," Chuck said, "then this murder case is a lot more complicated than we thought."

"If the drone shows Billow's car in the lot," Chuck said, "I'll visit the printer as a potential customer. I'll ask for a tour like I did with Bald Eagle Printing in Chicago. I could bump into Billow inside."

Hank shook his head. "Bad idea, Chuck. If he meets you unexpectedly, he'll bear-hug you and apologize for not calling. No, it should be somebody Billow doesn't know. We can't risk that he'll tip the bad guys we're suspicious."

"Bad guys?" Cleveland said. "Now that you mention it, if Billow helps an unknown party print counterfeit currency, doesn't that make him a bad guy?"

Hank waffled his hand. "Depends on why he's doing it and how he intends to use the funny money."

"If the counterfeit currency is to finance freedom fighters in Kazakhstan," Chuck said, "they might be allies of the USA. They'd be the good guys."

"Unless they're Islamist radicals and they hoodwinked Billow," Snoop said. "Or they might be crooks. Aisha's blog posts might be cover for a scam. Sometimes the simplest explanation is correct. Could be easier to pass counterfeit money in Kazakhstan."

"It's a moot point," Chuck said. "First, we don't know Billow is doing it. Second, if he is printing funny money, we don't know why. Third, we don't know who the ringleaders are. It couldn't be Billow, but it might be Aisha or her brother or the Kusainov family that owns the print shop. By the way, have we confirmed the Kusainovs are from Kazakhstan? With that name, they might be Russians, or Ukrainians, or Belarusians. Buster, you or Lissa better check that out."

Chan lifted a hand. "I checked them out. They're from Kazakhstan."

"And let's not forget the main reason we're here," Chuck said. "We don't know who killed Phillip Franks, or if his murder is connected to the printing company. We don't have a motive."

"And why are the Russians hunting Aisha?" Hank asked. "Why didn't they figure out how to pick up her trail across the bridge the way Chuck did?"

"Perhaps the first time we tailed her was the first time the Russians did too," Chuck said. "I confirmed her location this morning. She's back at the printer."

"How do you know?" Cleveland asked.

Chuck regarded him without expression.

Chan touched Cleveland's forearm. "Buster, you and I don't need to know how."

Cleveland stared at her. "Oh."

"Moving along," Chuck said, "the Russians may post a second chase car across the drawbridge today the way I did yesterday. Buster, I suggest you post a squad car on the east side of the bridge this afternoon. They can stop the new Russian car on a pretext. Take a peek at the driver's license, or ask for the car's insurance card."

"How do you know they'll be there?"

"It's what I would do. Hell, it's what I did do yesterday. You lose nothing for trying. I'll be across the bridge. If your squad car can't manufacture a reason to stop them, I'll trail them home."

"We know they came from San Marco Island."

"Buster, the *Suburban* came from San Marco Island. We know nothing about a possible second vehicle. Let's not make unwarranted assumptions. There may be people involved in this who we haven't encountered yet."

"What about Aisha?" Cleveland asked.

"I'll assign Gunner to shadow Aisha from the printers," Chuck said. "Snoop, if you're not working another case, could you pick her up on the east side of the bridge?"

"No problem."

Chuck handed Cleveland the business card Special Agent Valery Villa had given him. "I suggest you call Villa. Perhaps she'll cooperate better since they came up blank at my office."

"What do I tell her?"

"Tell her everything," he said. "Can't hurt."

———

On their way to Southeast Printing and Binding, Snoop and Chuck passed Shiva Indian Cuisine. Shiva was in a neighborhood Chuck seldom visited, so he drove into their parking lot. "It's lunch time, Snoop. How about Indian food?"

"I ate Indian food once and my stomach rebelled. Let's eat Cuban, or Mexican, or barbecue, or a hamburger."

"You can order Indian food mild, without the hot spices. Trust me, you'll love it."

Snoop chuckled, "There's an old joke: 'Trust me. I'm from the government, and I'm here to help.'"

"Order a chicken dish. They can make those mild as a baby's smile."

Snoop unfastened his seat belt. "I hope I don't regret this."

———

After lunch, Snoop drove the white Caravan. He followed NW 162nd Street past the printer. From the passenger seat, Chuck snapped pictures of the license plates on the cars parked in front. Rule Six: *You never know what you'll need to know.*

"Hang a right at the corner, Snoop. Let's pick a space to park while we fly the drone."

"Aren't you supposed to keep the drone in line of sight?"

"Yes, but once the drone is a hundred feet up, I can spot it a long way —even from the other side of the block. Don't worry about it. Circle the block."

Snoop made the turn, eased off on the accelerator, and pulled to the curb. "That Indian lunch is back to haunt me. I have to find a restroom. Fast."

"Go, go, go."

He hung a tight U-turn, sped back to 162nd Street, and located a convenience store with gas pumps in the next block. Slamming the van into park at the pumps, he bailed out the driver's door. "You could fill the tank while I'm gone," he said as he scurried into the convenience store.

The van needed five gallons of gas. Snoop hadn't returned. Chuck cleaned the windshield...the rear window...the side windows. Still no Snoop. Chuck hoped he was okay. He parked the van at the air pumps and checked the tires.

Fifteen minutes later, Snoop returned. "Sorry, but Indian food doesn't like me."

"I'm the one who's sorry, Snoop. I didn't listen to you."

Snoop circled the block around the printer.

"The engineering and architecture firm on the east side is the place. They use drones for aerial inspections of their projects. I bet they test and calibrate them in their parking lot. Park backwards next to that wooden fence. Leave room to open the rear hatch."

The parking lot was large and half-filled with vehicles. Mostly crew-cabs and work vans. Chuck doubted anyone would notice them.

Before exiting the van, he gave Snoop a burner phone and explained his new email address. "Before I go anyplace the Feds or Buster Cleveland don't know about, I'll remove the battery from both my regular cellphones." Chuck always carried a business cellphone and a personal cellphone. Now he was juggling three. It was hard to keep them straight.

Snoop reviewed the contact list in the new phone. "You have Gunner on the list. What about Hank?"

"I don't want to tell Hank about the new phones and email. I won't put him in a compromising position unless there's no alternative. Now let's go fly a drone."

Chuck popped the back hatch of the van and unpacked the drone in the cargo space.

"What's that?" Snoop asked.

"Remote control." Chuck removed it from the bag. "It attaches to my cellphone with this USB cable. Once I link it, whatever the drone's camera views, it displays on my cellphone."

"That's pretty cool. What if somebody walks by?"

"Let them. We're not bothering anybody. The worst that happens is they ask us to leave. You worry too much."

After pausing for a passerby to enter the architect's building, Chuck set the drone in an empty parking space. "Here we go, Snoop. Upsy-daisy."

The drone buzzed like a hundred angry bees and rose to hover four feet above the pavement. Chuck eased the remote's joy stick and the drone rose to twenty feet altitude. The buzz was softer, but still noticeable. Aiming the camera toward the employee lot, he scanned the area.

A woman wearing a blue Southeast Printing and Binding tee-shirt and khaki shorts stood in the back door, staring at the camera. She gesticulated at the drone and twisted her head to shout to someone inside. Chuck heard her over the combined buzzes of the drone and the traffic.

He tilted the toggle. A split-second later, the drone rocketed skyward at max acceleration, its buzz screaming then fading. It soared to its max altitude of 400 feet.

"What's happening?" Snoopy said, a touch of anxiety in his voice.

"Keep your voice down. The only thing between us and the employee parking lot is this fence. A woman standing in the back door eyed the drone. Couldn't you hear her shouting? I'm flying it out of sight so she won't know where it originated." Chuck piloted the drone three hundred yards west and dropped it to thirty feet, hovering over the flat roof of a large building where no one should notice it.

"We'll stay a bit," he said. "She'll go back inside."

"How long will that thing fly?"

"About fifteen minutes on a charge, depending on how hard I push the drone. That moon shot to 400 feet didn't do the battery any good."

"If the drone is out of sight, how will you know when she goes inside? We need a way to look over the fence. You can stand on the van's roof."

"Too obvious. We don't want them to suspect they're under surveillance. We watch and hope. I'll monitor the battery indicator. Once it indicates five minutes remaining, I'll bring it back and try again."

Snoop eyeballed Chuck's cellphone. "Why not land the drone on the roof? Wouldn't that save the battery?"

"Good idea. I'm new at this drone surveillance."

Chuck parked the drone on the warehouse roof. The battery drain almost stopped; all the battery did was maintain a link to the controller.

Snoop shifted his weight from one foot to the other. "I hate to say it, but I need to use that restroom again. Sorry."

"Take the van, Snoop. I'll wait here."

Chuck looked for a crack in the fence. A warped board or a loose knothole. Nothing. The fence was maybe a year old, but it was better built than the typical backyard fence. *Hmm.* The printers valued their privacy more than any ordinary business ought to.

The architects/engineers building was one story, so a second-story window wasn't available. Had to use the drone.

Snoop returned soon. "Sorry. I wish I knew why Indian food affects me that way."

"No problem. I'll fly the drone and take another run at the parking lot."

Chuck flew the drone close enough to observe the parking lot from a distance. From 85 feet he recognized Snoop and himself standing beside the fence. The printer's back porch was empty. He brought the drone closer and flew into position to video the license plates.

The back door flew open. A man stepped onto the back porch and aimed a shotgun. He pointed it straight at the camera.

Chuck watched his cellphone screen in horror.

He stabbed the lever on the controller.

Pow!

Before the drone responded to Chuck's command, the shot nicked the drone. The view on his phone spun around and Chuck lost control.

A second blast. *Pow!*

The camera view tilted crazily and the picture went black.

There was a third shot. *Pow!*

Chuck figured the drone was blown into a zillion pieces of plastic and electronics.

Snoop stared at him. "What sort of business keeps a shotgun on hand?"

"The sort that's hiding something very valuable."

"Or very dangerous."

———

Two blocks east of the drawbridge, a Port City police cruiser lurked behind a croton hedge in a used car lot with a good view of the traffic.

Chuck parked under a palm tree in the McDonald's lot again and buzzed the windows down. The weather was what the Tourism and

Visitors' Office loves to brag about. Mid-seventies, easy sea breeze. South Florida in the winter. On the other hand, if Chuck's relationship with Ruby required it, living in Austin would be great. Chuck could learn to cheer the Longhorns, unless they were playing the Gators, and he loved the Texas Hill Country.

Snoop parked his old but shiny-clean Toyota across the street in a convenience store lot. He had swallowed a big dose of anti-diarrhea medication and swore he would be okay. Chuck waved; Snoop waved back. No need to talk or text. This wasn't their first rodeo.

Chuck tuned to a local news station. Politicians denouncing each other, murders, fires, terrorism. Same old, same old. He switched to a satellite radio classic country station. Better for killing time, and better for the soul. *Go, Kelly Clarkson, go*, he thought. *Lift my spirits.*

The clock on Chuck's dashboard said it was 5:30. Sunset in twenty minutes. If Aisha left work now, she'd be there before the 6:15 bridge opening. *If.* Was Billow working and sleeping at the printer? It would help if Chuck knew where the hell Billow was.

He started the GPS tracker app on his tablet. Yep, Aisha's car was on the move.

Across the street, a black GMC Yukon with Virginia license plates rolled into the parking lot on the opposite side of the convenience store where Snoop was parked. There were three empty spaces closer to the store and several available at the entrance. Why did they park that far away? Why did the car park facing the street? And why did no one get out of the car?

Chuck slipped his camera with the telephoto lens from the console and stared through the viewfinder at the Yukon.

Two Asian men sat in the front seat, wearing dark suits, white dress shirts, and unremarkable ties. The passenger consulted his watch, stared in the direction of the drawbridge, and spoke to the driver. The driver responded with a single syllable.

The light was waning, but Chuck snapped a picture, paused until the passenger twisted toward the driver and snapped another. He photographed the license plate and sent the images to Buster Cleveland and Hank Ramirez with a request for Cleveland to run the plate and Hank to run the faces. He sent it to Snoop's regular phone also. Good to keep him current.

Virginia plates? Why were so many people from Virginia interested in Aisha Aubakirovna? And where were the Russians?

Chuck called Snoop on his burner.

"There's a black Yukon with Virginia plates parked on the other side of the store. Two Asian guys might be waiting for Aisha."

"Thanks for the heads-up. Any change in plans?"

"You shadow Aisha, and I'll shadow the Asians."

"I haven't spotted the Russians. Do you suppose the Asians are working with them?"

"Unlikely. Perhaps the Russians are lurking farther down North Bay Causeway."

Twenty minutes later, Cleveland texted.

Yukon registered to Yu Chang, the Communist Chinese military attaché in Washington. Yukon listed at his home address in Arlington, Virginia.

Chuck noted that Snoop's old cellphone also received the text. He didn't mind if the Feds read it because it came from Buster Cleveland. It was good to show case-related traffic on his old phone. Otherwise, Special Agent Villa might get suspicious.

Chuck sent Snoop's burner phone a text from his burner:

The previous text came from Buster. Things the Feds already have access to are okay to share. Let's not send any messages from our old phones to the new ones or vice versa. I don't want any links between unsecure phones and the burner phones.

Snoop replied with an *okay* emoji.

Hank texted Chuck.

We drew a blank on the two guys in the Yukon. They're not in any photo database.

It was cloudy over the Everglades and the light was fading fast. By the time the bridge dinged the warning bells for the 6:15 opening, it was dark enough that most vehicles switched on their headlights.

As expected, Aisha's Toyota was the last car across the bridge before the barricades dropped.

The passenger in the Yukon tapped the driver's shoulder. The car started and the Yukon's lights switched on.

Snoop let three cars get behind Aisha before he left the convenience store. The third car was the Chinese Yukon. They made an interesting parade: Aisha, the Chinese, Snoop, and Chuck. All they needed was the Russians and Port City Police. The more the merrier? No, the more to make Chuck worried. The longer the caravan, the more to go wrong.

There was no way Snoop would lose Aisha's car; he used the same GPS tracker app as Chuck. He need only observe where she walked after parking at her destination. The previous week she had parked a half block into the Village of Seeti Shores.

Chuck let two more cars in after Snoop, then joined the parade. This was beginning to be a sit-com farce. Where were the Russians? Can't stage a farce without overdoing everything.

Three blocks later, the Russians joined the parade. All they lacked was a laugh-track.

The Russians inserted their black Suburban two cars behind Aisha. A hundred yards later, the police cruiser moved behind Chuck, its red and blue lights flashing.

Check merged over one lane. The cruiser advanced. One by one the cars ahead of it pulled over until it was behind the Russians' Suburban. The Suburban edged over. The cruiser did too. The Suburban kept moving. It expected the cruiser to pass.

The cruiser beeped its siren and the Russians pivoted into a furniture store parking lot. The cruiser parked behind them, lights flashing.

Chuck almost waved at the Russians, but resisted the temptation.

The Chinese Yukon settled in to follow.

Aisha chose the route she had before. Right on Clendening, south on A1A.

Snoop passed Chuck and drove a block ahead of Aisha. He curved right on 91st Street, and Aisha and the Chinese trailed. Hanging a left on Madison, he parked at the curb where Aisha had parked the previous week.

The traffic thinned, and the Chinese tipped their hand by stalking too close. Their pursuit of Aisha became obvious. Any second, Chuck expected her to spot the tail, paranoid as she was about being tailed.

Chuck wondered what she would do when she learned she was being followed.

After Aisha's Toyota passed Snoop, the brake lights flashed and she slowed as if she intended to park. Then she accelerated and continued south on Madison.

Damn. She'd made the Chinese. No telling what she would do.

The parade behind Aisha shrank to two cars: the Chinese and Chuck. He dropped back fifty yards and called Snoop on the burner.

"What the hell? She didn't park."

"She spotted the Chinese tail. Get back in your car and monitor her on the tracker app."

"The Chinks are subtle as a fireworks show."

"Chink is a racist term, Snoop. Not supposed to say that anymore. All the best people say so."

"My father called them Chinks during the Korean War. That and 'slants.'"

"They were the enemy, like the Japanese in World War II. We don't call the Germans Krauts anymore either. Nowadays Chink is considered offensive to Asians. Blame the twenty-first century. Or maybe the media."

"People call me a Polack, so I call them Chinks."

"You can't say Polack anymore, either."

"You ask me, bud, you spics are too sensitive about this stuff."

"A conversation for another time." Chuck stifled a laugh and disconnected before Snoop could reply.

Aisha went east on 90th Street, then north on A1A. She wanted to shake the Chinese before she went home.

Chuck dropped back a hundred yards.

She looped around several blocks.

Chuck figured she was heading for the Seaside police station. He called Snoop again. "She's heading to the Seaside police station on 94th. That should scare off the Chinese, then she might return to the block where you are."

"Okay. I'll stay. Keep me posted."

"I'm a block behind the Chinese."

Aisha rolled up the driveway to the police visitor lot. The Chinese didn't hesitate; they continued past Aisha and curved south on Madison again.

"The Chinese are driving back down Madison. They'll pass you in a couple of minutes. I'll be a block behind them."

"I'll stay where I am until Aisha comes back. You think she'll go inside to tell the cops she was stalked?"

"No. She's keeping a low profile. If I were her, I'd sit in my car until the Yukon abandoned the chase, then I'd continue home. I'll hang up. Call me once you learn something."

Chuck removed the batteries from his old phones. He didn't want the Feds to learn where he followed the Chinese.

The Chinese rolled along A1A and onto Beachline Causeway. Fourteen miles later, they turned into a modest residential neighborhood south of Port City International Airport.

Snoop called. "Aisha returned and parked in a different apartment lot across the street. She's definitely living in this neighborhood. I'll track her on foot. I'll call you later."

"Okay. Remove the battery from your old phone. Let's keep Aisha's location between us."

The black Yukon reached SW 4th Street. It was seven-thirty and the neighborhood's two-lane streets were empty of traffic. Chuck stayed on 52nd Avenue another block so the Chinese wouldn't make him. He made three right turns to wind up on SW 4th Street east of where they had been.

The Chinese were somewhere on SW 4th Street between 52nd and 53rd Avenues.

Studying the houses on the south side, Chuck idled the length of the block to the roundabout at the next intersection. No Yukon. He circled the roundabout and retraced the block examining what was visible of the houses on the north. No black Yukon.

Chuck's phone rang and Snoop's picture flashed on the screen.

"I need good news, Snoop."

"I don't know how good it is, but it's news. Aisha was not alone in the car. A man was in the passenger seat. When they got out, Aisha took his arm."

"Could you tell whether it was Billow?"

"Billow is six-foot-five? This man was half a head shorter than Billow."

"Is Aisha two-timing Andrew?"

"I couldn't tell. I tailed them to a second-floor apartment. I'll text you the address and the pictures I snapped. The pictures aren't great because it's night, but you'll get a good idea of the setup. You can enhance one and get a picture of the man's face. How did you make out with the Chinese?"

"I lost them somewhere on the 5200 block of Southwest 4th Street. There are twelve houses on the north side of that block and nine on the south. Four houses have eight-foot privacy fences, and two have dense hedgerows higher than that. If I were a sneaky Chinese spy, I would pick a house where people couldn't look into the property."

"How many houses? Twenty-one?"

"Yeah. I'll send Gunner to stake out the neighborhood tomorrow morning. He'll spot them. If not, I'll research the ownership of twenty-one houses, or ask the Port City cops to do it."

"About the Port City cops, Chuck..."

"What?"

"If you give Aisha's address to Buster Cleveland, he and Melissa will interview her."

"So? What are you thinking, Snoop?"

"I don't know Melissa Chan, but I do know Buster Cleveland. He's a plodder, not a runner, and he has the imagination of a snail. Until our conference in police HQ this morning, I don't believe he'd clicked that this case is about counterfeiting. Buster might screw up this investigation big-time."

"How so?"

"Once Buster interviews Aisha, she'll realize we're onto them. Buster's next step will be to get a search warrant on the printing plant, which will require a few hours, even with a friendly judge. Suppose Aisha tips off the Kusainov brothers. The whole gang could relocate except for the Heidelberg press, and buying one of them is a matter of money and time—the counterfeiters could disappear. If your buddy Billow is a captive patsy instead of a conspirator, they could make him disappear too."

"The way Phillip Franks disappeared?"

"Yeah. We don't want more of your friends washing up headless on a beach. The counterfeiters can hire or kidnap another press operator. We still haven't found who killed Franks. Might be the Russians. Might be the Chinese…" Snoop let the sentence hang in the air.

"Or it might be the Kazakhs," Chuck finished.

———

Chuck found an electronics store still open and went drone shopping. This time he bought two. Rule Eighteen: *Always have a backup.*

Switching his old phone on, Chuck received a text from Hank.

The man with Aisha is Duman Aubakirovich, her brother. Where did you take those pictures?

Another turning-point in the case. Should Chuck level with Hank? For the time being, Chuck didn't respond to his text.

Chuck plugged both drone batteries into car chargers and headed back to Southeast Printing and Binding. Between the electronics store and the print shop, Buster Cleveland called.

"Hey, Buster. Did your guys learn anything from stopping the Russians?"

"Yeah. We learned the driver had a Virginia driver's license. We stopped him for failure to signal a turn. He accused us of running a scam to exploit northern tourists by writing traffic citations. How about you? Did you determine where Aisha is living?"

Decision time. Tell Buster Cleveland or keep it to himself? And what should Chuck tell Cleveland about the Chinese? Was Chuck willing to assume responsibility for the entire case and cut Cleveland adrift? Could Chuck do better without the detective than with him? Buster Cleveland, Melissa Chan, and Hank Ramirez, to the extent he was involved, were LEOs–Law Enforcement Officers. They were sworn to obey the legal folderol: due process, probable cause, *Miranda* warnings, and warrants. They must respect the diplomatic immunity of the Russians and of the Chinese if it came to that.

Chuck didn't begrudge LEOs their oath to uphold the law. He wouldn't want to live in a country where you couldn't trust the cops to uphold the law impartially. But…here he was!

Sometimes jumping through legal hoops made it difficult or impossible for LEOs to catch the bad guys. Chuck remembered his case where a foreign diplomat ran a sex trafficking ring. One powerless cop referred a missing girl's father to Chuck. The cop knew Chuck would ignore the kidnapper's diplomatic immunity and treat him like the scumbag he was.

Once Chuck took a case, he never worried about legal and illegal. He fixated on right and wrong, and weighed the consequences if he got caught breaking the law.

Chuck's internal debate was over as quickly as it had begun. If he cut Cleveland out of the loop, he had to cut Hank Ramirez out also. It would kill Hank's career if his superiors learned that Chuck told him things that he didn't pass along to Cleveland. Chuck wouldn't burden his friend with knowledge he couldn't share.

"Well?" Cleveland said. "Did you find out? Where can we find Aisha?"

Chuck hated to lie to a cop but…

"Sorry, Buster. Aisha caught on that the Chinese were hunting her and fled into the Town of Seaside police parking lot until they drove away. That scared the Chinese into abandoning the chase. I trusted Snoop to tail Aisha, and I tracked the Chinese. Aisha must have been too scared to go home. Snoop said she drove back to the mainland and lost him with the drawbridge trick again. I shadowed the Chinese toward the airport but lost them." He made a mental note to fill Snoop in on his lie so he could back up Chuck's false narrative with Cleveland.

"Chuck, couldn't you monitor her on the tracking device? Don't confirm or deny whether you placed an illegal device on her car. Simply tell me where her car spent last night."

"There is no tracking device, Buster. I have no idea where she went last night."

"Iacta alea est," Julius Caesar said when he defied the Roman Senate's rule that a general could never bring his army into Rome. It means "The die is cast." Caesar led his army across the Rubicon river and sparked the long Roman civil war. Chuck had passed the point of no return. The Port

City Police Department didn't realize it, but this was no longer their case; it was Chuck's.

He hoped his shoulders were broad enough to carry it.

———

Chuck arrived at the printing plant after 10:00 p.m. He should have better luck investigating the employee lot at night. Fewer cars.

The printer was sandwiched between an air conditioning contractor and an engineering and architecture firm. Both companies' parking lots were lit. The tall lights bled into the printing company's back lot. It wasn't daylight but it was light enough for a drone camera to operate.

Chuck parked at a warehouse a block behind the printer. Okay, he intended to fly the drone out of sight. That was against a Port City ordinance, a Florida state law, an FAA regulation, and maybe the Ten Commandments. Big deal. Chuck figured he had exigent circumstances.

The battery charges showed fifty percent on one and sixty percent on the other. He debated charging them another hour, but his stomach won the battle.

Scanning the industrial street, all he observed were dark windows and empty parking lots. That figured; it was past business hours. Chuck assembled a drone, tested it, flew it to 300 feet, and scanned toward the printer. The employee lot was visible. A half dozen cars were scattered across the large lot. Awfully busy for this late at the night.

Chuck tested the zoom feature on the new camera and flew the drone closer to the target. The camera read the license plates from fifty yards away. It was a geometry problem of flying the drone high enough to see over the cars parked in front of the target plates.

The drone's battery gave an alarm. It was at ten percent power—three minutes flying time. Chuck located two cars with Illinois plates and videoed them first, then videoed the rest.

The battery indicator flashed red. Not enough power to return to base. Fortunately, the videos were recorded on his cellphone. He rotated the drone, searching for a safe area to land. He flew over the air conditioning contractor. The battery died and the drone dropped hard on the roof.

It should be safe there until Chuck figured a way to retrieve it. If not: Win some, lose some.

No matter how long it took, or what he had to do, Chuck would catch the people who butchered Phillip Franks. His killers would never meet a judge and jury. They had declared a war as serious and deadly as the one the Triple Seven fought in Iraq and Afghanistan. The war the killers had started would rebound on them like an echo.

After scanning the surroundings again, Chuck returned to the minivan, flipped on the interior lights, and played the drone video. Freezing the image of the first Illinois license plate, he zoomed in. It was one of Aisha's brother's autos.

He played the video in slow motion until the next Illinois plate showed. Pausing, he zoomed in. It was Billow's U.S. Army Veteran's license plate on his 2017 blue Chevy Blazer. Chuck had finally confirmed that Billow worked for the Southeast Printing and Binding Company.

The dashboard clock said *11:04.* Too late to call Gunner. Chuck texted him.

I have another assignment. If you're available, call me first thing in the morning. Any time after 6:00 a.m.

———

Chuck staked out Aisha's apartment before dawn. Gunner called at six sharp, or as he would say, *Oh-six-hundred.*

"What's the mission, boss?"

Chuck briefed him on the two Chinese men who stalked Aisha the previous night. "They live somewhere in the 5200 block of Southwest 4th Street. Stake out that block and watch for their black GMC Yukon with Virginia license plates. Last night they drove in from the south on 52nd Avenue and turned left. They ought to come out the same way. Call when you ID them and we'll figure out what they're doing. If they both leave their SUV at any time, plant a GPS tracker on it."

"Hooah, boss. What are you doing now?"

"I'm at Aisha's apartment. Snoop tailed her last night and discovered where she lives. She was with her brother, Duman. He might be a handler or he might be something else. I want to catch her alone and ask questions without Duman around. The Russians, the Chinese, and the Kusainovs are interested in this, whatever 'this' is. It's as tangled as a bucket of worms. The U.S. Secret Service is involved now. I hope Aisha will tell us what they are doing and who killed Phil Franks."

"If I can capture a Chinese for questioning, should I?"

"Gunner, their car is registered to the People's Republic of China Military Attaché in Washington, D.C. These guys are People's Liberation Army soldiers—armed and dangerous."

"That's okay, Chuck. So am I."

That Gunner, Chuck thought. *What a character.*

"If you can catch one *quietly* without causing a fight that drags in the cops or the Feds, go for it."

He disconnected and Chuck opened his takeout breakfast from McDonald's: three sausage-egg-McMuffins with orange juice and coffee. That might hold him until lunch.

He ate the first sandwich and settled back to wait. Aisha's apartment building was what Chuck's Grandma McCrary in Texas called "mid-century modern." Boxy lines and pastel colors, three stories, flat roofs that overhung the external corridors, exposed concrete stairways, no elevators. There were a million identical buildings along the Atlantic coast from Miami Beach to Jacksonville.

Aisha and her brother descended the stairs at 8:10 a.m. Chuck snapped pictures of the brother in the daylight.

They walked to Aisha's Toyota. Duman took the driver seat. Aisha sat in the passenger seat.

Chuck let them drive practically out of sight before he followed. The GPS tracker ensured he wouldn't lose them. He needed only stay close enough to observe if either one left the car. Duman drove. Perhaps he would drop Aisha somewhere Chuck could talk to her. A mall or a grocery store would work.

No such luck. Duman drove straight to the print shop and dropped Aisha at the front door at nine o'clock. He didn't park. Instead he drove away without a backward glance.

Okay. Chuck couldn't barge in and interview Aisha, so he applied Rule Two: *When in doubt, follow somebody.*

Duman Aubakirovich was a good lead also.

Ten minutes later, Duman pulled into an industrial neighborhood wedged between two runways of the Oklahatchee Airport, a private general aviation facility not far from Southeast Printing and Binding. A utilitarian sign pointed arrows toward the local police substation, U.S. Customs & Border Protection, U.S. Coast Guard, the FAA Control Tower, and a host of other operations servicing the airport.

The Toyota paused at the sign, then turned left.

There was no other traffic on the street. If Chuck trailed close enough to keep Duman in sight, the Kazakh was sure to notice him. Chuck pulled into a parking lot at the first business he encountered, a flight training school, and snatched a pair of binoculars from the glove box.

The street ended at a hangar that said *Port City Reliable Jet Maintenance.* The airport's security fence commenced at the corner of the building. Duman paused at a gate and held something against a card reader near the driver's window. The gate opened. He rolled through, waited while the gate closed, then drove out of sight around another hangar three hundred yards further into the airport.

Chuck followed his path to the gate, stopping thirty yards away. Signs on the chain link fence said *Security Gate 40, No Access Without I.D.* A sign on the gate instructed visitors to proceed beyond the yellow line and wait until the gate closed. Another sign told the public that airport ID was required to enter.

Chuck parked in the Port City Reliable Jet Maintenance lot and monitored the Toyota's tracking transmitter on his tablet. Duman stopped at the third hangar. Chuck booted his laptop and scanned for a public Wi-Fi. He found several from nearby businesses. Selecting the strongest signal, he launched Street View for an aerial view of the airport. Zooming in on the third hangar, he read the label: Atlantic County Air Charter Service. The Toyota was still parked. Chuck researched Atlantic County Air Charter Service's website on the internet.

They specialized in air freight all over the world. *Hmm.* Did Duman pick up something or bring something to ship? If he brought something, he locked it in the trunk all night because he did not pick up anything at the print shop.

Twenty minutes later, the Toyota retraced its path. Duman exited Security Gate 40. Chuck watched him in his rearview mirror as he drove the street behind Chuck's Caravan. As usual, Chuck let him drive two blocks ahead before backing out of the parking spot.

Duman returned to Southeast Printing and Binding. Stopping at the entrance to the employee's parking lot, he waited while the chunky, gray-haired man opened the gate. Duman entered the lot and Chunky locked the gate again.

Chuck decided to poke around at Atlantic County Air Charter Service.

TWELVE

Gunner Knutson cruised the 5200 block of Southwest 4th Street from SW 52nd Avenue to SW 53rd Avenue. He looped the roundabout at the corner, rolled back to 52nd, shielding his eyes against the rising sun that blinded him. He hadn't expected to find the black Yukon in a driveway because it had not been visible the previous night. Nevertheless, someone might have moved it in the night to let another car out.

Gunner parked on the north side facing west. Anyone driving east from the target block would stare into that rising sun, effectively obscuring him. If his quarry hadn't appeared by the time the sun rose higher—say another hour—he would drive to the west end of the block. The landscaping in the roundabout would hide his Jeep there.

His reconnoiter complete, he laid the binoculars on the center console. He tilted his seat back to a comfortable posture. This also lowered his visibility to anyone who passed.

By 8:30, a dozen or more vehicles, mostly commuters, had passed down the street toward his position. One was a blue Suburban that passed him and continued east on 4th Street.

Soon the sun was high enough to no longer blind the eastbound commuters. Gunner cranked the Jeep and drove to the other end of the block.

Curving past the roundabout, he made a 180 and parked on the south side facing east. Yes, the sun was high enough that it didn't interfere with his vision. Plus, tall trees on the block shaded his location. His sightline passed between the trunks of the six palm trees that landscaped the roundabout.

At 10:17, a black Yukon nosed out of a circular driveway on the north side and drove east.

Gunner snatched the binoculars and read the license plate. Virginia plates with the correct numbers.

Booyah, he thought. *Target acquired.*

He started the Jeep and called Chuck's new burner phone. It rang four times and switched to voicemail. "Chuck, this is Gunner. I have the quarry in sight. It is 10:19 a.m. They were staying at 5221 SW 4th Street. Call me and we'll run a leapfrog tail. Gunner out."

Why didn't Chuck reply?

———

Chuck was in the middle of his third set of bench presses with free weights when the phone rang. *Damn. It was precisely the worst time to talk.*

Kennedy Carlson, the owner, was spotting for Chuck and reached for the barbell. "You need to answer that, pal?"

Chuck's muscles burned like glowing coals. "Four reps to finish the set."

He coaxed four additional lifts from his weary arms and eased the free weights onto the rack. Reaching to the floor for his towel, he rolled off the bench and grabbed his gym bag. "Thanks for spotting, Ken,"

"Anytime. I'll wipe the bench. You answer your phone."

Chuck tossed him the towel and reached into the bag too late. The phone stopped ringing. He checked the call log: Gunner. He didn't play the message, just touched the redial button and Gunner answered.

"The Chinese were staying at 5221 SW 4th. You want to use a leapfrog tail?"

"Yeah. I'm at the gym. I'll drive your direction and call you when I'm closer."

———

In the Caravan, Chuck cranked the air conditioning to *Max*. He hadn't had time to shower and he was sweating as if he'd just finished a half-marathon. He figured he'd be okay if he didn't get close to anyone. And if he stayed downwind.

Ten minutes into the trip, Gunner called again.

"They drove west on the Beachline, not east. Could be they'll take the 895 Loop around to the print shop."

"One way to find out. Stay with them. I'll catch you."

"Whoa, daddy," Gunner said. "Traffic stopped dead. Too many commuters, not enough freeway. You'll catch up sooner than you thought."

"Until I hit the back of the same traffic jam."

Chuck managed to drive close to the speed limit another ten minutes, then the traffic backed up like a clogged sink.

"Where are you, Gunner?"

"They exited at State Highway 824, past the airport."

"Traffic on the Beachline is a four-lane parking lot. Keep the line open."

"Roger. Wilco."

In the next seven minutes Chuck's Caravan crawled one mile.

"Boss," Gunner said, "they're turning into a car rental place."

"That makes sense. Last night, Aisha made them. She's sure to be alert for their black Yukon. They'll switch vehicles and try again."

"Boss, I drove a block north of the rental office, made a 180, and I'm stopped at the curb watching for them to come out in their new vehicle."

"The paperwork takes ten or fifteen minutes. If I can join you before they rent the new wheels, I'll park a block south of the car rental. No matter which way they come out, one of us will tag them. If I'm still jammed in traffic, you're on your own."

"Got it, boss. Changing the subject, where did the Chinese pick up Aisha last night?"

"They picked her up past the drawbridge. I made them when they parked at a convenience store across the street."

The eighteen-wheeler blocking Chuck rolled ten yards. Hoisting his foot off the brake, he idled after the truck.

"How did they know Aisha would cross that bridge?"

Sometimes, Chuck thought, *I am so blind I don't know how I manage to solve a case.* Gunner's question was so obvious Chuck should have thought of it the first time he identified the Chinese. How *did* they know to wait across the bridge? And how did they know which car was Aisha's?

"Gunner, they learned Aisha's bridge trick the way we learned it. They had another car full of soldiers stalk her another time from the print shop to the bridge."

"They need two vehicles to do that, and we only know about the black Yukon."

"They also need at least four soldiers."

"Let's hope the two of us don't bump against four of them today."

"Four bad guys against two Triple Sevens sounds about even."

"If I had a rifle, I'd say yes. With pistols, not so much. Stand by...They rented a white Ford Expedition. No plates on the front, so it's Florida. That sucker is a damn tank rolling down the driveway."

"It weighs four-and-a-half tons."

"Let me grab the binoculars...Yeah, one of the Chinese is driving. A black suit jacket and a red tie. He looks like the head hoodlum. Their original black Yukon is shadowing...They're driving this way. How close are you?"

"I see the Highway 824 exit ahead. Say, five minutes. Too far away to help."

"Too bad. Okay, once they pass me, I'll flip around and follow...Stand by...Oh, no! A blue Yukon pulled in behind me. Oh, crap, he's trying to block me. Three vehicles! Six men!"

Over the phone, Chuck heard a thunk. Then the roar of spinning tires. A crash and screeching metal. Then nothing.

The phone call had dropped.

They had Gunner, Chuck thought. *And it was all my fault.*

———

The Ford Expedition pulled crossways in front, blocking Gunner in.

Dropping his phone on the passenger seat, Gunner threw the Jeep into gear and stomped the accelerator. He hammered into the front passenger door of the Ford hard enough to crush the door but not to set off his air bags.

Dammit! Their air bags didn't blow up either.

All four tires spinning, Gunner spun the steering wheel left. The Jeep's bumper scrapped along the Ford's rear door toward the rear wheels, ramming the larger vehicle sideways.

Gunner bulldozed the rear of the Expedition out of his way. His own hood and fenders bent and crumpled from the stress on the front.

Jerking the steering wheel further left, he freed his bumper from the Ford and skidded the Jeep into a screeching half-donut 180° turn. He aimed at the front tire of the blue Yukon that had been blocking behind him. He crushed the fender into the tire, knocking it off the rim.

That'll keep those bastards out of the fight, he thought.

He spun the wheel right and powered the wrong way up Highway 824, now heading north, gaining speed with every turn of the Jeep's massive tires.

Gunner veered to the right lane of the highway and glanced in the mirror. The black Yukon pursued from a hundred yards behind him. The white Ford was closing in the lane beside it.

The Jeep's engine made a whacking noise. The temperature gauge climbed into the red. Warning lights on the dashboard blazed.

Damn. I hit the Ford too hard. Or maybe it was when I rammed the blue Yukon. Whatever, the damage is done.

Steam poured from the opened seams on either side of the hood.

Gunner kept the accelerator crammed to the firewall, but the Jeep was no longer responding. The vehicles behind closed the gap as the Jeep lost power.

Slamming on the brakes, Gunner popped the seat belt and pulled his Glock from its holster.

He would go down fighting. It had been a good life. He had fought for his country and then for his friends. He had faced many dicey situations in the Middle East and the USA and never lost a battle. The law of averages had finally caught up with him.

I wonder how many Chinese PLA soldiers I can take down before I die.

He remembered the legends of Valhalla, the Vikings' hall for heroes killed in battle. For an instant, he wished he believed in that.

Prepared to meet the enemy, he pulled the door handle and pushed on the door.

Nothing happened. Holding the handle in the open position, he rammed the door with his shoulder. It moved an inch with a metallic bang. Hitting the other vehicles must have driven his own fender into the door, preventing it from opening. He lunged against the door, wedging it open a hand's width.

The vehicles that had been chasing him jammed to a stop, blocking his vehicle.

Gunner tried to lower his window. With the ignition off and the door partially open, the power had switched off.

He was trapped in the driver's seat.

Three large Chinese wearing denim jackets, khakis, and running shoes stood in a semicircle six feet from the Jeep with pistols aimed at him through the windshield and driver's window. The Chinese wearing a black suit and red tie said, "Drop your weapon and you will live. We only want to talk."

Gunner turned the situation over in his mind. He was propped against the door. The closed window prevented him from taking good aim with his own pistol. If he raised the Glock from his lap, three men would shoot him before he got it over the steering wheel. Not good enough odds to gamble his life.

"Okay." He dropped his weapon to the floor and raised his hands.

One of the soldiers yanked on the door until it opened.

Black Suit said, "Get out."

Gunner complied.

Two of the soldiers seized his arms with grips like shackles. They hoisted him into the air as if he weighed no more than a child. Professionals, well-trained and very strong.

Black Suit opened the Jeep's passenger door and picked up Gunner's phone. He threw it to the pavement, stomped it under his shiny black Oxford, and trotted back to the white Expedition.

With practiced movements, the other three abductors lugged their captive to the black Yukon's open door. One man jumped into the back seat, grabbing a cable tie from his pocket. The other two pushed Gunner in. A second bad guy jumped in beside the Triple Seven veteran and jammed a pistol into his ribs.

"You move, you die," the gunman said in heavily accented English.

The two men jerked his arms behind him.

Gunner didn't resist.

These men are professionals, he thought, *and I'm well and truly up shit creek. But at least I'm alive to fight another day. If I can only survive this one.*

As the first man passed the cable tie around Gunner's wrists, he slipped his cellphone from his back pocket and wedged it into the gap between the seat cushions. He curved his wrists apart to keep the tie from being yanked too tight.

Finishing with the cable tie, the first man slipped a black cloth bag over Gunner's head. If they intended to kill him, they would have shot him in his car. On the other hand, if these were Phil Franks's killers and they questioned him the way they questioned Phil, he was in for an excruciating imprisonment followed by a ghastly death.

Gunner sensed the Yukon accelerating straight ahead. They were northbound on Highway 824, not back to the Beachline Expressway. They were not returning to the house on SW 4th Street.

Gunner swiveled his head from side to side, concentrating on every sound and its direction.

A voice spoke from the front passenger seat. The man spoke in Chinese to the driver, who responded from the front left. Gunner spoke no Chinese, but it sounded from the pace and tone of the words as if the passenger gave instructions to the driver.

Or they could be discussing how to torture me to death. No, I'd better hope he's giving the driver instructions.

One gangster removed Gunner's holster clipped to his belt. He found the Ka-Bar knife strapped to his calf.

"Any more weapons? If you lie, you die."

"That's all." Unfortunately, that was the truth. The one weapon he had left was his wits.

A jet roared overhead on its descent to Port City International Airport, which sprawled a mile to the east.

Did anyone witness the kidnapping? Unlikely. Highway 824 was a commercial and industrial street. Not many people. No one wants to live under the airport flight path. Businesses weren't picky.

The SUV rumbled across two sets of railroad tracks.

Industrial railroad spurs, Gunner thought. *A manufacturing or warehouse neighborhood. No one to hear me scream for help.*

The passenger spoke again. The Yukon slowed and turned. The SUV jittered across another pair of tracks. When the passenger spoke again, the driver eased off the accelerator.

The nose of the vehicle tilted up. Must be entering a driveway.

More Chinese. To Gunner, it sounded as if the passenger said, "We're almost there." Or was it his imagination?

Rolling at idle speed a short distance, the Yukon made a wide loop to the left and stopped. The driver's window buzzed down. Four clicks. The driver must have punched a keypad.

A tinny voice outside the window responded in Chinese. It was an intercom to someone inside the building.

Another jet roared over.

The passenger raised his voice so his short sentence carried through the open window.

A two-syllable reply.

A metal door rattled open. The driver buzzed the window closed.

The driver tapped the accelerator. The Yukon's tires bumped over a low threshold. The metal door closed behind him.

Into the belly of the beast.

Something would happen soon. Gunner's pulse thumped faster.

The Yukon rolled to a stop. Three doors opened.

Adrenaline coursed through his blood, kicking off the fight-or-flight reflex, but he could neither fight nor fly.

————

Chuck leaned on the horn and gunned the Caravan onto the shoulder. Ignoring the honks and obscene gestures, he burned rubber up the shoulder to the Highway 824 exit. He bluffed an exiting sedan and jammed into the queue. Reaching the bottom of the exit ramp, he bulled across three lanes of vehicles on the frontage road until he could bump up onto the sidewalk. Driving on the sidewalk to Highway 824, he bounced back to the roadway, jerked a right, and stomped the accelerator to the firewall. His Caravan leapt ahead with a roar of its oversized engine.

If Gunner was running this direction, Chuck might meet him as the Chinese chased him south on Highway 824. If he was running north, Chuck might not be able to catch them.

I should have hired another operative to leapfrog with Gunner from the get-go, Chuck thought. *The Chinese wouldn't have made the tail, and Gunner wouldn't have faced six armed men alone.* Mentally, he kicked himself. *Shoulda, woulda, coulda...but didn't.*

Weaving his way through the traffic, Chuck broke every traffic law until he saw a blue Yukon with a crumpled fender across the street. Gunner had mentioned a blue Yukon pulling in behind him. The Yukon was empty. A half-mile farther Chuck found Gunner's Jeep abandoned at the curb. Both front doors were open. He parked behind the Cherokee, jumped out of the van, and rushed to the driver's open door.

Gunner's Glock lay on the floorboard of his Jeep. Chuck stuck it in his pocket and scanned the pavement around the Jeep. Nothing. Moving to the passenger side of the Jeep, he saw Gunner's phone lying on the pavement. He picked it up and flipped it over. The screen was smashed into splinters where someone had stomped it.

Shoving the phone in his pocket, Chuck peered both ways down the street, hoping to spot a white Expedition or a black Yukon.

Nothing. The street of this industrial area held two cars and one truck.

5221 SW 4th Street. That's what Gunner said, Chuck thought. *I know where to start looking. Unless...*

Chuck had been watching for a black Yukon, a blue Yukon, or a white Expedition as he drove north on Highway 824. They hadn't come south.

What was to the north?

Chuck had one asset the Chinese didn't know about: Gunner carried two cellphones. They had smashed the burner phone Chuck had given him. Maybe Gunner's original phone was still in his pocket.

If only they hadn't searched him thoroughly enough to uncover it...

———

Chuck returned to his Caravan, turned on his laptop, and logged into Gunner's Google account. *Bingo.* There was Gunner's phone, three miles north and moving.

Placing the laptop on the passenger seat, he monitored his friend's phone.

But with six kidnappers, Chuck needed backup. He reached for the phone...

———

Hank Ramirez connected on the second ring.

"What's happening, Chuck?"

"Six Chinese soldiers have kidnapped Gunner."

"The guys you tailed last night?"

"Yeah. He managed to hide his phone from them. I'm tracking it from my van now."

"You mean *now* now? You're tracking six kidnappers as we speak?"

"Yes. I'm driving north on Highway 824 west of the airport. I need backup."

"Sure, I'm in. Have you called the FBI? Kidnapping is a Federal crime."

"For reasons I can't discuss, we can't involve them or the Secret Service or the Port City cops."

"But you called me, and I'm a Port City cop."

"I need you to do this off the books."

"Why off the books?"

"If you'll meet me in person, I'll explain everything. It's for Gunner."

"I'm on my way, but for six kidnappers, you need more than me. I'm good, but I'm no Superman."

"I'll call Snoop, the Martinez cousins, and Tank."

"Tank's a civilian."

"He's had his baptism by fire. You remember the Doraleen kidnapping."

"True, but it's tax season. Tank's a CPA. He's as busy as a one-armed juggler."

"Tank will come anyway. He owes me big time."

"Okay. Should I call Angelina Curtis? She's always ready to go to war."

"Good idea. Tell her to wear a vest."

———

Snoop answered on the second ring.

"How's it hanging, bud?"

"Snoop, Gunner's been kidnapped." Chuck gave him a swift rundown of the day's events. "Gear up and meet me west of the airport on Highway 824. I'll text you the exact location once Gunner's phone stops moving."

———

Pedro Martinez and his cousin Morris Martinez were former cops and current private investigators. Pedro lived in Miami-Dade and Morris lived in Palm Beach. Even if they were in town and available, it would still take an hour or more for them to drive to Port City. That was okay. Chuck would use the time to reconnoiter and plan.

He called Pedro first.

"Sure, I'll be on my way in ten minutes, but Morris is in Orlando on assignment. Won't be back for a couple days. What about Desiree Clover? I could call her. If she's available, I can pick her up on my way there."

"Good idea. We need the extra manpower."

"With Desiree, it's womanpower."

———

Thomas "Tank" Tyler answered his private line on the third ring.

"Tyler Asset Management. How may I direct your call?"

"Tank, it's Chuck McCrary. I'm calling on a burner phone."

"I wondered how someone got my unlisted number. Why are you on a burner phone?"

"It's a long story."

"Your tax appointment isn't for another month. You wouldn't call my private line unless this was urgent."

Tank was Chuck's good friend, and his CPA and financial advisor.

"Tank, fifteen minutes ago, six Chinese PLA soldiers kidnapped Gunner Knutson. I need to rescue him before they question him. They're not real big on recognizing a prisoner's civil rights. Remember how my buddy Phillip Franks was killed."

"Who could forget?"

"I don't want the same thing to happen to Gunner."

"You suspect the Chinese killed Phillip Franks?"

"I have no proof, but it's something they would do without a second's hesitation."

"And you need my help?"

"Yes. If we wait for the FBI or the cops, Gunner might be dead. Delaying his rescue is a risk I'm not willing to take. I'm mounting a private rescue op, like we did for Momma Dora. Are you in?"

"Naturally. I have a client waiting in reception for an appointment in five minutes. Give me ten minutes to reschedule her, another fifteen to gear up. Where do I meet you?"

That's Tank for you, Chuck thought. Tank was one of the most successful (meaning "rich and busy") financial and tax advisors in the country. It was the middle of February and Tanks was hip-deep in work for mega-millionaire clients, which Chuck was not one of. Chuck's modest investment portfolio must be the smallest one Tank managed, but he did it because they were friends. And he would drop all that to help Chuck.

"Highway 824 west of the airport. I'm tracking Gunner's phone. I'll text you the location once I know it. Drive this direction."

"Did you call the FBI?"

"For reasons I can't discuss on an unsecure phone, we can't involve them or the Port City cops."

"If you're on a burner phone, it's secure."

"My phone is secure, but your phone is not."

"Oh, yeah. That's why I'm the CPA and you're the world's greatest detective. I'll be underway ASAP."

"Bring the Red River rifle and three extra magazines. And wear your jumbo-sized vest."

"Are we fighting a war, Chuck?"

"I hope not, bro, but remember Rule Nine: *You can never carry too much firepower.*"

————

Chuck switched the map view to "satellite." Gunner's phone was in a medium-sized metal building with a smallish parking lot and a two-story office section in the front. The satellite view revealed a large loading dock and truck lot in the back. Chuck located the building on Google Street View. It had been a tile warehouse, so it was a warehouse-office combination. The three-year-old image showed a neatly-trimmed orange Ixora hedge growing between the parking lot and the building front. The parking lot had spaces for thirty-six cars.

Chuck emailed Flamer:

I need to know the current ownership and occupants of the building at 6612 NW 29th Street. Also, its blueprints. I'm looking for vulnerable points if I have to invade it and capture criminals inside. Send me anything else you learn in the next seventy minutes. Time-sensitive with life-and-death consequences.

Chuck did a drive-by. The Ixora hedge was so tall he couldn't look in the first-floor windows, but they were all dark. The second floor was where a sentry would be. Those windows were dark also, but Chuck peered extra hard for a lookout behind them. There wasn't one. He paused long enough to snap telephoto shots of each window for later analysis.

Chuck pulled into the parking lot of the Atlantic Worldwide Cruise

Lines office a half-block from the tile warehouse and across the street. The building was gaily painted with murals of cruise ships in exotic ports on the side toward Chuck and on the front above the second-story windows. A collection of national flags ringed the property. He recognized a few: Jamaica, Puerto Rico, Mexico, and the Bahamas. Maybe someday he and Ruby would cruise to those countries. That would make a good honeymoon. Something to bookmark in his mind for future reference.

In his mind he heard Vicky cautioning him. *Watch it, Chuck. There's that Norman Rockwell painting again. It may be your painting, but not Ruby's.*

After parking in the far corner of the lot in the shade of a live oak tree, Chuck fished his telephoto camera from the center console. Studying the front and east sides of the warehouse, he snapped a half-dozen photos and emailed them to Flamer. They might aid his research.

Chuck sent a group text to the entire assault team he was assembling with the address of the Atlantic Worldwide Cruise Lines office, telling them to muster under the oak tree.

As he finished the text, his stomach complained. "Feed me. Feed me *now*," it said.

Truth be told, Chuck's stomach had begun to protest in the middle of his gym workout, but he'd ignored it. Until now.

He called Snoop. "You received my text?"

"Yeah, bud. My GPS says I'm twenty-one minutes out."

"Stop at a fast-food joint and buy a couple dozen hamburgers and two dozen bottles of water. Hold the onions."

"A bunch of godless Chinks capture Gunner, and you're hungry? Bud, food is the last thing you should be thinking about."

"Don't get your panties in a knot, Snoop. One thing I learned in the army was you don't send troops to fight on an empty stomach. I haven't eaten in seven hours, and I doubt the other folks I recruited have eaten either. You're the nearest to our staging position. You can buy the food and still be the first one here. *Capisce?*"

"Hooah. No onions. You want fries with that?" He disconnected before Chuck could give him a witty retort. Knowing Snoop, Chuck figured he would bring a humongous order of French fries.

Swapping the camera for binoculars, Chuck studied the target. Above the second-story office windows a row of faded plastic letters spelled out "Atlantic County Tile Expo." The windows on both floors were bare and dark. If anyone was using the offices, they worked without lights.

A "For Sale or Lease" banner hung from the top of the east wall of the building. Another sign stood in the grass between the sidewalk and the street. It gave the name and phone number of the real estate agent.

Chuck ate two energy bars from a door pocket, washing them down with a half-liter bottle of water. He called the leasing agent.

"Port City Commercial Real Estate. How can I help you?"

"I'm interested in the building at 6612 NW 29th Street near the airport."

———

Gunner sat statue-like, analyzing every sound as if his life depended on it.

Why did they leave the Yukon's doors open? he thought. *Do they plan to return soon and haul me someplace else? They will want to question me. If not here, where?*

In any event, it was better not to attract their attention. Out of sight, out of mind. He would be content to remain motionless until Chuck McCrary rescued him. He was certain that Chuck would mount a rescue. His job was to survive until then.

Simply survive.

The metal door rattled open again. One more vehicle bumped over the threshold and parked to Gunner's left. The engine sounded like the Expedition. Three doors opened on the Expedition, two of them with metal grinding. Must be the right-side doors Gunner had trashed. Three doors meant Black Suit had gone back to the blue Yukon for the other two soldiers.

Six Chinese were present, including Black Suit, the boss. But one voice answered the keypad when they first arrived, so at least one person was inside.

Maybe Black Suit is the only one who speaks English.

Gunner listened to distant conversations in Chinese and recognized the squeak of rubber-soled shoes and the rustle of unidentified movements and actions. It was impossible to tell how many people were in the building.

Another jet roared over, but the sound was muted. There was soundproofing on the ceiling wherever he was.

No news is good news, Gunner thought. *Survive. Chuck will come.*

Gradually, his pulse and blood pressure returned to normal.

Scraping noises. Metallic bangs. *Folding metal chairs?*

Clicks and scrapes. *From the echoes, the room sounds large and empty. No sound-deadening fabrics or furniture. An empty warehouse?*

Among the jumble of noises, a set of rubber-soled footsteps moved closer.

A voice on the left said, "Get out."

"Okay." Gunner scooted to his right and paused at the edge of the seat, waiting for his captor to come around and open the door. The longer he stalled, the better his survival chances.

The door opened. Swinging his legs to the right, Gunner bent over to make sure his head cleared the top of the door. He leaned out and stood straight. His elbow nudged the open door.

A torrent of Chinese. The thug who fetched him was probably cursing him in Mandarin. Screw him if he couldn't take a joke.

Gunner smiled inwardly. *Score one for the good guy.*

Footsteps came around the Yukon. Strong hands seized his right arm and tugged at him. "You come."

"Okay." He would be agreeable. Stall and survive.

He accepted the guidance of the man holding his arm for twenty-seven steps until his shins rapped against something. A metallic clatter and scrape told him it was a folding metal chair.

The unseen hands cut the cable tie holding his hands behind him and spun him around. "You sit." His captor pushed on his shoulders.

"Okay." He sat, squeezing between the chair arms. He rubbed his wrists to restore the circulation.

The unseen hands grasped his arms and fastened them to the chair with new cable ties at wrists and elbows. Next, they shackled his ankles with more cable ties.

The footsteps receded three paces. His keeper was expecting someone.

The boss.

Other footsteps with harder soles arrived. *Maybe it's Black Suit and his Oxfords with leather soles?*

A new voice spoke in Chinese, commanding.

He heard one footstep and a massive blow slammed the left side of his jaw. Someone had punched him with a fist, a right-handed man. Another blow from the other side. A third blow to his left.

So, the interrogation had commenced, but they intended to soften him up first.

More blows. He lost count of the number of times he was pounded.

He dropped his head to his chest. Make them believe he was unconscious. Stall and survive. He thought about Phil Franks. *Was this what happened to Phil?*

A needle pricked his arm.

————

Snoop parked near Chuck's Caravan, leaving an empty space between. He popped the door behind Chuck and set several sacks of hamburgers on the seat in the second row.

"No onions."

Returning to his car, Snoop hefted a case of twenty-four bottles of water in plastic wrap and deposited it on floor behind the driver's seat. "I'm a water boy during timeout at a football game."

"Thanks for the help, Snoop. I'm starving."

"You're always starving. Speaking of food, there are no onions on the hamburgers, but I smell plenty of onions in this van." Shoop wrinkled his nose. "Wow, you smell like old sneakers. Did you come straight from the gym without showering?"

"Sorry about that. Gunner was in danger, and I didn't have time. Stay upwind and you'll be okay. Hank should be here soon. Angie Curtis arrives in fifteen minutes. Tank is a few minutes behind her. Pete Martinez and Desiree Clover arrive in forty-five minutes. Eat now, if you want. I intend to."

"I'll eat, but I'll do it in my car."

"Picky, picky," Chuck said.

By the time Angie Curtis arrived, four vehicles had gathered in the far corner of the cruise line's parking lot.

A man in a pale blue guayabera marched out the front door of the cruise line and approached Chuck. He wore an oblong badge with the Atlantic Worldwide Cruise Lines logo, the name *Marco*, and a small Bahamian flag beside his name. He glanced nervously at the group gathered in his company parking lot. "May I help you, sir?" he asked with an islander's accent. "Do you have business with Atlantic Worldwide Cruise Lines?"

Hank walked over and held up his shield. "I'm Detective Captain Hidalgo Ramirez, Port City Police, sir."

Marco snapped to attention. "Yes, sir. How may we be of service?"

Hank smiled. "This is my team of plainclothes cops. We intend to stake out that building down the block. We believe the occupants are involved in a criminal activity, and we need to assemble where they won't notice us and become suspicious. Your parking lot is the perfect spot for us to blend in. Is it okay to use this corner of your lot for another hour?"

Chuck thought it was nice to have a real cop with a real shield with his team. It avoided awkward questions.

"Uh, what criminal activity do you suspect? Are we in danger? We've never had trouble in this neighborhood in the twelve years I've worked here."

"Possible smuggling. Your people aren't in danger."

Tank Tyler's maroon Mercedes parked in a neighboring space, and the former NFL defensive lineman unfolded his six-foot-six frame out of the car.

Marco's gaze traveled across Chuck, Snoop, and Angie Curtis, lingering on Angie. No surprise there; her wide brown eyes, mocha-colored skin, and curly brown hair affect most men with a pulse. His focus returned to Hank. "If this is a stakeout, why are your people wearing bulletproof vests?"

Tank walked over.

Marco, who was five-foot-six if he wore cowboy boots, stared at the giant black man. "I know you. I mean, I don't *know* you, but I know who you were. Didn't you used to be Tank Tyler?"

"Last time I checked my ID, I still am," Tank said with a smile.

"I mean, uh…You were defensive tackle for the Port City Pelicans. Super Bowl MVP, NFL Hall of Fame. I'm a big fan, Tank."

Tank extended his ham-sized hand. "It's nice to meet you, Marco."

Marco seized it in both hands and shook it like a pump handle. "Imagine that. Tank Tyler in my parking lot."

Marco considered the rest of them and squinted one eye. "If you people are undercover cops, why is Tank Tyler here? He's no cop."

Hank smiled. "That's a reasonable question with a mundane answer. Among his many community service activities, Tank is a reserve police officer. He's joining our surveillance team as volunteer service."

Marco looked at Tank, who smiled, then at Hank. "But why the bulletproof vests?"

"It's policy that officers wear body armor on duty, regardless of the duty. Even parking enforcement officers wear body armor. It's a crazy world out there."

Marco rubbed his hands together and glanced at Tank again. "Okay. *Mi casa es su casa.* If any of your task force need to use the restroom or get a drink of water or anything, come inside. Is there anything else we can do to assist the Port City Police?"

"No, sir, and thank you for your cooperation."

Marco bowed to Hank. "Thank you all for your service."

Pete Martinez and Desiree Clover arrived. The rest of team had done serious damage to the hamburgers and French fries, and torn open the case of water. Chuck had put the remaining food and water in Snoop's Toyota for Pete and Desiree or anybody else who wanted seconds. That kept them out of range of Chuck's stinky B.O. too.

Chuck couldn't use the laptop outside. The sun's glare, even in the shadow of the oak, made the screen difficult to see. Flamer had emailed blueprints from the Port City Building Department and aerial photos and building notes from the Atlantic County Property Appraiser's website.

Turning to Hank, Chuck said, "Why don't you and Snoop sit in the second-row seats where you can observe the laptop over my shoulder. You're the West Point graduate. You take command."

"My first command is let's lower the windows. Your van smells like a locker room."

Chuck buzzed the windows down and popped the rear hatch. He twisted halfway in the driver's seat so he could talk to both men. "I called the leasing agent. She rented the building to an outfit called the East-West Trading Company, LLC. They booked a short-term monthly rental on January first. The LLC was organized in Virginia on December 27th last year. The LLC's registered owner is a law firm in Washington, D.C., that often represents the Chinese embassy. The building owner gave them a special deal for paying three months' rent in advance, and the owner continues to market the property. The REIT that built the building twenty-seven years ago still owns it. The Chinese agreed to vacate on short notice if the agent snags a buyer or long-term lessee. It's been empty two years."

Chuck loaded his photo of the building front.

"All the windows in the office section are dark. There was no sign of a sentry. It's likely that the Chinese are using only the warehouse space in back. The warehouse contains seven rows of steel shelves with aisles wide enough for forklift access. The shelves are in fourteen sections ranked on either side of a fifteen-foot wide central aisle that runs from the front to a work and loading area at the back."

Chuck switched to a photo of the east wall.

"The warehouse space has windows twenty feet in the air. There will be natural light if the lights or electricity go off. The satellite view shows numerous skylights in the roof. The back wall has two metal overhead doors for trucks and one steel personnel door. The personnel door has four small windows measuring twelve by eighteen inches with wire reinforcement. There's no easy way into the warehouse."

"Show me the front again," Hank said. "Zoom the photo to the ground floor windows. Watch for burglar alarm contacts."

"I asked the leasing agent whether the property has a security system. She said no."

"That doesn't mean the Chinese didn't install one."

"Good point." Chuck zoomed the picture. "No alarm contacts."

"Did you do a drive-by before you parked?"

"Yeah. No sign of a sentry in the front windows. I made telephotos and zoomed to max. No sentries in any of those dark windows."

"If they're PLA, they're not well-trained if they don't post a sentry."

"They're over-confident."

"Good," said Hank. "We'll enter through a front window."

"Why not the door?"

"Breaking a steel door makes more noise than breaking a window, and picking the lock while standing on the front porch risks a passerby calling the cops. It's quicker and quieter to break a window. Less likely to alert the people in the back. Also, the blueprints indicate the front door opens to a corridor that funnels sound straight to the back. They would hear the break-in if the warehouse door is open. We'll pick a window that opens on an office. Much quieter."

"And that's why you were commanding officer of the Triple Seven and I was a grunt," Chuck said.

"When the Pentagon issues Captain's bars, they come with a twenty-point increase in IQ," Hank said. "Okay. You know everybody on the team. Pick the two best snipers to cover the two truck doors and the people door in case they attempt to escape out the back. The rest of us will infiltrate through a window. Have you seen traffic in or out of the building?"

"Not since I've been here. Nobody in, nobody out. We're safe to park in front."

Hank turned to Snoop. "Sound okay to you, Snoop?"

"You're the Army captain with the Pentagon-issued IQ. I'm a grunt like Chuck. You ready to brief the rest of the team?"

Hank opened the van door. "Let's do it."

Chuck assembled the team in the shade of the oak. "Most of you know Hank Ramirez, but for those of you who don't, Hank was my commanding officer in Special Forces. He's a Detective Captain with the Port City Police though this mission is personal, informal, and off the books. Hank has saved my life more times than I can count and I asked him to command this rescue mission…" Chuck smiled, "…though I'm the one who's paying you."

Chuck briefed the team on how Gunner was kidnapped. "Any questions before I turn the floor over to Hank?"

Desiree Clover stepped up. "If these six Chinese kidnapped your friend Gunner, why not call the FBI? Kidnapping is a federal crime. Why risk our lives?"

"Two reasons. Calling the FBI or the cops wastes time for them to organize and put a team on site. Gunner could be dead by then. Secondly, the men who kidnapped Gunner are solders in the People's Liberation Army."

Another jet roared over. Chuck stopped talking until it passed.

"The soldiers work for the military attaché of the Chinese embassy in Washington. If the FBI arrests them, they'll flash their diplomatic passports, and United States law can't touch them."

"Surely there would be diplomatic repercussions if Chinese diplomats kidnap a U.S. citizen," Desiree said.

"Sure," said Hank, "but the Chinese kidnappers would still be free, and we couldn't question them about Phillip Franks's murder."

"That's why I haven't officially involved any sworn LEOs." Chuck scanned the group. "Any other questions before Hank gives us our assignments?"

"I'm not finished," Desiree said. She glared at Pete Martinez. "Pete, you didn't tell me this was a military assault on professional soldiers. I'm a PI like you. I didn't sign up to be a mercenary in a private army. I'm outta here."

Pete glanced at Chuck. Chuck shrugged. Pete fished his keys out of a pocket. "Use my car. I'll catch a ride home with someone. No hard feelings."

Desiree accepted the keys and shook Pete's hand. "Good luck."

She walked away.

Chuck felt uneasy about Desiree Clover. He didn't know her well; she was Pete Martinez's operative. Chuck's team was engaged in a mission of questionable legality, and Desiree knew all about it. If the shit hit the fan, there was nothing he could do to prevent legal repercussions. But Gunner's life was at stake. That was worth the personal risk. He decided to cross any bridges that Desiree burned when he came to them.

Chuck had six team members remaining. *Should be enough*, he thought. *We have the element of surprise*. Chuck counted on that. Stealth and surprise. And six bulletproof vests.

———

Snoop was the oldest team member by fifteen to twenty years. At his age, Chuck figured Snoop had no business climbing through windows, running after bad guys, or hand-fighting with Chinese solders. On the other hand, Snoop was the best pistol shooter on the Port City cops before he retired, and he was great with any firearm, so he would make an excellent sniper.

Chuck posted Angie as the second sniper. Angie was a former Marine sharpshooter. Snoop and Angie would be less than a hundred yards from the warehouse. An easy shot for Snoop with the Rock River Arms Varmint rifle that Chuck loaned him. Chuck carried one himself. Angie brought her own Springfield Armory M1A National Match Rifle with a twenty-round magazine.

Chuck drove the two snipers to where the tracks crossed the side street two hundred yards from the warehouse. The three of them stepped to the rear of the Caravan where their equipment was stowed.

"You and Angie sneak up the tracks and hide behind the hedge near the railroad spur. One on each corner."

Snoop hefted his rucksack. "Bud, lugging forty pounds of armaments makes it hard to *sneak*. How about I *trudge* or maybe *plod*?"

Angie lifted her rucksack as if it were a loaf of bread and slung it over one shoulder. "I can sneak with my pack and yours too, Snoop. I have a spare hand." She reached for Snoop's rucksack, but he jerked it out of the way.

"Thanks, Angie, but once I'm too old to lug my own gear, I'll retire. Again." He winked at Chuck. "I like to give Chuck a hard time. Keeps him humble."

Angie tilted her chin Chuck's direction. "That one will never be humble."

Snoop clapped her on the back and hitched his pack into position. "Okay, bud. Send us each a text before you breach the warehouse."

The other three crew members were at the parking lot of the warehouse.

As Chuck opened the driver's door, his body prepared for action. His pulse accelerated. His blood pressure elevated. His mouth went dry. *Showtime,* Chuck's body said.

Not yet, he told it.

The orange Ixora hedge that once accented the front had grown uncontrolled in the years the building had been empty. Branches grew seven to eight feet tall. Hank stepped between the hedge and the building and was invisible from the front. In the quiet neighborhood, he rustled from one window to the next behind the hedge.

Another jet roared overhead. The rumble of its engines vibrated in Chuck's chest.

Hank returned. "All the windows show empty offices behind, but most of them have doors open to the lateral hallway beyond. The second window from the left has the office door closed. That door will suppress the sound inside when we break in. We'll infiltrate there while a jet is passing over."

He surveyed from one end of their group to the other. "We're outnumbered, so we depend on stealth and surprise. That means no talking and no noise. Let's roll."

Hank paused at the second window. Pete, Tank, and Chuck wedged themselves and their equipment bags into the space between the hedge and the wall. Another jet on approach roared over and Hank broke the pane with the butt of his pistol. Working shards of broken glass loose with his gloved hands, he reached inside and unlocked the window.

Hank reached through, dropped his rucksack inside, and interlaced his fingers for a step-up. Pete positioned his foot in the improvised stirrup and crawled through the window. Hank handed Pete's rucksack after him. Chuck handed his rucksack through and followed Pete.

Tank stepped up to Hank and laughed. "Hank, I weigh 285. I'll give *you* the boost." With his height and reach, Tank set his rucksack inside the window. He interlaced his own fingers. "Upsy-daisy."

Hank tapped Tank's shoulder and stepped into the massive hands. "Thanks, pal," he said as he vaulted through the window.

Tank stuck one of his size-sixteen boots through the window up to his knee followed by his hands and arms. Chuck was surprised he folded his massive bulk so easily. On the other hand, he fit into his Mercedes, so he was used to tight spaces. Ducking his massive head and wedging his shoulders through the window, he squirmed through like a giant contortionist.

Glancing back through the broken window, Chuck surveyed the street through the Ixora leaves. No one had noticed them. Stealth and surprise.

Tank fastened the straps of his rucksack. "I'm glad I don't need to exit this way. Lead on, Captain."

"Leave the lights off," Hank said. "Chuck, I got us inside. You should re-assume command."

"Okay." Chuck lowered his voice. "Don't use your helmet lights. In this darkened hall, the lights make us easy targets. Your vision will adjust to the dim light. Once we're in the warehouse, we'll have ample natural light. There are six shooters or more. Don't ease up after we account for the six. We'll need to search the warehouse to ensure there aren't more Chinese soldiers hiding God-knows-where. We make up for our smaller numbers with stealth and surprise. Are we on the same page?"

Pete said, "Hooah."

Tank fisted Chuck.

"Okay, folks," Chuck said. "Let's crash the party."

Chuck opened the door and slipped into the hallway. Glancing both directions down the shadowy passage, he tiptoed toward the central corridor. Each step from the open door behind them got darker, but their eyes dilated to compensate. In the Triple Seven, Chuck had led attacks into plenty of dark rooms and buildings. This was nothing new to Hank and him. He hoped Pete and Tank didn't screw anything up. Stealth and surprise.

Pausing at the junction of the two halls, Chuck listened before stepping into the central corridor. Nothing.

The long passage was bare except for old pictures of tile samples hanging on the walls. Good, no furniture to trip them in the gloom. Chuck

led the way, removing the old pictures he passed and leaning them again
the walls.

They stopped at the door to the warehouse.

Chuck motioned Pete closer and lowered his voice. "Go close the door
we entered through. I want this hall pitch dark when I open the door to the
warehouse. We will charge from the dark into the light."

Pete gave Chuck a two-finger salute. "Hooah," he whispered.

"And, Pete, get a mental picture of this hall imprinted in your mind.
Use that picture mentally after the last light goes out. For God's sake, don't
knock any of the pictures over when you come back."

Pete retraced his path and disappeared into the lateral hallway. The
squeak of his boot soles grew fainter. Chuck composed a text to Snoop and
Angie:

Going in ten seconds.

He paused, his finger on the *send* button. The last dim light seeping
from the lateral hallway went dark, and he sent the text.

The soft squeak of Pete's rubber soles on the tile floor grew louder. A
scrape as he grazed a picture leaning against the wall. "Oh, shit," Pete said.
The picture frame crashed to the floor and echoed in the corridor.

So much for stealth and surprise.

———

"Maybe they didn't hear the crash," Pete said.

Chuck twisted the doorknob. "Too late now; we're committed."

Throwing the door open, Chuck met three Chinese in denim jackets and
khaki pants running at him down the central aisle. The leader stopped and
aimed his pistol. The two behind him fired without stopping.

A slug slammed Chuck's vest over his belly-button, slowing his rush
into the warehouse and knocking the breath from his lungs. It felt like he'd
been kicked in the gut.

He couldn't return fire accurately because he didn't know where
Gunner was. The punch to his gut didn't help either. Instead, Chuck fired
twice in the general direction of the shooters, but aimed high enough to not
hit anyone, good guy or bad guy. One bullet banged a metal shelf and rang

it like a gong. Chuck pivoted and stumbled at a right angle down a side aisle, gasping for air.

The three Chinese soldiers leapt to either side into the gap between the shelves.

From the leasing agent's description, Chuck expected to find empty shelves that they could look through from the front to the back wall. Instead, the previous tenant had abandoned the warehouse with its inventory still there. Hundreds of boxes of tile filled the shelves.

A shout in Chinese echoed though the vast room. Another shout responded. With the echo, Chuck couldn't tell where either shout came from, and he observed no one. He slinked along the aisle, struggling to stand upright.

Chuck heard the other team members behind him. They spread out, searching for shooters. They made their way between the shelves lined in neat ranks on each side of a central aisle.

About the time Chuck caught his breath, he reached the second side aisle.

Two shots rang out. A bullet clanged on the shelf near his head and flashed a shower of sparks.

Chuck whirled and fired a three-shot burst. The shooter screamed, fell, and rolled out of sight. Chuck had wounded him, but not fatally.

There were more shots. One of the team members shot him too.

Chuck broke into a trot toward the far end of the aisle. A Chinese soldier leapt into view and fired a pistol. Chuck returned fire. Two of the three rounds riddled the soldier's chest. Chuck knelt to feel his pulse. Dead.

Tank stepped up. "I got that other one."

"That's two," Chuck said. "Spread out. And be careful of the track behind your shots. We don't know where Gunner is."

Rounding the shelves, Chuck crept toward the back, expecting another gunman to jump out. The warehouse echoed with shouts in Chinese and small arms fire. He reached the end of the shelving and peered to the rear of the warehouse.

Amongst a scattering of a half dozen folding tables and a dozen assorted chairs, Gunner lay on his side on the concrete, tied to an overturned chair. He was either dead or unconscious or playing possum. Chuck hoped he was playing possum.

Another denim-jacketed shooter and a man in a black suit stood on either side, trying to haul Gunner's chair upright. Two hundred pounds of dead weight is hard to lift using one hand to hold a gun.

Chuck aimed at the denim-clad gunman. One through the chest and he fell backwards, firing wildly. Why were they not wearing body armor?

Chuck's ears were ringing from the noise of the gunshots. Another jet roared overhead.

The black-suited man stopped tugging on Gunner and dropped to his knees, attempting to hide behind Gunner and the chair. Gunner had a black bag over his head. Black Suit shoved his pistol against Gunner's temple.

Chuck pointed his rifle in the general direction of Black Suit. He didn't want to spook him into shooting Gunner.

Black Suit and Chuck stared at each other while the gunfire around them slowed, then stopped.

Hank rounded the far rack of shelves with his arm around the neck of another man in a denim jacket. He held a pistol to the man's head. "I killed one and this one surrendered."

Black Suit switched his focus to Hank, then back to Chuck.

Probably can't decide which of us is the bigger threat, Chuck thought.

"Stop where you are or I will kill him," Black Suit shouted in good English.

Tank dragged another man in a gray suit around a corner. The man was limping from a bleeding leg wound. "There's another dead one at the back end of this aisle," Tank said.

"How was he dressed?"

"Same as that guy." He pointed at the denim-clad man on the floor near Gunner.

Pete returned. "I shot a man dressed like that dead one," he said, pointing.

"Stop where you are," Black Suit repeated, "or this one is a dead man."

Chuck motioned Tank, Hank, and Pete to stay where they were. "You guys stop, but keep that one covered."

He walked toward the man in the black suit. "What's your name?"

"You stop. I will kill him."

"I believe you." Chuck walked closer, stopping fifteen feet away. "That won't be necessary. I'm Chuck McCrary. What do I call you?"

Black Suit jammed his pistol into Gunner's throat. "If you come closer, I will kill him." His hand shook so hard Chuck was afraid he might inadvertently fire a fatal round.

Chuck lifted his free hand in a peaceful gesture and rotated his rifle where it wasn't pointed at the Chinese. "I'm sure you could, and if you do, those men there will kill you the next instant. Nobody else needs to die today, okay? Nobody. We all can walk out of this alive. There's been enough killing for one day. Let's take a breath."

He drew an exaggerated breath to demonstrate. "Just breathe."

Chuck needed time for his hearing to recover. He fought the urge to shake his head. He knew from experience that it doesn't help.

Black Suit's hand stopped shaking. That was good.

Chuck turned to Pete. "Check the rest of the warehouse. Make sure we found them all, then text Angie and Snoop to come in. Open the back door." To Tank: "Keep your weapon pointed at the guy in the suit. If he pulls the trigger, kill him."

"With pleasure."

Black Suit gawked from one of the Americans to another, calculating his chances of dodging their bullets. He arrived at the identical conclusion Chuck had: He was thoroughly screwed. He placed his pistol on the floor and stepped away. "My name is Kang. I am a Chinese diplomat, with a diplomatic passport in my jacket pocket."

Chuck glanced at Gunner's motionless body. A fist squeezed his heart. Best case, Gunner was unconscious. Worst case, he was dead.

Kang straightened himself taller and smirked. "I have diplomatic immunity. You must allow me to call the Chinese Embassy. This is the law in the United States."

Chuck stepped closer to Kang and smashed his smirk with the barrel of his rifle, knocking him further from Gunner.

"Too bad, Kang," he said. "I don't care about your diplomatic passport. We're not cops. We're private. And this isn't business; it's personal."

THIRTEEN

"Hank, please cut Gunner loose," Chuck said. He covered Kang with his rifle.

Hank sliced through the cable ties with a Ka-Bar knife and Gunner fell from the chair.

Chuck yanked off the black hood. Gunner's face was bruised, bloody, and cut but he grunted and his chest moved.

Chuck must have been holding his breath, because suddenly he breathed again. Gunner was alive.

Hank knelt beside Gunner and checked his pulse. "Pulse is slow but solid. He's been drugged."

Hank tugged up Gunner's left sleeve to reveal a needle mark on the bicep.

Chuck recalled his and Hank's visit to the medical examiner's office. "Same place as Phil's injection. Secure the three prisoners with cable ties. After Pete finishes looking for more Chinese, search again for a syringe and vials of sodium thiopental. Until then, I'll attend to Gunner's wounds as best I can."

As Chuck finished with the disinfectant and the bandages, Pete returned. "The building is clear. We found them all: five bodies and three prisoners. I texted Snoop and Angie. I'll open the back door."

"Thanks, Pete. Did you notice any syringes or vials of sodium thiopental?"

"No, but I was searching for Chinese gangsters."

"Okay, thanks. Search the building again. This time for drugs and syringes. Look for blood stains or cutting tools. A crosscut saw or a machete or hatchet."

"Is this where they killed your friend?"

"If they killed him, this could be the crime scene. Anything you find, don't touch it. You have evidence gloves?"

"Sure," Pete said. "I carry nitrile gloves, but why worry about preserving evidence? What about these guys never living to stand trial?"

"Let's keep all options open. Replace your utility glovers with nitrile gloves. Don't contaminate evidence. *Capisce?*"

"Hooah."

Gunner moaned and rolled his neck.

"He's coming around," Hank said. "I wish we had someplace he could lie down other than a concrete floor. How about the back of that SUV?"

Chuck unhitched his pack. "Too small. Empty the rucksacks and make a pallet."

Snoop and Angie joined them.

Hank arranged six empty rucksacks and they laid Gunner on the pile. It was the best they could do.

Kang slumped on his side on the concrete with his hands fastened behind him and his ankles cinched tight. "My man is wounded. You should tend to him also."

The leg wound of the man in the gray suit was through-and-through in the fleshy part of the calf. It was bleeding, but the flow had slackened. If the bullet clipped an artery, he would be dead before Chuck could call an ambulance. Not that he would have called an ambulance for those killers. Besides, Chuck needed someone to question, someone who spoke English. This guy wore a suit. Chuck figured he was an officer.

Chuck applied an Israeli emergency pressure bandage. He had kept Israeli bandages in his first aid kit for years, but the only time he'd used one was when Serbian gangsters shot him in the Florida Everglades. It kept him alive until Snoop got him to a hospital. This bandage would hold until they decided what to do with him.

"What's your name?"

He glanced at Kang and shook his head.

Chuck tapped the bandage and he jumped.

"I put that bandage on and I can rip it off again. You want to bleed to death?" He grasped the bandage and gave it a tiny tug. "What's your name?"

He shrugged. "Bohai."

"You speak English?"

"A little. I am diplomat." He gestured with his chin. "We are all diplomats."

"What is your interest in the woman you followed last night?"

His gaze unfocused as if he were translating Chuck's question into Chinese, then translating his response back to English. "We want find where she live."

They were making progress. "Why do you want that information?"

Kang spewed a torrent of Chinese. He was not a happy camper.

Chuck walked over to the pile of equipment Hank had dumped from their backpacks. He selected a roll of duct tape and ripped off six inches. He taped Kang's mouth shut.

"As I was saying, Bohai, why do you want to know where she lives?"

"To...take her. We want take her."

"You mean to capture her the way you did my friend?"

"Yes, *capture*. We want *capture* her."

"Why?"

"If we capture woman, her man...do what we say."

Kang grunted and tried to speak.

Chuck walked over to him, seized a handful of his hair, and banged his head against the concrete hard enough to get his attention. "Kang, if you want to say anything, wait until I finish with Bohai. In the meantime, shut up."

Once Bohai realized he was vulnerable to bleeding to death, he was remarkably talkative. His English was good enough to communicate. It was like tugging on a thread to unravel a sweater, but Chuck learned useful information. Eight men were dispatched here in two SUVs from the Chinese embassy in D.C. They rented the house on SW 4th Street the same time as the warehouse. The house was their dormitory and mess hall, the warehouse their base of operations. Bohai didn't know why they were in Port City or even Aisha's name. He didn't know who Antarion Billow or Andrew Billow was either. Bohai was a lieutenant in the Chinese People's Liberation Army. Kang said he was a captain, but Bohai—who never met Kang before this mission—thought Kang was in military intelligence. The six other soldiers were enlisted men—grunts. They had flown to Washington, D.C., from Beijing for this mission.

Gunner sat up. "First time I've seen what this room looks like. They put the black bag over my head before I got out of the Yukon. Thanks. I knew you guys would come."

"We don't leave any soldier behind. How do you feel?"

"My head is a wooden box full of cobwebs. Help me stand up."

Chuck assisted Gunner to his feet. Gunner shifted his weight from one foot to the other, lifted his arms one at time, then touched his face.

"Those are band-aids," Chuck said. "I gave you first aid while you were unconscious. Somebody used your head as a punching bag."

He glanced at Kang. "No kidding."

"That's Kang. He's a captain in the Peoples Liberation Army. He's in charge of this bunch."

"That figures."

"How do you feel?"

"Well enough to interrogate Kang. Let's put him in the chair. We'll see how *he* likes it."

Kang glared at Chuck.

Chuck slipped his Ka-Bar from its scabbard, and cut the cable ties around Kang's wrists and ankles.

"If I were you, Kang, I'd do what Gunner says. He's not in a good mood."

Kang came to his feet, stretching his arms and flexing his shoulders. He feinted at Gunner, pivoted, and sprinted toward the back door, ripping the duct tape off his mouth.

Chuck ran after him, but Angie beat him to it. She ran the angle straight to the back door and tackled Kang as he reached the emergency bar. She dropped a knee between his shoulder blades and leaned close to his ear. "You're a fool, captain. You can't outrun a bullet. You're lucky I didn't shoot you instead of tackling you."

Chuck wrapped a fresh cable tie around Kang's wrists.

Angie stood and Chuck gave her a high five. "Thanks, Angie. I can run all day, but I'm no sprinter."

"I was NCAA Women's All-Southeast-Conference sprinter in college. You should have seen me run the 200-meter hurdles. *Zoom*." She sneered at Kang. "Stand up, fool."

She herded Kang back toward Gunner.

Gunner picked up the chair off the floor.

Kang sat in it without expression, arms awkward behind him.

Gunner held out a hand. "Give me some cable ties."

Chuck fished a bunch from his pocket.

Gunner fastened Kang's ankles to the chair legs. He cut Kang's wrists loose and fastened them to the chair arms the way he had been fastened: once at the wrist and once at the elbow.

Kang was trussed like a calf at a rodeo. He wasn't going anywhere.

Chuck thought of Phil's body in the morgue, visualizing those disturbing grooves on his arms and ankles. Had Kang trussed Phil up the same way? Was Phil killed in this building?

Gunner walked to a folding table that held a case of water. He twisted the top off a water bottle. "I heard these guys open water bottles, but they didn't offer me any." He drank half the bottle, then pivoted to Kang. "What did you inject me with?"

Kang stared straight ahead, stoic and unmoving. A neutral observer would think he was alone in the room.

Gunner stepped in front of Kang. "Last chance. What did you inject me with?"

Kang displayed no reaction.

Gunner pivoted toward Chuck. "Can I borrow your leather gloves?"

Chuck peeled off his utility gloves and handed them to Gunner.

Gunner stood in Kang's line of site and drew the gloves on. "I intend to question you the way you questioned me, Chinese style."

Kang's eyes flickered.

Gunner lifted the black hood that had been over his head. He waved it at Kang, then slipped it over his head.

"What drug did you use?"

Kang said nothing.

Gunner back-fisted him, knocking Kang sideways and scooting the chair a few inches. "You know you're going to tell, don't you? Make it easy on yourself."

Kang shook his head.

Chuck almost admired the guy's guts. Almost.

Gunner slugged Kang three more times, but Chuck could see his heart wasn't in it. Gunner didn't relish torturing a helpless man any more than Chuck did. Plus, he had drugs in his system. He might not be back to full strength for a couple of days.

"Hey, Gunner," Chuck said. "Take a break. Pete Martinez is searching the building. He'll find the drug paraphernalia."

Gunner hauled up another chair and finished the bottle of water. He looked as if he needed twelve hours' sleep.

Pete returned. "We have them all."

Chuck slipped the Ka-Bar back in its scabbard. "What do we do with Kang, Gunner? Keep beating him up?"

"Nope. I got that out of my system. This is your party, Chuck. You decide."

"Okay. I gave you first chance since you were the aggrieved party." Chuck slipped the hood off Kang. "Kang, we won't beat you to death." He opened a bottle of water from the Chinese supply and drank. Kang stared at the bottle and licked his lips, but didn't ask for any. Chuck put the hood back on him.

"Snoop, would you and Angie collect everyone's car keys and bring our vehicles from the front parking lot and park them in here? Any hamburgers left?"

"What, are you hungry again?" Snoop said.

"Yeah, but they're not for me. Gunner hasn't eaten since he was kidnapped. Gunner, you hungry?"

"I could eat."

———

Chuck emptied the pockets of all eight Chinese soldiers, living and dead. He sorted the loot into eight piles on three folding tables.

"Hank, you read the passports for anything useful. Snoop, search the wallets. Angie, determine which keys operate which vehicles. You match one, set the keys or keyfob on the dashboard. There will be keys to this building and everyone will carry a key to their house on SW 4th Street."

Chuck arranged the cellphones by which soldier had them. He began with Kang's phone, which was locked. Undoubtedly, they all were. He turned to Bohai. "Do they have the same password?"

"011049," he replied.

That's the one Chuck would have tried if they had killed all the Chinese. It was the date of the founding of the Peoples Republic of China, 1 October 1949. Not a secure password, but Chuck figured these guys were over-confident to the point of arrogance. No sentry, no body armor. Chuck's second guess would have been 261293, Chairman Mao Zedong's birthday, 26 December 1893.

He had begun to review Kang's call log when Pete returned. "I found something you ought to see. Actually, you and Hank and Gunner should all see it."

Chuck's gut sent him a warning. The sole reason Pete asked the three of them to come was that it related to the Triple Seven. Pete must have uncovered a clue to Phillip Franks's murder.

The three of Triple Sevens trailed Pete to the office section of the warehouse.

Pete stopped where the central corridor crossed the lateral hallway. "These doors on the right, they open to windowless rooms for files, storage, and stuff." He walked down the hallway. "The last room is where I uncovered the stuff you wanted."

The door was open and light from the room spilled into the hallway.

Pete led them through the open door. There were three office supply cabinets on the left wall and a rank of six file cabinets on the back. A three-by-eight metal table sat in the middle of the room, surrounded by eight cheap office chairs. "When I checked the building the first time," Pete said,

"I didn't look inside the cabinets because they aren't big enough to hide a man. This time I opened everything. The file cabinets were empty. What I found is in the first two cabinets."

He swung open the doors to the first cabinet. "You asked about drug paraphernalia. I found this opened box of syringes and these vials of sodium thiopental."

The box had a drugstore logo on it. The label said it held 90 insulin syringes with ultra-fine needles. Chuck pulled on a pair of nitrile gloves and opened the box. About a dozen syringes were missing. If he checked the trash cans in the warehouse, he would bet he would uncover at least one used syringe near where they rescued Gunner.

Gunner stepped over. "Can I have a pair of gloves?"

Chuck handed him a pair and Gunner removed a new syringe and held it to the light. "The needle Kang used was single-use. I won't catch AIDS from a second-hand needle." He placed the syringe box back on the shelf.

On the next shelf was a cardboard box that once contained a case of Mexican beer. Pete slid it out far enough to open the flaps on top. The box contained dozens of vials of sodium thiopental. The vials were labeled in Chinese and English. It was a brand name Chuck didn't recognize. No telling how many had been used. The box was not the one the vials were originally shipped in. Chuck assumed Kang brought them from the Chinese embassy in the rear of his SUV.

"Good work, Pete. That's a nice catch."

Pete slid the box back and stepped to the next cabinet. "You asked about cutting tools." He opened both doors.

A hacksaw was on the top metal shelf, below eye level. Something brown had dried on the blade. More brown drips had congealed beneath the blade. Chuck recalled the medical examiner commenting on the weapons used on Phil's body. A weird sensation scratched the rear of Chuck's throat.

He leaned in closer but didn't touch the saw. "What do you think, Hank?"

"I bet a case of twenty-five-year-old Puerto Rican rum that it's blood."

"No bet. The key question is, whose blood?"

"We don't know who else these bastards have killed," Hank said. "Phil is the only body we have, but there might be others. We haven't located

Billow." His voice sounded like he had a frog in his throat. "We need a, a DNA test..." He cleared his throat and paused to bring his voice under control. "...it's probable that hacksaw was used on Phil's wrists."

Pete pointed to the shelf below. "But look at this."

On the shelf below the hacksaw lay a machete. A simple killing tool made from a twenty-four-inch piece of thin high-carbon steel with a wooden handle fastened on one end. This one was sharpened until a man could shave with it. In the English-speaking islands of the Caribbean, the sugar cane harvesters call it a *cutlass*, and they use it like a short sword to cut cane. In Latin America, it's often used to cut through underbrush or in the home as a cleaver.

This machete had been used as a cleaver. Chuck could tell by the tiny nicks in the cutting edge.

It lay on the shelf, somehow elegant and brutal in its ruthless, deadly simplicity. The handle had absorbed something that deposited a brown stain on the wood. More dried brown stains marked the blade and drips on the shelf. The weird sensation in Chuck's throat threatened to gag him. He fought it to a draw.

"The ME said Phil's head was hacked off by a hatchet or..." He glanced at Hank, but Gunner responded. "A machete," Gunner said with a harsh voice. "They would have used that on my neck if you guys hadn't gotten here in time."

The four of them stared at the simple tool, thinking their own thoughts. Chuck's thoughts were uncomfortable. Probably the others were too.

Pete broke the awkward silence. "You need to get lower to see this next tool. It's at the back."

Hank and Chuck leaned over and peered into the shadows at the rear of a waist-high shelf. "It's a pair of pruning shears." Chuck shined a flashlight. "A brown stain on the blades."

Gunner wedged between Hank and Chuck and grabbed the flashlight.

Chuck's stomach churned. He swallowed hard. "Those pruning shears are too small to cut off Phil's hands. Besides, a toothed blade severed his wrists. It could be that hacksaw. I didn't notice any wound on Phil's body that those pruning shears could make. Did you, Hank?"

Hank drew back from the cabinet. His countenance appeared dark and lethal. "Neither of us saw a wound consistent with pruning shears. Either those shears were used on another victim we don't know about, or…"

Chuck finished the thought. "The Chinese soldiers sheared off Phil's fingers before they cut off his hands."

Gunner rushed into the hallway and lost his lunch. Chuck's stomach was empty, but it was all he could handle not to follow Gunner's example.

Pete closed both pairs of cabinet doors. "The rest of the building was clear."

Chuck raised a hand. "Open that door again."

He did. Chuck reached into the cabinet and snatched the pruning shears in his gloved hand. He wouldn't spoil any fingerprints on it nor leave any of his own.

Pete closed the cabinet door again. "What's that for?"

"Threatening Captain Kang with these shears might motivate his cooperation."

"You sneaky bastard." Hank grinned. "We both know you would never do that, but…"

"Kang doesn't know me. I might be as pathological and sadistic as he is."

"Are you that good an actor, Chuck?" Pete asked.

"I guess we'll find out."

Chuck stepped back into the hallway. "Get the lights will you, Pete."

Gunner stood a few steps from the remnants of the two hamburgers he had eaten.

"Let's go back to the warehouse, guys," Chuck said.

Tank had set Bohai and the other enlisted man against the last row of steel shelves, but twenty feet apart. Kang was hooded and hog-tied to the chair in the middle of the staging area.

Chuck jerked the hood from Kang's head. "Look what we found in a storage cabinet." He waved the shears before the Chinese soldier's eyes.

Kang leaned away from the bloodstained tool as if it were a venomous snake about to bite. To him, it was.

"Are you familiar with karma, Captain Kang? It's the principle that 'what goes around comes around.' Good actions a person does influence a good future for him. Likewise, bad actions—say torturing someone by cutting off their fingers with garden shears—would cause that bad action to be directed at that individual, say you, with me cutting off your fingers with these garden shears."

Chuck flicked open the catch and the jaws sprang open with a click. The serpent's mouth was open. "Notice that brown stain? That stain is blood from you cutting off Phillip Franks's fingers, isn't it?"

Sweat broke out on Kang's forehead. He didn't act so stoic now. He stared at the stained blades as if they were serpent's teeth dripping venom.

"How did you do it with Franks? Did you cut the whole finger off —*bang*, like that?" Chuck snapped the shears closed inches from Kang's nose. He flinched and whimpered.

"Or did you remove one joint at a time? You know, use three cuts to remove a finger." Chuck held the jaws near Kang's left hand, and squeezed them: *snick...snick...snick.* "Which method did you use, Captain Kang?"

Kang's breathing came so fast that he panted like he had run a mile. "I never cut off anyone's fingers. What is that thing? I never see that before." He clenched his hands into fists.

"Personally, I believe it would be effective to remove your fingers one joint at a time." Chuck tapped the back of Kang's hand with the outside edge of the bottom blade. "That will give you ample opportunity to answer my questions..." He held the shears six inches from Kang's nose. "... before you bleed to death."

Chuck stared at Kang's fists. "Did Phillip Franks stop you by clenching his fists? That didn't stop you, did it? It won't stop me either. Or I skip your fingers and start by cutting off your nose." Chuck held the tool's jaws over the end of Kang's nose. "What is your mission in Port City?"

Kang jerked his head back further. "Okay, okay, okay. Take those things away. I'll tell you everything."

And he did. He talked for twenty minutes straight. Chuck didn't need to ask many questions. Kang was a trained investigator and he knew what Chuck wanted to know.

————

Chuck finished with Kang and put the hood back on his head.

He waved his teammates over. "Let's powwow."

Snoop and Angie had parked all the team's vehicles in the warehouse. With their vehicles and the three large SUVs, the staging area was crowded.

The six of them moved far enough away that the kidnappers would not overhear them.

Snoop, Tank, and Angie had observed Chuck questioning Kang. Chuck told them the rest of what Pete found in the file room and what the medical examiner had said about the condition of the body and the manner of Franks's death. "The evidence Pete uncovered convinces me beyond doubt that these eight Chinese tortured Phillip Franks to death. Even if Captain Kang had not confessed."

"Me too," said Hank. "I'm one hundred percent certain they are guilty."

"They would have killed me if you folks hadn't come," Gunner added. "I owe you all big time for the rest of my life. And I mean that."

"Glad we could help, Gunner," said Snoop. To Chuck: "I suggest we dump them and their vehicles in the old phosphate mine at the end of Highway 888 like those hoods from Chicago. No one would ever locate the vehicles or their bodies."

"But we called the cops following that gunfight and gave them our statements," Chuck said. "We didn't break any laws."

Snoop shrugged. "This time we don't call the cops. We dump the vehicles and the bodies. That would drive the Chinese military attaché crazy. His eight soldiers vanish without a trace. *Poof.* A cloud of smoke in a hurricane. It would serve the bastards right." He brushed his palms as if dusting them off. "No muss, no fuss, no diplomatic immunity to U.S. laws."

"It chaps my ass, Snoop, but we need to call Buster Cleveland. Let the Port City cops handle this. We have no choice."

"What about you swearing Phillip Franks's killers would not go to trial," Angie said. "We heard every word that bastard Kang said."

"I never swore, but I understand your meaning. We still need to call Buster."

"What about not letting diplomatic bullshit get these guys off with a slap on the wrist," Hank said. "Remember what happened with Tony

Crucero, that gangster from San Cristobal, with his diplomatic immunity. I never want to attend another funeral like that."

"How about justice for Phil Franks?" Gunner asked. "Sometimes vigilante justice is the only justice available."

"This isn't Afghanistan, Gunner. This is America, and it's too late for Wild West frontier justice. We need to call Buster. We broke Rule Twenty-five by asking Tank and Angie and Snoop to help."

"What's Rule Twenty-five?" Angie asked.

"Rule Twenty-five says: *The best way to keep a secret is to not tell anyone. Second best? Tell one other person. Any more than that, you're kidding yourself.*"

Angie bobbed her head. "I understand, Chuck. You don't know me like you know Snoop, but you can trust me. I won't tell. In fact, I'll pull the trigger on the three prisoners so I'm guilty also."

"I'll do that too," said Tank. "I vote guilty. If you can make their bodies and vehicles vanish without a trace, I say let's do it."

"Guys, it's too late for 'without a trace.' Maybe I need a new rule. Rule Ninety-nine: *Eventually, everything becomes known.* Consider the clues that we've already left. For one thing, Desiree Clover knows what the mission was and where we did it."

Pete said, "You can trust Desiree to keep her mouth shut."

"Forever, Pete? Forever is a long time. Killing the first five soldiers was self-defense. Killing the three remaining prisoners may be justice, but legally it's murder. There is no statute of limitations on murder. Thirty years from now, you might be playing with your grandkids one day and there's a knock on the door."

Chuck motioned to Hank. "The guy at the cruise company read your badge, Hank. Hell, you introduced yourself. If he doesn't remember your name, he'll never forget meeting Tank Tyler. Any little thing can unravel the case, and there are traffic cameras and security cameras everywhere nowadays. Like the company that rented the Expedition. That's a $60,000 car. They can track it with built-in GPS. So can the cops. Once the Chinese Embassy learned their soldiers were missing, the FBI would investigate. I don't want the FBI on my trail. I'd be peeking over my shoulder the rest of my life. So would every one of you."

Chuck shook his head. "Without a trace? That train left the station when we mustered in the parking lot of Atlantic Worldwide Cruise Lines, if not before."

He scanned the group and caught each one's gaze. "You people performed better than any other team I could ask for except the original Triple Seven. You risked your lives for Gunner, and I am so proud of you that I have no words to express my gratitude. I am indebted to each of you forever."

"I'll call Buster," Hank said. "It will be a local investigation, since we rescued the kidnap victim. Buster won't call the FBI. We can keep it a local case."

"Except for the Secret Service," Chuck said. "We mustn't forget the Secret Service. I'm sure they flagged my name. My name will appear in a crime report, and the NSA computer will flash a warning. I expect another visit from Special Agents Valery Villa and Lionel Welsh. If they come, I'll tell them about the counterfeiting."

Hank called Buster Cleveland, then gathered the team together.

"People, once Buster and his team arrive, our explanation is that Chuck called to ask my advice about the imminent danger to Gunner's life. I decided we did not have time for an organized police response. Gunner might be dead before the cops arrived. I assumed command and recruited all of you to rescue Gunner. The building we breached was not someone's home, so the Fourth Amendment protection against unreasonable search and seizure doesn't apply. We had exigent circumstances. Gunner's life was in imminent danger."

He grinned. "Hell, they'll give me a medal for initiative instead of a black mark in my personnel file."

Too late, Chuck realized Gunner's kidnapping had kept him from arranging to tail the Russians that afternoon. It was already dark. Had they discovered where Aisha lived? Chuck couldn't do anything about it, but it bothered him. A lot. There was no predicting what the Russians would do if they cornered Aisha. Chuck couldn't warn her since he didn't have her phone number.

Chuck spent the half-hour until Cleveland's crime scene team arrived copying the Chinese soldiers' cellphone SIM cards and memory chips. He hooked each phone to his laptop and copied the contact lists, call history, text messages, and so forth to the hard drive. Might be useful later. Rule Six.

Chuck sent Snoop and Angie to move the team's vehicles back to the front parking lot. He wouldn't leave them inside the warehouse where they might be impounded as evidence.

Angie examined all eight key rings. "Chuck, each soldier had copies of these two Kwikset house keys," she said, holding them up. "Probably one for the doorknob and one for a deadbolt. This brand is commonly used on rental property. It's easy to rekey the locks for new tenants."

"Let me have Kang's keys."

She handed them to him.

One key looked like a padlock key. He removed it and shoved it in his pocket. He gave the key ring back.

"Okay, remove those two keys from every key ring except Kang's and give them to me."

Angie removed the keys and handed them to Chuck. "If there's the one set on Kang's key ring, it won't be obvious to the Port City cops that those are keys to the house on SW 4th Street. Those might be keys to his apartment in D.C."

"Or Beijing," Chuck said. "That's the idea."

She handed Chuck two more keys. "Why obscure the fact that those are keys to their house?"

"Better you don't know, Angie. Eventually they'll figure it out; just not until tomorrow."

———

Buster Cleveland and Melissa Chan arrived with the CSI crew and an extra van because of the volume of evidence to transport. Chuck walked Cleveland and the CSI videographer around the building for a quick tour to familiarize the detective with the background for the statements Chuck's team would give.

Captain Kang flashed his diplomatic passport and demanded to speak to the Chinese Embassy. Cleveland replaced Chuck's team's cable ties with handcuffs and moved Kang and the other two survivors aside. He called the FBI.

Kang regarded Chuck with eyes black as midnight and equally menacing. "You treated me with disrespect, McCrary. This isn't over."

"It's over for you, Kang. The Port City cops will turn you and your men over to the FBI. The U.S. State Department will declare you *persona non grata* and give your government 72 hours to get you out of the country."

"That is true," Kang said, "but this is not over. Not between you and me. You were disrespectful to me and to the Chinese people. That will not stand. Airplanes that fly from Washington to Beijing also fly back. Look over your shoulder, McCrary. One time when you look, I will be there."

Once Kang had the Port City cops here to protect him, Chuck thought, *he got very brave. Still, I hope that's just bluster.*

The ambulances hauled the wounded off to the nearest hospital and the bodies to the Medical Examiner's office. Kang glared at Chuck until the FBI hauled him away.

Cleveland hauled over a folding chair and sat near Chuck. "We'll need to run prints and do ballistics and fill out a ton of paperwork, but it's clear you solved the murder of Phillip Franks. It's a shame we have to invest department resources to prove the Chinese murdered Phil Franks. We can't hold them. They have diplomatic status. But regardless of that, you did a hell of a job and I thank you."

Cleveland peered both ways. The two men were off to themselves. "Sometimes you cut corners, but if you and Hank hadn't jumped on Gunnar Knutson's kidnapping when you did, he would have wound up floating in Seeti Bay like your friend Phil Franks. You may have a reputation as a loose cannon, but sometimes a cannon ball is the best way to bust through obstacles."

He shook Chuck's hand. "Okay. Now I have to get back to work and close out this crime scene."

———

Cleveland and Chan finished the team's statements at midnight. The CSIs were photographing, measuring, and bagging everything from the tools in the storage room to the shell casings scattered around the warehouse. They bagged Chuck's armored vest with the slug embedded in it. Oddly, Chuck was the only person shot in the vest. Lucky him. They collected the guns the team had fired to do ballistics tests. They would document who shot who and reconstruct the entire rescue mission. Chan dropped Chuck's gun in an evidence bag. "I'll return this to you ASAP, but it will be two or three days."

"No problem, Lissa. I keep spare guns and ammo in a gun safe built into my van."

Chuck sent his people home for a good night's rest after a job well done.

It had been a long and eventful day, but—to quote Robert Frost—he still had promises to keep and miles to go before he could sleep.

FOURTEEN

Returning to his Caravan, Chuck opened the bag of burgers which Snoop had brought. The one that remained still smelled good, but it had sat in the van for ten hours or more. No way Chuck would eat that burger. Too big a risk of food poisoning.

He stopped at an all-night fast-food restaurant. He hadn't eaten since afternoon. Two cheeseburgers, a large order of French fries, and two cups of coffee later he felt like a new man. Well, almost. Every time he moved, he felt that hellacious bruise where the bullet had slammed into his armored vest.

At 1:30 on a Wednesday morning, SW 4th Street was deserted and the neighborhood was quiet. Chuck stopped in the circular driveway at 5221.

Chuck didn't know what he would learn, but this was his best—maybe only—opportunity to search the house. Kang had threatened to assassinate Him. He might learn something useful to defend himself from Kang if push came to shove.

Exiting the van, he scanned the surroundings. A dog barked twice in the distance. A gentle breeze ruffled the palm fronds. The stars were visible despite the light pollution from a city with millions of people. The house was dark. Both Kang and Bohai swore they brought eight men, but Chuck believed Rule Twelve: *People lie. If they don't lie, they can be mistaken.*

He wasn't worried about mistakes, but he figured someone lied about something. They always do.

Best to assume the house was occupied and the occupants were expecting him.

Chuck drew his spare Glock 17 before he unlocked the dead bolt and the doorknob. Throwing the door open, he dived in low and rolled to the side, avoiding the dim light spilling through the doorway. He lay still and listened.

Nothing.

The burglar alarm beeped. The keypad was where Kang said it would be. Holding his Glock, Chuck keyed the alarm code and the beeping stopped.

The air in the entry smelled like a men's locker room mixed with a Chinese restaurant and a hint of ashtray.

Chuck cleared each room. After confirming the house was empty, he returned to the entry and did a systematic hunt.

The house was the worst bachelor living arrangements he could imagine. That accounted for the locker room whiff.

Did soldiers live like pigs in the People's Liberation Army? American army barracks were cleaned every day.

Chuck was glad he had worn nitrile gloves. He tossed the unmade beds and the dirty clothes piled in corners. He inspected the dirty dishes on every counter. He peeked in the overflowing trash cans and eyeballed inside the tanks of the filthy toilets.

In the toilet tank in the master bedroom, Chuck fished out a plastic bag with two currency straps of U.S. hundred-dollar bills and an envelope full of loose hundreds. Each of the straps held $10,000. He stuffed both straps in his pocket. The envelope held another fifty bills. He counted out ten, left them for the CSIs to find, and folded the other $4,000 into another pocket. The Port City CSIs would impound the $1,000. Months from now, after the case was closed, the U.S. State Department would return the money to the Chinese government.

The money Chuck confiscated would cover part of his expenses for the rescue mission. Spoils of war, which he would split with Gunner.

Three closets held pistols, machine guns, cases of grenades of various types and boxes of ammunition. Chuck had flash-bang grenades and smoke grenades, but he didn't own a fragmentation grenade. He stole four to add to his own armory. Rule Nine: *You can never carry too much firepower.*

Chuck didn't find any armored vests and they hadn't found any in the gang's SUVs. Perhaps life is that cheap in the People's Paradise. Why else would they not provide body armor?

Another closet with built-in shelves contained spy gear: binoculars, telephoto cameras, GPS trackers, two-way radios, and syringes and vials of assorted drugs.

The five bedrooms and the living room had ashtrays on every flat surface. Some had been emptied but none had been washed.

The pantry and refrigerator were filled with Chinese food ingredients. That accounted for the Chinese restaurant aroma. The gang did its own cooking rather than eating out. That made sense; they kept a low profile.

The dining room table had eight chairs arranged around it. The table had been cleared and was reasonably clean.

Light from the streetlamps seeped through the trees into the backyard. Chuck shined his Maglite at the swimming pool. It was green and cloudy. The pool was too dirty to see the bottom. The CSIs would drain it to reveal any evidence it contained. The grass in the fenced backyard was over a foot high. Since the front lawn was well-trimmed, Chuck assumed someone had been hired to maintain the sections the public saw.

Returning to the kitchen, he opened the door to the garage, reached in, and flipped on the lights.

The garage smelled…different. Not exhaust fumes or rubber tires or lawn equipment with dead grass in it. Just…different. Something in the back corner of Chuck's brain woke, but he couldn't place the odor.

A concrete platform four inches tall and four feet wide stretched the length of the back wall. A water heater was installed on the platform near the kitchen. Next to the water heater, an air-conditioning unit reached its duct through the ceiling.

A washer and dryer were centered on the platform beside a laundry sink. On the other side of the sink a waist-high cabinet with a chipped laminated countertop had empty shelves above. No detergent, no fabric softener, no dryer sheets.

As Chuck stepped to the washer and dryer, the mysterious odor became stronger. That back corner of his mind complained.

He peeked inside the washer and dryer. Empty. Who did the Chinese soldiers' laundry?

Opening the cabinet doors, he squatted to check inside. A built-in shelf stretched across the storage space. It was empty of everything but a pervasive odor.

A storage closet was built into the far corner of the platform next to the counter. It had a shiny new steel hasp and a serious padlock.

Nothing else in the house was locked. Why this closet?

Chuck found the key from Kang's key ring. It fit the lock. He popped the lock and opened the closet door.

The odor became a stench.

The closet was empty except for a gallon-sized glass jar on the floor in the back corner. Perhaps it was the stench, but that lone jar sitting in the shadow seemed sinister. Whatever it was, Captain Kang considered it important enough to install a padlock. The jar was filled with a yellow liquid. It reminded Chuck of specimen jars he handled in his high school biology class, the ones with a pig's heart or a calf's brain.

That back corner of his mind screamed a warning.

He edged closer to the jar and shined a Maglite on it.

Chuck's stomach rebelled. He barely made it to the utility sink before he barfed his midnight meal.

The jar contained severed finger joints.

––––––

After the shock of finding Phil's finger joints in a jar of formaldehyde, Chuck cleaned the vomit from the utility sink. Luckily it washed down the drain. He ran the water another five minutes to wash all trace of vomitus to the sewer.

Chuck retraced his steps in the house to ensure there was no evidence he had been there.

Sitting in the Caravan, he composed himself before he drove home.

Chuck had been under unrelenting stress for eighteen hours. He was close to exhaustion. *I'm the World's Greatest Private Investigator,* he thought, *but I'm not Superman.* The aftermath of an adrenaline high lasts until you decompress. Chuck usually chilled in a couple of hours. He'd lived through several adrenaline-charged events in the last twenty-four hours with not enough decompression in between. The discovery of Phil's finger joints was the straw that broke the camel's back, or, in this case, the gag that made not-Superman Carlos McCrary toss his cheeseburgers.

Would Kang want to collect Chuck's finger joints if he returned to Port City? He couldn't enter the USA as a diplomat because of the *persona non grata* status. He would either enter illegally or as a private citizen. Either way, he would be fair game. Chuck almost hoped Kang would return to hunt him. Kang and Chuck had unfinished business.

Chuck fell into bed at 3:15 a.m. and slept ten hours. He dreamed of bloody pruning shears and Chinese soldiers ten feet tall.

―――――

Chuck ate a late breakfast and drove to Jerry's Gym to work out. Kennedy Carlson motioned him over to the reception desk.

"My newsfeed this morning said you and your friends had a gunfight with a dozen Chinese soldiers who kidnapped Gunner. How is he? Gym members are asking. He doesn't answer his phone."

"Gunner will be okay. It was eight Chinese, not twelve. They injected him with sodium thiopental and beat him up. Once the cops finished taking his statement, I sent him home to rest. He'll be back to normal in a day or two."

"Normal?" Kennedy said. "What the hell is normal in the universe where you guys live? The news report said he was blindfolded in the middle of a freaking gun battle. I would have permanent mental scars if that happened to me."

"The good news is Gunner was unconscious from the drugs during the gunfight. He didn't learn about it until later. Gunner and I served in Iraq and Afghanistan. We're no strangers to gun battles."

Chuck clapped the Gym owner on the shoulder. "Thanks for asking, Ken, and thanks for caring."

"He's had enough sleep by now" Ken said. "I'll call him again."

Chuck put his hand over Ken's phone. "Don't bother trying. Gunner doesn't have his phone. When the Chinese shoved him into the SUV, he stuffed his phone behind a seat so I could track him. The CSIs impounded the vehicle and haven't released his phone. I told him I'd pay to buy him a new one today. He'll call us with the new number when he gets it. I haven't heard from him either, but I'm not worried."

Chuck walked toward Kennedy's office. "Now let's lock my weapons in your safe so I can work out. I have heavyweight thinking to do."

Physical exercise put Chuck's body on autopilot and allowed his mind to reflect on facts, options, and theories. He needed to warn Aisha and Billow. They had to contend with the Russians, even if the Chinese didn't send more men. But how to get in touch with them? Chuck didn't have Aisha's phone number or email address.

But he knew where she lived.

———

Chuck ate dinner early and waited for Aisha at her apartment, parking near the bottom of the stairs.

The traces of twilight had faded when she and Duman parked across the street.

Chuck opened the driver's door and stood beside his van.

Aisha and Duman paused for two cars to pass before they crossed the street. She wore the gold-trimmed hat she wore the first time Chuck tailed her. This time she wore an ankle-length white layered skirt and a dark gray vest reaching to her thighs. Duman was dressed in a Chicago Bears tee-shirt and blue jeans. They both wore plain leather sandals.

Chuck walked to the bottom of the stairs that led to their apartment.

As the siblings reached the parking lot, a black Chevy Suburban rolled into view. There were thousands of similar SUVs, but this one was so familiar that Chuck's gut clenched.

He jerked his jacket to one side and drew his Glock 17.

The black SUV squealed into the lot behind Aisha and Duman and slammed to a stop. All four doors opened and four men jumped out. They were focused on Aisha and Duman and didn't notice Chuck.

Chuck assessed the field of fire behind the bad guys. No one a stray bullet might strike. He sidestepped for a clear shot. "Police! You men, stop where you are. Hands up and get on your knees. *Now.*" Holding a two-handed grip, he walked smoothly toward the men. "I've called backup. Down on the ground."

Aisha and Duman spun to the men behind them but neither one moved.

All four men drew pistols.

Oh, crap, Chuck thought. *Now they've done it.*

"Aisha," he shouted, "Duman, run!"

Two men charged toward Chuck and two dodged behind the open front doors of the Suburban. *That was a boneheaded move,* Chuck thought. *Bullets slice through those doors like tissue paper.*

Chuck squeezed off two rounds at the charging man closest to him. The shooter fired in the air as he fell.

"Run, dammit," Chuck shouted again and leapt to one side. He landed prone on the pavement, rolling sideways.

The other three fired. Bullets whanged off the pavement.

A bullet ripped through Chuck's jacket, missing his ribs by inches.

"Run like hell."

Chuck fired from a prone position, hitting a second man in the leg, and rolled behind a parked car. Bullets whizzed past him. Others punched holes in the car he lay behind.

The siblings ran toward the apartment building.

Chuck crabbed around the parked car and fired three rounds through the Suburban door on the near side. The man behind it fell to the pavement. Chuck couldn't see the fourth man, but he had to be crouching on the far side.

The man with the wounded leg struggled to stand. Another stupid decision; he could shoot sitting on the pavement. Chuck shot his other leg and he collapsed again. His pistol scooted across the pavement out of reach.

Chuck dropped prone on the pavement. He saw the fourth man's feet underneath the SUV. No hurry; the fourth man wasn't going anywhere. Chuck's ears rang like church bells. *Easy squeezy, nice and easy,* he thought. Chuck hit him with the third shot, and the gunman fell to a sitting position.

Chuck changed to a full magazine, walked over to the SUV, and kicked the weapons away from the shooters. He frisked each of the shooters, but found no weapons. Two were wounded and two were probably dead. He backed away until he covered all four with the pistol in his right hand. Chuck used his left to call 9-1-1.

"9-1-1. What's your emergency?"

"Four men attempted to kill me. I wounded all four. My name is Carlos McCrary. I am a licensed private investigator with a concealed weapon permit." He gave the operator the address. "We're in the Village of Seaside city limits. Send Atlantic County sheriff's deputies."

"Was there anyone else hurt, sir?"

"No. I am holding the four attackers at gunpoint until the deputies arrive."

"Please keep this line open until help arrives."

"Okay."

Aisha stood behind the concrete stairway next to Duman. "Is it safe to come out?"

"Yes. I disarmed them and the police are on the way."

She walked over to Chuck. "Who are you? Are you the police?"

Chuck smiled. "Nah. The odds were four to one. I tried to counterbalance bad odds by pretending to be a cop. I'm Carlos McCrary. I was in the army with Andy Billow and Phillip Franks. Here, hold this phone. I need to take something from my pocket."

Chuck had brought an eight-by-ten of the Triple Seven, the photo that hung on his office wall—identical to the one in Phil Franks's sock. Chuck held the picture where the light from the stairway lit it. He handed it to her and retrieved his phone. "That's me in the picture. I was in the Triple Seven Special Forces Unit."

Aisha touched the surface of the photo. "I recognize that picture. Andy has one just like it." She spoke with a trace of an accent.

"Soon, the police will arrive to investigate the shooting," Chuck said.

"They will interview you both and me too. That requires an hour or longer. After they finish, I'd like to talk with you and your brother."

Duman Aubakirovich stepped in front of her, protectively Chuck thought. "How do you know my name?" He had a pronounced accent.

"It's my job to know your name. I'm a private investigator searching for Andrew Billow. I hope you and Ms. Aubakirovna will help me."

Aisha touched Duman's arm. "Andy speaks well of Carlos McCrary. We should invite him in for tea after the police finish with us."

"Not here," Chuck said. "The Russians know you live in this building. If we're lucky, they don't know which unit is yours, but it won't them take long to figure it out."

"But they're dead or captured. We're safe."

"No, Aisha. There are more gunmen where they came from. They will send more after you. You and Duman and Andrew remain in danger."

Two patrol cars arrived, trailed by four ambulances.

"For now, let's cooperate with the police."

The police that came were Atlantic County Sheriff's Deputies. The Village of Seaside didn't have its own police force. Like many smaller towns and villages, it contracted with Atlantic County to provide police services.

———

Two hours later the deputies finished with them. Chuck lingered until both patrol cars left.

"The Surfside Diner is a good local restaurant. I'll drive."

Aisha glanced at Duman. "Since the Russians found us, we'll need to rent another apartment." To Chuck: "Yes, restaurant is fine." She opened the front passenger door. Duman got in back.

The dynamic between the two siblings was clear. Aisha spoke first. Aisha decided to talk to Chuck. Aisha decided they would change apartments. Aisha sat in the front seat. Aisha was in charge.

After they parked at the Surfside Diner, Aisha exited the car and led the way inside. She picked a booth without asking Chuck's opinion. Yes, Aisha was in charge.

She patted the bench beside her and Duman slid in. Chuck wondered if he resented his younger sister bossing him around.

Chuck sat across.

Aisha interlaced her fingers on the table. "Andrew is fine. He is working at Southeast Printing and Binding."

The server brought them menus.

It was hours since Chuck had eaten his early dinner and he was hungry again. "We should eat. I'll buy."

Aisha smiled at the server. "Please give us a minute to decide. You might bring us three glasses of water." The boss-lady, bossing again. If it made her comfortable that was a good thing. Women had bossed Chuck around since he was a baby. Didn't bother him.

The server walked away.

Aisha leaned toward Chuck. "As I said, Andy is fine. But let's order." She studied her menu. Duman and Chuck did too.

The server returned with three glasses of ice water and utensils.

"I'll have the chef's salad with Thousand Island dressing," Aisha said.

Chuck waited for Duman. "Sirloin steak, please, and mashed potatoes and zucchini squash, please."

"How would you like your steak?"

Duman said something to Aisha in a language Chuck didn't recognize. Kazakh or Russian or maybe Turkic, if that was a language.

Aisha replied in what Chuck assumed was the same language. Her sentence ended with "well done" in English.

Duman smiled. "Ah, yes."

He pivoted to the server. "Well done, please."

The server scribbled on her pad. "And you, sir?"

"I'll have what he's having. Make mine medium rare."

She noted the order and walked away.

Once she was out of earshot, Chuck said, "Billow's cellphone was disconnected and he hasn't spoken to his parents in weeks."

"He is busy," Duman said.

"Billow is in great danger. Do you know what happened to Phillip Franks?"

Aisha's erect posture deflated. "Unfortunately, yes. When Phil disappeared, we realized something bad had happened but we didn't know what. Then we saw on the television that his body had been found." Tears glistened in her eyes. "To die that way..." She daubed her eyes with a napkin. "He was a hero."

Duman sat, oblivious to their discussion. Chuck wondered how well he got by when Aisha was not with him.

"Where did you last see him?"

Aisha fought back the tears. She signaled Duman to speak.

"At the shop. Many of us order pizza for dinner and Phil drive to pick up pizza. He never come back."

"When was that?"

"Friday, January 10. I remember because Kusainovs pay. It was... celebration?" he said to Aisha.

She nodded.

He faced Chuck again. "Yes, *celebration* that work for week was finish. But no more pizza."

"You don't do it anymore?"

"After Phil disappear, we are more...careful. We do not celebrate end of week after Phil's death. We work weekends now, so the work week do not end. And we buy guns. Lots of guns. Everyone in shop is armed."

"How many of you?"

"We are ten men plus Aisha and two other women."

"Are you all from Kazakhstan?"

"One man from Kyrgyzstan."

"How many of you are trained soldiers?"

"Andrew and one other man. He was in the Kyrgyzstan police."

Oh, great. Lots of guns in untrained, but dedicated hands. What could possibly go wrong? This would make a good lead-in for a funny home video.

"Were you aware that I captured the people who killed Phillip Franks and turned them over to the Port City police?"

They glanced at each other. She shrugged.

"It happened last night so it wouldn't be in today's newspapers or television news until later. If you worked all day, you wouldn't have known."

Chuck told them about Gunner being kidnapped and about the rescue. Midway through his story, the server brought their food. They stopped talking while she served and left.

Aisha began to toss her salad. "That was very dangerous for you and your men."

"And woman. One team member is a woman."

Chuck cut a bite of steak. It was perfectly cooked and smelled delicious.

"It was dangerous, yes, but Gunner is a Triple Seven. We are brothers." Chuck lifted the bite to his mouth. The aroma made his mouth water.

"And since you caught the killers, why are you here?" Duman said. He cut his steak into pieces.

"The Chinese will not give up. We killed or captured the eight they sent. Next time they will send more men. There are over 2,000,000 soldiers in the People's Liberation Army. What's ten or twelve more? They intend to kill Billow and anyone else involved with your...*project*. That's why I need to talk to Andy. To make sure he is safe and stays that way. His parents worry about him, not to mention Gunner and Hank Ramirez and me."

"Andy is safe," Aisha said. "As I said, he works at the print shop."

Chuck lowered his voice. "The Chinese captured and killed Phil Franks. He was a professional soldier in the most elite fighting force in the world. Yet they captured him. They also captured my friend Gunner, another highly-trained professional soldier. They want to capture and kill Andy also. These men are serious and they are expert. The Chinese are the enemies who located you first."

"And they are gone, yes?"

"Only until the Communist Chinese government sends more men. But that's not the only danger you face. The four gunmen who tried to kidnap you tonight were Russian. They have located you."

Duman said, "Russians too. This is bad."

"I understand the Chinese interest in your, uh, *project*. But why the Russians?" Chuck asked.

Duman sipped his water. "What project?"

"The counterfeiting of Kazakh currency to finance the Turkic Liberation Army."

"We don't know what you're talking about," Aisha said.

Of course not. Well, it's never easy.

"Before Phil died, the Chinese learned everything he knew about you, the print shop, and your project. I captured the leader of the Chinese kidnappers, and I forced him to tell me everything he knew and everything he learned from Phil Franks. I know about the paper from Xinjiang. I know about the Heidelberg printer. I know Andy prints the money."

Duman ate without looking up. How much did he understand?

"I'm not a cop. I don't care if you counterfeit foreign currency." That wasn't true. Chuck wanted to stop the whole mess, but he also wanted their cooperation. "My mission is to make sure Andy doesn't end up floating headless and handless in Seeti Bay. Andy is a brother to me and Hank and Gunner. We will do anything we can to keep him safe. We are not your enemy. It's true that we are not your ally, but at least we want to keep Andy safe."

Chuck ate a little zucchini and added pepper while the two of them pondered what he had said.

"Do you know what the Secret Service is?"

"They guard the president of the United States," Aisha said.

"That's true, but that's not all. They are responsible for preventing counterfeiting and for capturing counterfeiters. Like you two, Andy, and the Kusainovs. Were you aware Vladimir Kusainov served time in prison for counterfeiting?"

Duman said to Aisha, "I did not know this. Did you?"

"No. He said he was an experienced printer on highly technical print jobs."

"Vladimir is on probation for his counterfeiting conviction," Chuck said. "Do you understand what probation means?"

Aisha said, "He cannot commit another crime or he goes back to prison with no trial."

"That's correct. The Secret Service does not know about this current project, but they are suspicious. They keep surveillance on Vladimir electronically. I investigated Vladimir on the internet and the Secret

Service found out. The next morning, they had gotten a search warrant, and they swooped down on my office like a hawk on a field mouse. They questioned me about Vladimir. Now they know my interest in Vladimir, they will have an electronic alarm set for any mention of me in the news or in police reports. They will hear of my rescue of Gunner Knutson and the involvement of the Chinese Peoples' Liberation Army. Tomorrow morning, they will learn about my shootout with the Russian gangsters and they will have your names from the police report. Knowing you two and Andy are involved with Vladimir, the Secret Service will investigate you all." Chuck cut another bite of steak while he let them chew on that idea.

Duman broke the silence. "We do not print U.S. dollars."

"I would bet that a U.S. treaty forbids counterfeiting other nations' currencies," Chuck said. "The U.S. government has long arms. They reach everywhere. Believe me: Your counterfeiting scheme is over. It's only a matter of hours before the Secret Service finds out what you've been doing."

"Surely, it does not violate U.S. law to print a foreign currency?" Aisha said.

"Are you willing to serve fifteen or twenty years in a federal prison if you're wrong? Believe me, Aisha, I don't want that to happen to you or to Andy. To prevent that, I need to talk to Andy. By tomorrow, the Secret Service will be tapping your phones. If I give you a burner phone that the Secret Service can't tap, will you give it to Andy and ask him to call me?"

Aisha glanced at Duman. He shrugged.

Chuck extended a burner phone to her. "You have nothing to lose."

She accepted the phone. "I will give it to him in the morning."

"And Aisha and Duman, do not tell the Kusainovs I am here or that Andy is communicating with me. Tell Andy not to confide in the Kusainovs."

"But Duman and I work with the Kusainovs. They help us finance the liberation army."

"Perhaps. Or else they're using you to make a fast fortune for themselves. It is better for you and Duman and Andy to have options. If the Kusainovs know I'm here to help you, you have fewer options."

After dinner, Chuck took the siblings back to their car.

"You are no longer safe in your apartment. I don't know why the Russians are after you, but the reason isn't important. The fact is: They want you. More Russians could come for you tonight. You both should stay in a hotel tonight. Just abandon the furniture and clothes in your current apartment."

"We can't afford to lose our furniture and clothes," Aisha said.

"Can you afford to lose your life? The Russians will have the building under surveillance. Start fresh in another apartment. Get rid of the Toyota, and buy a different car. These Russians are not amateurs. You were lucky I was there tonight. Next time, they will be expecting me or someone like me."

———

Billow called at 8:30 the next morning.

"Are you alone?" Chuck asked.

"Yes. Aisha said not to tell the Kusainovs about this phone or about you."

"How long can we talk without them becoming suspicious?"

"I'm in the bathroom, so…five minutes?"

"Were you aware that we caught the men who killed Phil Franks?"

"Aisha told me. I haven't had a chance to catch television news. She said it was the Chinese."

"Yeah. And we killed five of the eight men who did it." Chuck didn't feel as satisfied with that outcome as he sounded, but he wanted Billow to drop the whole revenge thing.

"Aisha told me the other three have diplomatic immunity," Billow said.

"Yes. Actually, they all had diplomatic immunity, but they were shooting at us, so it was self-defense on the five we killed. The other three surrendered. There were too many witnesses for us to execute them. We would never get away with it, so we turned them over to the Port City cops. They gave them to the Feds. The Feds released them. The Feds have expelled them from the U.S. or will in the next couple of days."

"Too bad."

"The good news is we accomplished our mission. We caught the men

194

who killed Phil, and we did kill five of the eight in rescuing Gunner. Now we need to extricate you from this counterfeiting mess. The Secret Service is sniffing around. They interrogated me. You face twenty-five years in prison, bro. Get out of there before it's too late."

"Can't do that, Chuck. Aisha and Duman are fighting to free an oppressed people. I'm in this for the woman I love."

Oh, crap. That was what Chuck was afraid Billow would say. Billow was motivated by duty, honor, and love. It was a heady brew of ideals that Chuck couldn't fight over the telephone. He needed to talk face to face with his friend.

"Okay," Chuck said. "Do you have private access to the internet?"

"No. The one computer I can access is in the office. They would know if I logged onto their Wi-Fi with this cellphone. There's a workaround: I can mute the phone and you can text me. That's the only way to communicate. We're staying incommunicado in the shop since Phil disappeared. His murder freaked us out. The Kusainovs are serious as a funeral about security."

"And for good reason. Both the Russians and the Chinese are sniffing around the print shop probing for weaknesses. Did Aisha tell you that the Chinese kidnapped Gunner? That's how we proved they were Phil's killers."

"Yeah," Billow said, "and she told me about your gunfight with four Russians last night. You saved her ass. Hers and Duman's. Thanks for being there."

"Sometimes it's better to be lucky than smart. I was in the right place at the right time. But I may not be there the next time they attack."

"She's out renting a new apartment today. Those bastards are getting close."

"And we can't be sure who 'those bastards' are, Andy. Might be the Russians or the Chinese. Might be someone we haven't thought of. Whoever the bad guys are, they know Aisha's car."

"Don't worry. She borrowed a car from a guy who works here. She's using it to rent a new apartment."

"The Russians and the Chinese will both send more men. Also, I guarantee you the Secret Service will be all over Southeast Printing and

Binding like a cat on a June Bug. We need to meet in person, Andy: you, me, Gunner, and Hank. We have some planning to do."

If Chuck got Billow alone, away from the influence of Aisha and the Kusainovs, he hoped he could talk sense into him, especially with Gunner and Hank to help. "We need to battle plan. Can you get away from the Kusainovs?

"Sure. I take the night off every Friday. I go home with Aisha. We go out to dinner, then we spend the night together. We joke and call it our 'conjugal visit.' That's tomorrow night. If Aisha hasn't rented a new apartment by then, I'll meet her at a nice hotel."

"Can you get away from Aisha for a couple of hours?" Chuck asked. "Maybe meet at the house of one of my friends? It's three or four miles from your current apartment."

"Why not meet at your condo? It's closer."

"After the Chinese and Russians both shot me, I'm as serious about security as *two* funerals. The Chinese spotted Phil Franks and Gunner. And the Russians are still around. Someone might know where I live, and the location of my office is public record. It's not safe to meet either place. I have a friend who lives on a secure private island. No one gets on that island without an invitation. I'll clear it with him and text you the address."

"Oh, geez. Tomorrow is Valentine's Day. No way I can blow off Aisha on Valentine's Day. How about Saturday morning?"

"I forgot Valentine's Day," Chuck said. "I'm sure Hank wouldn't leave Mariana alone tomorrow night either. Yeah, we'll meet first thing Saturday morning. Say, eight o'clock?"

"Nine would be better."

Chuck thanked his lucky stars Billow had mentioned Valentine's Day. In typical Chuck McCrary style, he had forgotten. He ordered two dozen roses sent to Ruby's lab at the Austin Police Forensic Science Division building and two dozen to Vicky Ramirez at her office. That way, both women's colleagues would know they had an admirer. Couldn't hurt.

He also sent a dozen to Bettina Simpson, a Houston cop who had helped him with a case a few years before. Bettina and Chuck also had a brief fling. Chuck had sent her flowers every Valentine's Day since.

FIFTEEN

Chuck understood China's interest in the counterfeiting. They wanted to prevent a revolution in Xinjiang province. But why were the Russians interested? So much had happened that it was hard for Chuck to believe he had discovered the George Alexander connection only a week ago.

It was time to shake the bushes and pursue anything that flew out. Or slithered out. The target: George Alexander at his office.

Chuck set up Snoop to stake out Alexander's building until he flushed Alexander from his office.

Snoop was skeptical, but that was typical. "How will I recognize this guy stepping off the elevator? A twenty-year-old college yearbook picture is worthless. I might tail somebody who sneaked off early for a weekend in the Keys. Should I call you if the guy I tail passes Key Largo?"

"That's what I love about you, Snoop. Always the optimist. I'll snap a picture of him with my phone and text it to you. How's that?"

"That's real subtle, bud. I can picture it now: Say cheese, George. I want your picture for my scrapbook. There's gotta be a reason no one's photographed him in the last twenty years."

"Sure, it may not work, but give it a shot. If it doesn't work, we're no worse off than we are now."

He grumbled, but that's Snoop's hobby—grumbling. He was a Certified Grouch as far as Chuck was concerned. Once Snoop got a few years older, he would be eligible for the Grand Curmudgeon title.

Chuck parked in the garage next to George Alexander's office building and walked to the building lobby. The building directory didn't list any major-league tenants: no big banks or insurance companies or major law or accounting firms. Offices of start-up businesses, engineers, surveyors, small insurance agencies, small law firms, and lots of empty space. The building was Class B space when it was new. Time had passed it by. Soon a developer would buy the twenty-story building and replace it with a fifty-story condo with a swimming pool and an expensive restaurant on the roof.

Rising to the twelfth floor, the noisy elevator vibrated and shook. Chuck hoped it was up to the challenge. He put his faith in the Atlantic County elevator inspector and assumed the building management wasn't bribing anyone. The doors creaked open to an empty corridor in need of a fresh coat of paint.

The plaque on the door said *G. Alexander, Esq. Suite 1212.*

The door was locked. Not many offices were locked at 10:45 a.m. on a Thursday. Alexander must not get drop-in business. Or he worked by appointment only. Or he was visiting the two Russian gunmen in the jail ward at Port City Medical Center. Or arranging funerals for the other two.

Chuck set down his briefcase and rapped on the door with a cop knock. *Bam-Bam-Bam* with the side of his fist. Nothing.

Next, he thumped the door with the butt of his pistol. *Bang-Bang-Bang.* He reholstered his Glock and paused twenty seconds. More nothing.

Calling Alexander's office number, Chuck heard his phone ring inside. Fifteen rings later, it went to voicemail. A computer told him the mailbox was full. Alexander's listed office number wasn't the one his clients, friends, and family used.

Glancing at the empty hall, Chuck donned a pair of nitrile gloves and picked the lock.

Suite 1212 wasn't a suite. It was a single room with no outside window. Alexander must not be claustrophobic. Chuck stepped in and shut the door.

Alexander's desk had a thin, almost invisible, film of dust on top. He hadn't been in there for weeks.

Chuck called Snoop. "You can go home. He isn't here. I'll ransack his office. Perhaps I'll discover where he lives. If I do, I'll call you back."

Chuck set his briefcase on the desk. He carried burglar tools in it. Nobody suspects a briefcase if a man in a suit is carrying it.

Alexander had officed in the building for nineteen years. His computer equipment and his desk chair were late model, but the remainder of his furnishings and equipment was at least nineteen years old, including the locks on his desk and file cabinets.

Chuck began with the desk. The lock on the center desk drawer would yield to a paper clip. The center drawer held the customary assortment of office sundries and junk. Amidst the junk, Chuck found a key ring with a dozen keys on it. Door keys? They could be extra keys to the buildings he was trustee of.

Chuck used modeling clay from the briefcase and molded impressions of the keys. He had an *I-know-this-guy* relationship with a former Green Beret. After he retired from the army, the Green Beret became a locksmith. He would make Chuck keys from the impressions, no questions asked.

The top left drawer held a Soviet-made Tokarev TT-33 semi-automatic handgun with the Soviet Star and CCCP initials on a round medallion molded into the grip. The pistol was a museum piece from the Soviet era. An ancient box of Soviet-era ammunition sat behind the pistol. The pistol and ammo were far older than Chuck was. Since it was in the left drawer, Chuck surmised that Alexander was left-handed. He sniffed the barrel. It hadn't been fired recently, maybe never. Could be a gift from Alexander's father that laid forgotten in the drawer for nineteen years.

The other thing of interest in the left drawer pedestal was a half-full bottle of 18-year-old Johnnie Walker Gold Label Scotch and four glass tumblers. No vodka. Chuck held the glasses to the light. Polished clean with no fingerprints.

The top drawer on the right held personal mail. Most was addressed to his office, but one envelope was addressed to him at 26 San Marco Drive in a distinctive cursive handwriting that looked foreign. Chuck never knew an American with handwriting in that style. There was no return address, but the envelope was postmarked in Washington, D.C., in 2008, after the anonymous new owner bought the San Marco Island mansion. The envelope contained pictures of a much-younger Alexander and an attractive blonde with three small children. Other photos were vacation pictures in a forested campground and at an amusement park. On the backs were handwritten notes in Russian. They probably said "Here are little Dmitri and Sasha in the Soviet Youth Camp forest outside Minsk. Here are Olga, Dmitri and Sasha at the Che Guevara People's Hero roller coaster at Stalin World Amusement Park." Those were the kind of things Chuck's grandparents wrote on their family photos before the age of digital photography.

Flamer hadn't mentioned anything about Alexander's family or marital status. Why hadn't his family history appeared on Flamer's report? The photos were old. Had the family stayed in Russia? Chuck photographed the front and back of the pictures.

The second drawer held business and personal checkbooks and extra deposit slips. Both accounts were with a large local bank. Chuck photographed blank checks to record the account numbers.

The bottom drawer contained spare printer cartridges and extra paper for the printer-copier-scanner on a side table.

Chuck stuck an eaves-dropping bug underneath the desk's leg space and another one under the side table where the printer-copier-scanner sat.

Alexander's two file cabinets looked original to the office. They had the four-pin cabinet locks that were common at the end of the last century. Easier to pick than his office door. Three drawers of the eight were used. One held folders of his office leases dating back nineteen years. Another drawer held insurance policies, paid bills, and other office files.

The third drawer held twelve folders, one for each Florida Land Trust property for which he was trustee. Chuck opened them on his desk and photographed the pages. Twelve pieces of property and twelve unidentified keys in his desk. *Hmm.* By hook or by crook, Alexander was making money. Would these twelve properties be the key to unlock the source of his income?

Chuck emailed copies of the twelve files to Flamer, asking him to dig deep into the properties, their tenants, their owners, and anything fishy regarding the tenants or leases, if any.

Chuck overturned the desk chair and the four side chairs to check underneath. Nothing there. He emptied all eight file cabinet drawers and all seven desk drawers. He removed them and examined all sides and the bottoms.

He removed the files on the Florida Land Trusts and discovered another file underneath them. It was unlabeled. It contained the Articles of Incorporation for 26 San Marco Drive, LLC. The Registered Agent was George Alexander. The Managing Member was Aleksandr Borisov, George Alexander's father.

George Alexander and his father had run the $6,500,000 scam on Kommerzbank Sachsen. Maybe that's what Alexander did for a living—he was a thief, assisted by his father, Aleksandr Borisov, the Commercial Attaché of the Russian Embassy. What other properties was Alexander trustee for?

Taped on the bottom of the third drawer in the empty file cabinet Chuck found something useful: a list of passwords and two lists of numbers that appeared to be combinations to safes. He photographed the list.

Chuck peeked behind the file cabinets. No safe built into the wall. The safe was likely at 26 San Marco Drive.

Chuck's stomach complained while he waited for Alexander's computer to boot. He hadn't eaten since breakfast, and it was one o'clock. Way past his feeding time. He told his stomach to suck it up, he had work to do. His stomach didn't appreciate that.

Chuck input the PIN code from the password list and copied Alexander's hard drive to an external drive he had brought in his briefcase. If Alexander were sufficiently paranoid, he might keep useful clues on his hard drive.

That would need ninety minutes to copy.

Using Alexander's computer, Chuck logged into the attorney's Cloud files. *Bingo.* He added them to the copy list for his own hard drive.

Having combed the office, Chuck had time to kill.

Calling Tank's regular office number, he told his receptionist his call was not urgent and Tank could call back anytime today, no matter how late.

Chuck read his email on his phone while the hard drive continued copying.

Tank called. "My last appointment didn't use the full time I scheduled. I have ten extra minutes. You called?"

"Yeah. Thank you again for helping me rescue Gunner. You always come through for me, and I appreciate it."

"What are friends for if you can't use and abuse them occasionally? Don't worry; I'll get you back. But that's not all you called about, is it?"

"I reached Billow. I want to meet with him, Gunner, and Hank at your house Saturday morning early to do battle planning. Pink Coral Island is the most secure location in South Florida besides a bank vault."

"How early?"

"Eight o'clock okay?"

"Sure. I'll tell Gregory. How many people will be here?"

"The four of us, unless you want to join in."

"Not unless you need me. It's tax season and I work Saturdays until after April 15th. I will be your muscle whenever you need backup, but battle plans—that's too much for this old pecan farmer. Financial plans, tax plans, and estate plans are my bread and butter. I'll tell Cook to feed the four of you breakfast."

Chuck knew that Tank loved to pretend he was a simple Alabama sharecropper's son. In real life, he passed all four sections of the Certified Public Accountants licensing exam on the first sitting, his IQ was so high it was hard to measure, and he was wealthier than most of his professional athlete financial planning clients. Last year Tank had made *Forbes's* list of the 400 wealthiest Americans. Not bad for a retired professional football player.

"Thanks, Tank. Tell Gregory we'll be there at eight a.m. Tomorrow is Valentine's Day. You have any special lady in your life?"

"Holy crap, I forgot Valentine's Day. I owe you."

The operation in Alexander's office spent five hours and Chuck was hungry enough to eat the plastic mat under the desk chair as he locked everything up.

Since Chuck couldn't provoke George Alexander in his office, he decided to provoke him at his home.

———

Distracted people can make mistakes. Maybe Chuck could force Alexander to make a mistake. He texted Gunner and Snoop to meet him at 26 San Marco Drive.

Gunner replied:

Hooah.

Snoop called. "Bud, there is no way George Alexander will let three strange men into that fortress."

"You and Gunner park on the street outside the wall. One of you shadow him if he makes a break. I'll go in alone."

"Have you been eating nuts from the crazy tree? You would attack the gates of hell with a water pistol. Did you forget this guy sent four gunmen to kill you last night? Do you have a freaking death wish?"

"I wasn't the target, Snoop. They tried to kidnap Aisha."

"To-*may*-to, to-*mah*-to. Where he had four gunmen, he must have more. That's a helluva big house. It would house a private army."

He grumbled again, but he was parked on the grass beside San Marco Drive when Chuck arrived.

The walls around 26 San Marco Drive seemed more forbidding in the late afternoon sunlight than when Chuck first encountered them in the dark. The security cameras loomed ominously, and the steel gates at either side of the property seemed formidable. He was breaking into a fortress. It reminded him of a similar stronghold he once visited on a mountaintop overlooking the capital of *La Republica de San Cristobal* in the Caribbean.

Snoop had parked his Toyota on the grass beside the street. Gunner's Jeep was across the street pointed in the other direction.

Chuck curved into the first of the two driveways. Edging his silver 1963 Studebaker Avanti forward to the call-box, he lowered the window and pressed the call button.

The box clicked. "Yes?"

"Carlos McCrary to see George Alexander."

"Is he expecting you?"

Chuck smiled for the camera he knew was recording him. "Why don't you ask him?"

"Wait there." *Click.*

As if he had a choice. A Jeep Cherokee could crash those gates, but not his precious Avanti with its irreplaceable fiberglass body.

Three minutes later, the box spoke again. "Call Mr. Alexander's office tomorrow for an appointment." The box clicked off.

Chuck pushed the call button again. "I need to talk to him today."

Click. "Mr. Alexander doesn't see anyone without an appointment and he doesn't meet anyone at his home. Ever. Call his office." *Click.*

Chuck pressed the button. "I called his office earlier today. There was no reply and the voicemail box was full."

Click. "Call his office tomorrow." *Click.*

Call button. "No, thank you. I'll wait here until he agrees to see me. I'm in no hurry." He lifted a paper bag and smiled. "I brought sandwiches." He figured Alexander would cave eventually. Chuck lowered the windows and killed the engine. It was a beautiful winter day on fabulous Port City Beach.

He rang Snoop. "Park your car in the other driveway. If he won't let me in, he can't get out."

Ten minutes later, Chuck opened the paper bag and unwrapped a sandwich where the camera could observe him. He toggled the call button again. "I'll eat my first sandwich. I brought several. I'm not moving until I see Alexander, and he's not using these driveways until he sees me." He smiled and took a bite. "Just saying."

That wasn't quite true; Alexander might escape in the 60-foot yacht Chuck noticed moored at the gangster's dock as he drove across the bridge.

Two minutes later, the gate rolled open and Chuck got his first good examination of 26 San Marco Drive. The aerial photos he found online did not do it justice.

In the center of the brick-paved circular driveway, a stainless-steel abstract sculpture was mounted in the middle of a round pool with six gushing fountain jets surrounded by six Royal Palm trees. The so-called artwork resembled a pile of twisted wreckage remaining after a tornado. Somebody had wasted good money to watch jets of water splash on a pile of rubble every day. The landscaping was attractive though.

Chuck cranked the engine and let the Avanti bump over the gate track. The antique car rolled around the circular driveway to the main building.

The steel gate clanged shut behind him. Yep, he had broken into a prison. How would he break out if the visit went to hell? He would improvise something. Perhaps he could dive off the T-shaped dock and swim away.

Outside the steel gate, Chuck heard Gunner's Jeep pull into the driveway to replace the Avanti. With both exits blocked, Chuck was safer. Right?

The circular drive served a parking area large enough to host a frisbee tournament. Mediterranean-style buildings rose on three sides.

It was a house like a famous actor would have built in Beverly Hills during Hollywood's golden age. Chuck expected Bruce Willis or Tom Cruise to greet him at the front door, or Marlon Brando. Yeah, Marlon Brando as the tuxedo-clad Godfather in the opening scene of the movie. This house was perfect for the Godfather's mansion. How do you say "Godfather" in Russian?

At the center, coral stone steps rose to a wide terrace with an Italianate balustrade. The mansion was balanced with matching two-story bungalows with multi-car garages on both sides of the parking area. The whole tableaux made Chuck think of a Moorish castle or maybe a five-star resort in the South of France.

Behind the second-floor windows of one bungalow, three men tracked Chuck with expressionless eyes.

The good news: They weren't aiming rifles at him, and the windows were closed.

The other bungalow had two pairs of matching French doors with gauze curtains and two garage doors. The red-tile roofs reminded Chuck of a monastery he toured during a collegiate summer spent backpacking through Spain.

Chuck locked the Avanti. The classic car was a college graduation present from his grandfather, Magnus McCrary. Magnus named it the *Silver Ghost* back in the days when it had a Citizens Band radio. He bought it used after he mustered out of the Army in the 1960s and kept it for fifty years. Chuck didn't want anyone working for the Godfather to molest the *Silver Ghost* while he was in the lion's den. Or the Russian bear's den.

Chuck stopped at the top of the steps and pivoted a slow 360. No snipers lurking, but you never know. He waved at the three men on the second floor. They didn't wave back. He guessed they weren't the neighborly type.

The carved wooden door on the right opened. Chuck figured he must not be important enough to get the full welcome with both doors.

A stocky fortyish man in a good suit held the door. Chuck thought he could cast him as a villain in a James Bond movie. The suit was tailored to fit both the broad physique of a fighter and a shoulder holster. His scarred face was expressionless as a pile of rocks. He was shorter than Chuck but outweighed him by twenty pounds, all muscle. Hard as a bowling ball. Chuck hoped he never met him in a dark alley. As a boy, the man's light brown hair would have been blond. Now he wore a buzz haircut. Pale blue eyes, cold as marbles. Serviceable black dress shoes with rubber soles. Chuck owned an identical pair of Rockports, except Chuck's were size 12.

"I always say that J.C. Penney makes a nice suit," Chuck said. "The fit is in the tailoring, isn't it?"

Scarface didn't respond. Maybe he spoke only Russian, or he wasn't a conversationalist.

He motioned Chuck inside. The door closed behind Chuck with the sound of a vault door. At least it didn't clang like a prison cell.

The foyer was round and soared to a thirty-foot ceiling with six skylights spaced around the center. Walkways circled the atrium at the second and third floors. Another *James Bond* thug stood on the second-floor walkway and aimed a handgun at the bridge of Chuck's nose.

Chuck waved at him, but the thug ignored him. Probably not accepting new Facebook friends.

A three-tiered wrought iron chandelier hung from the ceiling with lights at each of the three levels. The chain seemed strong enough to hoist an eighteen-wheeler. Or to hang a troublesome Private Eye.

Scarface held out his arms and gave a head jerk for Chuck to do the same.

Chuck extended his arms. While the thug bent over to frisk Chuck's legs, he looked for cameras. Two of them were aimed to capture everything that entered or exited the front doors. That's all Chuck saw.

Frisking Chuck, the thug removed Chuck's Browning .380 from its ankle holster, the Ka-Bar knife strapped to Chuck's left calf, and the Glock clipped behind his back. He found all three of Chuck's cellphones. He arranged each of the weapons and the phones on a tray that sat on a gilded table beneath a decorative mirror the size of a pool table.

All he missed was the ceramic knife strapped to Chuck's left forearm and two wireless bugs in his pants pocket. Scarface patted them while frisking Chuck. "Car keys," he said. The thug bought the lie. Nobody's perfect.

The thug cracked the slimmest of smiles. "You may have your equipment back if we let you leave."

Boy, what a joker.

Chuck glanced up and the thug on the second floor had disappeared. He had stood guard until Scarface finished disarming Chuck.

Scarface did an about-face, his shoes squeaking on the white marble floor. "Follow me."

Chuck shoved both hands in his pants pockets and palmed a wireless bug.

The thug led the way across an interior atrium with a traditional fountain in the center of a garden. Chuck didn't spot any cameras, but they were walking pretty fast. They passed through a living room the size of a tennis court, also no cameras. Alexander didn't want his security people to see what he did inside the house. What happened in the Godfather's mansion stayed in the Godfather's mansion.

That could work to Chuck's advantage if push ever came to shove.

Chuck stuck a bug under a mirror table as he passed. A wall of sliding glass doors across the living room opened to a back garden with amenities any five-star resort would feature, complete with a fifty-foot dock with the giant yacht Chuck observed earlier.

Everything fit the image of the Godfather, but Florida-style instead of New York. Would Chuck find Alexander wearing a tuxedo like the opening of the movie? Perhaps he should have worn his own tuxedo.

Scarface curved down another Mediterranean loggia and stopped three yards from a man seated at a glass-topped table with six fiberglass chairs.

George Alexander was a Russian Godfather, but he was no Marlon Brando. No Al Pacino, either. He was more Jabba the Hutt than John Wayne.

The years since Godfather Alexander smiled for his law school yearbook portrait had treated him harshly. The braided gold necklace he wore was swallowed in the folds of fat on his neck. His thinning hair was dyed a dark brown that conflicted with his wrinkled cheeks and jowls. He was a caricature of a man fighting middle age. And losing. His white guayabera and white pants revealed fat arms and ankles that ended in feet stuffed into white woven-leather sandals.

Chuck was glad he hadn't worn a tux. He would have been overdressed.

Half the table was covered with the remnants of a meal. It was too late for lunch, too early for dinner, but perfect for a fat, aging gangster's mid-afternoon snack.

The Godfather swallowed a long drink from a glass beer mug and wiped his lips with a linen napkin. He belched and stared across the table at Chuck. "Well? You're here. What do you want?"

Chuck dragged a chair out too far, palmed another bug, and sat opposite him.

"I didn't ask you to sit, McCrary."

"You didn't ask me to come see you either, but here I am." He scooted the chair closer to the table, using the motion to mask him sticking a bug underneath the chair.

Scarface reached toward his shoulder holster, but Alexander waved him back. The Godfather belched again. He shrugged. "Who cares? Okay, what the hell do you want? I'm a busy man." His index finger tapped on the table.

Chuck surveyed the opulent surroundings. Except for the leftover mess on the glass-topped table, the uninhabited tableau was an ad from *House & Garden* magazine. "Yeah, I can tell how busy you are."

Alexander regarded him with lizard eyes but said nothing. Chuck looked twice to make sure he was breathing. He was. More's the pity.

"Why did you try to kidnap Aisha Aubakirovna last night?"

He gave Chuck a pretty good poker face, but his eyelids widened a millimeter. His finger stopped tapping, then resumed.

"Who?"

"Aisha Aubakirovna. The woman your four thugs tried to kidnap last night. Why do you want her? What's she to you?"

"I don't know what you're talking about, McCrary. Now, if that's all, you are free to go. Terrence will show you out."

Terrence? Scarface's name was Terrence. How disappointing for him. Hard to intimidate people who knew your name was Terrence. Maybe he wouldn't be so tough in that alley at midnight after all.

"Why did you import those four thugs from Washington six weeks ago?"

"What thugs?"

"The four thugs I videoed driving that Suburban with stolen D.C. plates. The four thugs the Port City Beach cops recorded on video driving that Suburban out your gate with its new Florida license plates. The Suburban that is currently in the Atlantic County Sheriff's impound lot where the criminalists are processing it with a fine-tooth comb."

Chuck looked at his watch.

"I'd bet they show up here within 24 hours with a search warrant. Would you take that bet?"

Alexander's eyes slitted.

"I have nothing to say to you, McCrary."

"Okay, let's consider the $6,500,000 you and your father looted from Kommerzbank Sachsen on the phony foreclosure on this property in 2007 and 2008. How would the Florida Bar Association feel about a member participating in a bank fraud?"

"Number one: Every part of that deal was legal. Number two: If there were fraud, the statute of limitations is five years, six years in some cases. Screw you, McCrary."

"Do you believe your two gunmen in the jail ward at the hospital are willing to take the fall for you? If the Feds don't prosecute them for attempted kidnapping, they face state charges for attempted murder. Even second-degree attempted murder is fifteen years. And discharging a firearm in the commission of a crime draws a minimum twenty years. Your guys were shooting like we were at the pistol range."

Alexander cut his eyes to Terrence, then back to Chuck.

"You've said enough, McCrary. You've overstayed your welcome. Get out." To Terrence: "Be sure to return McCrary's property to him."

He chugged the rest of his beer, stood, and stalked off.

Terrence stepped from the wall. "Follow me."

They retraced their steps to the foyer. Terrence stopped near the front door and gestured to the tray with Chuck's weapons and phones. "Help yourself."

He opened the door and watched Chuck retrieve his gear.

Chuck didn't learn until later that his visit to the bear in his den had not caused Alexander to make a mistake. On the contrary.

SIXTEEN

Friday morning was Valentine's day, and Chuck's girlfriend was fifteen hundred miles away. He might as well work. It was better than moping.

He called Hank at eight a.m. "What did you learn about those four Russians?"

"The Deputy Sheriff on the case is a golf buddy. I'll call him and get back to you."

Hank called ten minutes later. "My buddy identified all four shooters. It's bad news."

"How bad?"

"About as bad as it gets. Two were former Moscow cops, working as enforcers for an oligarch in St. Petersburg—that's in Russia, not Florida. You killed one and the one who survived is thirty-one years old and doesn't speak much English. He's sitting in the jail ward, stalling for his attorney, who he claims is out of town, but will be there to advise him on Monday. Both of them arrived in Washington, D.C., on tourist visas on December 27. The other two shooters are former *Stasi*, the East German secret police. The one you killed was fifty-seven years old. The one in the jail ward is fifty-six. They grew up in Communist East Germany, where the schools required everyone to learn Russian. After East Germany collapsed, these two worked for Kommerzbank Sachsen in Dresden, Germany. Isn't that the bank George Alexander's father owns?"

"Yeah, him and two other former oligarchs."

"They've been on the bank's payroll over thirty years. He says his attorney is out of town and will fly in to advise him on Monday. They came to Washington on tourist visas on December 28."

"Are both using the same attorney?" Chuck asked.

"That's not clear, but we assume so. Doesn't matter. They aren't talking until Monday."

There was nothing Chuck could do about the Russians. At least not now, unless he learned more about the enemy and found a weak spot. If they had one.

For all Chuck knew, George Alexander and his father had an endless supply of Russian gunmen they could turn loose on him.

––––––

Next, Chuck followed up with Buster Cleveland.

"Buster, did your CSIs process the house on SW 4th Street?"

"Yeah, they finished last night. I was about to call you. You want to read the report?"

"Depends. Did they uncover anything useful?"

"Guns, ammo, and some hand grenades, believe it or not. An envelope with ten hundred-dollar bills."

"Anything to tie them to Phillip Franks's murder?"

"Yeah, but I hate to tell you—it's gruesome."

Chuck paused long enough for Cleveland to think he was considering the possibilities. Lowering his voice, Chuck asked, "Did they find his head in the freezer?"

"No, but what they found was almost that bad."

"Let's not play twenty questions, Buster. I'm a big boy. What did they find?"

"Are you sitting down?"

"Geez, Buster, just tell me."

"They discovered a big jar of formaldehyde with a bunch of severed finger joints in it. Medical Examiner ran the DNA. They were Phillip Franks's."

"Jesus Christ," Chuck said, and he wasn't acting. Contemplating his friend's fate again was unnerving. "What was this Kang guy, a demented collector?"

"We don't know why he kept them, Chuck. We found them in a locked closet in the garage. You want a copy of the CSI report?"

"No. I don't need reminding, but thanks for telling me. This can't be easy for you either."

"Over thirty years on the job and I never worked a murder case this gruesome. Anyway, I'm ready to wrap the investigation. A tad more paperwork and we'll tie a red ribbon around it."

"Have you contacted Phil's family in Denver?"

"They're two hours behind us. I'll call them around ten a.m. Colorado time. I suspect this is all of the victim's body we'll recover. I'll ask them what to do with the...You know, years ago folks used to call a dead body the *remains*. With this case, that is in fact true. We have remains."

"Yeah, I never thought of remains that way. Send Hank and me a text after you talk to them. Hank was commander of the Triple Seven and he will call Phil's family on behalf of the unit. He'll contact the other members of the Triple Seven also. Most of us will attend the funeral."

Cleveland disconnected and Chuck ticked another item off his mental to-do list.

Next item.

Three days earlier, Chuck had tailed Duman Aubakirovich to Atlantic County Air Charter Service where he either delivered something or picked something up. Or both.

Southeast Printing and Binding was receiving paper from Xinjiang, and they were shipping counterfeit currency to someplace in Kazakhstan.

Somehow the Atlantic County Air Charter Service was involved in one or both activities.

And the Russians owned a bank in Kazakhstan that was mixed up in this somehow. If Chuck could just uncover that connection, maybe he could unravel this whole ball of string.

Oklahatchee Airport was ten minutes from Southeast Printing and Binding. Handy for both types of transaction.

It was time to pay them a visit.

———

Chuck entered at the main airport gate. A guard holding a clipboard slid open the glass door, "Driver's license and destination, please."

Chuck handed the guard his license. "Atlantic County Air Charter Service."

"Do you know how to get there?"

"I have a GPS."

"Be sure to use it. The sign blew off and it hasn't been replaced. Are you flying out today? Or will this vehicle be leaving the property today?"

"I'll be back within two hours."

"Okay." The guard stepped away. He returned with a piece of paper with the date and time in large print. He handed Chuck the paper and returned his license.

"Display this permit on your dashboard. You scan it at the exit to raise the gate when you leave."

"Thanks." Chuck situated the permit on the dashboard of his Caravan and followed the GPS directions. The two-lane street curved around a car rental building, the U.S. Coast Guard Station, and past a jogging track and outdoor exercise area. The road passed several aviation-related businesses, and ended at a parking lot for a two-story steel building.

The building butted an airplane hangar. Chuck's GPS said he was there. At the edge of the property, a steel fence separated the cars from the airplanes. The numbers above the double glass doors said he was at the right address. Above the door he identified where a sign had once been mounted. *This must be the place.*

Chuck opened the glass door, and a *ding-dong* sounded. A half dozen utilitarian steel-framed, vinyl-seated chairs lined the wall. A waist-high counter with a computer terminal divided the room. Two steel bar stools sat empty at the counter.

The walls were adorned with generic travel posters: The Great Wall of

China, the Eiffel Tower, the Great Pyramids, Mount Fuji in Japan, and others Chuck didn't recognize. Perhaps countries the company serviced. Was one of the mystery posters a scene in Kazakhstan or Xinjiang?

A speaker mounted on the wall spoke. "I'm in the hanger. Be right with you."

Switching his cellphone to audio recording, Chuck shoved it in a jacket pocket and sat on a bar stool.

A couple minutes later a swarthy, middle-aged man in a white dress shirt with epaulets and captain's bars opened the door. His close-trimmed hair was salt-and-pepper and his neat goatee was going gray. His black tie was held with a tie clasp with a gold emblem of a generic airplane. He wore khaki pants and white sneakers that had endured a lot of use.

Extending his hand, he approached the counter. "I'm Captain Adam Kushner."

Chuck reached across and shook his hand. "Chuck McCrary."

"How can I help, Chuck?"

"Does your company service Kazakhstan?"

Kushner's gaze flicked to a poster where a snow-covered mountain rose by the shore of a big blue lake surrounded by evergreens. *Aha*, Chuck thought.

"We fly anywhere there's an airport. What did you have in mind, passengers or freight?"

"Freight."

"How big a load?"

"A couple of tons."

"Sure, we can do that. Are we flying it there, or getting it there and flying it somewhere else?"

"Don't know. Performing my due diligence. Where in Kazakhstan is the best airport facility to handle freight?"

"Beats me. I didn't say I'd flown there. I said we can fly anywhere there's an airport. You say where and that's where we'll fly."

"Oh. Someone told me your company had worked in Kazakhstan."

"Nope. We've flown to Russia and we've flown to Mongolia, but I've never been to Kazakhstan. Got a nice picture of Lake Almaty there on the wall. My wife collected those posters when we started the company eight years ago."

"Any of your other pilots flown to Kazakhstan?"

"Nope. One pilot flew to Uzbekistan twice. I'd love to fly to Kazakhstan though. Lake Almaty looks pretty with those snow-capped mountains. I'd love to see it from fifteen thousand feet."

Everybody believes they're a good judge of character. Not Chuck. That's why he made Rule Twelve: *People lie. If they don't lie, they can be mistaken.* Kushner acted sincere enough, but Chuck had been fooled more times than he cared to remember.

Chuck fished out his phone, found a picture of Duman Aubakirovich, and held it where Kushner could see. "You ever notice this guy around here?"

Kushner studied the photo. He stepped back. "Who the hell are you? Are you a cop?"

Handing him a business card, Chuck watched him read it. Chuck wondered if he should add a logo to his card? Perhaps a knight on a white charger.

"You got ID?"

Chuck showed him his PI license and concealed weapon permit.

"A private investigator, huh. You armed now?"

"I'm always armed. It's no biggie." He showed Captain Kushner Duman's picture. "Have you seen this guy?"

"Don't think I've met a private investigator before. What are you investigating? Is this guy a criminal? Who the hell is he?" He gestured at Duman's photo.

"Have you seen him?"

"Yeah. A few days ago, it was. He come in with a box about yay-big." He spread his hands about two feet apart. "The way he held it, it seemed heavy. He plunked it on the counter and asked for Pavel Nurbayev. Pavel was a pilot who worked here for a few weeks. This guy told me Pavel had done some shipping for him. I told him Pavel didn't work here anymore. This guy," he tapped the photo on Chuck's phone, "said Pavel had shipped other boxes like the one he brought with him. Asked me to ship two more just like it. I told him what I told you. I said we fly anywhere there is an airport. Then he told me Pavel did it off the books. Bypass customs on the other end. Somebody greases some palms and collects the box on the QT."

Kushner made a face. "I told him to go fly a kite."

"Spell Pavel's name."

He did.

"And he doesn't work here anymore?"

"No. There was something...*off* about him. He was sloppy with paperwork, shipping manifests, customs declarations, and mundane stuff, as if he didn't consider regulations important. Our company can lose its license to fly if we screw up that stuff. I fired him last week."

Kushner shook his head. "Business may not be great, but life's too short to be nervous all the time, hoping a bad decision you made won't bite you on the ass. I told him if I ever saw him again, I'd report him to the FAA."

"Where did he go?"

"Don't know and don't care. I gave him his final paycheck on the spot, took his keys and company ID, and sent him on his way. Good riddance."

"You said he was sloppy with paperwork. Is there a chance he might file a flight plan to somewhere else in Central Asia—you said somebody flew to Uzbekistan—and then fly to Almaty instead?"

"Holy shit. That's what the bastard did." Kushner's face reddened. "Pavel flew to Tashkent—that is: He said he was flying to Tashkent. He flew there twice, maybe ten days apart."

"Any idea where I might find Pavel?"

"Yeah. Wait here." Kushner stormed through another door, leaving it open behind him. It was an office. He flipped through a file drawer and pulled a manila folder. He waved it at Chuck.

A minute later he returned and tossed it on the counter. "Help yourself, Mr. McCrary. It's Pavel Nurbayev's personnel file. Hell, copy the whole damn thing."

So he did.

———

Pavel Nurbayev lived in the Palm Grove District, a neighborhood in Oklahatchee that journalists call "disadvantaged," but people in the real world call "high crime." The District was often the lead story on the *Eleven O'clock News* as the site of a drive-by shooting, or a domestic disturbance that led to a murder-suicide, or a major drug bust with hundreds of thousands of dollars of illegal narcotics seized.

It was a neighborhood where fearful parents wouldn't let their children play outside at night.

Nurbayev didn't come to the door, but the building manager said he lived there. Chuck invested a fifty-dollar bill with the manager and learned that Nurbayev rented the apartment furnished, after Christmas. He paid three months' rent in advance in cash.

Interesting. Bunches of people arrived in Port City after Christmas: the Chinese, the Russians, Aisha and Duman, Andrew Billow, and Phil Franks. The timing was no coincidence.

Chuck parked on the street to pass the time. He had copied a good photo from Nurbayev's pilot's license in the personnel file. Blue eyes so pale they were practically white. Shaggy blond hair worn over his ears. Five-foot-ten. One hundred ninety-five pounds. The eyes reminded Chuck of Vladimir Putin's—warm as an iceberg.

Chuck wasn't afraid the neighbors would notice him. It was a neighborhood where strange men hung out in parked cars. Neighbors minded their own business if they valued their safety. The pedestrians who walked past faced the other way passing Chuck's van.

Chuck unwrapped the first half of a foot-long sandwich he bought on the way from Atlantic County Air Charter. A spicy Italian combo of pepperoni and Genoa salami. He had added Provolone cheese and Ranch Dressing to the lettuce and tomatoes. No red onions though; it might be a long afternoon, and Chuck didn't need the agita the red onions cause. He bit off a chunk and washed it down with Diet Dr Pepper.

Vicky Ramirez called.

"Your wonderful roses arrived. All the women in the office are jealous. Come over tonight and I'll demonstrate my appreciation with Chicken Marsala and Calvados. You'll love the dessert."

"What a nice invitation. One potential problem: I have an eight o'clock meeting at Tank's house tomorrow morning so I can't spend the night."

"No problem. I can be through with you in ten minutes, dinner optional. Just kidding. Seven o'clock okay?"

"It's a date."

Chuck dragged out the copy of Nurbayev's personnel file and studied it again. Born in Kazakhstan when it was part of the Soviet Union. Spoke Russian, Kazakh, and English. Forty-three years old. Four years in the Kazakh Air Force, followed by four thousand hours of multi-engine flying in Eastern Europe and Central Asia. He demonstrated the technical qualifications to fly anything, anywhere, anytime. No wonder Adam Kushner hired him. On paper, he was quite a catch. The paperwork didn't reveal a criminal record.

Chuck texted Nurbayev's birth date and place, legal name, and pilot license number to Flamer. He asked Flamer to send what he found.

An hour later, Ruby called on a video call. "Happy Valentine's Day, Chuck. The flowers are beautiful. I love the color combination." She aimed her phone where he could view the flowers on her desk. Chuck had ordered two dozen red roses and the florist sent a dozen red and a dozen white which Ruby had mixed in the vase. They appeared fresh and beautiful. He kept his mouth shut. "I'm glad you like them. I wish I were there."

"I miss you too. I enjoyed our trip to Chicago and Fort Benning and Port City Beach. How is Phil Franks's murder case going?"

Chuck brought Ruby current on Gunner's kidnapping and the rescue from the Chinese army.

"So that's over," she said, "and you're a hero again."

"It's nothing Superman couldn't do."

"You're my Superman."

"I'm on a related case." Chuck told her about the counterfeiting of the Kazakh currency. "One of these days I hope to get a case that pays money."

They chatted about everything and nothing. "If you're free next weekend," Ruby said, "why don't you come to Austin. Or I can come there. Either one."

"It's my turn to fly there. What's the long-term forecast for the weekend of the twenty-second?"

"It's supposed to snow again in three days, then the cold front will head toward Florida. Today it's a freezing drizzle coating everything with ice."

"The front will be rain when it gets here, not a blizzard. When the weather is bad in South Florida, it's still pretty good. Since it's my turn to fly; I'll buy your ticket. If it rains, we'll spend the weekend cocooning."

"It's a deal."

"Text me your flight details and I'll pick you up at the airport next Friday."

"I will. Okay, I need to get back to work. Kisses." She disconnected.

Flamer emailed an extensive dossier on Nurbayev. At the end he added an editorial comment: "This guy is so low he could walk under a snake without removing his hat. Watch your six, soldier."

The dossier revealed that Nurbayev had never been convicted of a crime. He testified three times against co-conspirators to avoid spending time in prison. He was guilty, but he slithered away unscathed.

Two hours later, Chuck opened another Diet Dr Pepper and ate the rest of his spicy Italian sandwich. He stuck a small piece of tape at the bottom edge of Nurbayev's door and drove to a gas station to use the restroom. When he returned, the windows to Nurbayev's apartment were open.

He was home.

After locking his van, Chuck tapped on the audio recorder on his phone and slipped it in a pocket.

He knocked on the door. It opened to the length of the security chain. Nurbayev's pale blue left eye appraised Chuck through the slot. "Yes?"

"I am told you have a commercial pilot's license and are qualified to fly overseas. I may have a job for you."

"Who are you?"

Chuck shoved his Carlos Calderone business card through the opening, the one with the Mexico City address. Carlos Andres Calderone is an alter-ego Chuck maintained. An internet search for Carlos Calderone would reveal that he owned a copper mine in Chile, a cattle ranch in Mexico, a marina in Fort Lauderdale, and pieces of two casinos in New Jersey and the Bahamas—none of which was true. It made a good cover for some of Chuck's undercover activities.

Nurbayev accepted the card. "Let me remove the chain." He closed the door, slipped off the chain, and invited Chuck in. He wore a tight tee-shirt; what Chuck's friends called a muscle shirt in high school. His biceps bulged from the sleeves and his trapezoids sloped from the sides of his neck to his shoulders. He was solid muscle. This guy could arm wrestle a backhoe.

Chuck trailed him inside.

Nurbayev's apartment was old and dingy. Either he was not a successful criminal, or he was stuffing his profits in an offshore account somewhere. There were no family photos, no artwork on the walls, no souvenirs of his travels on a shelf, nothing of a personal nature. It was as if Nurbayev didn't live there, but was camping. If Chuck tossed his bedroom and closet, he would bet Nurbayev could grab everything he owned in three minutes, stuff it in one backpack, and carry it on a dead run. And according to Flamer, he had done that in Ukraine, Algeria, and—no surprise—Kazakhstan.

"Would you care for something to drink, Mr. Calderone?"

"Always have time for a friendly drink. What are you having?"

"Amstel, but I got wine, liquor, and soft drinks." He gestured Chuck toward an upholstered chair whose seat had collapsed from years of use. The furnishings explained why the apartment rented so cheaply.

"Amstel is fine." Sitting in that chair was like falling into a shallow grave. The springs were shot and Chuck's butt was halfway to the floor.

Nurbayev strutted to the kitchenette with the rolling gait of an Olympic weightlifter. His glutes and thighs were as well-muscled as his neck and back. Chuck figured he had a hard time buying blue jeans to fit those immense thighs.

Nurbayev returned from the kitchenette with an Amstel in each hand. He handed Chuck one and sat on a worn-out sofa across from his visitor. He drank from the bottle and wiped his mouth on the back of his hand. "What job do you need done?"

"The same job you did for this guy." Chuck showed him Duman Aubakirovich's photo on his phone. It felt like reaching up out of a bathtub.

Nurbayev recognized the photo and froze in the middle of reaching for his Amstel. He eyeballed the dreary apartment as if he was planning to run for it.

Nurbayev glanced at Chuck's screen. "Who is that?"

Surprise, surprise. He planned to deny everything.

Chuck attempted to lean forward in the chair but couldn't. Once it was time to leave, he would have to hoist himself like he'd been sitting in a bushel basket. "The guy who hired you to fly boxes to Kazakhstan. Twice, before Atlantic County Air Charter fired you. I want to start the shipments again and I'm not picky about going through customs. You interested?"

"You got an airplane with trans-Atlantic range?"

"Yes."

"I'm interested. For a price."

"Tell me how the previous trips went."

"Sure," he said, rising to his feet. He raised his Amstel to drink. Instead he hurled the bottle at Chuck. He leapt across the coffee table and grabbed Chuck's throat.

Chuck had time for one breath before Nurbayev rammed him like a freight train. The momentum of his rush scooted Chuck's chair back a few inches on the tile floor. Nurbayev thumped Chuck's abdomen with both knees, then straddled Chuck's lap and wrapped his hands around the PI's neck. From his position in the chair, Chuck was pinned like a butterfly specimen. He couldn't reach the Glock behind his back nor the Browning on his ankle.

Chuck clasped his hands together and shot them upward between the pilot's forearms, intending to wedge them apart. Nurbayev locked onto Chuck's neck like a vise, cutting off his breath and blocking the blood flow to his brain.

Chuck had mere seconds of consciousness remaining.

Chuck unclasped his hands and grabbed Nurbayev's crotch. The Kazakh's blue jeans were stretched drumhead-tight between his thighs, and Chuck couldn't get a grip on his testicles. Chuck's vision began to red-out.

Chuck ripped his left sleeve open. His fingers gripped the ceramic knife strapped to his forearm.

From that position, Chuck could gut Nurbayev like a deer, but he needed information. Pulling the knife, he stabbed the fleshy part of Nurbayev's right forearm. The razor-sharp point lanced the skin and cut through the muscle the way a submarine carves the sea. The forearm bled on Chuck's wrist and shirt, soaking through to Chuck's ribs. He twisted the knife to widen the wound. Chuck stabbed at the pilot's right thigh. His blue jeans resisted the knife point.

Chuck sliced instead of stabbing and the fabric gave way. He stabbed again. This time his blade punctured the muscle. Blood flowed hot onto Chuck's pants, soaking through to his own thigh.

The Kazakh's hands loosened. He screamed like an actor in a horror movie and spittle sprayed Chuck's face. "I'm bleeding!"

Chuck threw a short punch to Nurbayev's throat and the Kazakh released the PI's neck. Chuck yanked the knife from Nurbayev's thigh and tossed it across the room. Seizing his belt with one hand and a fistful of his shirt with the other, Chuck threw him off. He fell away, collapsing the coffee table beneath him. "I'm bleeding." It was a whimper this time.

Chuck struggled out of the chair, retrieved his knife, and examined Nurbayev's wounds. Chuck had avoided the arteries in the muscled man's arm and leg, but the wounds were deep and serious.

"I'll be back. I carry a first aid kit in my van."

"Don't leave me. I'll bleed to death."

"Don't worry, Pavel. I'm not abandoning you. I may not let you die."

In two minutes, Chuck was back.

Nurbayev's eyes widened when he noticed the bandages.

"What's that stuff?"

"These are Israeli emergency pressure bandages. One of these saved my life once. Aren't you the lucky one?"

"Hurry before I bleed to death."

He wasn't bleeding much, but some people get freaked out at the sight of blood. Especially their own.

Chuck cut off the rest of Nurbayev's pants leg and bandaged his thigh, then his forearm. Chuck rolled him over on the tile floor and fastened his hands behind him with a cable tie. The PI shackled his ankles. The son of a bitch wasn't going anywhere.

Chuck selected a kitchen chair that wouldn't swallow him and dragged it over, sitting near Nurbayev's head.

"Call an ambulance. I'm wounded. I'm bleeding, for God's sake."

"I might call an ambulance if you cooperate. If you don't, I'll duct tape your mouth so you can't call for help. Then I'll rip off these bandages and abandon you to die alone. Your choice."

"You can't do that. You gotta call an ambulance. It's the law."

"That might be true if I were a cop, Pavel. Your bad luck that I'm not. I'm a private citizen whom you attempted to murder. Needless to say, I'm not a happy camper."

Chuck placed his cellphone on the floor near Nurbayev's mouth. "Shall we have a productive conversation? Or shall I remove my bandages and let you bleed to death? Alone."

Nurbayev tried to negotiate. Chuck shook his head and tugged on the bandage. The Kazakh caved and told Chuck everything.

They finished in time for Chuck to haul him to the Cedars of Lebanon Hospital Emergency Department. Chuck called the cops while transporting him. They handcuffed him to the bed in the ED. Chuck gave them a statement and rushed home in time to change and make it to Vicky's apartment before seven-thirty.

Only later would he learn his mistake.

SEVENTEEN

It was seven o'clock the next morning when Chuck reached his Avanti in the condo garage. He switched on his radio scanner to learn if anyone had stuck a GPS tracker under the *Silver Ghost*. The scanner light flashed and the dial lit.

Damn. Someone had tagged it.

Chuck had driven the Avanti two places in the last two days: George Alexander's Marco Island estate on Thursday and Vicky Ramirez's condo last night. He used his mirror on a stick and discovered the tracker clinging to the metal chassis of the fiberglass sports car.

George Alexander's crew had tagged the Avanti while Chuck was annoying their boss.

The Russian-American gangster knew which building Chuck lived in and which building Vicky Ramirez lived in, even if he didn't know Vicky's identity. Chuck might have prevented both those discoveries if he had scanned after he left the Godfather's mansion two days ago.

Instead, he had left the Godfather's estate proud of himself for leaving a couple of bugs inside.

The Book of Proverbs was right: Pride goeth before a fall. Chuck was so busy patting himself on the back that he forgot to scan for trackers after he left. Damned stupid mistake.

Chuck walked to the main entrance and picked a delivery truck to stick the tracker on. That might distract the bad guys.

The one bright spot in Chuck's dismal performance was that he had parked in a visitor space at Vicky's condo. Still, a good detective might learn Vicky's identity and address knowing where Chuck had parked. He hoped Alexander didn't know any good detectives.

Chuck's own high-rise condo had a large parking garage. Alexander knew the building he lived in, but not the unit.

Chuck was pissed off at himself. Returning inside, he washed his hands and changed the clothes he had soiled removing the tracker.

Chuck took the Avanti anyway. If someone tailed him, it would confirm that Alexander's thugs had staked out his condo building.

Chuck left at 7:30 for Tank Tyler's house. It was a cool crisp winter morning in South Florida. On Port City Beach seventy degrees qualifies as cool and crisp in February.

Chuck chose Highway A1A alongside the sunrise joggers on the beach. He drove toward North Bay Causeway. Two blocks later he spied the SUV behind him, this one dark blue.

Damn again.

Chuck cut across the island to the Seeti Bay side and took Navasota Drive to the Port City Beach public golf course. He took the service road across the golf course and lost the tail.

Chuck had shaken them this time, but the Russians would be back.

He called Vicky. "I'm sorry to call this early, but I needed to reach you before you left your apartment. Did I wake you?"

"No, I was doing my yoga. I enjoyed last night. I hope you're not calling to change plans for this weekend."

"No, no, nothing like that. I forgot to radio scan my Avanti after I left Alexander's house Thursday. This morning I discovered a GPS tracker under the Silver Ghost. The gangster hid it while I was parked at his house. I have placed you in danger."

"What danger?" she asked. "Unless he saw you enter my apartment, he won't know which condo is mine."

"But he knows I spent the evening at your building. I parked in a visitor space. He doesn't know which unit I visited, but he could narrow it to ten

226

units. I left my parking garage this morning, and someone tailed my Avanti. I'm afraid someone will be in your visitor space this morning to tail whoever shows up."

"Should I call the police?"

"No. I'll send Snoop over to learn whether anyone staked out your parking lot. When you are ready to leave your condo, order an Uber to pick you up on the other side of your building, away from the visitor space I used last night. That way, if somebody is watching for you, they won't see you. To be doubly sure, take the Uber to the Bayside Mall east entrance and walk across the mall. Call a Lyft from the west entrance to come to my condo. And bring your Monday work clothes. I'd like you to spend Saturday and Sunday nights. And bring your tennis racket."

"Are you up for the embarrassment?" Vicky asked.

Chuck laughed. "Someday the law of averages says I will beat you. Sunday could be that day. See you at my place for lunch."

"You have hamburger fixings? I'm in the mood for grilled burgers.'

"Great. You'll find everything in my refrigerator. I'll be there soon."

Chuck's next call was to Snoop. He explained what happened and asked Snoop to postpone the lecture on his mistake. Chuck sent him to stake out Vicky's apartment and tail anyone who shouldn't be there.

That was all he could do. *Damn, damn, damn.*

Okay, enough worrying. He had done what he could. Chuck focused his attention on the plans for today.

———

Billow thought the meeting started at nine a.m., but Chuck was meeting Hank and Gunner at eight.

Pink Coral Island was built in the 1920s. It was a gated community reached by a private bridge from North Bay Causeway. Pink Coral Way, the one street, circled two-thirds of the island like a horseshoe with the Pink Coral Golf Club on the land side and a necklace of about four dozen multi-million-dollar mansions on the bay side. A hundred years ago, the rich residents hadn't worried about terrorism or being kidnaped for ransom. The only security required was to keep out the nosey public.

Since the last time Chuck had visited Tank's house, the owners of the island had built a substantial guard house and extended it onto the bridge. The old wooden security gate was gone. It was more for appearances than for security. Any vehicle, even a motorcycle, could drive through it.

Stopping the Avanti at the new gatehouse, Chuck handed over his driver's license. "Carlos McCrary to see Tank Tyler. He's expecting me."

The guard consulted his computer screen, scanned the license, and returned it. "Nice to see you again, Mr. McCrary."

Chuck shoved the license in his wallet. "Thanks. You improved security."

"Yes, sir. One of our residents drove home drunk one night and drove smack through the old security gate. It wasn't the first time. The security committee approved the new double gate system. He'll need a heavy truck to get past these new steel gates. Have a nice day, sir."

The first gate rolled sideways and Chuck idled forward. The first gate closed. The second gate opened. Nice. The gatehouse guard was armed with a taser and a Glock 17 like the Port City cops and the World's Greatest Private Eye used.

Chuck followed Pink Coral Way. It was lined with palm trees on the left and giant live oaks and bougainvillea on the right. The golf club grounds crew were mowing the fairways and raking the bunkers. The fairways glistened in the morning dew. The street ended at a circular turnaround that served four waterfront mansions on a peninsula.

The wrought-iron gates to Tank's estate swung open. The curved lane stretched fifty yards through a manicured jungle of tropical foliage to another circular driveway with a three-tiered fountain in the middle. Hank's car was parked beside the coral steps to the front door.

The butler opened the door just as Chuck reached the top of the steps.

"Good morning, Gregory."

Gregory wore his customary light blue guayabera, navy-blue Bermuda shorts, and sandals. "Good morning, Chuck. Mr. Ramirez is at the pool. Cook prepared a special breakfast buffet for you and your friends and apparently the rest of the neighborhood, judging by the amount of food."

"Thank you, Gregory. Is Tank still home? I'd like to say hello."

"No, sir. Tank left for the office. He sends you his best regards and hopes you and your friends have a productive meeting."

Gregory shuffled his way across the circular foyer. He was far past retirement age, and Tank needed a butler like a cruise ship needs an outhouse, but Tank let the old man stay on after he bought the mansion. Gregory had worked in the house over thirty years and had no place else to go. He had no other family, and he lived in the servants' quarters on the property.

Hank was sitting on a wrought-iron chair at a glass-topped table set for four. The sun had not risen above the house and the pool area was still shaded.

He waved at Chuck. "There's a school of dolphins in the bay." He pointed. "I count six. They're throwing a party out there."

Cook had arranged two catering tables in the loggia, complete with white tablecloths. She stood behind the tables in a traditional chef's toque, white jacket, and a new apron that said *Queen of Everything* with a crown embroidered above the slogan. She kept a steady guard over the coffee urn, two pitchers of orange juice, and a tray of assorted pastries in case the pastries made a run for it. Metal racks for the hot dishes sat empty. Knowing Cook, she kept the hot dishes in a warming station in the kitchen.

"Good morning, Chuck," Cook said. "I'll serve the hot dishes when you're ready."

"Good morning, Cook. I'll have coffee and orange juice while we're waiting, if you don't mind." Chuck always felt awkward calling her "Cook." Her name was Gretchen Wilder. He'd called her "Ms. Wilder," then "Gretchen," but she convinced him her preferred title was "Cook." The way you would call your physician "Doctor." To each her own.

Perhaps with the new apron, Chuck thought, *I should call her "Your majesty."*

Cook smiled and poured the coffee, then the juice.

Gregory pulled out a chair for Chuck. He was old enough to be Chuck's grandfather, but he would be offended if Chuck hadn't let him do his job.

"Thanks, Gregory. We'll be fine. Gunner arrives at eight. I don't expect Andrew Billow until nine o'clock."

At 7:59 Gunner arrived. He practically came to attention at the table. "It's 0800. Where is Speedy?"

"I told him to be here at nine. I want to talk to you and Hank without him. Also, I have a present for you, a donation from the Chinese Peoples' Liberation Army."

Chuck handed him an envelope stuffed with hundred-dollar bills. "I ransacked the house on SW 4th Street and uncovered a money stash. I kept enough to cover the expenses of your rescue. You deserve the rest as damages from the Chinese government. This is war reparations."

Gunner stuffed it in his pocket without counting. "How much is it?"

"Sixteen thousand dollars."

A big smile creased his face. "For that much reparations, it was almost worth getting the snot beat out of me. Thanks."

"Don't thank me. You earned it."

Chuck nodded to Cook. "We'll eat breakfast now, Cook. Thanks."

Cook loaded the table with enough quiche, waffles, scrambled eggs, poached eggs, and corned beef hash to feed all twelve of the original Triple Seven soldiers. Cook's motto was "Nothing succeeds like excess."

Snoop texted Chuck.

Four men in blue Yukon with crumpled fender are in visitors parking space. I'll shadow when they give up and see where they go. Cheers.

The four friends filled their plates and sat where they could view the bay and the dolphins cavorting. You gotta love South Florida.

"I scheduled this meeting on Thursday, but yesterday, I learned new information that we three should discuss before Billow gets here."

Hank poured maple syrup on his pancakes. "What new information?"

"Aisha's and Duman's father is a corrupt police commissioner in Almaty, the capital of Kazakhstan. Yesterday I interrogated another Kazakh living in Port City who works with him and Duman to steal the counterfeit currency before it gets to the Turkic Liberation Army. Duman is part of the theft. Billow may be hard to convince that his future brother-in-law is a crook and a turncoat."

"How did you find out?"

Chuck briefed Hank and Gunner on his actions at Atlantic County Air

Charter and at Pavel Nurbayev's apartment. "I recorded my interrogation of Nurbayev. I'll play it while we finish eating."

The recording finished and Gunner said, "Play the recording for Billow. When he hears what we heard, that will convince him."

"Billow's a smart guy," Hank said. "But I'm interested in the guy who just tried to kill you. Where is he?"

"I took him to Cedars of Lebanon ED and called the Port City cops. They charged him with assault and attempted murder."

"They can't make attempted murder stick, and they'll be lucky with the assault since you were in his apartment under false pretenses."

"Win some, lose some," Chuck said. "My goal today is to get Billow to quit this project. Even if Duman weren't a turncoat, it's an ill-fated mission. We tried nation building in Afghanistan and Iraq. It didn't work there, just like it didn't work in Somalia, Viet Nam, yada, yada, yada. I want Billow to come to his senses. Then we can dump the whole Southeast Printing and Binding Company into Seeti Bay for all I care."

Gunner said, "I have time to eat another crepe before Billow gets here."

Cook beamed with delight. "I'll make you some fresh ones."

Billow arrived at five minutes to nine. He noticed the dirty dishes on the table. "Am I late? You said to be here at nine."

"The rest of us got here at eight," Chuck said. "We had bad news to discuss and didn't want to wait for you. Don't worry, I'll eat again to keep you company."

"I will too," Gunner said.

Cook beamed again.

"What's the bad news?"

"Let's discuss it in Tank's conference room after breakfast. For now, let's enjoy this Triple Seven reunion."

As they sat down again, Chuck realized this was the first time the four of them had been together since Afghanistan. Hank and Chuck met several times a month. Gunner now lived in Port City. But Billow had lived in Chicago for ten years. The last time he visited Hank and Chuck in Florida was before Gunner moved from North Dakota.

After they finished eating, Chuck stood at the head of the table and lifted his coffee cup. "Guys, this is the first time the four of us have been together since Afghanistan. Let's lift a glass or a cup to Hot Dog and Packy. Rest in peace."

The other three stood with Chuck. "To Hot Dog and Packy. Rest in peace."

"Okay, let's adjourn to the conference room. Cook plans to pass the leftovers to the homeless shelter."

———

Tank's conference room was on the third floor. The elevator opened to a room large as a squash court, which it was before Tank remodeled. A mahogany conference table with twelve office chairs dominated the room. Two white walls featured a corkboard, a whiteboard, a sixty-inch computer monitor, and a projection screen. Everything a modern corporate meeting required, including its own Wi-Fi router, a bar, and coffee counter in one corner of the room. The conference room God would design if He could afford it.

Two pairs of French doors thrust out in a wide dormer on one side of the sloped ceiling and half-wall. The doors were closed, but Chuck remembered they opened to the balcony overlooking the pool and Seeti Bay.

Cook wheeled in a trolley with coffee service and an assortment of Danish pastries. "If you need more, Chuck, call me. I'll be back from the shelter in a half-hour."

"Thanks, Cook. In case of emergency, I can brew coffee." He winked at her, and she blushed.

Before departing, she arranged the coffee service and pastries on the counter.

They sat at the table.

"Andy, why don't you tell us how your counterfeiting plan was supposed to work."

"Early November, I met Aisha Aubakirovna. We dated a few weeks and there was this immediate connection, like I'd been waiting for her all my life and didn't realize it until we met. Eventually she told me about the Turkic Liberation Army. Her brother Duman has a contact in Xinjiang

Province of China where the paper is manufactured that the Kazakh Tenge are printed on. That's where we got the idea of financing the revolution with counterfeit money."

"The idea was Duman's?"

"Yeah, but we all support it."

"How did you wind up in Port City?" Chuck asked.

"Duman knew the Kusainov brothers, Daniyar and Aldiyar. They and their father owned Southeast Printing and Binding Company, and it had a Heidelberg Printing Press. The Heidelberg could print virtually perfect currency if we had the right paper and an expert operator like me. The printing company offered an obscenely high salary. The three of us decided to relocate to Port City and start a revolution."

"What about Phil Franks?" Hank asked. "How did Phil get involved?"

"We were worried for the physical safety of the company and its employees once anyone in Asia got wind of the project. The Russians have dominated Kazakhstan for the last hundred years, since the Communist Revolution in 1917. After the Soviet Union fell, the Russians still interfered in Kazakhstan. Partly because of Baikonur, the old Soviet space launch facility. The Russians kept it when the Soviet Union dissolved and leased it from Kazakhstan until 2050. But they don't intend to give it back. They want to make it part of Russia. The Chinese want to drive a wedge between the Kazakhs and Russians to increase China's influence in the area."

"The Russians and the Chinese are both fighting for influence in Kazakhstan?" Hank asked.

"Yeah, and both countries play dirty. None of the employees at the print shop are ex-military. We needed more muscle than just me in case the shit hit the fan. Phil's enlistment was ending and he was bored at Fort Benning so I invited him to be head of security. The Kusainovs doubled his U.S. Army salary, and Phil relished the idea of helping a democratic revolution." Billow grinned. "The South Florida sunshine helped his decision also."

"How much currency have you printed so far and where is it?" Chuck asked.

"We've been getting four boxes of paper, weighing 35 pounds per box, each week for the last four weeks. That's all the people in Xinjiang can divert without red-flagging the operation."

"How many tenges does one box make?"

"We print notes worth 10,000 tenges. That's equivalent to about twenty U.S. dollars. We get eight bills from one 14-by-20-inch sheet of paper. That's 80,000 tenges worth $160 dollars per sheet."

"Why not print 20,000s?"

"Duman says that's too obvious. People notice a 20,000 tenge bill the way an American notices a hundred. The 10,000 is common and nobody gives them a second glance. With 500 sheets of paper per box, we get 40,000,000 tenges per box of paper. We print 320,000 U.S. dollars' worth of tenges a week."

Billow leaned back in his chair. "We need the equivalent of fifty million U.S. dollars to finance the revolution. With that money, we can buy heavy weapons from Pakistan."

Chuck made a quick calculation. "That's 625 boxes of paper, weighing 22,000 pounds. That'll require more than three years at the rate of four boxes of paper a week. And there's the problem of getting the funny money to Kazakhstan."

"That's our logistical problem," Billow said. "We need to get more paper faster and ship it faster."

"Back to the original question: 'How much have you printed, and where is it?'"

"We've received sixteen boxes of paper from Xinjiang, and we printed twelve boxes, or 480,000,000 tenges. Equivalent to 960,000 good old U.S. dollars. Duman hid it off site in a fireproof storage unit. After we print enough for a down payment on the revolution, we'll charter a plane and ship it to our contacts in Kazakhstan."

"How long since you visited the storage unit and counted the money?" Chuck asked.

Perhaps Billow heard something in Chuck's voice, but he did a slight double-take. "That's a funny question to ask. What do you know that I don't?"

"That's the bad news I learned yesterday and discussed with Gunner and Hank before you arrived."

Chuck held out his phone with a picture of Pavel Nurbayev. "You know this guy?"

"No. Who is he?"

"Pavel Nurbayev, a pilot who used to work for Atlantic County Air Charter Service. Have you heard of them?"

"No."

"They fly people and cargo all over the world. Duman knows them well enough that he uses a pass to get through the security gates at Oklahatchee Airport and drive up to the airplanes without using the public entrance. Tuesday morning, I followed Duman after he dropped off Aisha at work. He drove to Oklahatchee Airport and used his own access card to open this gate." Chuck showed Billow a picture of Gate 40 that Duman used.

"He visited Atlantic County Air Charter Service, spent a few minutes, came back out the gate, then drove to Southeast Printing, where he parked Aisha's Toyota in the employee parking lot."

Billow frowned. "What was he doing at the airport?"

"I didn't learn that until yesterday when I questioned Pavel Nurbayev. I recorded our conversation."

Chuck placed his phone on the table and played the recording.

———

They listened to Pavel Nurbayev spill his guts for a half hour.

Aisha and Duman's father, Aubakir Yakovlevich, was Pavel's uncle, which made the siblings cousins to Nurbayev. Aisha's Papa was head of the Kazakh security police, and he hatched the scheme to feed fake tenges into Kazakhstan to buy gold. The gold was flown to Switzerland where Duman, Pavel, Vladimir Kusainov, and Papa Yakovlevich all had bank accounts. Pavel got a fee for every ounce of gold he flew to Zurich.

Pavel said Duman's supposed break with Papa was a fake. Papa wanted him as a sleeper agent in America.

Pavel had flown 320 million tenges to Kazakhstan using the charter service's airplane. Both times, Papa met him at the airport, bypassing customs. Papa bought gold with the fake tenges, brought the gold back to the airplane, and Pavel flew it to Zurich.

Duman had carried another four boxes—160 million tenges—to Atlantic County Air Cargo in the trunk of Aisha's car. He expected to find Pavel, but the pilot no long worked at the charter company.

The recording finished. Andy Billow scowled. "Duman lied to Aisha and me the whole time. My future brother-in-law—my *family* for God's sake. He's no patriot; he's a thief and a turncoat."

"Better that you learned from the co-conspirator in his own voice," Chuck said.

"Why are the Chinese and the Russians interfering?" Billow asked.

"The Chinese interest is strictly politics. The Russians are in it for the money."

"What Chinese politics?" Billow asked.

"Papa Yakovlevich isn't the only one with spies in Kazakhstan. It's the Wild West of Central Asia. The guy I knew as Captain Kang was actually a colonel in the intelligence service of the Chinese Army. The PLA plants spies in the Uighur Muslim 'reeducation camps' in Xinjiang. One spy learned that a paper company in Xinjiang manufactures the paper that Kazakhstan uses to print its currency. According to the spy, a portion of this paper was being redirected to the USA. Last December, the Chinese PLA learned about this. They want to keep the Turkic Liberation Army from starting a revolution in Xinjiang. They searched for the counterfeiting operation in the USA. They located the Kusainovs just after Christmas."

"That accounts for the Chinese. That's why they rented the house and the warehouse," Hank said. "But where do the Russians fit in?"

"Two days ago," Chuck said, "I planted bugs in George Alexander's office and his home. Since then I've recorded several conversations in Russian. I'm meeting Tuesday with a professor who teaches Russian at the university. He'll translate them, but I think I know what they say. I don't believe the Russian Embassy sent the four guys I had the gunfight with. That's why the Russian gangsters didn't carry diplomatic passports. George Alexander and his father run their operation as independent criminals. The Russian Embassy doesn't realize their commercial attaché runs an organized crime side hustle."

"Or the embassy does realize," said Gunner, "and they don't care. Maybe they look the other way and treat this as a fringe benefit for him."

"Either way, I think George Alexander and his father intend to highjack the counterfeiting operation. They will use the bank they own in Kazakhstan to launder the fake money into real cash. They have the perfect setup to do that."

"This thing with the Turkic Liberation Army is a hoax?" Billow said.

"I'm afraid so, Andy. The TLA might be real, but Duman and the Kusainovs scammed you and Aisha."

Billow shoved his chair back. "That's it. I quit."

Chuck gave him a palms-down. "Don't be hasty, Andy. Both the Chinese and the Russians have figured out that Aisha is involved in this screwball project. That's why they tried to kidnap her. At the least, the Chinese and the Russians have painted a bull's-eye on Aisha's back. If you quit and walk away, they may still go after her. But what about you? The Chinese realize you are involved, because they tried to kidnap Aisha to get to you. The Russians may not be aware you exist, but I wouldn't count on it. They and the Chinese might both target you and Aisha."

"Why do they want me?"

"The Chinese want to destroy the counterfeiting operation root and branch. Their goal is simple: Kill you, Aisha, Duman, the Kusainovs, and anybody else connected to the counterfeiting scheme. The Russians' goals are complicated: They want Aisha as leverage with her father, the head of the Kazakh security police. They want you because you can continue printing the fake tenges for them. You're backup for Vladimir Kusainov."

Billow poured more coffee. "I don't worry so much about me, but I need to protect Aisha. How do we get her out of this?"

"We bring down the counterfeiting scheme in such an obvious way that the Chinese and the Russians will realize you and Aisha are no longer involved in it. In fact, they need to comprehend that the entire operation is history."

"How do we do that?"

"We use the Secret Service," Chuck said. "We let them arrest the whole team."

Billow clunked his coffee cup on the table. "Just a damned minute, bro.

Remember that Aisha and I are both on the team, and I'm the main guy who runs the printing press. How do we keep the Feds from sending me to prison, too, huh? And Aisha, as an accessory?"

"You both need a good attorney. First, we need to move you and Aisha physically away from Southeast Printing and Binding. While either of you are there, you can be tailed and targeted."

"That's easy. Aisha and I planned to eat lunch together and go back to work. Instead, we won't go back."

"That's good thinking, but where would you stay?"

"We can stay in the hotel Aisha rented yesterday."

"Does Duman know where you two stayed last night?"

"Sure. He stayed there also."

"Then the Kusainovs know. Staying there makes you sitting ducks. You need to be somewhere Duman and the Kusainovs and the Chinese and the Russians—and the Secret Service—can't find you. Someplace you didn't use a credit card to pay for. Someplace you haven't discussed on Aisha's phone, which the Secret Service listens to."

Billow was bobbing his head while Chuck talked. "I bet you have someplace in mind."

"I have a friend. I'll give him a call at eleven a.m."

"Why so late?"

"He's an old man, and he works until midnight on Friday and Saturday. He needs the rest."

Billow left his car at Tank's house and rode with Chuck. Chuck didn't know if his car was being tracked by person or persons unknown, and he didn't want to take the time to search under it. Simpler to drive the Avanti since it no longer carried a GPS tracker.

Damn. Chuck told himself that was water under the bridge. He couldn't change the past. Focus on present opportunities.

Billow opened the passenger door. "Where does Aisha sit?"

Chuck's Avanti was a two-door car, but the back seat was miniscule.

Most two-door cars made in America disappeared by the 1980s. It was possible that Billow had never ridden in one.

Chuck gestured with his thumb. "In the back."

"How is she supposed to get in there? Crawl over the front seat?"

Chuck walked around the car and flipped the passenger seat forward. "Like this. You get out of the car and fold the seat forward. The passenger climbs in back."

"I never saw anything like that," Billow said. "That's amazing engineering."

"That's why the 1963 Studebaker Avanti is a classic. Climb in, and let's pick up your fiancée."

Chuck didn't let Billow call Aisha, even with the burner phone, because he hadn't given Aisha a burner phone. Instead, they parked in a visitor space at the modest hotel where he and Aisha and Duman stayed the previous night. Chuck sat in the car while Billow fetched his fiancée.

Billow called. "She's at the pool with Duman. How do I get her away from him?"

"Tell him you want to steal your fiancée away for a romantic lunch, just the two of you. And wink at him. If he asks, tell him you'll pick him up after lunch."

Four minutes later, the two of them strolled out the front door hand-in-hand. Billow opened the passenger door and flipped the seat forward. "You sit in back, honey. I'm too tall to fit back there."

"What is this?"

"It's a two-door car—a classic made in 1963."

"Okay. I'll squeeze in." She wedged herself into the back seat by rotating her knees sideways. "It's awfully small back here. What are these things?"

"Those," Chuck said, "are the 1963 version of seat belts. There is no shoulder harness and no tensioner for the lap strap. Pull it snug and you'll be okay. I wouldn't dare have an accident. Parts are so hard to locate that my antique car mechanic pitches a hissy fit when I get the smallest ding on it."

As Chuck drove away, Duman stood in the hotel lobby, observing. He suspected something was up. Chuck gave no indication that he noticed him. Let the bastard wonder.

Chuck stopped at a discount store for Billow and Aisha to buy clothes and toiletries and suitcases.

"Why can't we buy stuff at this place we're staying?" Billow asked.

"The place we're going sells similar items with a cutesy Mango Island logo for three times the price. It's like shopping at Rodeo Drive in Beverly Hills, compared to Main Street in Des Plaines, Illinois. People who shop on Mango Island are so rich they seldom ask what anything costs."

Aisha leaned forward. "And your friend owns a condo there which he doesn't use?"

"They use it a few times a year. It's available right now."

"Why would this man who never asks what anything costs, why would he say, 'Sure, I own the perfect condo I am not using. Your young friends need to hide from assassins? No problem. I shall loan these strangers my million-dollar condo.' He's that kind of friend. Really?"

"You and Andy aren't strangers. I vouched for you with the owners."

"Still," Billow said, "you call without notice, and he loans it to us? Just like that?"

"I saved a family member of his from a long prison sentence. Ever since, he and his wife do me favors. I tell them I did what I was paid to do, but they'll have none of that. This couple is very generous."

Chuck stopped at a grocery store and let his friends buy enough food for three or four days.

Aisha's phone rang. "It's Duman calling. What shall I do?"

"Let it go to voicemail. We'll discuss this later. A little mystery won't do us any harm."

Duman called twice more before he gave up.

"Aisha, may I have your phone please?"

She handed it to Chuck, and he removed the battery.

"We don't want anyone to track your phone." Chuck shoved the battery and phone in his pocket and handed her a new burner phone. "Use this one until we get your deal with the Feds sorted out. Then I'll return your other phone. But don't call anyone who is not on the phone's contact list. If the Kusainovs or the Secret Service or the Chinese or the Russians get this number, they can find you. Don't call anyone you don't absolutely have to."

It was a short trip to the Mango Island ferry terminal. Like Pink Coral Island, Mango Island is built around a golf course, except Mango Island is twice the size and has hundreds of high-rise condos and resort facilities and dozens of single-family mansions. Being a barrier island between Seeti Bay and the Atlantic Ocean, it has world-class beaches. Mango Island is reachable by boat, seaplane, or helicopter. Chuck had visited several times, typically as an invited guest, but once or twice trespassing in the middle of the night. But that's a story for another time.

Chuck stopped in the visitors' lane at the ferry terminal's guard house. "Carlos McCrary. I'm a guest of Hank Hickham." Chuck handed his driver's license to the guard.

The guard consulted a computer terminal, scanned Chuck's license, and handed him a pass. "Please display the pass on your dashboard. Do you need a map of the Island?"

"No thanks. I've been here before."

"Very good, sir. Enjoy your stay on Mango Island."

Chuck joined the queue to board the ferry. The *Islandhopper II* glided into the dock. The cars departing from the island drove off the ferry, and their queue drove on. As the last car boarded, the ferry pushed off.

Aisha gawked at the *Islandhopper III* cruising the other direction. "Are these ferries the only way to the island? There's no bridge?"

"Boat, helicopter, or swim. That's it. That's one thing that makes it exclusive. And expensive."

When they reached the Hickhams' condo parking lot, Chuck stopped at the condo's concierge and got Billow and Aisha guest cards for the island. The concierge gave them a Mango Island Paradise Map and explained the various shuttle routes and hours of operation.

They rode the elevator up. Chuck gave them a tour of the condo, then handed them the keys. "You can ride the shuttles all over the island. This building has its own pool and the beach club is across the street. If you get tired of cooking, buy food and drinks at the beach club or any restaurant on the island with your guest cards."

"Since everything on Mango Island is so expensive, how do we pay your friends back?" Aisha asked.

"You don't. I offered to pay them. They won't accept it. Like I said, they are generous people."

———

Valentine's night Chuck had promised Vicky they would spend the weekend at his condo. He hoped his fiasco of not finding the GPS tracker wouldn't shake her up too badly to enjoy the getaway.

She planned to go to Chuck's condo before lunch. Chuck expected that the next weekend he would raise the stakes in his long-distance relationship with Ruby by asking her for an exclusive arrangement. That would lead to more frequent-flyer miles and sooner or later one of them would relocate—either him to Austin or Ruby to Port City. Chuck was quite happy to do either one.

If that led to marriage, this would be the last romantic weekend Chuck spent with Vicky. If this were to be their last time together, Chuck wanted it to be special. He started the Avanti and texted Vicky he was on the way.

In case anybody had staked out his condo again, he parked the Avanti in the parking lot at a busy motel on the Atlantic side of Port City Beach where it wouldn't be noticed and Ubered across to his condo on the Seeti Bay side.

Chuck opened the front door and smelled burgers grilling. Vicky had opened the sliders and ocean breezes swept through the apartment.

"How did your impromptu tour of Bayside Mall go?"

"As planned. Don't you worry, big guy, 'cause I'm not worried. Let's focus on us, on the weekend, and on a good time. We can start worrying again Monday morning. Deal?"

"Deal."

They bumped fists.

Following lunch and what they jokingly called a "nap," they spent an hour at the pool.

Snoop texted Chuck again.

It was the Russians. They gave up at 3 p.m. I

tailed them to 26 San Marco Drive. I assume you are through with me, and you and Vicky are enjoying your weekend. Give her a hug. Call if you need me.

"Was that Snoop?"

Chuck showed her the text.

"Let's follow his advice and enjoy our weekend."

They motored Chuck's boat *The Gator Raider Too* out to admire the sunset and dine at Vicky's favorite waterfront restaurant.

As they cruised home at idle speed, Chuck brought Vicky up to date on the situation with Billow and Aisha.

"They'll need a good negotiator," Vicky said. "Someone who knows how to horse-trade with the U.S. Attorney for them to testify against the Kusainovs and against Aisha's brother."

Chuck smiled. "I know the world's greatest criminal attorney: Abe Weisman."

A few years back Chuck had been charged with murder. Vicky didn't handle criminal cases nor did anyone in her boutique firm. She introduced Chuck to Abe Weisman, who represented him in that case. Although Abe didn't get Chuck off—Chuck did that by catching the real killer—Abe impressed Chuck with his skill. He had represented other clients of Chuck's since then.

"Do you think Abe will represent Aisha and Andy?"

"Do they have money? Abe's not cheap."

"Andy and Aisha have been drawing big salaries for a couple of months and have nothing to spend it on. If necessary, I'll front them the money."

"This is the type of case Abe lusts after. He loves to butt heads with the U.S. Attorney. If he's busy, Diane can handle it as well as Abe."

Diane Toklas was Abe's partner.

"I'll call them first thing Monday morning," Chuck said. "Now, could you please hustle your sweet ass up to the bow and tie us off? In case you didn't notice, this is our dock."

———

Monday morning, Vicky and Chuck finished a Western omelet he cooked for breakfast. "Chuck, thank you for a lovely weekend. We did everything I wanted this weekend: sunsets, boating, eating, and tennis, even though tennis isn't your favorite sport."

"That's because you always beat me."

"It hasn't escaped my notice that you've been catering to me more than usual. I mean, even a foot massage?"

"I'm glad you enjoyed yourself. I enjoyed every second of this weekend, except for losing in straight sets yesterday afternoon."

"I am the gazelle on the Africa veldt, and you're the elephant, a magnificent beast that will never catch a gazelle."

She reached across the table and squeezed his hand. "Is this weekend your way of saying goodbye? You wanted to send me off with a bang, if you'll excuse the pun?"

Chuck didn't know what to say, so he didn't.

"Chuck, this is the first Valentine's Day you've sent me flowers. I'm not faulting you for that; you're just not a man who remembers those things. I'm guessing you sent Ruby flowers for Valentine's because you plan to make a major advance in your relationship, and you decided to give me a weekend to remember."

"For a family law attorney, you make a good detective."

"It's not my business. We don't get jealous of each other's relationships, and you haven't said a word about Ruby all weekend, but I'm curious—are you going to propose? If so and if she says yes, then, as a *former* friend with benefits, I want to be the first to congratulate you. Hank met her. He says you two are great together."

"No proposal yet. She's flying in Friday to spend the weekend. I intend to suggest we have an exclusive relationship."

Vicky began clearing the table. "I've never made a long-distance relationship work more than a couple of months. How does Ruby feel about relocating to Florida?"

Chuck carried his dishes to the sink. "We haven't discussed it, but I believe she would be amenable, especially with the bitch of a winter they're suffering in Austin. Or I'd be happy living in Texas. Heck, I lived there the first eighteen years of my life."

Vicky washed her hands in the sink and dried them. "Your friends are here in Port City. Your business contacts. You'd have to start over in Austin. I don't want to see you get hurt again. You get sloppy sentimental when a girl breaks your heart. I should know. I'm the one who puts you back together again."

Chuck rinsed the dishes and loaded them in the dishwasher.

"True, but I'm going to make the question very low key. Besides, she might say yes. When I moved here, the only people I knew in Port City were you and Hank. I can make more friends in Austin. Plus, my family lives in Texas."

He closed the dishwasher door.

"I'm sure Ruby and I will have a busy discussion this weekend. At least, I hope the conversation gets that far. Hell, she may not be ready for an exclusive relationship."

Vicky checked the time on her phone. "I need to get dressed for work. Let me know how you make out with Weisman."

EIGHTEEN

A be Weisman was tied up for a week with the defense of a corporate CEO against insider trading charges by the Securities and Exchange Commission. Chuck wasn't worried that Abe was unavailable. His partner, Diane Toklas, was plenty smart and brave enough to represent his friends.

Monday afternoon, Diane drove to Mango Island to interview Billow and Aisha. Chuck didn't attend because having a third party present would waive their attorney-client privilege.

Diane called Chuck afterward and said she would represent them. She had an appointment with the U.S. Attorney for Tuesday and wanted to eat dinner with Chuck Tuesday night to discuss his possible role. Chuck hadn't met with Diane since she made partner and the firm changed its name to Weisman and Toklas. He looked forward to their dinner.

While that was happening, the FBI interviewed Pavel Nurbayev in the jail ward at Cedars of Lebanon Hospital on Monday. On Tuesday they filed new federal charges against him for money laundering. Special Agent in Charge Eugenio Lopez bought Chuck's lunch on Tuesday.

Chuck figured he must be doing something right.

Now all the Feds needed to do was execute a search warrant on Southwest Printing and Binding and arrest a bunch of people. That was like saying that all Napoleon needed to do was invade Russia and capture Moscow. Easy to say; difficult to do.

Flamer sent Chuck a report on each of the twelve properties that George Alexander was the trustee for. The attachment to his email was over a hundred pages long. Chuck decided to study it in detail that night when he got home.

———

Chuck parked in a visitor space at the College of Language Arts and Sciences of the University of Atlantic County. Chuck's appointment with Dr. Anatoly Kuzmich was at 1:30 in his office on the third floor of Meacham Hall.

He stood in Kuzmich's office door and rapped twice on the jamb.

Professor Kuzmich stepped around his cluttered desk and extended his hand. "You are Detective Carlos McCrary, yes? You are prompt. I appreciate a person who is prompt. It demonstrates respect for others."

He pumped Chuck's hand with both his and gestured at a wooden chair that might have come from the UAC library. It had a worn brown cushion like the ones at the University of Florida library when Chuck studied there. Good times and good memories.

"You want me to translate a conversation you, uh, shall we say 'overheard'?"

Kuzmich's UAC biography said he was 63 years old and had been a naturalized U.S. citizen over twenty-five years. He was bald on top with a fringe of gray hair and an obvious comb-over. The wrinkled collar of a blue and white plaid shirt showed above his gray V-neck sweater. He wore a Glen Plaid sport coat, khaki pants, and scuffed brown brogans. His blue-green eyes twinkled with intelligence.

"Yes, Professor, I do. Or do you prefer to be called Doctor?"

"My students call me Doctor or Professor. Either one. But you—" He waved a hand and returned to his desk chair. "—you are not a student. You are a *client* and a public servant. You should call me Anatoly, yes?"

Chuck handed him a business card, one without the crossed swords. "I am a private investigator, not a detective. I was a detective with the Port

City police for two years. Now I run McCrary Investigations. Everyone calls me Chuck."

He studied Chuck's card. "Aha, I appreciate the nickname. Chuck is a diminutive for Charles, and Charles is the English translation of Carlos. Very good, Chuck."

He handed Kuzmich the flash drive. "There are four conversations on this drive. Two are one side of telephone calls and two have both sides of a live conversation. I'd like you to translate."

Kuzmich plugged the flash drive into his computer.

"I saw on the news that four Russian men were involved in a gunfight on Port City Beach last Wednesday night. Your name was mentioned as the Good Samaritan. Do these conversations relate to those Russian gangsters?"

"Yes, sir, they do."

"After you made the appointment, I called a woman with the Port City Police Department to make inquiries. This woman is a friend from my synagogue. She said you were, uh, unconventional and operated so—I believe the word she used was 'informally'—that you might break the law sometimes. Is this true?"

"Yes, sir. I am more interested in right and wrong than in legal and illegal. The man I recorded is the employer of the four gunmen. I don't intend to use the information in a court of law, but to protect the woman from further attempts to kidnap her. I assume the woman you spoke to from your synagogue was my training officer when I was a Port City cop, Lieutenant Joyce Weiner?"

"She sends her regards and says you owe her a lunch for the nice things she said about you."

Kuzmich inserted the flash drive in the side of his laptop. "Please close the door, Chuck."

As he closed the door, a conversation in Russian played from the external speakers.

Chuck lifted his phone and pointed to the Audio Recorder icon.

Kuzmich nodded as he listened. He paused the playback and Chuck started his phone's audio recorder.

"The speaker is talking on the telephone to a man he calls 'Misha,' a diminutive for Mikhail in Russian or Michael in English. He is speaking in a manner that tells me Misha is subservient, probably an employee." He played the audio awhile. "He instructs Misha to discover where 'the goddamned detective' lives. He did not say the name of the detective. Might it be you?"

"Gotta be."

He played the flash drive again, stopping to translate. Alexander had made the first phone call within minutes after Chuck left his home. Misha was to use the GPS tracker to stalk Chuck. The second call was Misha reporting the building in which Chuck lived. Alexander told Misha to take three men to stake out Chuck's building and follow him. They were to kill him at the first opportunity. That was just before Chuck drove to Vicky's apartment.

Learning he led four gunmen close to Vicky's home was a "butt pucker" moment. A frisson of fear ran down Chuck's spine as he realized the Russians were closing in on one of his dearest friends.

He resolved to do something about this Russian Godfather.

The final two conversations were between Alexander and Terrence, sitting in Alexander's loggia, and Alexander's father, Aleksandr Borisov, speaking from the Russian Embassy on the speakerphone. Borisov castigated his son for wasting resources on a fruitless attempt to assassinate Chuck. He called the young PI an "insignificant window-peeping nobody of an agent for ambulance-chasing lawyers."

Kuzmich was amused at translating that description. "It is more insulting in the original Russian with its nuance of derision and contempt."

"Everybody says that about me, Anatoly, but typically in English or Spanish."

"Then the father says you are not worth the price of the bullets to shoot you."

"Everybody says that too."

Borisov told Terrence to scout the printer and return with a plan to invade the print shop. The final conversation was on Monday between the three men. Borisov listened to Terrence's plan to kill everybody in the print shop. He'd steal the completed fake tenges and the printer plates and the blank paper for printing them.

Borisov modified the plan. "Take eight people in four SUVs. You'll have space to haul the paper and currency. Burn the shop to the ground when you finish. Scrub all clues. Do it at three o'clock in the morning. I'll send the extra men and vehicles on Wednesday. Attack the print shop as soon as the men are ready."

It was a fifteen-hour drive from D.C. to Port City. Would they split it into two days or switch drivers and travel non-stop? The answer would determine how long Chuck had to plan his response.

Chuck called FBI SAIC Eugenio Lopez and Special Agent Valery Villa of the Secret Service and arranged a conference.

———

That night Chuck met Diane Toklas on the top floor of the Port City Palace for dinner. She briefed him on the non-confidential facts of the case and what his role would be. Chuck asked that his role be small. He had finished his mission to catch Phil Franks's killers. At this point Chuck wanted only to make the counterfeiting charge against Billow disappear. That way, Chuck's life could return to the chaotic weirdness that passed for normal in his world.

Chuck didn't tell her about George Alexander's plans to kill him, but he told her about the Russians' plans to assault the printing company. "That's another reason to keep Andy and Aisha away from that shop."

"Have you notified the proper authorities?" she said.

"I have an appointment with the FBI and the Secret Service tomorrow. All you and I need to worry about is keeping Andy and Aisha out of jail."

"We're making progress." Diane told Chuck she had spent much of that day in a dogfight at the Miami office of Harding Louis Jefferies, the U.S. Attorney for the Southern District of Florida. "Jefferies is a pompous blowhard who tries to prove how smart he is. He agreed to five years' probation with no jail time. You are to take Aisha and Andy to the FBI office tomorrow morning. They will transfer them to a safe house and I'll represent them tomorrow afternoon at the FBI interview."

"Do you trust the FBI not to question them before you get there?

Perhaps a 'casual conversation' with their handlers while they wait for you to arrive?"

"Good point. After you fetch Andy and Aisha, pick me up at my office on the way to the FBI office. I'll stay with them."

———

Chuck studied Flamer's report on George Alexander's Florida Land Trusts until almost midnight. Just when his eyes were going buggy, he figured out where Alexander was stealing the money. It was the slickest scam Chuck had ever seen.

———

The next morning, Chuck collected Billow and Aisha on Mango Island. He drove the Caravan so they had more room. "The FBI has a safe house for you two to stay in until the bad guys are in custody. I'll fetch Diane on our way to the FBI office. She'll escort you during the transfer to the safe house, and she will be with you when the FBI interviews you. Did you pack everything?"

"There wasn't much," Aisha said, "but we got it all. We did splurge on matching Mango Island tee-shirts." She held one up for Chuck to admire before folding it into her suitcase. "And yes, we paid three times what we normally pay. But the memory will be worth it." She and Billow handed Chuck the keys to the condo and their guest cards. "It was nice to see how the other half lives."

"To meet the owner, you'd say he was a good ol' boy from a small town in the Deep South without two nickels to rub together."

Chuck walked with Billow, Aisha, and Diane into the lobby of the Federal Building. "Aisha, in case I don't see you and Andy again until your wedding, congratulations to you both. Andy, I assume you and Aisha will move back to Des Plaines after this takedown at Southeast Printing and Binding is over?"

"Yeah. We both have family in Illinois. I talked to Esther Florence at

Bald Eagle Printing. Last week they fired the guy they hired to replace me. She offered me a raise to take my old job back."

"Win-win all around," Chuck said.

"We'll be married this spring," Aisha glanced at Billow and smiled, "after baseball season starts. We'll pick a date when the White Sox play another series with the Pilots. You men can catch a couple of baseball games while you're in Chicago."

"I love the idea. I now leave you in the capable hands of Diane Toklas."

Aisha hugged Chuck and kissed his cheek. "I can never thank you enough for saving me from the Russians."

"You just did."

Billow shook Chuck's hand, then bear-hugged him. "Watch your six, Chuck," he whispered. "I wouldn't put it past the Russians to seek revenge for the two thugs you killed." He broke the hug. "If you need me, I kept that special cellphone, bro."

"You won't be involved in the arrest of the Kusainovs and Duman?" Aisha asked.

"I had two missions: Catch Phil Franks's killers and make sure that Andy was safe. I accomplished both. It's time to get back to running my own business."

Chuck didn't tell them that the Godfather had sent a team of killers after him. That was his problem, not theirs.

———

Agents Valery Villa and Lionel Welsh walked into Eugenio Lopez's office in the Federal Building at 3:00 p.m.

Welsh was dressed in the same gray pinstriped suit and yellow tie. Or he owns a closet full of identical suits and ties. Like Superman.

Villa wore a tan, raw silk jacket over a yellow silk blouse and white linen pants. This time she wore gold loop earrings and a matching gold chain necklace. Her hairstyle seemed less formal to Chuck, although he knew nothing about women's hair styles other than whether he liked them. To him, she seemed like a normal Floridian, not a Federal agent. No pantyhose this time. White sneakers so clean they might have just come from the shoe box.

In other words, today she looked hot. Chuck considered offering to let her strip-search him, but his better angels prevailed.

SAIC Gene Lopez was casual today, at least for him. Navy-blue sport coat and khaki pants to go with his light blue, button-down dress shirt, red tie, and black shoes shined so bright you could spot the fluorescent ceiling lights reflected in them.

"Have a seat Special Agents," Lopez said. "Did the receptionist offer you some refreshment?"

"We're good, Gene," Villa said. To Chuck: "The U.S. Attorney's office said you have information on the Kusainovs, Mr. McCrary. That's why we came."

"Call me Chuck," he said, "and I'll call you Special Agent Villa."

She almost smiled. Maybe she wasn't a robot after all.

"There was a miscommunication regarding the purpose of the meeting, Valery," Lopez said. "Chuck's information concerns a planned attack on the Southeast Printing and Binding Company building and personnel."

"Don't worry, Special Agent Villa," Chuck said. "I'll tell you about the Kusainovs, but if you Feds don't handle the planned attack, you won't find anyone alive to arrest."

"So, tell us what you know, Chuck," Lopez said.

"Treat this as an anonymous tip. Make notes while I play this. I can't give you a copy of the recording."

Chuck played them his audio recording of the two telephone conversations with Dr. Kuzmich's translation.

"Driving straight through, they would arrive tonight," Chuck said. "If they take two days, they'll arrive tomorrow afternoon."

"How do you spell Aleksandr Borisov?" Lopez asked.

Chuck spelled it.

"That's part of the translation," Lopez said, "or I should say, part of the recording."

"Yes, there were two one-sided telephone calls before those that didn't concern the printing company. I didn't bother playing them."

"Since this is a counterfeiting operation, the Secret Service should be in charge," Villa said.

"Since this involves eight armed men who crossed state lines to commit a planned mass murder," Lopez said, "the FBI should clearly be in charge. We have the trained agents in South Florida, and we can be ready tomorrow."

"We can get the armed agents we need," Villa said. "They can be here tomorrow morning."

Welsh kept his mouth shut.

Lopez and Villa stared at each other, each waiting for the other to blink.

Chuck stood. "I'm getting another coffee. You dedicated public servants work this out between you. But play nice; I faint at the sight of blood."

He exited the room with them still staring at each other.

Chuck returned ten minutes later, and Lopez said, "It will be a joint task force."

What a stupid idea, Chuck thought. He managed not to say that out loud, but the FBI and the Secret Service were both federal bureaucracies, fighting turf battles between the Justice Department and the Treasury Department. What else should he expect? The operation would be a two-headed mule. An animal that can't make up its mind and is stubborn about it to boot. Better if they had flipped a coin.

Chuck kept his opinion to himself. It wasn't his neck on the line. Besides, he had his own troubles. But Chuck planned to warn Hank Ramirez and Buster Cleveland and Joyce Weiner and Jorge Castellano and anyone in the PCPD hierarchy he knew to avoid this risky mission. Too easy for good people to die unnecessarily.

"Let's take a short comfort break," Lopez said, "before we get Chuck's briefing on the Kusainovs."

"And we can take a piss," Chuck said.

Agent Villa seemed shocked, but perhaps Chuck read more into it than he should. Lopez looked amused. He had worked with Chuck before.

Fifteen minutes later they reconvened.

Chuck briefed the agents on the kidnapping of Gunner Knutson and the rescue mission, although he was pretty sure they had read the police reports. "In the course of that mission, I captured the leader of the gang and asked him why the Chinese military attaché sent eight PLA soldiers to South Florida to hunt Aisha Aubakirovna."

"That's your friend's girlfriend you told us about last time we met?" Villa said.

"She's his fiancée. The leader of the kidnappers said he was Captain Zhao Kang of the People's Liberation Army of China." Chuck spelled it. "That's the name on his diplomatic passport. I later learned from the Port City cops who ran his prints that he is a Colonel in the PLA intelligence division. In other words, he's a military spy."

Chuck didn't tell the Feds about Kang's last threat to him. They couldn't help Chuck, but they might handicap him.

"You saw his diplomatic passport?" Villa asked.

"Sure. I made pictures of it with my phone. Shall I text them to you?"

"Not now. But this Colonel was willing to let you interrogate him?"

"Yes. Anyway—"

"He is a Chinese diplomat, and he did not claim diplomatic immunity from questioning? I find that hard to believe."

"I was very persuasive."

Villa regarded Chuck with manifest disapproval.

Lopez smirked. He was enjoying this.

"Very Special Agent Villa," Chuck said, "do you want to learn what I know or don't you? I might have kept my mouth shut. Instead, I volunteered to cooperate with you. Now you act as if you don't want to know."

Villa forced her lips into a thin line. "May I record this interview?"

"No, but you can take notes. According to Colonel Zhao Kang," Chuck spelled the name again, "the Kusainov family planned to counterfeit millions of Kazakhstan tenges—that's the name of the Kazakh national currency."

"Why does the PLA care about Kazakhstan?"

"The Kusainovs claimed to be active in the Turkic Liberation Army. The TLA is an underground political movement to create an independent Republic of Turkistan from parts of Kazakhstan and the Xinjiang region of China. The TLA plans to overthrow the current Kazakhstan government, then create the Republic of Turkistan. Assuming that succeeds, they'll invade Xinjiang. Needless to say, both the People's Republic of China and the current leaders of the Republic of Kazakhstan treat the TLA as terrorists."

"I know the People's Liberation Army," Villa said, "but this is the first I've heard of a Turkic Liberation Army. Are the Kusainovs using this counterfeit money to fund the TLA?"

"No. They are stealing it to buy gold for their Swiss bank accounts. They and Duman Aubakirovich. But the PLA doesn't realize the counterfeit scheme is a hoax which the Kusainovs are playing on the TLA. Neither does the TLA. The Kusainovs are not patriots or revolutionaries. They are thieves. So are Duman Aubakirovich and his father."

"The PLA fears the TLA movement will spill over into China."

"Kazakhstan and Xinjiang are Muslim majority regions with cultural ties reaching back hundreds of years, long before the founding of either the Soviet Union or the People's Republic of China. The Kusainovs are from Kazakhstan and have many criminal contacts there, including Duman's father, the Police Commissioner of the Security Police in Almaty."

"Did Colonel Kang have proof of the counterfeiting scheme?"

"Special Agent Villa, we're talking about the PLA. The Communist Chinese government doesn't care about civil rights and fair trials. When they suspect someone is guilty, they don't need proof. Hell, their whole operation in Florida violated a bunch of treaties and international laws. After we rescued Gunner, the Port City cops turned the Chinese over to the FBI."

Chuck pivoted to Lopez. "What did you do with them, Gene?"

"Our State Department contacted the Chinese Ambassador. We declared the three survivors to be *personae non grata*. They have been expelled from the USA."

"And Gene won't say this," Chuck said, "but I will: Both the U.S. and the Chinese government decided to keep quiet about it to avoid their mutual embarrassment."

"Our people are interviewing Aisha Aubakirovna and Andrew Billow at an FBI safe house. We'll get probable cause for a search warrant."

"Can you get the warrant before the Russians attack the print shop?"

Chuck asked. "They might attack at three a.m. tomorrow. Ten hours from now. If they took two days to drive from Washington, they could attack by three a.m. Friday."

"It'll be tough to get the warrant before tomorrow," Lopez said.

"Your best bet is to execute the warrant tomorrow, arrest the group at the printers, and haul off the evidence. Then hide near the printing company for the Russian attack."

"Let's take another break," Lopez said. "I need to make a phone call."

Ten minutes later, they reconvened. "We'll have the warrant tomorrow afternoon. We'll hit the printer tomorrow evening." Lopez glanced at Villa. "Does that meet with your approval, Special Agent Villa?"

"Sounds good to me." To Welsh: "Get our agents ready to go tomorrow at six p.m."

Welsh left.

Chuck said, "If the Russians arrive from Washington, D.C., this afternoon, they will attack the print shop at three o'clock tomorrow morning, fifteen hours before you serve your search warrant. You would arrive to a burned out building full of corpses. You need agents to guard the shop tonight."

"You're right. Valery, I'll stage ten FBI agents near Southwest Printing and Binding by midnight. Can you arrange ten Secret Service agents?"

"I'll make it happen," she said. She telephoned Welsh and gave him instructions.

Villa turned to Chuck again. "Why didn't the Chinese attack the Kusainovs' operation once they found it. They could kill everybody there. The Russians plan to do it with eight soldiers."

"It will be more than eight. George Alexander already has a gang who live in Port City. I don't know how many men he has. There could be a dozen or more gunmen in the assault team."

Lopez wrote a note on a pad in front of him.

"Still," Villa said, "eight PLA soldiers should have been enough."

"I disagree," Chuck said. "The Chinese located the Kusainovs the first week in January. They got lucky and kidnapped and interrogated Phillip Franks. From that, they learned the operation was stronger than they'd thought. They were casing the plant and gathering intelligence when I spotted them stalking Aisha."

"Still, with eight professional soldiers, they would make quick work of everyone at the print shop."

"Whatever," Chuck said, "that's in the past. Today, the people in the print shop are armed. One of them shot down my drone with a shotgun. Andrew Billow, the main offset press operator, is a former Green Beret and the Chinese may think that other employees have military backgrounds. The rank and file weren't in on the theft. They think they are genuine revolutionaries. There's no telling how many people and guns they have inside. I don't blame the Chinese for being cautious after learning what they did from Phillip Franks."

"Do you think we'll meet resistance serving the warrant?" Lopez asked.

"Did Napoleon meet resistance invading Russia?"

―――――

Gene Lopez called Chuck the next morning. "The Russians didn't attack the printer last night. They must be taking two days to drive from Washington. Just thought you'd like to know."

"Thanks, Gene. Did you get your search warrant yet?"

"Not yet. We're pushing, but it's like wading through mud."

"Did you ever hear of Murphy's Second Law, Gene?"

"The only Murphy's Law I ever heard was 'Anything that can go wrong will go wrong'."

"Murphy's Second Law says: Everything take longer than you expect."

Lopez laughed and disconnected.

Chuck didn't feel too confident. He had intercepted another conversation between the Russians.

―――――

"Anatoly, this is Chuck McCrary. I intercepted another conversation yesterday afternoon. Would it be possible for you to translate it?"

"Sure. One-thirty this afternoon still okay?"

"Thanks. I'll be there."

Ruby was due at eight-thirty the next night. Chuck didn't want George Alexander's thugs to mess up their romantic weekend. Chuck needed to learn what the Russians had planned. The way Alexander talked about Chuck to his father made Chuck pretty sure that Alexander would continue his attempts to kill the PI.

Chuck got to the UAC campus as the cold front arrived. The wind freshened from the northwest and the clouds rolled in like an invading army.

Chuck parked in the visitor space he had used before.

He handed the professor the new flash drive, and Kuzmich clicked it into his laptop. "You shared my earlier translation with the FBI, yes? They are preparing for the attack on the printer?"

"Yes, I shared it with them, and it's in their hands. But I couldn't discuss the FBI's plans if I knew them. Operational security."

"You are not at risk, yes?"

"No, I'm not involved, and I'm glad it's out of my hands. You translated the Russians' attack plans. You know what it will be like. This action reminds me of the wars I fought in Iraq and Afghanistan. Small skirmishes with unpredictable irregular troops in urban settings."

"Okay, let us translate what the Russian-American gangsters say this time." He clicked the mouse. A torrent of Russian played from the speakers.

Kuzmich listened, then paused the playback. "Your man George does not obey his father—he is not finished with you. George looked at a condo for sale in your building. He met the Harbor Master of your marina to discuss putting his yacht there."

The Harbor Master. Chuck's gut clinched like he'd been punched in the stomach. The Godfather had discovered a gap in Chuck's condo's security —the marina. Or, more specifically, the Harbor Master. The condo Harbor Master was a retired Navy Chief Petty Officer who loved to talk about boats and swap stories with anyone who showed an interest.

Chuck already knew what the rest of the conversation would say:

Boaters like to talk about boats. The Godfather would get the Harbor Master to talking. And talking, and talking, and talking.

The professor played the recording again. "In conversation with the Harbor Master, Alexander said you and he were friends and you recommended the building and the marina."

Somewhere in the dialog Chuck heard the name of his boat, *Gator Raider Too.* Kuzmich paused it. "Alexander learned from the Harbor Master that the *Gator Raider Too* belongs to you. The Harbor Master showed him where your boat was moored. Alexander will send this person named Terrence with a sniper rifle to locate a nearby apartment with a view of your dock. He will shoot you next time you use your boat."

Kuzmich ejected the flash drive and handed it to Chuck. "I am sorry, my friend. You are in great danger still."

That news could ruin your day.

Chuck's mind raced down alternate paths.

Alexander didn't know which unit was Chuck's, but he knew where Chuck's boat was. Several high-rises in Chuck's neighborhood had good views of his marina. Alexander might rent an apartment with a window or balcony overlooking the marina from anywhere within, say, four hundred yards. Hell, he might buy a unit in a neighboring building. Terrence would watch until Chuck walked to his boat. *Bang.* An easy shot.

The Godfather might buy a unit in *Chuck's* building. Hire a hitman to ride in an elevator with Chuck and kill him there. There were always strangers wandering in and out of the building. If the assassin couldn't get Chuck alone in an elevator, an owner could easily determine which unit was his. Then post Terrence on any of dozens of balconies on the building next door. *Bang.* An easier shot.

Chuck was a sitting duck. When Ruby came, she would be also. Or Clint or any of Chuck's friends or family. *Bang. Bang.*

"Anatoly, I have a favor to ask: Please keep this conversation confidential. Don't mention it to anyone—especially not Joyce Weiner."

The professor gazed at him. "Reading between the lines of what Lieutenant Weiner told me, I assume you plan to take…preemptive action against this Alexander person."

It wasn't a question so Chuck didn't reply.

Kuzmich shook his hand. "Go with God. This meeting never happened."

The next thing Chuck knew, he was sitting in his car. He didn't remember walking there. He was stunned. Chuck didn't know what the hell he was going to do.

Alexander had all the options; Chuck had none. Alexander would be patient and wait for an opening. He could wait days or weeks, then strike without warning.

Okay, Chuck, keep calm, he told himself, *you need to think about this. You'll come up with something. Just take a breath.*

NINETEEN

Ruby would arrive the next day. Chuck had to act fast, with little time to plan.

Surveying the dozens of apartments that Terrence might choose would be impossible. Chuck had one option, which was no option: a preemptive strike in the Godfather's fortress.

Chuck couldn't make a citizen's arrest in Alexander's own home. His alternative was a citizen's execution. George Alexander was like a rabid dog. Chuck needed to put him down before Ruby arrived.

Chuck had to wage war again. Otherwise, it was a matter of time before Alexander killed Chuck, or, God forbid, Ruby.

The Russians planned to assault the print shop with at least eight men and probably some of Alexander's local crew. If the men departed Washington on Wednesday, they had arrived late last night or would later that afternoon. Either way they would shelter and stage the attack from one or both of Alexander's bungalows. The Feds would be surveilling the San Marco mansion. They had heard the recording Chuck made. They knew Chuck had one or more listening devices in Alexander's mansion. God only knew what spy technology the Feds had available. Even tapping phones and hijacking the bugs Chuck planted inside.

Chuck had been inside once and walked through three rooms. The

Godfather and his thugs lived on premises. Talk about home field advantage.

To top off the difficulty, Chuck assumed the Feds were listening to everybody in the house. Chuck faced two adversaries: The Russians and the Feds.

How the hell could he assassinate George Alexander and not get caught or killed?

The time for the attack was easy: Chuck's best chance was after the Russian invasion force left the estate. That would be about midnight that night. Once they departed the mansion, the Feds' attention would shift to the printing plant.

Maybe the Godfather would be alone in a command post back at the estate. No, not alone, but his bodyguard cohort would be small, perhaps two or three men.

It was doable.

Then the cold front slammed with full force and the rain fell in buckets.

———

San Marco Island had one bridge. Hank parked a half-block from the bridge at 11:00 p.m. At 12:30 a.m. he called Chuck. "It's raining like you need Noah's ark here. Visibility is impossible. Four dark-colored SUVs with what might be Virginia license plates crossed the bridge. No one sane would be out in this weather. I say it's 'go' time."

At that time of night, the caravan of gunmen needed 45 minutes to an hour to drive to the print shop. With the rain, longer.

"Thanks, Hank. I agree; it's 'go' time."

Chuck tugged on his wetsuit and packed his gear in a dive bag. Gunner was in his Jeep Cherokee in the condo parking garage at 1:20 a.m. Chuck threw his gear in the back and buckled into the passenger seat. Chuck felt his blood pressure rising and the adrenaline pumping. They reached San Marco Island, and his body was on full alert.

Gunner stopped on the grass at the San Marco Island pocket park. A hundred years before, the developers of the Venetian Isles reserved one lot on each island for a neighborhood waterfront park. The homeowners' association added colorful playground equipment for the children and grandchildren of residents. At 1:50 on a Friday morning, the park and the streets would be deserted even without the storm.

The Russian assault team would be on site at Southeast Printing and Binding. Chuck hoped the Feds would too.

Chuck slid the hood over his head. In the event anyone was outside in the storm, his face and neck should not glow white in the dark. He slathered waterproof black grease paint on his face, then wiped his hands on the thighs of the wetsuit before pulling on black gloves. Removing his gear from the dive bag, he donned a buoyant armored vest, and rapped on the driver's window.

Gunner lowered the window two inches.

"You and Hank park out of range of the security cameras. Don't charge in unless you hear gunshots or spot extra lights inside the estate."

"With the noise from this rain, we wouldn't hear the Crack of Doom."

"It can't rain forever. If it does, watch for extra lights. If the Godfather or his crew discover I'm in the house, I'll need backup. You and Hank smash the gate with everything you've got and save my worthless butt."

"You exhibit a great deal of confidence in my Jeep as a battering ram."

"I've used Jeeps on other cases. It could knock over the whole damned wall. Knocking over a steel gate ought to be a walk in the park."

"And if we don't hear shots or observe extra lights from inside…"

"It will mean I hit the target and didn't make a sound. Stay out of range of the cameras and I'll swim out the way I swam in. I'll call your cellphone to pick me up. No one need know we were here."

"Hooah, boss. Good hunting."

Gunner raised the window, slipped the Jeep in gear, and rolled around the corner.

Chuck stood alone in the pouring rain and thought of his high school in Adams Creek, Texas. In high school, the U.S. Army had run recruiting ads with the slogan "An Army of One." Chuck always thought that was pretty cool, and when he graduated, he joined the Army. He was never an army of one when he was in the army because everything was teamwork. But it was a great slogan.

Ironically, more than a decade after leaving the Army, now Chuck truly was an army of one.

———

Lugging his diving bag, Chuck stepped over the seawall and picked his way down the riprap into the canal. The riprap stacked against the seawall prevents erosion from boat wakes, tides, and waves. It gets encrusted with barnacles and coral that cut like walking on broken bottles. If you don't wear tough shoes, it shreds the soles of your feet. Chuck wore hard sole neoprene diving boots.

He adjusted the buoyancy of the diving bag to zero. Thrusting it ahead of him, he waded where he could and swam through the deeper spots. He glided parallel to the seawall past the first three docks. Black bag, black vest, black wetsuit in a black night. Even on a normal dry night, he would be almost invisible to the security camera on the Godfather's roof. The rain would work to his advantage.

Chuck reached the riprap behind 26 San Marco, his body in full attack mode.

The estate owned 170 feet of waterfront. Lush foliage hid the walls on both sides and stretched from the canal to the house.

The Godfather's yacht was unmistakable in the faint ambient light. It was a giant white balloon floating above Chuck's head. He swam between the yacht and the dock to the other end of the dock. He continued to the other end of the seawall where the landscaping hid his approach from the rooftop camera.

The cacophony of the rain splashing on the water made it difficult to concentrate.

Chuck infiltrated at the only spot along the waterfront where bougainvillea grew. They were beautiful, but he knew from painful experience that beneath the blossoms, the giant hedge held a world of hurt.

Chuck unpacked his diving bag behind the bougainvillea, avoiding their two-inch thorns. Removing each item of gear from its waterproof bag, he strapped it on like a suit of armor. Ka-Bar knife on his left calf. Browning .380 pistol in its holster on his right ankle. The ceramic knife on his left forearm. Glock 17 belted around his waist. Extra magazines for both pistols in an ammo bag fastened to the vest. A pry bar and a fanny pack of other goodies and gizmos he hoped he wouldn't need, like a silencer for the Glock.

It was 2:20 a.m.

Wedging his way between the wall and the landscaping, Chuck crabbed toward the main house. The rain pounded against the wall, the palm fronds, the hedges, the pool deck, not to mention his wetsuit hood. The sound was a relentless drum roll punctuated by cymbal clashes of thunder.

As Chuck neared the mansion, he noted two night-lights in the rear loggia, one on either side of the wall of windows from the living room. The sliders were shut against the storm, but were they locked? *Probably not the best place to break in anyway*, he thought.

Chuck had studied the mansion's floorplan and satellite photos online. He moved to the foot of the stairway that led up to the master suite.

The master suite on the second floor overlooked the pool and the water. A large deck with an Italianate balustrade that matched the front terrace opened off the bedroom. A curving stairway descended from the deck to the pool area. The sliders between the master bedroom and the deck were buttoned up. It made a cozy lovers' nest, but Chuck had encountered no mention or evidence of a girlfriend, or a boyfriend for that matter, for the Godfather. Perhaps the old family photo he found in Alexander's office was all that remained of a younger George Alexander's family.

The deck was beneath the field of vision of the rooftop security camera. That made sense: The deck was perfect for the owner's romantic trysts on a starry night. Or would be on a normal starry night for a normal owner.

Chuck pulled a pair of night vision goggles from his belt and studied the deck. A motion-detector was mounted on the balustrade. If anyone climbed those stairs, they would light up like opening night on Broadway. That the rain did not trigger the motion-detector was a tribute to the technology. Perhaps if it rained harder. Like in a hurricane.

Besides, the Godfather wouldn't be asleep. He would monitor his assault team from a command center somewhere.

Where would Chuck put a command center if it were his house? Even for a smartphone conference, he wouldn't invite employees into his bedroom. One maintains a certain distance and mystique with the subordinates.

Chuck wouldn't waste a prime waterfront room on a command center. It would be toward the front of the house. It didn't require an outside window, but with the South Florida climate, all rooms are built to open to the outside. The Godfather's bulk indicated that he wouldn't climb stairs when he could avoid it, and using an elevator was time-consuming. It had to be on the ground floor.

The logical choice: Put the command center on the ground floor of the west bungalow. Chuck had noted the sitting room the previous week when he barged into the fortress uninvited.

The aerial photos Chuck had studied revealed sidewalks on both sides of the mansion that allowed visitors to both bungalows to access the pool without walking through the mansion.

The walkways on both sides of the mansion would not have motion detectors; there was too much lush vegetation to activate them when the wind gusted.

Chuck sneaked along the coral stone walkway toward the front of the mansion. He reached the loggia that connected to the west bungalow. To the left, the loggia ended at the bungalow wall with two doors: an ornate wooden door that was the obvious entrance, and a white metal door beside it with a plaque that said *Utilities*. Passing the loggia, Chuck mounted the side steps to the front terrace and sidestepped beneath the overhanging balconies where he stood out of the rain. From there he looked into the sitting room through the French doors on the front of the bungalow.

Yes. The sitting room was the command center.

The wind was out of the northwest. While the rain did not hit the French doors, rain spatter flecked the glass.

In the daylight, gauze curtains on the French doors admitted natural light and maintained privacy in the sitting room. But with Chuck standing in the dark, the lights inside made the room as clear as if the curtains weren't there.

The Godfather, Terrence, and the second thug that had covered Chuck while Terrence frisked him sat in easy chairs around a coffee table. On the wall behind them, a bank of four, high-definition monitors were mounted above a control panel and an empty desk chair. A coffee bar stood against the back wall.

At the far end were an elevator door and another interior door that led to the garage.

One monitor featured images from the four cameras mounted on the front wall—San Marco Drive with the waves of rain snaking along the street in the wind. A second monitor showed four views of the driveway and garages with the rain making puddles in every imperfection of the brick paving. A third monitor showed twin views of the foyer from above. The fourth and final monitor showed one broad view of the back garden, dock, and yacht. The wind buffeted the rain and made wavy patterns on the canal. The yacht strained against its dock lines.

The three men paid no attention to the monitors. They were intent on the phone on the table.

It was 2:55 a.m. The attack on the print shop would commence any second. Did it begin early? Had the Feds already arrested them all? The Godfather and his merry men didn't act very merry.

The rain was so loud Chuck couldn't have eavesdropped even if he spoke Russian, but he could read their body language like a Russian-English dictionary. They were as tense as the strings on a Balalaika.

Something had gone wrong for the Russians. Too bad.

———

There was a simple solution to the Godfather's contract on Chuck: Kill all three of them. From where Chuck stood under the balcony he was out of range of the driveway and garage cameras. He could fire through the French doors. With a silenced Glock, the shots wouldn't be audible outside the walls of the estate without the rain. With the rain, Chuck could fire a cannon and no one outside the walls would hear it.

The glass would deflect the first bullet a fraction of an inch, but for the second bullet, the glass would not be there. The gauze curtains would have no measurable effect on the slugs.

Since the three gangsters were seated several feet apart, Chuck would shoot each double-tap through a different pane of glass. He would aim at the center of each man's chest. A deflection of an inch or two wouldn't save them. *Bam-bam. Bam-bam. Bam-bam.* No-brainer for a good shooter.

Terrence was Alexander's right-hand man. That made him the most dangerous man in the room. Kill him first. Lounging deep in their upholstered chairs, sluggish in the early morning hours, none of them could reach their weapons in less than two or three seconds. The shooting would be over before they drew their pistols. Kill Thug Two while the Godfather fumbled for his weapon if he even had one. He might not be armed in his own fortress.

After executing all three, Chuck would collect the spent brass. Then drop the brass and gun barrel and silencer in Seeti Bay on the way home.

The next day, Chuck would buy a new barrel and silencer for the Glock. He was wearing gloves and a wetsuit hood. He hadn't appeared on any camera. No evidence.

The perfect crime.

The one insurmountable problem with committing the perfect crime was that Chuck could not bring himself to do it. That was a bridge too far.

Yes, Terrence intended to assassinate him without a qualm. He would hide several hundred yards away with a high-powered sniper rifle. He would screw on a silencer, mount a telescopic gun site on the barrel, and blow Chuck's head into a red paste. Terrence would kill Chuck, not because he hated Chuck, but because that was his job. Probably Thug Two had the same lack of emotion and scruples.

The two thugs bore Chuck no ill will. They were the trigger on a gun; the Godfather was the assassin who would point that gun and squeeze the trigger.

The Godfather ordered it done against the wishes of his father. He was the guilty party, not his men.

For Chuck to kill a person, the bad guy must threaten an innocent person. Shoot at Chuck. Threaten to shoot someone else. Hold a hostage. *Something.*

But shooting a person who was not an active, immediate threat? It wasn't in Chuck's character to be an executioner.

How to solve this dilemma?

In a perfect world, Chuck would hide and wait for justice to catch up with George Alexander. He was guilty of attempted murder for ordering the attack on Aisha and Duman. After the assault on the printer, he would be guilty of federal crimes also. Either the State of Florida or the U.S. Government would put the Godfather in a dark hole for the rest of his life. With him out of the way, the other thugs would have no incentive to attack Chuck even if they didn't go to prison.

But the Godfather would be free on bail for the weeks or months awaiting trial. Ample time to have Chuck killed.

Chuck could never hide long enough for justice to be meted out to Alexander.

So how to kill George Alexander without first killing the two bodyguards?

The trick was to get them to come out one at a time. Knock each one out, duct tape his mouth, and secure him with cable ties on his wrists and ankles. If Chuck silently subdued them one at a time, he wouldn't need to kill them to assassinate the Godfather.

The plan was not simple like shooting through the French doors, but it was doable. He hoped.

———

Chuck sneaked to the rear of the west bungalow where the air conditioning compressors were mounted on concrete footings in the space between the eight-foot wall and the rear of the bungalow. Low hedges surrounded the units, hiding them from casual view. The night was cool, but there are always heat sources in a house and the humidity was 100%. Both units were running.

Chuck broke off two branches of croton from a bush and shoved one through the vent of the first unit until it thumped the fan blades of the compressor. It looked as if the storm tore the branch loose and it fell into the fan. The fan chewed at the branch with a fast *whump-whump-whump*, but the blade kept churning and ate the branch away.

Chuck pushed the branch in farther. *Whump-whump-whump*, and the blade chewed the branch away again.

What was this thing, the Energizer Bunny?

Time for Plan B.

Chuck unsheathed his Ka-Bar knife and hacked off a thumb-sized branch. He used the knife handle to widen the space between the vent blades on the housing. He rammed this bigger branch into the compressor. *Whap-whap-whap.* The blade stopped. *Yes.* Chuck gave himself a fist pump. If at first you don't succeed, bang it with a bigger hammer.

Chuck couldn't tell which unit was for upstairs and which for downstairs. He cut off another thumb-sized branch and disabled the other compressor.

Chuck sneaked back to the front terrace and regained his position under the balcony to observe the command center.

The three gangsters were having a heated discussion. The Godfather leaned toward the coffee table. Perhaps he didn't like what he was hearing. Or not hearing.

Evaluating their body language, Chuck imagined their argument. "Why aren't they talking? Is the volume turned up?...It is? Maybe the call dropped and we don't know it. We should disconnect and call them again...No, don't disconnect. If you do, we would get their voicemail... Yeah, let's wait. Something is bound to happen...I don't agree, but you're the boss."

While they argued, the rain slackened. Chuck heard voices, but in Russian. So much for eavesdropping.

They didn't notice the air conditioning had stopped. The rain had cooled the air. It might be morning before the room temperature and humidity got muggy enough to send someone to search for the cause.

Okay, time for Plan C.

Sneaking back to the utility room, Chuck eased the door open. The utility room shared a wall with the sitting room. Ceiling lights spilling from the loggia faintly illuminated the room.

Metal shelves on one side held a leaf blower, two hedge trimmers, and other gardening supplies and equipment. The wall opposite had four timers labeled for different zones of the landscape irrigation system. Other shelves held four DVRs with cables leading to the ceiling and another set leading to a metal box labeled *Security System.*

On the floor were a fertilizer spreader, a two-wheeled hand trolley, and two pair of rubber boots.

Three breaker boxes were imbedded in the back wall. A silver box was labeled *Cable TV*. A brown plastic box with an ancient AT&T logo from the days the estate used a half dozen land lines. The third box was an industrial gray Square D breaker box labeled *West Bungalow*.

Bingo.

Chuck closed the utility room door and flipped on the lights.

Stepping over the fertilizer spreader, he accidentally kicked it. His heart stopped for a second. He moved the spreader into a corner, then the rubber boots and the hand trolley. He didn't want a bodyguard to trip over something and cause a racket.

Chuck opened the breaker box. Shining a flashlight on the labels, he analyzed some to determine what the abbreviations meant. They were pretty obvious. The two he would flip were *W Loggia lights* and *Living room W. wall 120V.*

Chuck switched off the loggia lights. His target would emerge from the command center to a loggia in darkness. The interior of the utility room would be dark also.

Chuck flipped the second breaker. That disabled the monitors and anything else plugged into that wall. He doused the utility room lights. The only light remaining was from the control panels of the security system. Chuck didn't have time to disable those dim lights. He hoped he had it dark enough in the room.

Through the wall, Chuck heard three voices exclaim in surprise. One barked instructions in staccato syllables.

Yanking a black leather sap from his carry bag, Chuck crouched in the shadows behind the door. The spider awaited the fly.

One of Alexander's thugs should come to the breaker box. Chuck needed to take him out instantly and silently. If he shouted, it would warn the other two, and a gunfight would be inevitable.

Special Forces training taught Chuck many ways to kill an enemy quietly: garrote, knife slash across the throat, or an icepick in the ear, to name three. But those are fatal. Even with a garrote, the victim's windpipe is crushed and he can't breathe after the pressure is released.

To give the bodyguard a reasonable chance to survive, Chuck would hit him with the sap.

A leather sap is a dangerous weapon. The safest way to use it is to whack someone on the hands, arms, legs, or shoulders. Police Academy taught Chuck not to strike anyone on the head with an "impact weapon" such as a sap or a police baton unless you were required to use lethal force. That meant you were under attack or in fear of your life.

The effect of smacking someone's head with a sap is unpredictable. Swing too hard—you kill him. Don't swing hard enough—you give him a knot on the head and piss him off. Finding that sweet spot is a bitch.

Television and movies make knocking someone unconscious appear easy and almost harmless to the victim. Punch him in the jaw with your fist. Bang the bad guy on the head with the butt of your gun. Bash him in the temple with a rock. Break a chair over his back. Whatever action the screenwriter invents, the actor collapses unconscious and later recovers none the worse for the experience.

That's not real life. A couple years ago, Chuck rescued a hostage. He surprised two of the kidnappers and walloped them with a sap. One was knocked unconscious. He later recovered and was spending twenty-five years contemplating the error of his ways. The other kidnapper died instantly. Maybe one of them had a harder head.

Chloroform on a handkerchief over the bodyguard's nose would do the trick, but Chuck hadn't brought any.

No, the sap was the best silent way available, but it was tricky.

It wasn't long before the fly entered the web.

The door opened. A flashlight shined on the back wall. The light tracked around the room. Chuck was glad he had cleared the path to the breaker box. Stepping into the utility room, Thug Two stepped toward the back wall.

Chuck swung the sap at the side of Thug Two's neck below and behind his ear. He dropped like a sack of wet laundry and crumpled to the floor with a *plop*.

After securing his hands and ankles with cable ties, Chuck slapped an eight-inch piece of duct tape over his mouth, making sure his nose was free to breathe.

Chuck dragged Thug Two out the door and to the clearing with the air conditioning units. He rolled his unconscious body into the bushes and stepped back. The body was invisible.

When the power didn't come back on and Thug Two didn't return, the Godfather would send Terrence to investigate.

Chuck returned to the utility room and waited for his web to entangle the next fly.

One major difference: Terrence would be suspicious and alert.

From outside the door Terrence shouted "Gregor" followed by a string of Russian.

The door swung inward and Terrence's gun hand emerged from behind the door. He said something in Russian that sounded like a question and stepped further into the room.

Chuck had to disarm him with one blow, because the Godfather would be behind him.

Chuck whacked the gun hand with the sap, breaking the bones where Terrence's wrist met his hand.

Terrence screamed and cradled his hand. His pistol fell to the floor.

Chuck kicked it out the door and swung the sap across the side of his neck. Terrence's huge trapezius muscle absorbed the blow. Terrence staggered into the steel shelves but didn't fall. He swung his right elbow backward like a scythe, striking Chuck's bicep with a blow that jolted like an electric cattle prod. The strike paralyzed Chuck's arm and he dropped the sap. Worse, Chuck couldn't feel anything with his right hand except the tingle of his entire arm. It felt like one giant funny bone.

Terrence continued the spin, pivoting on his right foot and swinging a roundhouse kick with his left that slammed Chuck like a battering ram across the ribs.

His armored vest absorbed the blow but the momentum of the kick knocked Chuck through the door into the loggia. Chuck fell against a column and rolled away. Regaining his feet and shaking his right arm,

Chuck tried to regain movement. Nothing. His right hand couldn't hold a gun or a knife. It wouldn't make a fist either.

Terrence darted toward his fallen pistol, reaching with his left hand.

Chuck kicked him in the ribs.

He fell sideways on his right hand and screamed again.

Chuck kicked him in the stomach, then the ribs again.

Terrence lowered his left arm to protect his midsection.

Chuck kicked him in the head hard enough to boot a forty-yard field goal.

Terrence rolled onto his back, blood pouring from his mouth and nose. He didn't move.

Chuck shook his arm again. This time partial control returned to the paralyzed muscles. Not enough to hold a weapon or make a fist, but not completely useless either.

Chuck pivoted toward the command center.

George Alexander screamed something in Russian. He stood silhouetted in the doorway pointing a Glock into the darkness.

The lights were out and Chuck wore a black wetsuit.

The Godfather had nothing to aim at, but that didn't stop him. He pulled the trigger repeatedly. Bullets sprayed the loggia, two thumping into Chuck's vest, staggering him. One ripped through the wetsuit hood near his ear.

Perhaps Alexander glimpsed Chuck's face in the darkness, despite the dark grease. It was pointless to wonder now. Chuck leaped into the foliage and crawled deeper into the bushes, struggling to draw his Glock from the holster on his right hip with his other hand. He managed to grip the pistol with the wrong hand.

Chuck turned to shoot at the Godfather.

He wasn't there.

The command center door slammed shut.

Using cable ties from his fanny pack, Chuck shackled Terrence's wrists and ankles. He wasn't sure the gangster was alive, but he stuck a strip of duct tape across Terrence's mouth.

Yes, he was breathing. Chuck hadn't killed him. Chuck hoped he didn't live to regret that.

The door to the command center was locked. Chuck tried it as a matter of habit, though he wouldn't breach that way. The Godfather was inside with a pistol aimed at that door. Better to breach the French doors. When it comes to security, French doors are like a beaded curtain—strictly ornamental. A twelve-year-old kid can kick in a French door. Hell, with modern safety glass, Chuck could run through the door without a scratch. Or course he might get shot instead of scratched.

Chuck returned to the utility room, opened the door to the security camera box and wrenched the cables loose. He jerked the DVRs off the shelf and ripped their cables loose. He hadn't appeared on camera yet, and if he did in the next few minutes, there would be nothing to record him.

Chuck followed the loggia toward the parking area. Carriage lights beside each garage door and the lights spilling from the east loggia lit his way.

The lights in the command center went out. The Godfather had switched the lights off. He could see out and Chuck couldn't see in.

Move, countermove.

Returning to the breaker box, Chuck flipped off every switch. The carriage lights were on at the east bungalow. He sprinted across the front terrace and down the east loggia. There was a duplicate utility room for the east bungalow. Chuck switched off all power to that building.

The entire front of the estate was dark, except for some light from a street lamp that reached the parking area. The landscaping cast large shadows across the view, but the Godfather could still see out better than Chuck could see in.

Chuck returned to the west loggia.

The Godfather had ripped the gauze curtains from the French doors. That gave him a clear view of the parking area, the front terrace, and the front of the mansion.

Advantage Godfather.

Time to stir the pot.

With no silencer, a Glock 17 makes a muzzle flash a foot long. With the silencer, there is almost no flash unless you're standing in front of the gun.

Then you observe a flash the size of a silver dollar. Using a silencer, the shot sounds as loud as a hand clap.

Chuck screwed the silencer on his Glock and stood in front of a garage door of the east house. He was sixty feet from the command center in the west house. Now to give the Godfather a target the size of a silver dollar... Chuck fired one shot through the French doors and sprang six feet to one side.

The Godfather fired three rounds at the spot where Chuck had stood a second earlier.

Chuck squeezed off a four-shot burst at the Godfather's muzzle flash, then sidestepped ten feet away.

The Godfather didn't fire back.

Chuck fired another four shots and sidestepped again.

This time the Godfather didn't fire back either. Either Chuck had hit him, or he realized Chuck was moving and that Chuck had a better chance to shoot him than he had to shoot Chuck.

Chuck fired a round through another French door then sidestepped the opposite direction.

The Godfather still didn't fire back.

Had Chuck hit him, or was he waiting for a better opportunity?

Chuck couldn't wait around to starve him out. He was using a silencer, but the Godfather wasn't. The more shots Alexander fired, the more likely it became that a neighbor would call the police. With the rain stopped, the shots were easy to hear.

Time to regain the initiative.

Chuck ran around the back of the mansion and jogged back to the west loggia. Hopefully, the Godfather thought Chuck was still near the east bungalow.

The west loggia was black as the inside of a coffin. Chuck kicked open the main door and jumped back to one side, expecting Alexander to fire at the open door.

Nothing.

A hint of light from the street filtered through the shattered French doors into the command center. Chuck paused until his eyes dilated, then eased sideways until he could see inside the room.

The Godfather sprawled across an easy chair. His pistol dangled from his limp trigger finger.

Chuck returned to the utility room and flipped the breakers on. The carriage lights cast enough light into the command center to observe the blood on the Godfather's shirt. The monitors lit the room with screens that said *No Signal*.

Was he dead or wounded?

Chuck shot him two more times. His body jumped with the impact of each bullet, but he didn't respond.

It was over.

The Godfather was dead.

TWENTY

C huck switched on the west loggia lights to check on Terrence. He was alive and stared at Chuck with basilisk eyes. If looks could kill...Lucky for Chuck, the basilisk was a mythical beast. Chuck frisked him and removed his wallet. Chuck photographed Terrence's driver's license with his cellphone.

"I know who you are, Terrence, and I can find you. I know George Alexander instructed you to shoot me with a sniper rifle the next time I use my boat. It wasn't your idea nor his father's. In fact, his father was smart enough to tell George not to try."

He leaned closer. "Terrence, I'm like Santa Claus: I know when you've been bad or good. I know about the eight men who drove down from Washington. I know they and the rest of your local men are attacking the printer. I knew about the four men your boss sent to capture Aisha Aubakirovna. That's how I was there to stop it. I know *everything*."

Chuck gave the thug a moment to absorb that.

"That's why I killed George and not you. You have nothing personal against me. That's why I haven't killed you. But if you threaten me, or I catch you around my friends, I will hunt you down like a rabid dog. I will kill you, and no one will ever find your body. Is that clear?"

Terrence didn't react.

Chuck kicked him in the ribs, but not hard. "You got that?"

This time he nodded.

"I have a couple things to do, then I'll see that you and Gregor get to the hospital."

Gregor had managed to wiggle out of the bushes.

Chuck photographed his driver's license and gave him the speech he gave Terrence. "Gregor, you don't want to mess with me. I am like radio waves; I can penetrate anywhere. You trusted this fortress was secure, but I got in. Stay away from me and my friends. You got that?"

He grunted. It sounded like *uh-huh*.

"I'll tidy up, then make sure you and Terrence get to the emergency room."

Chuck had fired two insurance taps into Alexander's chest. He located the first brass case. The second was hiding in the bushes at the edge of the walkway. The ten rounds he fired standing at the garage door were easy to find. They were scattered on the brick pavers.

Chuck's cellphone vibrated. It was Hank. "Is everything okay?"

"Mission accomplished. It took longer than I anticipated. I need fifteen minutes inside the main house, then I'll call you to pick me up."

"Hooah."

Chuck opened the door between the loggia and the foyer. He tracked through the atrium and living room retrieving a listening device as he passed. He pried the other one off the chair that he had sat in on the loggia.

Returning to the foyer, Chuck climbed the curving steps three at a time to the second floor and jogged to the master suite to search for the safe.

Most people lack imagination; therefore, Chuck checked the obvious hiding places first. The safe wasn't behind any painting on the bedroom walls. It wasn't behind any of the prints on the bathroom walls, nor behind either of the mirrored medicine cabinets. Chuck found it in the wall behind the clothes in the smaller of the two master suite closets.

Referring to the list of passwords and combinations he had photographed in the Godfather's office, Chuck tried the first combination. Nothing. He tried the second and the safe opened.

Bingo.

There were more straps of hundred-dollar-bills than Chuck had encountered in his young life. It reminded him of a display of one million dollars he had seen in the lobby of a Las Vegas casino, but with no armed guards standing alongside. This stack of cash made every drug bust he worked as a police detective seem like an office basketball pool. Chuck managed to stuff twenty-two bundles into the fanny pack. He stuffed thirty-three in an empty utility bag he brought along. Over a half million dollars. That much more remained in the safe, but he was out of space to pack it.

Hank texted.

Red and blue lights arriving over the bridge. Get the hell out. Alternate pickup site.

Time for this ol' boy to run like a scalded dog.

The second safe might have held the fabled Amber Room that the Nazis looted from Russia during World War II. Perhaps it safeguarded the Godfather's baseball card collection or held the missing Fort Knox gold.

Too bad, Chuck would never know.

He dashed to the back sliders, opened one and ran across the deck. The motion detector flipped the lights on. He ran down the steps to the pool deck, sprinted around the pool, and across the deck toward the water.

Behind him, flashlights flared in the mansion. Damn it, the Feds had arrived sooner than he expected. How did they get past the steel gates so quickly? Probably used a remote from one of the Godfather's men they captured or killed.

Squeezing through the landscaping, Chuck reached the east wall. He retraced his steps to where he had left the dive bag.

The Feds were in the house. Chuck had no time to repack his gear in the dive bag, but he didn't dare abandon anything.

No clues. This had to look like an inside job.

Chuck had to get out *instantly*, but he was too heavy to swim with the gear.

The Feds would secure the area to prevent witnesses or suspects from escaping the estate. They would post agents at the front and back at the seawall. They would secure the yacht in case someone was living on it.

Chuck had seconds before they arrived on the dock.

He slung the empty dive bag over his shoulder and perched on the edge of the seawall behind the bougainvillea. Inhaling a deep breath, Chuck jumped hard to clear the barnacle-encrusted riprap and sank straight to the sandy bottom.

He couldn't swim with the weight, but it made it easier to walk. Only he had to walk underwater. In pitch dark. With no air tank.

Circling, Chuck reached for the riprap with his right hand to get his bearings. He made his way toward the dock, groping for the dock pilings with his other hand.

Chuck's lungs protested. His blood pressure rose as the carbon-dioxide in his blood increased with each heartbeat. And with each breath he was missing.

After a dozen steps his fingertips touched a piling. He pivoted under the dock.

His lungs yearned to inhale. Instead he expelled some air from his nose.

Using the piling to guide him, Chuck angled back toward the seawall. Just when he couldn't hold his breath any longer, his feet bumped the base of the riprap. He climbed enough to get his head above water.

Chuck controlled his urge to gasp and pant because the Feds might be a few feet above him. Fresh air never smelled better. He breathed quietly in and out to re-oxygenate his blood. His blood pressure returned to almost normal.

The boards of the dock were three feet above Chuck's head. Two pairs of footsteps walked on the dock.

"Check if anybody is on the boat."

One pair of footsteps crossed the aluminum gangplank and walked away on the teak deck. The other agent stood on the dock. The boards creaked as he shifted his weight back and forth.

Inch by careful inch, Chuck unzipped the dive bag. One by one, working by touch underwater, he unclipped his knives, pistols, fanny pack, and other paraphernalia. He eased each piece into the bag. Chuck switched off the bugs and yanked out the batteries. The bag weighed over thirty pounds. It was over half a million dollars heavier than when he carried it in. A little over ten pounds of Benjamins. He blew softly into the tube and adjusted it to neutral buoyancy.

Chuck would wait until the Feds finished at the dock, then swim out. Piece of cake.

The footsteps returned from the yacht. "It's locked up tight and there are no lights."

"That doesn't guarantee there's no one on it. They might be asleep or hiding."

"I walked all the way around the deck. I didn't hear a generator or air conditioner. The boat is quiet as a tomb. Nobody's gonna sleep on a yacht with the windows closed on a muggy night without the A.C. on."

"Maybe, but we have to check the boat too. Look for the keys in the house."

"The sun will rise in a couple hours. Let's do it then. I'm so tired I may fall asleep standing up. I could use a coffee. How about you?"

"Thanks. Bring me back a cup. I've been posted here."

Damn, that means he isn't leaving now and doesn't intend to leave anytime soon.

The rain had stopped and the night was quiet, save for the rustle of leaves in the faint breeze.

What to do?

Chuck adjusted the buoyancy of the dive bag again. Guiding the bag ahead of him beneath the water, he swam under the yacht and surfaced on the canal side. The only thing visible above the surface was half his head from the nose up. Black on black. Chuck lightened the buoyancy of the dive bag again and swam straight across the canal, keeping the yacht between him and the FBI agent.

Chuck waded and swam along the bank of the canal farther and farther from Alexander's dock. He felt nervous as a pickpocket at a magicians' convention until he was a hundred yards down the canal.

The alternate pickup was the pocket park on Lido Island. Chuck had to swim an extra half mile to get there. With no flippers, the swim was a bitch. Barnacle cuts stung the fingers of his hand. His glove was shredded where he had dragged his fingers along the riprap. Minor wounds he would deal with later.

Finally, Chuck reached Lido Island.

Climbing halfway up the riprap, he removed the silencer and the barrel from the Glock and threw them hard toward the middle of Seeti Bay. He tossed the bugs he had retrieved from the mansion into the canal. Next, he fished the expended brass from his belt bag and threw the casings into the water. The Feds would extract the bullets from the Godfather's body and run ballistics on them. They would find nothing to compare to the distinctive markings made by the barrel and silencer.

Hank and Gunner were waiting when Chuck reached the top of the seawall.

"Guys, you all are not gonna believe what I found in the Godfather's safe."

———

Chuck's cellphone woke him that afternoon. He fumbled the phone into his hand.

"Chuck, it's Bernadette at reception. Two FBI agents are on their way up. They told me not to call you, so don't let on that I did."

The fact they told Bernadette not to call him was troubling. Perhaps they had come to execute a search warrant. If they brought a search warrant, they had proved to a judge that they had probable cause to believe Chuck had committed a federal crime. Had Chuck left some bit of evidence behind at George Alexander's mansion?

There was nothing he could do about that now.

Chuck hoped he was prepared for a search warrant. He had left all his gear and all his loot from the previous night's raid locked in the back of Hank's car.

"Thanks for the heads-up, Bernadette." Chuck made a mental note to send her flowers.

Mentally and emotionally, Chuck had been prepared for this visit ever since he returned home at six that morning. The near-certainty of an FBI interview didn't keep him from sleeping well. It just wasn't as much sleep as his body needed. Try staying up for twenty hours planning and executing a home-invasion assassination. Then swim three-quarters of a mile with no flippers in the middle of the night, pushing a forty-pound bag. It's physically tiring and emotionally debilitating. Fortunately, Chuck figured that, like Alfred Lord Tennyson, his strength was as the strength of ten, because his heart was pure.

Chuck threw on a robe and got out the coffee fixings. He finished grinding the beans before the doorbell rang.

It was Gene Lopez and a twenty-something, top-of-her-class female agent. Fresh out of law school, being trained by the old master.

"May we come in," Lopez said. It was a statement, not a question. They couldn't have a search warrant or they would have barged in. The knot in Chuck's stomach loosened a bit.

"Sure, Gene, I'm brewing a fresh pot of coffee. Let's go to the kitchen."

"This is my colleague, Special Agent Nicole Bloom."

She reached for her creds, but Chuck gave her the hundred-watt smile. "Not necessary, Special Agent Bloom. Gene and I have worked together before. If he says you're a Special Agent, that's good enough for me."

Chuck winked at Bloom. "Gene almost always tells the truth."

Usually his hundred-watt smile made women catch their breath and moisten their lips. Then they gave Chuck their phone number. That didn't happen with Bloom, even with the grin. Was it because he hadn't shaved and combed his hair? Yeah, that must be it.

Chuck led them to the kitchen.

"Y'all can sit at the island while I make breakfast. Would either of you care for a second breakfast? I'm cooking an omelet, but you choose whatever you fancy so long as I know how to cook it."

"We're good, Chuck. Coffee would be great."

Chuck dumped the ground beans into a filter and flicked the brew switch.

"Gene, since the receptionist didn't announce you, you must have badged your way past her and told her to shut up. You also brought a second agent with you. As the World's Greatest Private Investigator, I conclude from those subtle clues that this is a business call and not a personal one."

Chuck gave Bloom the smile again. "How am I doing?"

"We have some routine questions, Mr. McCrary," Bloom said.

"Please call me Chuck, and I'll call you Special Agent Bloom."

Bloom smiled and reddened. *Yes.* Chuck gave a mental fist pump. If he tried enough times, someone would get the joke.

The old "routine questions" tactic. It's nothing special, Chuck. We don't suspect you of anything, Chuck. Everything's fine, Chuck. We have some routine questions like we ask everyone, Chuck.

Everyone, that is, whom we suspect invaded a private home and murdered the homeowner.

Chuck wasn't kidding when he told Bloom that Agent Lopez almost always told the truth. *Almost always* meant *Sometimes he lies.*

"Routine questions," Chuck repeated to Lopez. "Sure, Gene. Or do I call you Special Agent Lopez today?"

Lopez smiled. "Gene is fine, Chuck. This is an informal conversation. We're not recording it."

Sure, they weren't recording it. Maybe. That's okay; this interview was a game. A serious game, but still a game. One of the game's rules: Even when a person is not under oath and has not been Mirandized, it's still a Federal crime to lie to an FBI agent. Another rule: The Feds can lie to a suspect. It didn't seem fair that the two sides played by different rules, but there you are: The Supreme Court had spoken.

Play the game carefully, McCrary, he thought.

Chuck took three eggs and a packet of bacon from the refrigerator. He cracked the eggs into a mixing bowl.

"I presume this is regarding the attack on Southeast Printing and Binding last night. Or should I say, this morning. They were supposed to attack at three a.m."

Lopez waffled a hand. "Not quite. It's more of a…tangential event."

"First, tell me how last night's bust went. No casualties to the good guys?"

Chuck ran a whisk through the eggs and added salt, pepper, and cayenne. Sometimes he added garlic powder, but he was in the mood for cayenne.

"Three agents were wounded—two Secret Service and one FBI. One Secret Service agent is not expected to make it. We killed three of the eleven attackers and captured the other eight. All the employees in the print shop are safe and we arrested twelve people who worked there."

Chuck was afraid the mission with joint leadership would be a clusterfuck. His misgivings had been justified. It was too bad about the three casualties to the good guys.

"Would I know any of the wounded agents?"

"I don't think so."

"I'm sorry to hear you had casualties."

"Thank you for that. Regarding this other issue," Lopez said, "where were you last night?"

Chuck reminded himself to be truthful with his retorts or lack thereof.

Opening the package of thick-sliced bacon, he peeled off three slices into a skillet, then added a fourth. He stuck two pieces of multi-grain bread into the toaster.

Positioning the skillet on a burner, he gave Lopez a smile which said *cat-with-feathers-on-chin*. "It's not nice to kiss and tell, Gene. A gentleman knows when to be discreet. I prefer not to respond to that question. Suffice it to say that I was not home, not until six this morning. That's why I'm eating breakfast in the afternoon."

Chuck glanced at the pot. "Coffee's ready."

He took three mugs from the cabinet and placed them on the island. He fetched a pitcher of half-and-half from the refrigerator and a sugar bowl and basket of no-calorie sweetener packets from another cabinet. He poured their coffee, then his own. "Help yourself to milk and sugar or whatever."

Chuck set a plate on the counter and doubled a paper towel across it to drain the cooked bacon.

Lopez tasted his coffee, added one level teaspoon of sugar. Bloom added three spoons of sugar and filled the cup to the rim with half-and-half. Obviously not a coffee afficionado.

The two Feds sipped their coffee in patient silence.

Chuck cooked. He flipped the bacon, straightened it with a fork, and watched for the perfect moment of crispness to stretch the rashers on the paper towel to drain. He got his tongs from the drawer, retrieved the bacon, and draped it across the towels. He poured the eggs into the skillet.

"Some people cook omelets with butter and oil. I use bacon grease. Pumping my blood past the cholesterol makes my cardiovascular system stronger."

The toast popped up. Chuck tonged the toast onto another plate and spread creamy peanut butter on both pieces. He debated adding strawberry preserves, but rejected the idea. The toast was perfect. Chuck loved peanut butter in all its incarnations: creamy, chunky, or with chocolate, jam, or jelly. But not honey—too sweet.

Chuck flipped the edges of the omelet over, let it cook for fifteen seconds, then folded it in half. He slipped the paper towel from under the bacon and tossed it in the trash. He slid the omelet onto the plate and set the dish on the island.

Nobody said a word. That suited Chuck fine.

He brought a jar of salsa from the door of the fridge and spooned a dollop on the omelet. He slid the plate in front of an empty stool and sat down, ready to eat.

Lopez said, "Who were you with last night, Chuck?"

"As I said, I prefer not to respond regarding last night." He smiled again. "It would be bad form to embarrass anyone."

"I really need to know."

This time Chuck didn't smile. "Sorry, Gene. We both know I'm not obligated to answer."

Lopez frowned. "George Alexander was murdered this morning."

"Really?" Chuck ate a bite of toast. "Do either of you want toast? This twelve-grain bread makes good toast."

"No thanks, Chuck."

"Suit yourself."

Chuck ate a bite of the omelet and chased it with a sip of coffee.

"I'm supposed to ask for details, right? When, where, why, and how was he murdered?"

"About three o'clock in the garage at his home."

Chuck imagined Lopez saying, "Mrs. Peacock, in the library, with the candlestick."

"I knew I forgot something." Chuck opened the refrigerator and poured himself a glass of orange juice.

Returning to his stool, Chuck continued eating. "It couldn't happen to a nicer guy. Alexander must have lots of enemies. Any suspects? Oh wait, you can't discuss an ongoing investigation, can you?"

"There were 9-1-1 calls from two neighbors about shots fired in the neighborhood," Lopez said. "The storm was thundering, and they weren't sure it was gunfire."

"Yeah, I heard thunder last night too." He kept eating.

"We had a search warrant on George Alexander ready to serve this morning anyway. We searched the house before dawn. That's when we found the body."

"Alexander's house?"

"Yeah. 26 San Marco."

"Kill two birds with one trip, huh," Chuck said. "How did Alexander die?"

"Four parabellums in the chest. Two from long range were the kill shots. Two up close were postmortem."

"Insurance bullets. Tough way to die, unless a jealous husband shot him. It wouldn't be so sad if he died happy. But he wouldn't be screwing around in his garage, would he?"

Lopez and Bloom drank coffee; Chuck ate.

"We discovered something else besides George Alexander's body."

"Okay, I'll bite. What else?"

"Two of his bodyguards were hog-tied with cable ties and gagged with duct tape. We took them to the hospital."

"Only two? I figured Alexander had more men than that."

"You captured or killed four last week and eleven more were killed or captured last night."

"Perhaps he was short-handed. What happened, Gene? Inside job? Or did someone know the house was vulnerable? Home invasion robbery that went wrong?"

"I doubt it. We found a wall safe in his closet with over half a million dollars in it."

Lopez didn't say the safe was open. He hoped Chuck would comment on it being open, then he would ask how Chuck knew. "Wow, did George Alexander deal drugs in addition to theft, kidnapping, and bank fraud?"

"We're still processing the mansion, but we finished with his office. His office is a one-room nothing, but the mansion is as big as a hangar. Over 10,000 square feet."

"Yeah, and that doesn't include the two bungalows."

Bloom jumped to her feet. "How do you know how big it is?"

"Atlantic County Property Appraiser's website, Special Agent Bloom. You can learn a lot on the internet."

Her face flushed.

Young and inexperienced, Chuck thought.

"I met Alexander last week. I did some research before I went. I took Snoop and Gunner as backup and went to talk to him. I'm sure you'll find my fingerprints in his house."

"What about?" Lopez asked.

"I asked him why he tried to kidnap Aisha Aubakirovna. He denied everything. He was quite rude."

"One other thing was strange at the crime scene," Lopez said, "the safe was open. The money was in plain sight."

"That's weird. You got a theory on why it was open?"

"I hoped you might enlighten us, Chuck."

"I'm no good at writing fiction. Talk to a mystery writer. She might invent a good reason for someone to leave a safe open with a fortune in it."

Lopez reached in his pocket and showed Chuck one of his own listening devices. "We discovered two of these in George Alexander's office downtown."

Chuck held out his hand and Lopez gave it to him. "I presume since you don't have it bagged and tagged, that it's not evidence?"

"Nah. It's been wiped clean. You can buy them anywhere: discount stores, online, hobby shops. Hell, Alexander might have used it to record conferences with legal clients. You own one of these?"

Chuck flipped the device over in his hand. "I seem to remember buying some of these. I fiddle around with a lot of electronic toys. I don't recall this one, but it looks familiar. I probably have a few just like it somewhere." Chuck handed it back.

Lopez stared at the band-aids on Chuck's right hand. "How did you hurt your hand?"

Chuck smiled. "Cut it shaving."

"Your *hand*?" Bloom said. "You cut your *hand* shaving? How could you do that?"

"I stood on a chair," Chuck said. "Oops. That was the punch line to a different joke. I meant to say I cut my hand shaving when I grabbed the wrong end of the razor." Chuck gave her his best boyish grin. She still wasn't impressed. He really should have shaved and combed his hair.

Chuck finished breakfast and carried his dishes to the sink. "You want more coffee, agents, feel free." He rinsed the dishes and put them in the dishwasher. "Since you don't have anything else to ask, I need to shower, shave, and change my sheets. My girlfriend is flying in from Texas to spend the weekend."

Lopez stood and motioned to Bloom.

"This isn't over, Chuck."

"Come by anytime, Gene. But not this weekend. I have a date."

Chuck barely had time to attend to one more loose end before Ruby arrived. But it was a very important loose end.

———

Hank met Chuck at his sister Vicky's office. He handed Chuck the plastic trash bag he had brought from home. He poured two coffees from the tray on the credenza and took them to the conference table. "You're gonna love this, Sis."

He pushed one cup over to Chuck.

Pulling on a pair of nitrile gloves, Chuck grabbed the bottom of the bag and dumped the hundred-dollar bills from Alexander's safe onto Vicky's desk.

Vicky looked from Hank to Chuck. "How much is there?"

Chuck sat beside Hank. "Fifty-five straps with $10,000 in each strap."

"What am I supposed to do with this $550,000?"

"Some of this is proceeds from a fraud against the Atlantic County Tax Collector perpetrated by George Alexander, a former attorney here in Port City."

"You say 'former.' He's no longer an attorney?"

"That's right. Alexander was the trustee of twelve Florida Land Trusts that owned twelve pieces of commercial property in various cities, villages, and unincorporated areas of Atlantic County." Chuck handed her a flash drive. "This drive contains photos of all the documents for each land trust. George Alexander was the beneficial owner of each property, but he certified to the Atlantic County Property Appraiser that each property belonged to St. Michael's Orthodox Church in Port City, Florida. They paid no property taxes."

"Why did he do that?"

"He rented all these properties for market rates, which included extra rent to cover any property taxes assessed on the properties. Then he pocketed that extra tax money. That's where some of this currency came from."

"How much?" Vicky asked.

"I don't know. It will take some research to find out how much tax was evaded. I suggest that the Atlantic County Property Tax Collector could calculate how long the fraud was going on and how much it cost the taxpayers of Atlantic County. Give him the flash drive without telling him where it came from. Once the tax collector calculates the amount lost, you pay it from this money. If there's any left over, donate it to the Port City Rescue Mission. You know the man who runs it. Brother Jim."

"Yes. I know him. Reverend James Holmes."

"That's the guy. And, since this is all for the public good and for charity, it would be nice if your firm could do it *pro bono*. If not, take your fee out of the cash. I've already absorbed a pot full of costs on this project and I can't afford any more."

"Where did you get the money?"

"Are we protected by attorney-client privilege?"

"Give me a dollar." Vicky held her hand out.

Chuck fished his money clip from his pocket. "The smallest thing I have are twenties."

"For Pete's sake. Then give me twenty dollars."

He did.

Vicky handed the twenty to Hank. "Hank, the firm is hiring you as a consultant on Carlos McCrary's case. That means that you are also covered by and bound by attorney-client privilege."

She tried to hide a smile. "Satisfied now, smart ass?"

"I took the money from a safe in George Alexander's closet at 26 San

Marco Drive."

"Did you have Mr. Alexander's permission?"

"No."

"You stole it?"

"I stole it."

"What about the Land Trust files on the flash drive? Did you steal those too?"

"Yes."

"I see lots of legal problems here, Chuck. Do you intend to break any more laws regarding George Alexander?"

Hank smirked but didn't say anything.

Vicky cut her eyes to Hank and back to Chuck. "Well? Answer the question."

"No, I won't break any more laws or steal any more of Mr. Alexander's property. One good thing about this case is that George Alexander doesn't know about the thefts, and he will never find out or complain about them."

"How can you be so sure of that, hot shot?"

Chuck looked at Hank and nodded.

"Sis, George Alexander was shot and killed early this morning by person or persons unknown," Hank said.

Vicky looked gobsmacked. "Did Chuck have anything to do with that?"

Hank sipped his coffee. He appeared to be deciding how to respond. "I don't think you need to know that to disburse these funds, Sis."

Vicky stared at the pile of money on the conference table and rolled her chair a few inches back from the table, as if to distance herself. "This is blood money, Hank. I won't have anything to do with it."

"Sis, I'm going to earn that twenty-dollar consulting fee now." He leaned forward. "George Alexander is the guilty party here, not Chuck. Alexander had no right to this money when he put it in his safe. Now that he is dead, if Chuck hadn't taken it, it would eventually be inherited by Alexander's father who is an organized crime figure with the Russian Embassy. It there's any blood on this money, it was spilled by George Alexander, not by Chuck."

He took Vicky's hand. "You have my word on that, Sis. Chuck is righteous in this."

Ruby smiled and waved from the top of the escalator.

She reached Chuck and threw her arms around his neck. "I can't believe how much I missed you."

They kissed, then Ruby stepped back. "What's wrong with your hand?"

Chuck wiggled the fingers with the band-aids. "I cut them on barnacles. I'll tell you about it when we get home."

Chuck realized he had said "when we get home," not "when we get to my apartment" or "my condo." He already thought of his condo as their home. He hadn't planned to ask her to move in with him. Or had he?

Ruby held his left hand walking to baggage claim. "It was 24 degrees and snowing as I departed Austin. I crave serious sunshine this weekend."

"Your slightest wish…" Chuck said. "I'll take your baggage stubs."

He collected her luggage and loaded it in the Avanti.

"Have you eaten?"

"I ate a barbecue sandwich at the airport before boarding. Currently, I'm hungry for food for the soul. And the heart." She trailed her fingertips down his arm and made him tingle all over. "Let's go, handsome."

Following their first round of energetic, tear-your-clothes-off lovemaking, Chuck cooked a late supper.

Afterwards they carried their drinks to the balcony and sat on lounges in the dark. The only lights were from the moon and stars and the city below.

"Earlier, I promised to explain the band-aids on my fingers. It's time to tell you the whole story."

Last Christmas Chuck had told Ruby how his fiancée Miyoshi Takashi had died. Ruby said that she believed the personal danger to herself was minimal and acceptable. She lived in Austin and Chuck lived in Port City. If they began an exclusive relationship, one of them would eventually move to the other's city.

This thing with George Alexander was a potential relationship killer. If

Ruby didn't accept his personal code of honor, they had no future together. It was better they learned now whether she could accept Chuck and his life as they were.

Chuck told Ruby about his confrontation with George Alexander, omitting nothing.

"So, you invaded this man's home, disabled his bodyguards, and assassinated him. You were judge, jury, and executioner."

"Pretty much."

Chuck gazed into her eyes but he couldn't tell what she thought.

"You want to give me a little help, honey? I can't figure out how you feel about that."

Ruby sipped her Pinot Grigio.

"I'm still processing it. This is a lot to absorb, kiddo."

"I suppose it is, but we've reached the point in our relationship where you deserve to know me, warts and all. You deserve to know the man I am when no one is watching. I answer only to myself when it comes to justice. I've been this way since grade school. Sometimes it's the only way to get justice."

"You've done this before?"

"Sometimes. Most times, the bad guys don't give me a choice. But with George Alexander, I didn't give him the chance to surrender because he would have had me killed before he ever came to trial. I executed him the way I would put down a rabid dog. I would have executed those Chinese soldiers without a qualm because there was no way to bring them to justice. The reason I didn't was simply that I couldn't get away with it. With Alexander, I knew I could kill him without getting caught."

"But Gunner and Hank know. Hell, they even helped you."

"I trust Gunner and Hank with my life."

"And now I know. Legally, you committed premeditated murder. I could turn you in. Many people would say I *should* turn you in."

"Yes, you might. I hope you don't, but you could." Chuck knew he was safe from prosecution because nothing he had told Ruby about the home invasion left any evidence.

"You're trusting me with your life too. Or the next twenty-five years of it. That's what you would get as a minimum sentence."

"I hadn't thought of that, but, yeah, I'm trusting you with the next twenty-five years of my life." Again, he felt safe saying that.

Ruby held his hand again. "This is a big responsibility, merely possessing this information. We've only been dating since October. That's less than four months."

"You want to sleep on this before you give me an answer?"

"Good idea. I shouldn't make a life-altering decision hastily."

———

Saturday was a lazy day of swimming, boating, grilling burgers on the balcony, a sunset cruise, and Florida lobster at Ruby's favorite waterfront restaurant. Ironically, it was Vicky's favorite too. Ruby and Chuck didn't discuss George Alexander's fate, but its influence draped a thin veil across the day, at least for Chuck.

Sunday morning at breakfast, the shadow of Ruby flying out at 6:30 that evening lurked in the background.

"Have you given any more thought to the life I lead and the things I do?"

"Yes. I thought about it, and I've decided."

This was it. The moment of truth. Chuck stopped eating. He didn't hold his breath, but it was one of those moments. The course of his life could swing in either direction.

"I processed a case once in Lockhart," she said. "You know Lockhart?"

"Sure. Smallish town 35 miles south of Austin. Famous for a bunch of good barbecue restaurants and the beautiful old Caldwell County courthouse. Why?"

"The Caldwell County Sheriff uses the Austin Crime Lab on account of they have a population less than 40,000 and can't support a major-league lab. Anyway, I analyzed a girl's handkerchief discovered under a pile of old clothes in the perp's closet. I found blood from the dead seven-year-old girl and DNA from the perp's semen on the handkerchief. The case revolved around this handkerchief. There was circumstantial evidence, but without the handkerchief, there was no case. I told the detectives and the prosecutor that I could testify that this blood was the dead girl's and the semen was the perp's. It was a rock-solid case—no doubt that the guy did it."

Ruby's voice cracked. Her eyes glistened with unshed tears. She paused a moment to regain her composure.

"I drove to Lockhart, ready to testify. The prosecutor moved to admit the handkerchief into evidence. The defense objected that the search of the perp's house had been illegal and the handkerchief should not be admitted into evidence. After a half hour of back and forth among the defense, the prosecutors, and the judge, the handkerchief was excluded from evidence. Without the handkerchief, the sheriff had no case."

The tears spilled and streamed down her cheeks.

"The killer walked. The Hays County Sheriff arrested him six months later in San Marcos. You know San Marcos?"

"About 25 miles west of Lockhart."

"This time the prosecutors in Hays County proved their case and sent him to prison for life with no parole. But not until the bastard killed two more little girls."

His tissues were across the room. Chuck handed her a fresh napkin to wipe her tears.

"If someone had had the guts and the skills to be judge, jury, and executioner after that child killer got off the first time, two little girls would still be alive."

Ruby sat straighter. "That's my answer. Yes, I accept you, warts and all, and I wouldn't change you if I could; that's who you are. And there's one other thing I decided."

"I hope it good news too, babe."

"I think you'll like it. This afternoon, could you chauffeur me around to look at rental apartments? Let's scout a few on the way to the airport."

"Forgive my confusion, but I am more brawn and balls than I am brains. What decision is this?"

Ruby raised her hand like she was being sworn in. "I decided I'm tired of Texas winters, which are too cold, and Texas summers, which are too hot."

She grasped his hands in hers. His right hand hurt from the riprap cuts, but he didn't show it.

"I intend to relocate to Port City and get a job as a criminalist here in South Florida. To tell you the truth, Chuck, partially it's to be closer to you, but I love the weather, the food, the culture, the...the excitement in Port City. Am I rushing things?"

Chuck squeezed her hands back.

"Honey, since I met you last October, each time I'm with you, it gets harder to say goodbye. Frankly, I considered relocating to Austin to be closer to *you*. So the short answer is 'no, you're not rushing things.' You and I are singing from the same song book. In fact, this afternoon I planned to ask whether you would contemplate an exclusive relationship with me. Now I won't need to move to Austin to make it work."

"Are you asking for an exclusive relationship?"

"Yes, but with this qualification: Since you decided to move to Port City before I asked, you don't need to make that decision now."

"Yeah, let's wait on that decision. Wait until I relocate and my life settles down."

———

After lunch, they loaded one of Ruby's bags in the Avanti, the one with the winter clothes she wore in Austin. The suitcase with her tropical wardrobe, she left in the closet where Chuck stored his suitcases. She would use the rest of her earned vacation days soon and fly to Port City to interview with various law enforcement agencies in South Florida. Good criminalists were in demand.

Ruby loved the first two apartments they visited, and she'd barely begun house hunting. Chuck was confident she would find the perfect apartment. The pressure was off. Well, almost. He still didn't know whether her attraction was to Port City Beach or to him. Vicky had warned him not to see things that weren't there.

As they said goodbye to the real estate agent, Chuck felt pretty damn good *vis-à-vis* the whole world.

Perhaps that's why he hadn't noticed the car that had been tailing them, probably all the way from his condo parking lot.

TWENTY-ONE

They visited another new high-rise. Ruby loved it also. They returned to the visitor parking lot and Check held the passenger door of the Avanti while Ruby folded herself into the low-slung sports car.

The first bullet shattered the rear windshield and the window on the passenger door.

"Get down," Chuck shouted. "Flat on the pavement."

A second later, another shot blasted through the fiberglass body and the passenger door, narrowly missing Ruby.

Sprinting toward the sound of the gunshots, Chuck drew his Glock and zigzagged across the pavement toward the shooter. He observed the third muzzle flash an eye-blink before he heard the third shot.

The quarter-second lag between flash and gunshot told him the shooter was two hundred fifty feet away. The flash looked round, like staring at a small sun. Chuck was viewing it straight on. The bullet was aimed straight at him at 2500 feet per second the instant it exited the barrel.

If Chuck hadn't been sprinting at an angle, it would have been a clean head shot. His head would have exploded like a ripe watermelon whacked with a sledge hammer, spewing blood and brains all over the parked cars. The wake of the air displaced by the bullet brushed his ear.

Chuck changed direction again and snapped off three shots in return.

That might make the shooter duck, or run to another spot, or crap in his pants. He didn't care which if it disrupted his rhythm.

Something was wrong with Chuck's shots. They were slightly off. *Oh, yeah*, he thought. *The band-aids on my first three fingers.* The one on his index finger interfered with the trigger squeeze. Fortunately, every week Chuck shot half his practice shots at the pistol range with each hand.

Switching the Glock to his other hand, he juked another curve and the rifle barrel slipped behind the hood of a parked car.

Chuck saw where the shooter fired from, but he would be gone before Chuck got there. Another ten seconds of zigzagging and Chuck arrived. Surveying both directions, he put himself in the shooter's head. Where was the next best place to make the ambush?

Thirty yards away, the parking garage entrance ramp beckoned. Yes, a desperate shooter would choose that. Chuck pounded up the ramp, alert for the rifle barrel to appear on the second floor. It did and he fired twice, his bullets hitting the concrete decking of the third floor. The barrel yanked back.

Chuck ran to the top of the ramp and looped a 180 back down the second floor. A brief image of movement, virtually subliminal, warned him. He zigged. Another small round sun flared forty feet away. The gunshot sounded instantaneous although it was a fiftieth of a second later.

The bullet nicked the side of Chuck's neck. He prayed it was only a nick. He was too pumped with adrenaline to feel pain. He sensed a faint pressure as the bullet peeled off a sliver of skin. The feel of warm wet blood trickled down his neck. At least he hoped it was a trickle. If the bullet had nicked his external jugular vein, he would be dead soon. No time to think about that now.

Chuck rapid-fired three return shots. Two of his shots pierced the hood of the pickup that the shooter was hiding behind.

Slowing to a stealthy tread, Chuck took a firm two-handed grip and approached the pickup truck.

He heard a clatter, then a grunt.

Dropping to his knees, Chuck shifted to a left-handed grip and leaned on his right hand to peer under the pickup.

A figure dressed in black sprawled on the pavement in a spreading pool of blood. He struggled to grasp his rifle. It was the barrel scraping across the concrete that Chuck had heard.

"Drop it," Chuck shouted.

The stranger managed to grip the rifle with both hands.

"Drop it now," Chuck shouted again. "You don't need to die. Drop it, for God's sake."

The shooter swung the rifle barrel in Chuck's direction.

He fired twice at the man's center mass. His body bounced with each shot. The rifle fell from his hands.

Chuck remained on his knees twenty seconds, observing whether the attacker moved again. He didn't.

Chuck glanced down before climbing to his feet. His blood had formed a large pool on the pavement. The wound was more than a nick, but Ruby was safe. Chuck had finished what the shooter started. He yanked a handkerchief from his back pocket and clamped it hard against his neck. He finished his approach around the front of the pickup.

The shooter was Colonel Zhao Kang, late of the Chinese People's Liberation Army.

Chuck kicked the rifle out of reach and checked Kang's pulse. Dead.

He called out to Ruby. She had heard the shots. "Don't worry, baby. I'm okay. Just a slight nick." He hoped like hell he wasn't lying. "I'm in the parking garage. I have to call 9-1-1 and wait for the cops."

"Is it safe to walk up?"

"Yes. The shooter is dead. Walk up the ramp. I'm on the second floor. I'm the handsome live one with the neck wound."

Chuck called 9-1-1.

———

"The Avanti is undrivable," Chuck said. "Call an Uber to take you to the airport."

"My God, you're bleeding. I'll stay. I'll call my boss in the morning and explain I have to take care of you."

"This is not a wound; it's a nick." Chuck applied more pressure to it. "I can't see my neck, but I'm sure it looks worse than it is. Blood always looks bad. Honey, this ain't my first rodeo."

"I know. I've noticed the scars all over your body." Ruby peered at the bloody handkerchief he pressed against his neck. "This is one of those things I have to get used to if we take this relationship to the next level."

She had said "if." *If we take this relationship to the next level*, Chuck thought. *Hell, she's moving to Port City. Doesn't that qualify as taking the relationship to the next level? Was Vicky right? Is Ruby more attracted to South Florida than to me?*

Two sirens sounded. That would be the Port City Beach cops and an ambulance. "The EMTs will bandage this and give me a ride to the ER where an intern or a nurse will put a few stitches in it. It's nothing."

Ruby seemed doubtful.

"Honey, I don't want anything to delay your relocating to Port City, not for one day. I'll be fine. My car is unlocked and the trunk release is in the glove compartment. Call an Uber, get your bag out of the trunk, and go catch your flight." Chuck patted her on the shoulder. "I'll be okay."

The black-and-white accelerated up the ramp. The ambulance was too tall to fit in the parking garage, but they would stand by in the parking lot at the foot of the ramp until the cops radioed that the crime scene was secure. Then they would wheel the gurney up the ramp.

"You better scram or the cops will make you give a statement. That might make you miss your flight. Ride the elevator down and they won't spot you."

Chuck kissed her goodbye and gave her a friendly pat on the butt. She walked away. He kept the pressure on his neck.

The black-and-white turned at the top of the ramp. It stopped in the driveway twenty yards away.

The front doors opened. A cop got out of each side, sidearms drawn. "Who are you?" the cop on the passenger side hollered. He wore sergeant stripes on his uniform.

"Carlos McCrary. I called 9-1-1. I'm the victim and I'm wounded. The shooter is dead and the scene is secure. I need that ambulance."

Both cops walked in Chuck's direction, their pistols aimed at him. "On the ground," the sergeant said.

This guy didn't know how to assess a situation. Better give him something productive to do, Chuck thought.

"I can't move my hand or my neck wound will get very bad, very quickly. I am a former Port City police detective and a licensed private investigator with a concealed weapon permit. The pistol I used to defend myself from the shooter is in a holster on my belt. You should place it in an evidence bag. Do you have an evidence bag?"

The sergeant glanced at the other cop. "Fetch an evidence bag."

"Could you call that ambulance up here? I'm bleeding like a gutted hog."

He keyed his microphone. "The scene is secure. You can come up. One guy has a bullet wound, and you'll need another gurney for one body."

The younger cop walked to the black-and-white and returned with paper evidence bags.

"Sergeant, do you prefer to remove my weapon," Chuck asked, "or should I?"

"I'll remove it." He kept his gun in his hand, but lowered it as he approached.

Chuck held his jacket out from his body, exposing the Glock in its holster. He twisted at the waist to make it easy to reach. "You ought to put on gloves before you handle my weapon."

"Oh yeah." He pulled a pair of gloves from a pocket.

"FYI, Sergeant, I have a Browning .380 in a holster on my right ankle and a Ka-Bar knife strapped to my left calf and another knife concealed on my left forearm."

"You're a walking arsenal." The cop removed Chuck's Glock, dropped it in the evidence bag, and holstered his own weapon. "Do I need to collect the other weapons?"

"I didn't use them in this case. I just didn't want to surprise you in case you frisked me."

He rotated to his partner. "It's okay. I recognize this guy. He's a friend of Captain Castellano in the City."

Two EMTs wheeled a gurney around the top end of the ramp. Later they told Chuck they reached him just in time to catch him as he lost consciousness.

Chuck's last thought was that he didn't want to die without kissing Ruby goodbye. He wondered if she felt the same way.

———

Chuck regained consciousness strapped to a gurney. "What happened?" He struggled to hear his own voice over the clamor of the siren. The ambulance driver was speeding like a NASCAR racer.

"The bullet cut your external jugular vein." The EMT wore a surgical mask which made it hard to tell, but Chuck hoped she was smiling. "We got to you in time. I would predict an overnight stay for observation and home tomorrow. It's a good thing we got there when we did. Another few seconds would have been bad."

"Thanks."

"Should I call anyone to meet you at the hospital?"

Chuck's head was swimming and the ambulance rocked back and forth. Ruby was probably on her way to the airport. "If it's not life-threatening, there's no need. This isn't my first trip to an emergency room."

"Yeah. I couldn't help but notice the arsenal you're toting," she said. "What are you, an undercover cop or something?"

"I'm something."

"The police sergeant said you were armed like Rambo but not to worry, because you're on the side of the angels. What's with all the hardware? Have we wandered into a private war?"

"Nah. You're in no danger. I'm just paranoid."

Then he passed out again.

———

Chuck regained consciousness. He knew he was in a hospital before he opened his eyes—the scent was unmistakable.

Renate Crowell, a reporter from the *Port City Press-Journal*, was sitting beside the bed. She didn't notice Chuck was awake.

Renate sat statue stiff. Her hands were clasped in her lap. If Chuck didn't know how cynical she was, he would have thought she was praying.

"How did you get here, Renate?"

Giving him a quick assessment, she decided he wouldn't die in the next few minutes, and she relaxed. She softened around the edges and became a person instead of a stone cutting.

"If I recall, I walked to my car. I drove to the hospital. I rode an elevator to this floor. Then I walked to your room."

Chuck smiled. Same old Renate.

"I meant how did you learn I was in the hospital?"

"You gave the 9-1-1 operator your name. We news sharks have spies everywhere. You being shot makes a great story for the *Pee-Jay*. Too bad you didn't die. *Hero Private Eye Killed by Chinese Spy*. The headline would have written itself."

"Too bad I survived and spoiled your story."

"That's okay, handsome. *Hero Private Eye Survives Assassination Attempt* makes a good headline too. The way you live, who knows what your next headline will be."

Good old sentimental Renate.

Chuck glanced out the window. It was dark. The last time he passed out in an ambulance, he was unconscious for a couple of days. "What day is it?"

"It's still Sunday. You've been here four hours. You lost a lot of blood, but nothing that buying you and me a steak dinner wouldn't fix. Will you tell me about the gunfight?"

Renate lifted her phone, asking whether she could record the conversation.

There was a rap on the door and a nurse walked in. "I'm nurse Patty Wales. Glad you're awake, Mr. McCrary. The front desk said they allowed a visitor in—a woman claiming to be your cousin."

Renate stood. "I'm Chuck's next of kin, Renate Crowell. You can tell me anything concerning his case. What's his prognosis?"

Nurse Wales chuckled. "Nice try, Ms. Crowell, but I recognize you. It's not nice to lie to the front desk. I've noticed you around the hospital before. You're a reporter for the *Pee-Jay*." To Chuck: "Is this woman bothering you?"

"No, Renate and I are old…acquaintances. She agrees this conversation is off the record. Isn't that right, Renate?"

She dropped the phone back in her bag. "Of course."

"Then you can stay. Okay, Nurse Wales, how am I doing?"

"You'll live, but it was close."

With the nurses wearing masks, Chuck couldn't tell when they were kidding. He missed the old days. Sometimes a pretty smile makes a patient feel better than a pain-killer.

"You lost a liter of blood from a GSW to your external jugular vein. You'll be weak for a few days. An intern in the ER gave you four stitches. The doctor will examine you again in the morning. If everything checks out normal, she'll discharge you."

"May I use the bathroom?"

"I'll help you. You could be dizzy." Nurse Wales walked to the side of the bed.

Chuck flipped back the covers and swung his legs off the side. He glanced at Renate. "No peeking at my derriere."

"A girl can dream, can't she?"

Nurse Wales grabbed his arm as he stood.

Chuck was woozy, but he had been worse. "I believe I can make it alone, nurse. Let me give it a shot."

She released his arm but walked beside him the four or five steps to the bathroom door. Chuck wobbled but he made it.

"I can make it from here, nurse. Thanks."

Chuck finished washing his hands, grasped both sides of the lavatory, and did a knee bend. A little dizzy, but not bad. He did another. That was better. He released the lavatory and did a knee bend without holding on. He fell on his butt. Not perfect, but alive. Colonel Kang had not exacted his revenge.

Chuck opened the door.

"Renate, will you take me home if I leave now?"

"Will I get a story?"

"You can't leave, Mr. McCrary," Nurse Wales said. "The doctor will examine you in the morning. I'm sure she will discharge you then. Let's get you back in bed so you can get a good night's sleep."

"Nurse, with respect, the last time I was in a hospital I would no sooner get to sleep than something would wake me. All night long there were *dings* of other patients ringing for a nurse that were broadcast through the whole wing. I didn't get a good night's sleep until I went home. I appreciate your professionalism, but no thank you. I'm going home where I can sleep. Will you bring my clothes?"

Renate said, "A ride home tonight in exchange for an interview tomorrow morning?"

"Deal, but make it *late* tomorrow morning."

———

It required a half-hour of folderol and foofaraw before Chuck was discharged *AMA*. No, that's not the *American Medical Association*; it's *Against Medical Advice*. Chuck signed a form agreeing not to sue the hospital, the doctor, the nurse, the Supervisor of the Department of Stubborn Private Eyes, and the population of Atlantic County, and they let him leave.

Renate stopped for takeout so Chuck wouldn't starve to death before morning. She helped him into bed about midnight, then offered to spend the night. She wanted to "take care" of him. There was no way in this universe Chuck would do that. She had a history with him.

Chuck slept until 10:00 a.m. The delivery of a beautiful flower arrangement from Ruby awakened him. She enclosed a Get-Well card. Chuck texted her a photo of the flowers with a message that he would call after she got off work.

Renate brought an entire Quiche Lorraine for his breakfast, along with bagels and cream cheese, and a quart of fresh-squeezed orange juice. Naturally, she put the breakfast on her expense account at the newspaper.

Renate interviewed Chuck for two hours, then she grilled hamburgers on his balcony. Once she figured he had enough of his strength back, she made a pass at him.

Chuck pointed out the flower arrangement from Ruby and explained he was in a relationship.

"Is it monogamous?"

There was that same damned question: What exactly was his relationship with Ruby?

"Not exactly, but she's moving from Austin to Port City."

"Lots of people move to Port City. Maybe she just wants to be a friend with benefits." Renate ran her fingertips down his arm. "Like us."

"You and I aren't friends with benefits, Renate."

"Well, you could have fooled me." She looked hurt.

Chuck felt like a heel. While he had accepted Renate's invitations several times to a home-cooked dinner and a friendly romp in bed afterwards, he had never reciprocated. If anything, he figured she was just using him for sex. Not that that was a bad thing.

"Look, I'm sorry, Renate. You and I are friends, yes. Let's just leave it at that."

"You can't blame a girl for trying, handsome."

Chuck locked the door behind her and slept four more hours. Loss of blood does that to you.

That evening he made a video call to Ruby. He steered the conversation to the flowers, her flight home, the melting snow in Austin, and whether the wet winter would improve the spring Bluebonnet season across Central Texas.

"Okay, hero. Enough idle chit-chat. I've been contemplating that bandage on your neck this whole time. How many stitches?"

"Four." He pointed the cellphone for a close-up.

"That's a ghastly bruise starting on your neck."

"Yeah, that happens. The blood below the skin turns blue. In a few days it becomes yellow or green. It's the leaked blood under the skin breaking down to be absorbed into the body. Nothing to worry about."

"My bruises never do that."

"Your skin is darker. The different colors are there, but you can't see them because of your brown skin."

"Does it hurt?"

"A little when I twist my neck. They'll remove the stitches in a week."

"Did the cops give you a hard time about the gunfight?"

"Not yet. They're coming tomorrow to take my statement."

"Not yet? Why didn't they take your statement yesterday?"

"I was in the hospital."

"Your neck wound being a 'nick,' as you called it, was wrong. Did you lie? Hoping not to worry me?"

"I thought it was a minor graze. Otherwise, I would have sought medical attention earlier. As it happened, the EMTs caught me as I passed out right after you left."

Ruby glared at Chuck with fire in her eyes. "Listen, you macho bozo. I will not be a girlfriend who plays Twenty Questions to pry details out of her boyfriend. To have a real relationship, we need trust both ways. Don't *ever* spare my feelings concerning danger to you. And never minimize the severity of a wound. It's far worse to not know whether you're telling the truth. You *will* be straight with me in the future. That's a deal breaker. Got it?"

"Yes, ma'am. You and I will be straight with each other." Chuck told her the whole story about the neck wound, and him passing out in the parking garage and regaining consciousness in the hospital.

"Renate Crowell, a reporter with the *Press-Journal*, was sitting beside my bed when I came to. The newspaper has spies in the 9-1-1 dispatch office. They told her where I was." He told Ruby about his complicated relationship with Renate, about their occasional trysts in the past, and that she drove him home. He told Ruby about Renate offering to spend the night.

"Does she have the hots for you?"

"In my defense, I never encourage her. Check out her photo on the newspaper's website. She's hot as a pizza oven. Most of the times she's come onto me, I've said no. If you and I agree to an exclusive relationship, I won't cheat on you."

"That's good to know."

"In the interests of full disclosure, Renate wouldn't take me home last night unless I gave her the story. She returned this morning to interview me. You'll find her story covering the ambush and the gunfight in the *Pee-Jay* tomorrow. It'll be in the online edition tonight, if you care to read it."

"I'll do that. Tell me: Why are the detectives waiting until tomorrow to get your statement?"

"Thank the security cameras. The detective assigned to the case sent me a text last night. Cameras from the apartment building parking lot recorded the initial attack and my chase after Colonel Kang. Kang's shot that wounded me was caught on two cameras in the parking garage. Since I'm recuperating, she's not in a hurry to get my statement since the shooter is dead."

"If Renate is that good a reporter, all the detective needs to do is print a copy of her article and clip it in the file."

"When the detective calls for an appointment, I'll pass your suggestion along."

TWENTY-TWO

C huck met Hank and Gunner for lunch at *El Sándwich Celestial*, a hole-in-the-wall Cuban place a mile from Jerry's Gym. You get your food at an outside stand-up window and eat it at a picnic table on the sidewalk. Gunner had an hour for lunch. *Celestial* was quick and the sandwiches were big and tasty.

"Did you get your wedding invitation?" Gunner asked.

"It came yesterday," Chuck said. "I suggest you and Hank and I fly up together and catch a couple of Pilots-White Sox games while we're in Chicago."

"Are the Pilots playing in Chicago then?" Hank asked.

"A three-game series," Chuck answered. "Aisha and Andy promised they would check the White Sox schedule before they picked the date. I'll send an email to the rest of the Triple Seven. Some of the other guys will want to go too. We can get a dozen seats together if we book early enough."

"We don't have a dozen Triple Sevens anymore," Gunner said. "Packy and Franks are dead and Billow will be on his honeymoon."

"That's the problem with you single guys," Chuck said. "You forget wives and girlfriends. There will be wives and girlfriends at the wedding. I'm going to invite Ruby to go. How about Mariana, Hank?"

"Yeah, Vicky will stay with the kids. They love their Aunty Vicky. She promised to take them to Disney World and Sea World and Universal Studios. Sometimes she misses having children of her own."

"But not enough to start her own family."

"Yeah," said Hank. "That's why she borrows my kids."

Chuck took another bite of his *media noche* sandwich.

"My buddy, the Atlantic County Deputy Sheriff, called yesterday," Hank said. "You remember the two shooters you wounded when they attempted to kidnap Aisha?"

"Yeah, the former Moscow cop and the former East German *Stasi*."

"They were killed in the Atlantic County jail awaiting trial for attempted murder. A brawl broke out and both were stabbed with shivs while the guards were occupied with the fight."

"I would bet the God-grandfather, Aleksandr Borisov, arranged those killings," Chuck said. "He didn't want them to testify about his organization."

"What's the big deal if they testified?" Gunner asked. "Borisov is the commercial attaché to the Russian Embassy. He has diplomatic immunity. No one in the U.S. law enforcement community can touch him."

"He doesn't dare embarrass the Russian government," Chuck said. "I'm glad you recommended this place, Gunner. This sandwich is *delicioso*."

"How is Ruby's job interviewing going?" Hank said.

"She's interviewing with the Port City Police Crime Laboratory as we speak. That's why she couldn't join us for lunch."

"Did she rent an apartment?"

"Yeah, but she can't move in until March sixteenth. She's staying with me until then. It's nice to have her around every day."

"You think she's the one?" Hank said.

Vicky's words of warning and Renate's comments about lots of people moving to South Florida rang in Chuck's ear. "I don't know. I've thought that before and been wrong. Right now, it's too soon to tell."

"Well, I hope you get the family you want," Hank said.

"Me too," said Gunner.

"Anyway, Ruby and I might have a problem I never anticipated."

"What's the problem?"

"I'm white and she's black."

"Hell, there's lots of people wouldn't call you white," Hank said. "Consider Gunner. He's so white that chalk makes a black mark on him. I'd call you *taupe*, or *tan*, or *fawn* colored."

"No, no, no," Gunner said, "Chuck is *beige* or a *light almond*. Definitely not white."

"And Ruby is no blacker than I am," Hank said. "She's *bronze*, or *russet*, or *auburn*."

"No, Hank," Gunner said, "she can't be Auburn. Auburn colors are *burnt orange* and *navy-blue*."

"She graduated from the University of Texas at Austin," Hank said. "She can be burnt orange."

"Guys, joke about this all you want," Chuck said, "but there are still people who believe skin color is important."

"Surely, your family doesn't have a problem with that."

"It's not my family with the objection," Chuck said. "It's hers."

Hank laughed. "You're a smart fellow, Chuck. You'll figure something out."

The End

SOMETIMES YOU LOSE

CARLOS MCCRARY PI, BOOK 10

Chuck's attention was drawn to Tommy's silver necklace with a coke spoon on it made from a crucifix. It was a twin to the one Chuck had found in Angie's closet.

"What are you doing here, asshole?" Tommy demanded. Apparently, Tommy wasn't looking to make a new friend.

"It's nice to see you too, Tommy," Chuck said with a smile.

Tommy's face reddened. "Look, buddy, me and Lola, we've already had enough trouble with Angie. Do me a favor. Just stay the hell away from Lola, okay?" He pushed past Chuck and melted into the crowd.

Chuck surveyed the room again, then saw Lola Salazar leaning against a wall chatting with a woman with purple hair. Both women were already high, Chuck thought.

Lola grinned as she pushed past the woman and tottered over to Chuck, clasping the front of his shirt in both hands and hanging on him. A cocaine spoon on a gold necklace hung between her breasts. It was made from a crucifix. "I'm glad you made it, Chuck. I was hoping you'd come." She stood on tiptoes and kissed his neck, too short to reach his lips.

She pulled out a small baggie with white powder inside. With practiced fingers, she dipped the coke spoon in it. She pressed a finger to one nostril, closing it. Holding the coke spoon to her other nostril, she sniffed the powder up her nose. Poof, it vanished.

Taking a deep breath, she smiled dreamily. "Want a hit, Chucky-lucky? This shit is the real McCoy."

Salazar's eyes started to close and she jerked them open.

Chuck wrapped both arms around her, propping her up. "I'd like to buy some of that 'real McCoy' myself. Where'd you get it?"

Salazar leaned against Chuck, nuzzling his neck. "Russell. He's been selling us high-quality blow since Thanksgiving."

"Is Russell his first name or his last?"

Lola leaned back and tried to focus on Chuck's face. "He's just 'Russell.' That's all. Would you like his number?"

"Sure."

"What the hell," she said, pulling out her phone. She thrust it into Chuck's hand. "I'm too high to find it. It's in my contacts."

She fell back on the bed, eyes closed, and began to snore.

Chuck scrolled through Lola's contacts and forwarded Russell's information to his phone. Chuck let himself out of room to look for Tommy.

Tommy was on the porch with a woman, leaning against the railing passing a joint back and forth. The joint was down to a nub.

Chuck stood a few feet away and waited for Tommy to move away from the woman. Chuck followed him as he walked to the Harley-Davidson parked in Angie's assigned parking spot.

Chuck stopped at arm's length and cleared his throat.

Tommy looked at him. "Why are you following me, asshole?" Tommy swung at Chuck.

Chuck stepped back and the punch swished harmlessly a few inches from his nose.

"Hold still, asshole." Tommy swung the other hand.

Chuck dodged it again. "I don't want to fight you, Tommy."

Tommy charged him.

Chuck stepped sideways and Tommy tried to stop his charge. He tripped and fell into the Mercedes behind Chuck, setting off the car alarm.

Chuck yelled over the car alarm. "There's no need to fight, Tommy. I just want to talk. Let's step away from this noise." He tried to help Tommy off the pavement.

Tommy jerked his arm away. His mouth was bloody where he had smacked into the car. "Leave me alone, asshole. I'm just fine here." He tried to sit up and fell back, bumping his head on the ground. His head lolled to one side and he stopped moving.

Chuck felt for Tommy's pulse. Finding it strong, he straightened Tommy's limbs to make him comfortable. He pulled the stainless-steel chain that fastened Tommy's wallet to his belt. Opening the wallet, Chuck photographed the driver's license. Interesting; Tommy's license was from Texas even though the motorcycle was from Mexico. He searched further in the wallet and found a Mexican driver's license which he photographed.

He frisked Tommy and found two cellphones, which he took.

Chuck checked the time. Eleven-thirty. Not very late for Saturday night. Maybe Bettina would still be up.

———

Available in Paperback and eBook from Your Favorite Bookstore or Online Retailer

ALSO BY DALLAS GORHAM

The Carlos McCrary PI Mystery Thriller Series

Six Murders Too Many

Double Fake

Quarterback Trap

Dangerous Friends

Day of the Tiger

McCrary's Justice

Yesterday's Trouble

Four Years Gone

Debt of Honor

Sometimes You Lose

ABOUT THE AUTHOR

Dallas Gorham's books combine murder, mystery, and general mayhem with a touch of humor—all done with a PG-13 rating. His Carlos McCrary, Private Investigator, Mystery Thriller Series can be read and enjoyed in any order.

Dallas writes in the mystery, thriller, and suspense genres. (Take your pick: His novels have all three elements) His stories will get your heart pounding and leave you wanting more. He writes to hit hard, have a good time, and leave as few grammar errors as possible (or is it "grammatical errors"? Hmm.)

In his previous life, Dallas worked as a shoe salesman, grocery store sacker, florist deliverer, auditor, management consultant, association executive, accountant, radio announcer, and a paid assassin for the Florida Board of Cosmetology. (He is lying about one of those jobs.) If you ask him about it, he will deny ever having worked as an auditor.

Dallas is a sixth-generation Texan and a proud Texas Longhorn, having earned a Bachelor of Business Administration at the University of Texas at Austin. He graduated in the top three-quarters of his class, maybe. He has also been known to lie about his class ranking.

Dallas, the writer, and his wife moved to Florida years ago to escape Dallas, the city, winters (Brrrr. Way too cold) and summers (Whew. Way too hot). Like his fictional hero, Chuck McCrary, he lives in Florida in a waterfront home where he and his wife watch the sunset over the lake most days. He is a member of Mystery Writers of America and the Florida Writers Association.

Dallas is married to his one-and-only wife who treats him far better than he deserves. They have two grown sons, of whom they are inordinately proud. They also have seven grandchildren who are the smartest, most handsome, and most beautiful grandchildren in the known universe. He and his wife spend waaaay too much money on their love of travel. They have visited all 50 states and over 90 foreign countries, the most recent of which was Indonesia, where their cruise ship stopped at Kuala Lumpur.

Dallas writes an occasional blog post at http://dallasgorham.com/blog that is sometimes funny, but not nearly as funny as he thinks. The website also has more information about his books. To get an email whenever the author releases a new title (and sometimes a free book), sign up for the VIP newsletter at http://dallasgorham.com/

If you have too much time on your hands, you can follow him at the following social media links:

www.DallasGorham.com

facebook.com/DallasGorham

twitter.com/DallasGorham

amazon.com/author/B00J4LISCS

www.ingramcontent.com/pod-product-compliance
Lightning Source LLC
Chambersburg PA
CBHW051332020726
47501CB00007B/2036